I0691948

Kingdom
Book Two

Shawna Ryan

ALL RIGHTS RESERVED

No part of this book may be reproduced or
transmitted in any form or by any means, electronic
or mechanical, including photocopying, recording,
or by any information storage and retrieval system,
without permission in writing from the author,
except in the case of brief quotations embodied in
reviews.

Cover Art:
MLC Designs 4U

Publisher's Note:

This is a work of fiction. All names, characters,
places, and events are the work of the author's
imagination.

Any resemblance to real persons, places, or events
is coincidental.

Solstice Publishing - www.solsticepublishing.com

Copyright 2015

Shawna Ryan

KINGDOM
BOOK TWO

By Shawna Ryan

*I dedicate this book to my grandmothers, great-grandmothers,
And great-great-grandmothers,
Courageous pioneers all,
Whatever their religion.*

Chapter One

New York City
Present Day
3:25 a.m. Saturday
April 24

Sprawled on the floor between thick steel bars for caging, amid shouts and mayhem, was the still and silent figure of a man. His eyes were wide and blank. His chin was unnaturally flat on the concrete, his head bathed in the spreading puddle of his own blood. His throat had been slit from side to side. The wound was deep and gaping. His life exhausting, he was in his last few seconds.

"What happened here?" a guard shouted from outside the holding cell door, as backup joined him. "Who is it?" he demanded. "Search them," he ordered, as a force of four rushed into the cell.

"Here," another guard said. His bare hand was holding a knife he found in the toilet, all bloodstains and fingerprints gone.

"Who did this?" the guard in charge asked of the three male prisoners pressed against the wall. Other guards pulled the prisoners' pants down to their ankles, ripped off their shirts and exposed everything, even their genitals.

"He did," the man who had been wearing a tuxedo said, pointing to the derelict in the corner.

The derelict's long, black hair was greasy and in tangles. His chin and jowls were densely covered with dark, dirty stubble. He glared at them as four guards stormed him. Forcing him to the concrete, jerking his arms behind his back, they cuffed him.

"Take him to the interrogation room," the guard in charge ordered, as barely noticed by anyone, Hank Blanchard convulsed, trembled and died. "Get these men out of here. Cordon off the cell and get CSU down here." He glanced fleetingly at Hank's body. "What was he in for, anyway?"

"Murder," someone shouted. "He's the one that offed that guy at the Garden after the basketball game."

"Good, doesn't make us look so bad when it's somebody who deserves it."

Paraded naked from the cell block by two guards, forced to display his genitals like an animal to anyone who cared to look, the derelict, reluctantly and belligerently, stumbled and faltered down a long, narrow hall of dingy beige walls and exposed fluorescent lights. "Shit. I'm cold. Either of you fucking eunuchs got a blanket? Beneath his bare feet, the ancient linoleum, cracked and worn in places where once there were black diamonds, was freezing and ripe with bacteria. "Don't push. I'm going," he protested.

"In here," one of the guards ordered him, as the other held open a heavy door marked 'Interrogation'. The derelict hesitated, and the guard shoved him though the doorway.

Standing very still, the derelict stared straight ahead into a plain, windowless room with a single table and three metal chairs, all bolted to the concrete tile floor. Leaving him alone, failing to turn on a light, the guards shut and locked the door behind them.

Handcuffed and unable to see, yet undeterred by the darkness, the derelict turned and backed against the table. Feeling along the inside rim near one of the rounded corners, he located a tiny, unsealed envelope taped to the underside. Opening the flap with his right index finger, he dumped the contents onto the table, scattering three distinct, silver keys. Feeling each of the keys, he chose the smallest and unlocked the handcuffs. Once free, he turned on the lights.

Crawling under the table, he identified and lifted four adjacent, concrete tiles tacked down with sturdy, two-sided tape. Beneath the tiles was a two-foot-square, steel storage compartment. He used the second key to open it. Within the hidden compartment was a gallon of bottled water, liquid bath soap, a bath towel, a ceramic washbasin, a shaving kit and clean clothes. He took off the long, dirty wig he had worn for hours, filled the washbasin with water, cleaned himself, and shaved. He then donned the casual slacks and print shirt folded neatly in the box and the gray, nylon socks and sandals beside them. He put everything he was not wearing back into the hidden compartment, locked it, removed the key, and replaced the tiles.

He was no longer the derelict who entered that room. He was someone else entirely. He used the third key to unlock the interrogation room door, slid all three keys in his pocket and, wearing an NYPD badge on his leather belt, stole away.

Chapter Two

It was dusk as Arthur Johnson's oldest granddaughter, nineteen-year old Molly Jeffreys, walked down the wide, expansive sidewalks of the Joseph F. Smith Building Quad toward the parking lot. She had been to see her advisor, Elder Roundtree, a gentle man with whom she felt she could confide. Day classes were over. Evening classes were just beginning, and there were only a handful of students nearby.

Susan's grandfather disappeared a little over a week ago, and she did not know what to do. Her grandmother told her he'd gone out of the country on business, but Molly didn't believe her. He never traveled. He was a lab technician. His closets were full, and he left Grandma all of his credit cards. When she quizzed her grandmother, all it did was upset them both. Worse yet, there were terrible rumors he'd moved to Guatemala with his boss, Wayne Hoffel, and might not be back for years.

None of it made sense to her. Why would he do that? He was always such a homebody. She went to Elder Roundtree hoping she could convince him to persuade her grandmother to tell him what really happened.

Feeling better because Elder Roundtree agreed, she walked at a clip, her blue dress swaying. She had curly red hair, tiny, feminine features, and a big friendly smile. She was packed and headed north to Little Cottonwood Canyon to meet friends at a private cabin for the weekend. Her red, Mustang convertible, a present from her parents the day after she was accepted at BYU, was waiting for her. Evenings in late April were still chilly, so she had the hood up. Resting her smart phone in its cradle, she selected her favorite rock album and headed north.

***

Carrying a large, green backpack over his shoulder, Elder Roundtree, a tall, middle-aged man with light hair and wire-rimmed glasses, walked to the edge of campus and climbed into the passenger seat of the black SUV waiting for him. "She's headed to Little Cottonwood," he told the driver.

***

Twenty-five minutes later, twenty miles south of Salt Lake City, Molly turned onto Highway 210, Little Cottonwood Road, a wet, narrow, paved highway with mountains on either side that sloped to its edges. There, she was alone, with no other vehicle in sight. As she left Provo, she had called her friends who were already at the cabin, so they were expecting her. What little daylight was left was blocked by the mountains and, in the dark, she turned on her brights.

Ten minutes down the road she saw car lights behind her, big lights, high above the ground and on bright. Brighter fog lights came on. Half blinded by them, she turned her mirrors so she could not see them. Slowing, she rolled down her window, stuck out her arm, and signaled the vehicle behind her to pass. When it didn't, she turned around to look. The vehicle was an SUV, and it was pacing her.

She was suddenly frightened. It was dangerous for her to drive into the mountains alone, especially at night. There was no help for her if something happened. Often, cell phone connections were blocked or not available. Mountains were havens for wild men, murderous men hiding from the law. Instinct demanded she run. She stomped on the accelerator, tore up the road and put the SUV a mile behind her. Yet even at that speed, it would take fifteen minutes more to reach the turnoff to the cabin. It would take another fifteen or more with her low riding sports car tediously working its way over bumpy mountain roads to get to the cabin itself. The rough roads would give the SUV an advantage, and it could easily overtake her. Maybe she should try for the ski lodge instead. That road was paved, and she could move faster. She gunned the engine, reaching a speed far in excess of that allowed by the road conditions. Fumbling for the rear view mirror, she put the SUV in sight and gasped. It was only a hundred feet away and closing. "Oh, God," she cried. "What am I going to do?"

The SUV was getting closer, the road was narrowing and the lodge seemed forever away. A designated passing lane was coming up. That's where they would get her. No matter which lane she took, the SUV could take her. She chose the right lane. The SUV took left. Quickly thinking, she slammed on her breaks and 'U' turned, speeding back the way she had come. She had gained only seconds, but hoped she could outrun them.

Her car was fast but had no traction. The road was wet from melting snow, and she had to slow down. Losing ground, she watched as the SUV closed in on her and came alongside her.

Jamming the accelerator to the floor, putting every other danger aside, she sped to ninety, the SUV hot on her tail. Looking back, taking too much time watching its lights in the mirror, she didn't see the oil slick in front of her and hit it. Out of control, the Mustang hit the rail, flipped twice in the air, and landed upside down in a thick growth of willows at the edge of a creek.

Chapter Three

Southern Utah
Early Summer 1857

It was near sundown as Anna and John Wickens walked beside their oxen out of a forest east of Cedar City with their wagon full of logs for their new cabin. The arid reaches of the Escalante Desert were some distance west of them, but the land they walked on was rich. The late spring grass was vivid green. Thousands of purple and red wild flowers were in bloom. To the left was a bright orange-yellow stand of ancient and gnarled bristlecone pine standing guard over a deep gorge cut through colorful limestone, pink and copper in the setting sun.

"Whoa, Bull. Steady, William," John called to the two lead oxen, and they pulled to a stop. John was a big, bearlike man but quite handsome, at least to Anna.

"Beautiful," she said, walking closer to the gorge. Her curly, copper hair was tucked neatly into a bonnet with a wide-brim tied down at the sides and to her chin.

John tethered the team of four oxen and joined her. "Look, the fir trees are way down there." He pointed to the very bottom of the gorge, his blue eyes smiling. "When we have some time, we'll come back here. Maybe bring Mum and the girls for a picnic."

Anna smiled and, as she enjoyed the view, gazed lovingly at him. His jaw was square and strong, chiseled, and with long, cavernous dimples. His hair was thick and dark brown. Three years ago, she and John were Mormon converts immigrating to Utah.

As Anna gazed over the gorgeous wilderness before her, that long terrible journey seemed as if it was only yesterday. When she met him, John was a fisher from England, traveling with his mother, Hattie, and his ten-year old daughter, Lizzy. Anna and her husband, Erich, were from Switzerland. Having left their families behind, she and Erich had begun their journey to Utah with two hundred other converts on board a ship crossing the Atlantic. It was only then that Jacob Tuttle, their elder, began to disclose some of the Church secrets he'd been keeping from them. When poor Erich argued with him, when Erich blasphemed by his refusal to accept these secret Church teachings, God struck Erich down and killed him.

Alone then and vulnerable, Anna was helpless to protect the monies Erich saved for them, helpless to keep Jacob from taking it for the Church. Impoverished, she had nothing except a few personal belongings and a small dog she adopted when she began her journey west across the prairies. Except for Jacob lending her money to buy supplies and Hattie and John's friendship, she might well not have made it to Utah.

Once there, the Church would not allow her to work to support herself, so she was forced to marry. Jacob demanded she marry him, but Jacob repulsed her. In the kindest of gestures, John married her so she wouldn't have to marry Jacob.

As the years passed in Salt Lake City, John and Anna built a home and adopted a little girl named Maybella. Maybella was one of the survivors John and other Mormon men saved from the handcart trains of converts who had been caught in the deadly mountain blizzards of last winter. This spring, John took Anna away from Jacob for other reasons. John and Anna were among those forced to move to Southern Utah. They would forfeit to the Church their home in Salt Lake City and anything else they could not take with them.

Brigham Young sent missionaries to Las Vegas to mine and smelt lead for ammunition and to Southern Utah to process iron from the mountains in preparation for war against the United States. John and Anna's mission, together with all the other Mormons sent south, was to strengthen the Mormon hold on these lands and to drive out the Gentiles. Brigham Young's orders were "to conquer the Kingdom of God."

Anna's thinking of the past, of Erich and of the hardships they suffered, took the shine off the bold and colorful vista in front of her. Suddenly the beauty around her was not beautiful anymore. Had Anna known their home and their belongings did not go the Church and went, instead, to Elder Jacob Tuttle and his co-conspirator, Elder Jeremy Gibbs, she would have been even more downhearted. "Too bad the gorge is right here and not closer," she coldly observed. "It'll take us hours to go around it and get home."

Their home near Cedar City was a tent they'd set up on land the Church gave them three miles out of town. Like that around them, the soil was rust colored clay, the land a wild desert garden before they cultivated. Covered with sagebrush, scrubs, and tall, dry grass it was alive with grasshoppers. When John and Anna got there about three hours after dark, their family was waiting for them.

"Finally used what they taught us in Iowa and made us an oven," John's mother, Hattie, told them in a heavy English accent, pointing to a mound of clay sod. Hattie was barely five feet tall. Although she had lost most of her girth since Anna first met her, she was still strong, as strong as Anna and as hardworking. "The girls helped me."

Now thirteen and becoming adept at grown women's chores, Lizzy proudly took from the crude oven a fresh baked loaf of bread. "It worked."

Anna looked lovingly at her. In a way, the move to Southern Utah was a blessing. Elder Jeremy had taken a keen, indecent interest in Lizzy. At least here, over two hundred miles away from him, they need not worry he would show up at their door any day to claim Lizzy as his fourth wife.

In the moonless night, the fire and one kerosene lamp were their only camp lights, though for miles around them in the distance, they could see other fires and the lights in town. Crickets chittered, and from the desert south, a pack of coyotes wailed. Hattie had set the large, outdoor table John built. "Maybella's already eaten," she told them, "but Lizzy and I waited for you."

Angel, Anna's adopted dog, a small, black dog with a patch of white on its chest and a tiny, white goatee, was at John's heels. Four-year-old Maybella was tugging at his shirt, her long red hair bouncing with the vibration. "Want to ride Bull into the corral?" he tempted her. "I promise I won't hold on to you." He picked her up and put her on Bull's shoulders.

Smiling, Anna lovingly watched. She and John traveled hundreds of miles with Bull, and she knew the dependable old ox would not hurt Maybella.

"Hang on to the yoke," John told the four-year-old, as with Angel's help, he led Bull and William to a small corral, the only structure on the property. Their time since their arrival had been devoted to plowing and planting, so their house and barn were not yet built. "Keep an eye on her, will ya, Lizzy, while I get Jasper and Jack?"

Bull, William, Jasper, and Jack, the four oxen, were as much members of the family as Angel, and Anna and John took very good care of them. The oxen would eat before they ate. He was giving them grain, when from out of the darkness and into the firelight, came four riders.

"Might not have been able to find you out here in the dark without that fire," one of the strangers said.

"Brother Zeb told us you were here."

Anna immediately relaxed. There was nothing to fear. These men were Mormons. "You want something to eat, Brothers?" she invited. "We've got beans and fresh bread."

"Thank you, Ma'am," the stranger responded. "Had supper hours ago. Food's scarce here, and yours just got planted. 'Lest someone's in real need, don't be givin' it away."

"Would you have a drink, then?" John asked.

"That we'd be obliged to." The stranger stepped down from his horse and offered John his hand. He was a stocky man, about forty-five. His hair was fair. Between his downward slanting eyes was a worry crease. "I'm Major John D. Lee." He turned to introduce the three men dismounting behind him. "These here are Brothers Hosea Stout, Philip Klingonsmith and Nephi Johnson. We're from a settlement up north a piece, and we've come to invite you to join our militia." He reached for the empty cup Anna handed him.

"Militia?" John asked, "What kind of militia?"

"Church militia," Lee told him. He grinned. "You go get me that drink, and I'll tell ya all about it."

Anna pretended not to be anxious when she invited them to the table while John went into the tent. "Please, sit down."

"Thank you, Sister, but we've been sittin' all day. Feels good to stand." Lee looked up at the stars, brilliant in the desert sky. "Nice evenin'."

When John returned, he poured a good splash of mash into each man's cup then stood next to Anna.

Lee seemed in no hurry. He sipped the liquor, took a look at the tent, the corral, and the wagon full of logs, then sized up Lizzy and Maybella. "Got a nice piece of property here. Nice lookin' family, too. Any boys?"

"No, there's just the girls."

Lee put his cup on the table and looked squarely at John, his manner grave. "Yer gonna want to make sure those girls are takin' care of. That yer ready to defend them."

Anna looked at John and saw the hair on the back of his neck stand. His back stiffened. He was studying John Lee. "What do you mean?" she blurted.

"There's a militia bein' formed under Brother Dame, William Dame, a colonel in the Iron Military District. Every able Saint in these parts has been ordered to join it."

"Why? Is there trouble with the Indians?" Hattie asked, her eyes wide, looking in the direction of what they thought only moments before were coyotes.

"No, Sister, the Indians 'round here won't hurt us. They're our friends. If there's trouble, they'll join us."

"Then, why do we need a militia?" she quizzed.

"Gentiles, Sister. Gentiles are our enemies. If this territory and our lives are threatened, it'll be 'cause the Gentiles want to challenge God's claim to this land. It'll be 'cause they want to keep us from forcing them out. We're gonna have to be ready." Lee looked expectantly at John. "There's a musterin' meeting in town right after Sunday services. You comin'?"

Anna knew that to refuse an order from the Church, to deny God's directive and Brigham Young's ambition was unthinkable. Anna squeezed his hand and John paused, not saying a word. Even if John didn't want to go, he wouldn't refuse.

"Yeah, I'll be there," he promised.

Chapter Four

Present Day Berkeley, California
8:00 p.m.

From a corridor window on the seventh floor of Dwinelle Hall, Sharon Marshall looked down at the parking lot at two men wearing sport coats, dress slacks, starched white shirts, and narrow dark ties. One was balding, muscle bound and short, the other a stocky redhead with a jaw that looked like it could bite through bone. The two were hurrying around the corner of the less than distinguished concrete hall and up the north steps. She looked closer. Hanging from their belts were holsters bulging with handguns. "My God," she blurted, suddenly aware. "It's the Impala, Alex," she shouted, bursting into Kevin's office, "they found us!"

Sharon was a corporate attorney out of San Francisco, a brunette, and slightly taller than average. She had brilliant green eyes with flecks of hazel.

Her companion was Alex Caldwell, an investigative reporter from the New York Post, tall and slender with deep cut dimples under his cheeks and along his jowls. They didn't know each other well, but they had one driving force holding them together. They were desperately trying to find out what happened to Wayne and Kim Hoffel. Kim was Sharon's sister. Wayne was one of Alex's best friends in college. Sharon had dinner with them just three nights ago. By six o'clock the next morning, without a word to her, they were gone, supposedly and expectantly having moved to Guatemala where Wayne was to continue his research on premature babies. While Sharon watched and followed, a moving van took all of Wayne and Kim's belongings to a storage facility south of town where Sharon was stopped by a cop, assaulted by him, and left lying in the gravel on the side of the road.

Neither she nor Alex could know that Wayne had already been murdered in a cruel and gruesome religious ritual. Wayne was known to the secret organization to which he belonged as 'Min, the Beekeeper'. He was found guilty by them of failing to deliver the vessel which they ordered him to surrender. He was also found guilty of most probably revealing to Hank Blanchard and possibly others secrets he had sworn before God and the Priesthood to keep.

Having violated the covenants of secrecy and obedience to which he swore, the only way Wayne could atone for his sins was by shedding his blood. Wayne was abducted in the night and driven into a mountain wilderness. One by one, his testicles were cut off. A cut was made across his belly and, as he watched, his guts unwound and slithered to his feet. As he lay next to his grave, while other executioners picked up and gathered his pieces, his throat was cut.

The same day Wayne and Kim disappeared, Alex and Wayne's friend, Hank Blanchard, was attacked by two men in the corridor at Madison Square Garden in New York as he and Alex were leaving a Knicks' basketball game. In self-defense, Hank killed one of his attackers and was charged with murder. The last time Alex talked to him, Hank was being ushered to a New York City jail. Alex did not yet know, Hank had been murdered in his cell.

Tonight, Alex and Sharon were at the University of California, Berkeley seeking Kevin James' help.

Kevin was not only a friend, he was a resource for some of Alex's investigative stories. Kevin's ash blond hair was long and thinning, uncombed and carelessly pulled back in a ponytail. His beard was short, dark and unkempt. He wore ill-fitting, khaki pants and a tan shirt covered with brown and black snake designs. Although he looked like a middle-aged, out of place student, he was a professor who was an expert in mythology.

In their search for Wayne and Kim, Alex and Sharon had broken into the storage facility and discovered a mysterious, gold medallion hidden in a crevice in Wayne's desk. One side of the medallion had a relief of an eagle, wings outstretched, head down, as if circling in search of prey. It was one of the symbols of the twelve tribes of Israel. The eagle, together with the tiny characters engraved in Hebrew just under the claws was a symbol of one of the twelve tribes' brigades, the symbol of the 'Dan Brigade'. On the other side of the medallion was an Egyptian symbol. It was a relief of 'Min', the Beekeeper, who carried the symbol of the bee the Egyptians called 'Deseret'. These symbols of the bee and eagle were also linked to the State of Utah, and in particular to the Mormon Church to which Wayne and Kim belonged.

In New York, after Hank's arrest, Alex found the strange inventory Wayne gave Hank in secrecy. It was in Hank's office in his wastebasket, hidden in a discarded pastrami sandwich. The inventory was a collection of numbers and letters apparently describing the condition and location of priceless vessels. It was entitled 'Project Samson Inventory'. Alex and Sharon believe the vessels identified must be similar to the Egyptian urn stolen from Wayne and Kim's home the night they disappeared. That vessel, too, bore the image of 'Min', the Beekeeper. Alex and Sharon believe Wayne might be involved in a black market for antiques.

Whatever significance the medallion and inventory had, whatever connections they had to Wayne and Kim's disappearance, it was obvious they were very important. Clearly others thought the symbols and inventory were vital, too. The very first time Alex and Sharon had a chance to examine the inventory, they were attacked by two armed and violent men who broke down their door, ransacked Alex's room, and gave chase to them in a white Impala. It was all Sharon could do to lose them.

There was something very strange going on. Alex and Sharon needed Kevin James' help to find out what that something was. Yet, Kevin couldn't tell them anything about the inventory. He needed more time to study it. The meanings of the combinations of numbers and letters were too obscure to understand without careful examination. The images on the medallion, however, were clear. Kevin had just finished explaining their meaning, when Sharon burst through the doorway.

"It's the Impala, Alex," she shouted, bursting into Kevin's office, "they found us."

"What?" Alex rushed passed her, into the hallway, and to the windows. He scanned the parking area. The white Impala was parked only feet from Sharon's red convertible. "So where are they?"

"On their way up. They've taken the stairs."

Kevin reached for the phone to call security.

"Forget that," Alex told him. "They won't get here in time. We've gotta' get out of here. Hurry."

Chapter Five

Kevin grabbed his laptop and an old, bell shaped, tan hat, and quickly followed. He and Alex had already decided he was going with them. Racing down the back stairs, the three of them ran to Sharon's sports convertible. The top down, Alex and Kevin did not bother with the doors. Kevin leaped in the back, and Alex took the passenger seat. Sharon started the car and was on the street before the two men pursuing them rushed out of the building headed for the Impala.

Retracing their route down Cross Campus Road and through traffic, Sharon drove west and then south. The speed and agility of her sports car, the many rights and lefts she took elusive, gave them the edge. The big, cumbersome Impala was no match for them, and they were out of sight and headed northeast in no time, the Impala lost somewhere behind them.

"How did they find us?" Sharon quizzed Alex. "You didn't tell anybody where we were going, did you?"

"Yeah," Alex hesitatingly acknowledged. "I told Herb Brown, my editor. I called him while you were in the bathroom just before we left the University of Utah."

"But why would your editor tell them?" Sharon asked. "Who are they?"

Obviously disappointed and stunned by the notion a man he trusted for years turned on him, Alex didn't immediately respond. Seeming to be searching for some logical, good faith reason, he offered an alternative. "Maybe Herb didn't tell them. Maybe they just figured that was where we went. We're looking for Wayne, and that's where is laboratory is. Makes sense doesn't it? They must have seen us there and followed us to Berkeley."

"Maybe so, but it's a little too scary and coincidental for me," Sharon observed. "I don't like it one bit. Maybe until you're certain you can trust him, you shouldn't tell Herb anything more. Maybe you shouldn't contact him at all."

"But, I was certain I could trust him," Alex protested. "Until now, I've never had any reason not to trust him. Damned if I'm gonna cut him off before I get an explanation." He was already calling Herb Brown's cell. After four rings, he got Herb's voice message. "Call me," Alex demanded, his voice almost as impatient as he was, "I need to talk to you." Angry and fidgety, believing he had been betrayed by a friend and not being able to find out why, he slumped in the passenger seat and looked away.

***

They were headed north to Portland, top up on the convertible, to see Sharon's mother. Kevin linked Wayne's medallion not only to the Twelve Tribe's Dan Brigade, but to the infamous Sons of Dan. Joseph Smith, founder of the Mormon Church, organized the Sons of Dan in the mid eighteen hundreds to kill and harass church members who didn't surrender their property to him. Kevin told them Wayne's medallion might well be evidence the Sons of Dan had revived and that Wayne was involved with them.

Sharon's Great Grandmother Anna may have mentioned the Sons of Dan in her diary, and Sharon's mother had it. They were on their way to Portland to get it. Anxious to learn what the diary contained, Sharon pushed the speed limit. Yet, she was not looking forward to seeing her mother. Her mother didn't yet know Kim and Wayne were missing, and Sharon would have to tell her.

About an hour after they lost the Impala, Alex still silently stewing about the possible betrayal of his editor, Sharon entered Interstate 5. It was a more obvious route to Portland for anyone chasing them, but the risk was worth it given it was considerably faster than any other route. Beginning to relax, Sharon set the cruise control.

Ready to get back to what Kevin told them, she said to him, "I want to remember and understand everything about the Sons of Dan. Tell me again."

Kevin nodded. What Sharon and Alex learned about the Sons of Dan might lead them to Wayne and Kim. "The Sons of Dan were basically thugs Joseph Smith used to do his dirty work. Smith was in all kinds of trouble. The Gentiles considered him a scoundrel and an adulterer who claimed he was having conversations with God, and they drove him out. Smith started a bank, issued his own paper money, and when he stopped payment on that money, his bank went bust. Substantial monies were lost, Church members deserted, and his settlement failed. He decided the only way out was to force his remaining members to surrender their property to him. His Sons of Dan thrived on violence and were more than happy to spill blood for him. Dissenters were forced out of the Church or worse, and when Smith finished with them, he turned the Sons of Dan on the Gentiles. He and Sidney Rigdon, his counselor, declared war on the Gentiles and ordered the Mormons to exterminate them, with the Sons of Dan taking the lead. They became the 'Army of Elohim' and were the scourge of anyone who got in the way. They survived Joseph Smith, and by the time your Great Grandmother came along when Brigham Young was in charge, the Sons of Dan were calling themselves 'The Avenging Angels'."

"I hope Wayne's involvement with them doesn't mean he's a murderer, too," Sharon wished aloud. "I told you my grandmother talked about the Avenging Angels," she reminded him, "and that they had something to do with 'bad things' and my Great Grandfather John." Kevin already told her because of Wayne's involvement with the Sons of Dan or Avenging Angels, or whatever they were calling themselves these days, Wayne might already be dead. Yet most dishearteningly for her, was his trying to prepare her for the worst by telling her Kim would not be the first woman they'd killed.

Nighttime traffic was still heavy on the interstate, the sun a desired companion they left far behind. Amidst the traffic, just south of the turnoff to Mount Shasta and still hours from Portland, they hit a ten-mile deluge that shut visibility down to a few feet, sending the fast moving, lowing riding sports car bucking and shimmying through standing water. Her hands tightly gripping the wheel, Sharon fought not only the road but the reckless, countless, fast moving semis that dangerously crowded her.

Chapter Six

Cedar City, Utah
Summer 1857

How ya doin', Sister Anna?" Brother Zeb was the owner of Cedar City's general store, a one room shop stuffed to the rafters with everything he could fit into it, cans and barrels, dry goods and skins, guns and ammunition, and an array of farm equipment. His tiny apartment was a shack out back. The livery stable he owned was next door.

Zeb was one of the men Brigham Young sent to Southwestern Utah six years ago to settle the area. He was well over fifty and bald, with a long and curly, ragged gray beard. "What can I get for ya today?"

"John's torn his Sunday pants, and I need some thread to mend them." Anna told him. Lizzy was with her, examining one of Zeb's new spools of ribbon. "Do you have any gray?"

"Yeah, think I do." Zeb took a dilapidated cigar box from one of the shelves behind him and placed it on the counter. Heaped inside the tattered box was a variety of hand wound spools of thread. He pawed through the spools, but there was no gray. "Don't worry," he assured Anna, "I'm sure I got it somewhere." He hunted in a neighboring cabinet filled with all kinds of tins and pulled from it a large tin of tobacco. Inside that tin was a much smaller tin of chewing tobacco, his personal stock, a hunk of pyrite, a nodule of turquoise, and two spools of thread. "Here ya are," he said triumphantly, handing Anna the gray one.

The store was a menagerie, a tangle of clutter. "How do you remember where everything is?" Anna asked, casually looking around.

"Jist got a way, I guess. Ain't a thing in here I can't find once't I set my mind to it." Zeb liked someone noticing how clever he was and usually tried to ply more compliments out of them, but not today. He furrowed his brow, and told her, disapprovingly, "Didn't see you and Brother John at the gatherin'."

"No," Anna confirmed, a little sheepishly, "we couldn't go."

"Got an invite, didn't ya?" he questioned. "Brother Brigham sent 'em ta every saint in the territory." The invitation to which Zeb referred was to an anniversary celebration. It was the tenth anniversary of the Mormon's arrival in Utah on July 24, 1847.

"We got the invitation. We just couldn't go," she explained. "Winter'll be here before long, and our cabin's only half finished. Couldn't afford to take the time."

"Too bad," he said, his voice still disapproving. "Ya really missed somethin.' There was over two thousand people there. Good people, too. Lots of 'em the first out here. Must 'a seen near everybody I knew outa' Missouri and Illinois. Great people. Great time."

"Was there a band?" Anna asked, quite envious.

"A band. Why, I ain't never seen so many bands. Bands playin' all day long. People dancin' and singin' twixt speeches of the grand kind. You know, the kind where somebody important gets yer blood ta boilin'.

"Wish we'd been able to go," Anna said.

"Me, too," Lizzy offered.

"Would have been nice to see everybody again."

Zeb thought of something else, and his voice turned grave. "John's comin' ta the meetin' next week ain't he? Everybody in the militia's supposed ta be there."

"I think so," Anna said. "He usually goes."

"Good. He better ought ta be there," Zeb scolded. "Whole town's supposed ta be there. This ain't goin' ta be no ordinary meetin'."

"Why, what's the matter?"

"Didn't ya hear?" The darkness in Zeb's face deepened. His lips drooped to a frown. "We was 'bout two days into the celebration when old Porter Rockwell comes ridin' in with three a' his partners. Road weary and solemn. Carryin' news to Brigham Young hisself."

"What news?" Lizzy asked.

As if measuring in every way a full grown woman, Zeb looked Lizzy up and down. His eyes filled with concern. "How old are ya, girl?"

Trying to look older than she was and more grown up, Lizzy stood on tiptoe and raised her chin. "Almost fourteen, why?"

"'Cause you're still a child."

Deflated, Lizzy's shoulders slumped. Her toes relaxed, and she lost two inches standing flat footed again.

"It's kids like her that's gonna suffer," he continued. "'Specially like her."

"What do you mean?" Anna asked. Zeb was frightening her. "What's happening?"

"Didn't know ourselves 'til that night, 'til we was bein' told how to break up camp, all the time dancin' and laughin' like fools."

"Didn't know what?" Anna demanded.

Zeb closed one eye and squeezed the other to a slit. Baring his teeth, he told her, "Them Gentiles have stopped all our mail 'tween here and parts east. Worse yet, that puke Buchanan's declared us rebels. He's sendin' an army against us."

Anna gasped, "An army?"

"Yep, twenty-five hundred troops of the Army of the United States on their way here. Comin' to put down what they're callin' a 'rebellion'." He seethed with bitterness. "Over my dead body."

"There must be a mistake," Anna argued, terrified. "There's no rebellion here. We're farmers." For months they'd been told the Gentiles would send an army against them, but still she was not prepared for it.

Hate burned in Zeb's eyes. "They're not attackin' us 'cause we're farmers. They're comin' after us 'cause we're Mormons. It's gonna happen all over again, the burnin', lootin', and murderin', just like in Missouri and Illinois." He sneered defiantly, "Ceptin' this time, it's not gonna be so easy, 'cause we'll be waitin' for 'em. We got us a bigger army than we ever had 'afore, and this time we'll use it."

Fear of war and invasion set the pace of her stride as Anna hurried Lizzy home. She no longer cared about the thread and had forgotten it. "John," she called, from nearly a quarter mile away. The wind was blowing in her face, and she was screaming. "John."

John was working in the field. Hattie was baking bread in the earthen oven in front of the cabin. When Anna's voice finally pierced the wind and reached them, they both looked up.

"Papa," Lizzy screamed. Anna's fear was contagious, and on seeing him, Lizzy was compelled to flee it. Breaking into a dead run, she cried, "Papa, the army's coming. We're being attacked."

"Anna," John shouted, he threw the hoe aside and raced to meet them, catching Lizzy by the shoulders. "What's Lizzy talking about?" he asked through the wind, but Anna was too far away and too breathless to respond. He pushed Lizzy away and, face to face, his hands on her shoulders, asked her, "What do you mean?"

"An army's coming." Lizzy breathlessly told him. "We're being invaded." They're going to murder us." Breaking John's hold, she buried her face in his shirt and sobbed.

Bewildered, he stroked Lizzy's hair. Anna was still several yards away. "Who told you that?"

"Brother Zeb."

"Is this true, Anna? An army's coming?" he asked, when she neared them.

Hattie joined them, and Lizzy was now clutching her.

"Yes, they're marching from Washington." Still out of breath, trying to keep her own fear in check, Anna related what they had learned from Zeb.

"He's gotta' be mistaken," John said. "If it's true, they'd have told me by now." As was required of him, he'd joined the militia and regularly drilled with them. This was news he would have expected to get from his commander.

"I hope you're right," Anna sighed.

Chapter Seven

Portland, Oregon
Present Day
April 24

Three hours after Sharon, Alex and Kevin hit the deluge near Mt. Shasta, they went through a second storm just as terrible. After they came out from under that storm they were enclosed in fog all the way to Portland.

They didn't reach Sharon's mother's house until mid-morning. It was a small rambler with red brick siding. There was no drive, so they parked at the curb beside her front yard. She'd been watching for them and came out to greet them. Smiling broadly, she took Sharon in her arms and hugged her.

Susan Marshall was tall, like Sharon's sister, Kim, perhaps even taller. Her dark blue eyes brilliant against her soft, pale skin and graying, blond hair, she appeared quite youthful. Her visitors, on the other hand, looked bedraggled and exhausted. "You must be tired," she said. "Have you eaten? Are you hungry?"

"We're all right, Mother," Sharon told her. Heartbroken for what she must tell her, she embraced her again. "I've missed you."

"I've missed you too, Honey. Are you sure you don't want something? I've got muffins and orange juice in the kitchen. I can make you some eggs. How about an omelet?"

As they walked to the door Sharon introduced them. "Mother, this is Alex Caldwell, Wayne's friend from the wedding."

"Oh yes, I thought I recognized you."

"And, this is our friend, Professor Kevin James."

"Nice to meet you, Professor James."

"Call me Kevin."

"You all look like you could use a sandwich."

"I'm fine, Mother, really. But, Kevin and Alex may want something. We didn't have much for dinner." As they entered the house, Sharon nodded toward the kitchen, so they would understand she wanted time with her mother alone.

"Come on, Kevin," Alex said, "let's see what's cookin'."

"There's coffee made," Susan called after them." Help yourselves."

"Don't worry about us," Alex told her. "We'll be fine." He glanced supportingly at Sharon and followed Kevin into the kitchen.

"Where are the kids?" Sharon asked. Kim told her Wayne brought their children up here to stay with her mother. Given how Wayne disapproved of Susan's not wanting to become Mormon, his bringing them here seemed odd when Kim told her. It seemed even stranger now.

"They're playing upstairs."

"Good, I can go up and see them later. Mother, I need to tell you something." With her arm around Susan's waist, Sharon guided her into the living room. "Let's go in here."

"I knew you hadn't driven all this way and all night just for a visit," Susan observed. The old style living room had a colonial theme. The upholstery was autumn-like with yellows and oranges out of the seventies, and there was an old upright piano in the corner. "What's wrong?"

"Sit down, Mother." Having come up with a dozen different ways of telling her mother Kim was missing and having rejected them all, words surprisingly tumbled from Sharon's mouth. "Kim's gone, and I can't find her."

"What do you mean, 'gone'?" Susan demanded, trepidation in her eyes.

"Mom, she and Wayne are missing. Everyone's telling us they moved to Guatemala, but that doesn't make sense. They would have told me. I had dinner with them the night before they disappeared. If they were moving, they would have told you, too. They would have taken their children. We think something has happened to them."

Susan was suddenly and surprisingly calm and deliberate. "Tell me everything." Alex and Kevin were hesitatingly standing in the hall with their muffins and coffee. "You come in, too," she told them. "Tell me what's going on."

Chapter Eight

Present Day Utah
April 21

It was after 9:00 p.m. and pitch black inside Little Cottonwood Canyon. Had they not seen where Molly's red Mustang landed, the two men in the Black SUV chasing her would never have found it in the dark. At least sixty feet from the highway, her Mustang was upside down in a thick growth of willows on the other side of a wide, swift moving creek. It had hit the rail at ninety miles an hour, flipped twice in the air, landed on its nose, and tipped over. The front end was crushed. The engine was dead.

Immediately jumping out of the SUV, her counselor, Elder Roundtree, trained a flashlight on the driver's side. "I can't see her," he shouted to Ralph, his companion. Not waiting for him, Roundtree stepped over the crumpled rail and into the dense growth of bushes. He was six-foot tall yet was only a head taller than the willows. His feet sinking into mud as he fought his way through the unyielding shrubs, he headed in a straight line toward the Mustang. His companion was close behind him.

"Can you see her?" Ralph kept asking. He was so close and nervous, he was breathing down Roundtree's neck and pushing him. "Is she dead?"

"I don't know." Roundtree answered impatiently. "Get off me." Twenty feet further, they reached the creek, and he shown the flashlight again on the Mustang. Willows were holding it up. A blue shadow was hanging from the driver's seat. As he trained his light on it, the shadow did not move or did it cry out when he called her. "Molly, are you all right?" There was silence. "We're coming, Molly," he shouted.

Struggling against the rapid current, holding their arms above the rough, water, they waded across the frigid, waist high creek, swollen from melting snow. Soaked, they scrambled up the bank on the other side into a second growth of willows. Still thirty feet from Molly's Mustang and exhausted, Roundtree kept talking to her. "Do you hear me, Molly? Are you all right? Is anything broken? We're coming Molly. We're coming."

Four feet above the ground, cradled upside down on dense willows, Molly's red convertible was totaled. The canvas convertible top was smashed and skewered by branches. Silent and unmoving, Molly was hanging upside from her seatbelt.

"She dead?" Ralph asked him.

Molly's door was bent at the top and had jammed. Roundtree tugged at it with all his might but couldn't open it. "Give me a hand here," he demanded, and he and Ralph tugged at it together.

"Can't get a decent grip," Ralph complained. The window was shut, the seams jammed tight by the collision, and there was no room for his fingers. The door did not move.

"We need the tire iron," Roundtree told Ralph. "Go get it. I'll stay here with Molly."

"You're kiddin' me, right?" Ralph argued. "I'm not going back through that jungle unless it's to leave." He was a burly guy but not much for doing any more than he had to do. "You go, and I'll stay here. I'll yell at 'ya if she says anything."

Roundtree looked at Ralph as if he didn't quite believe what he was hearing but didn't argue.

"Okay, but if she wakes up, tell her I'm here and that I'll be right back. Do you have a first aid kit?"

"Don't bother getting' that. If it turns out she's alive, we'll get her out of here and take her back to the car. You can patch her after we're underway. No use wasting time out here."

"Is it locked?" Roundtree asked about the SUV.

"No, but you'd better take my keys and lock it before you come back." The burly man reached into his wet pants pocket and pulled out a handful of keys.

Ten minutes later, the creek still troublesome, the trail they made going in making it easier to break through the bushes on the way out, Roundtree lifted the SUV's hatch, threw back the rug, and reached for the spare tire compartment. The tire iron was in his hand when the headlights of an oncoming car shown behind him.

Not turning around, he slowly closed the compartment and busied himself in the back, waiting for the car to pass without seeing his face. As the car behind him got closer, the lights grew brighter. There were suddenly flashes of red, emergency lights. Roundtree heard the car pull up behind him, and he froze. "It's a cop!" he murmured.

"Need any help?" A male voice shouted.

Roundtree turned. Behind him was an aid car and two medics walking toward him. He breathed easier. "No, I was just fixing a flat tire," he said.

"From the marks on the road and that bashed in rail, it looks like something happened here. You sure everything's all right?" the lead man, a middle-aged man in uniform, asked.

"Yeah, everything's fine," Roundtree told them. "Tire blew, so I swerved a bit. I'm all right, though." He glanced at the rail. "It was like that when I got here."

The medic walked to the rail and examined the damage. He drew his finger across a streak of red paint clearly from the car that hit it. "Don't remember it being like this when we drove up here," he observed, more to the other medic than to Roundtree. "You see it?"

The medic's partner shook his head. "No, but I wasn't lookin' for it, either."

"How'd you get so wet?" the medic asked. Roundtree's shirt, jacket, and pants were soaking wet. He was shivering.

"Ooogh. I dropped one of the lug nuts, and it rolled into the willows. It was like a rain forest in there, and I had to crawl on my hands and knees to find it."

"Sorry to hear that. Can we help you with the tire?" the middle-aged medic asked Roundtree.

"No, all fixed. I was just getting ready to leave."

"Want us to follow you?"

"No, I'll be all right. Besides, I've got to call my wife to let her know I'll be late. When I tell her what happened, she'll want to hear every detail. I don't like talking while I'm driving, so I'll be here awhile."

"Better turn your hazards on, though. We almost didn't see you. There's not much traffic out here, so anybody coming along won't be expecting you and might hit you." The medic and his partner walked back to the aid car, and as they opened the doors to leave, the middle-aged man turned back to Roundtree. "Just to be on the safe side, we'll let the police know you're here so they can check on you. Make sure you get off all right. You sure don't want to have to spend the night out here. Well, drive carefully."

Roundtree watched as the aid car moved back onto the road and drove away. He paused. "Shit." he swore. "Cops is all we need." Tire iron in hand, he turned, stepped over the rail and hurried back into the bushes.

Chapter Nine

Cedar City
July 1857

A blustery, evening wind blew dust in swirls down Main Street as the Meeting House crowded with jittery, angry Mormons. "What the tarnation they think they're doin'?" a man shouted. "Can't them damn heathens leave us alone?"

Brother Zeb, owner of the general store, led the meeting, shaking at them a rolled up copy of a newspaper. "I got an article here from the Deseret News recitin' Brother Kimball's sermon 'bout that army the U.S. is sendin' against us." Brother Heber Kimball was one of the twelve apostles of the Mormon Church and was Brigham Young's First Counselor. After Joseph Smith and Brigham Young, he was the most powerful man in the Church.

Zeb dramatically unrolled the eight page, ten-by-seven-and-a-half-inch tabloid to the front page and displayed to all of them the article containing Heber Kimball's speech. "Yes, that's right," Zeb encouraged, as his audience stared at words too small for them to read, "Brother and Apostle Heber Kimball is speakin' to us hisself. 'Send twenty-five hundred troops here,' he's sayin' to us, 'to desolate our people? God almighty help me, but I will fight until there's not a drop of blood left in my veins. Good God!' he tells us, not afraid, 'I have wives enough to whip the United States'."

Suddenly overwhelmed with worry, Anna wrapped her arms around Lizzy and Hattie's waists and held her breath. John was holding Maybella on his shoulders so Maybella could see and was standing behind them. Pressed against them, the crowd was quiet, loathe even to whisper. While outside, wind and dust buffeted the windows.

Continuing Kimball's tirade with his own, Zeb told them, "That Gentile army's gonna take over Utah. They got a new governor with 'em, and they're fixin' ta replace Brother Brigham. They're aimin' to turn the Gentiles against us, to murder us, and take all our lands away. Zion's gonna be destroyed.

"But don't you go fearin' now. Them soldiers may be thousands strong, but that don't mean they're gonna get us. We done been pushed far enough, and they ain't gonna push us no more. We gotta' be ready. You immigrants don't know what it's like to have the Gentiles against ya, but we know. Brother Thomas'll tell ya."

Brother Thomas was nearly forty. His brown hair was streaked with gray. His face was deeply scarred with pockmarks. He had lost both his index fingers to traps. As he took the podium, his eyes were downcast, his voice subdued. "I'm goin' to tell you what happened to me and mine at Nauvoo."

Stories about the sacking of the Mormon City-state of Nauvoo in Illinois by Gentiles just a few years before had been told and retold. Though Anna heard all the stories, including Brother Thomas', she listened intently. This time, his story might well become her own.

As if he could see nothing in the room except his memories of the Gentile's destruction of the Mormon capital and what they did to him, Brother Thomas paused. His face was a mask of anguish, gray and funereal, the corners of his mouth downturned to his chin. Glazed and vacant, his eyes stared at the open back door. He took a deep breath and in a low, somber voice began, "More than two-thousand drunk and violent vigilantes came huntin' us at night like wolf packs, and they whipped us. They licked us, they was drivin' us 'cross the Mississippi. Me and my kids were sick with ague, burnin' up inside with fever and shiverin'. My third wife was nursin' one babe and carryin' another. And we was defenseless. I carried my little girls into the tall weeds and hid 'em. My wives and our other children hid in the woods back a' the house. From there, we listened to the mobbers tear our home apart and burn it.

"My girls was cryin' they was so scared, makin' so much noise the mobbers found us. There was thirty of 'em, and they was armed with pistols and muskets fixed with bayonets. They found my wives and our other children, too." He sniffled, angrily wiped his eyes, and through clenched teeth, told them, "They was holdin' me, forcin' me to watch, when they raped my young wife, Jane. Hurtin' her so bad she was bleedin' and could barely walk when they herded us into the river, tellin' us they'd kill us if we ever came back. All the while carryin' their flag, that same Stars and Stripes that was supposed to protect us.

"We was swimmin', helpin' each other stay afloat, but we'd 'a been fish bait, drowned for sure, if a brother hadn't picked us up in his flatboat. By the time we crossed that dad blam river, we had nothin' but our faith. We was scorched by the hot sun durin' the day and frozen at night. We was tired, and we was hungry, with nothin' ta' comfort us but hope while we sat on the other side, waitin' two weeks for the wagons Brigham Young was sendin' to rescue us. My children was nothin' but shadows by the time the wagons got there.

"It was under the Stars and Stripes the Gentiles pillaged Nauvoo and drove us out. It's under the Stars and Stripes their army of over two-thousand advances on us now. Beware, and be careful. Be ready to defend your families with your lives. Fight 'em. Bring forth your weapons and fight 'em. Or you'll die!"

Anna could only imagine the horrors Brother Thomas described, but the picture he painted was vivid. All around her, aroused by his story, the congregation chanted, "Fight 'em! Fight 'em."

Strangely empowered by their voices, she joined the shouting. "Fight 'em. Fight 'em."

Zeb stepped to the podium and shouted over them, "Prove to God you'll defend yerselves against yer enemies. Fight 'em." With every heart willing to destroy the force set upon them, their chanting crescendoed, blocking out the pounding of the dust and wind beating against the windows. When the clamoring petered out, Zeb spoke again, this time inciting them to treason.

Again holding up the Deseret News, he told them. "Our Prophet, Brigham Young, has spoken. The time will come when this kingdom must be free and independent of all other kingdoms. We are to wait a little while to see, but Brigham has taken the hostile move by our enemies as evidence it is time for the thread to be cut. God wants a revolution, a struggle for freedom," Zeb encouraged, translating Brigham Young's message. "If we're gonna prove ourselves to God, we have ta take up arms and destroy the pukes comin' against us. We've gotta' free His Kingdom from mortal rule. We gotta' declare ourselves independent of the United States, and we gotta' reestablish our land as God's territory. We are Israel, and we shall triumph."

"We are Israel. We are Israel," everyone shouted.

"Curse them that comes," Zeb cried.

"Kill them. Kill them," the room chanted.

"Amen."

It was the summer of 1857. The states of the South were calling for secession and preparing for civil war. In Utah, the Mormons were preparing for their own war. When the war chants in the Meeting House died down that day, Zeb immediately began to prepare for it. "If we're gonna succeed in God's venture, we have ta' get ready. Our militia has ta' be ready. Major Lee," Zeb introduced.

John D. Lee took the podium, his written orders from Brigadier General Franklin D. Richards in hand. Summarizing, he reminded the attendees, "Our prophets and brethren have been imprisoned and murdered. Our people en masse have been exterminated from our midst," he told them. "Our appeals to the United States Government for the redress of those wrongs have been refused. We now appeal to God and our Prophets against the invaders.

"Our militia is required to hold our regiments in readiness to march at the shortest possible notice to any portion of the territory. Report any person who gives a kernel of grain to any Gentile merchant or temporary sojourner, or suffers it to go to waste. Take from passing emigrants their arms and ammunition. No one, and I mean no one, gives nothin' to the Gentiles. Brother Heber has promised there'll be plenty a' food for us."

Reclaiming the podium and interrupting Lee, Zeb shook the newspaper. "You can read his promise for yerself. The army that's comin' has some seven thousand head a' cattle and seven-hundred wagons each loaded with two tons of food and stores. Each of the twenty-five hundred soldiers carries a rifle, a coat, a blanket and personal things. We'll take it all from them, and what we take will be our manna. The soldiers' personal things will clothe our boys and girls. Their provisions'll last us fifteen months. After we whip those vermin, we can live on the spoils of our victory," Zeb encouraged. "By our own work and what God provides us in His cause, we can defeat our enemies and establish a nation free of Gentiles." He sighed, and everyone responded, "Amen."

Retaking the podium, Major Lee gave his own order. "Every able man in the militia will meet at Brother Zeb's store every night after supper until further notice."

The peaceful evening chorus of crickets in the desert brush was in sharp contrast to Anna's throbbing heart as the family walked home. Her people were on the cusp of war. Their very existence was in jeopardy. No one was in the mood for talking.

The family went to bed without wanting supper. Under the moonless night sky, the thick sod roof a barrier against light, the two room cabin was completely dark. In the bedroom, lying next to a restless John, Anna wondered if any of them were sleeping. Hattie and the girls, sharing a single bed, were in the main room. John and Anna were alone. She curled into his strong, stout body, and his arms enfolded her. "Do you think those army soldiers will rape us, like that mob did Brother Thomas' wife? Do you think they'd harm Lizzy? What about little Maybella?"

John spoke very softly so Hattie and the girls would not hear. "Not if I'm still alive, they won't. I won't let those soldiers get anywhere near any of you."

"What if you're off somewhere with the militia? How am I going to protect them?"

"The girls will have to do what they can. Like you, and me, and everybody else. They'll have to do whatever they're told to do. There'll be thousands of us if we stand together. If we don't, we won't have a chance."

Anna wanted comfort from John. She wanted him to tell her no harm would come to any of them. She knew he would be lying, but she needed to hear it anyway. Without his reassurance, her heart was sick, her mind restless with thoughts of the horrible ways each of them could die. Trembling from fear, she crowded into him.

Stories of rape and murder, violence and hate, were told and retold throughout Utah, agitating and provoking, making the Mormons restless and suspicious not only of Gentiles but of each other. Brigham Young and the Priesthood were adamant that Mormon traitors and sinners be purged and that the Gentiles in the territory be driven out. Members of the Church were disappearing.

John was attending a meeting with Zeb and some of the other zealots in town, those known to enforce the Doctrine of Blood Atonement. They called themselves the Avenging Angels and were proud of themselves for doing their duty to God. Many considered them valiant heroes and defenders of the faith. Though threatened with death if they told, Avenging Angels who murdered on orders let slip their activities to their loved ones. They spoke openly of the existence of secret tribunals held in the night, tribunals that convicted and sentenced

Mormon transgressors and Gentiles to die. Rumors spawned.

Mormon Albert Tilly had been seen talking to U.S. Marshals who were hunting a saint wanted for murder in Missouri. Brother Tilly told the marshals the saint they were hunting moved to San Bernadino, and he gave the Marshals bacon to keep them along the way. For helping those Gentiles and the government they represented, Brother Tilly was called 'Traitor'. He became a pariah, and then, he vanished.

Gone one night to look for stolen horses with Zeb and his nephew, Bud, Tilly was reportedly killed when his horse fell with him into a canyon. The bodies of horse and rider were said to have been lost. Yet stories abounded Tilly had been murdered by order of Brigham Young and Bud drove an ax through his skull. His body lay hidden beneath a landslide. His horse had been sold.

A second Mormon, Brother Baker, was a habitual thief and troublemaker. His loyalty to the Church had long been in question. Brother Baker was meeting with Gentiles who worked with the Federal Indian Agent telling them stories that made the Mormons look bad. The Avenging Angels' tribunal met and sentenced Brother Baker to death. Brother Stead, otherwise innocent, happened to be with Baker at the appointed time and was also executed.

Mormons who tried to leave, to get out of Utah, who had committed no other sin than that, were merely bankrupted. Letting them leave with all their cattle and portable belongings, the Avenging Angels robbed the deserters of everything along the trail, forcing them to return to Utah in poverty.

All over the territory, name after name was recited in the rumor mill. Brother Hanson and his mother were murdered. No one knew why. Brothers Jeffers and Tilman were killed for adultery with their stepdaughters. Brother Henry was executed for stealing a horse.

Anna noticed John was changing. Like a man in the midst of conflict, for no other apparent reason, he was agitated and impatient. An excitation was bubbling up in him that overflowed at the meetings with the zealots. He sometimes came home with blood on his clothes. Obviously involved in what was going on, he was no longer the man Anna married, and she found herself pulling away from him.

As time passed, the Mormon War of Extermination against the Gentiles continued. Avenging Angels threatened every federal official who caused trouble, making it clear that the Doctrine of Blood Atonement applied equally to them. Brigham Young publicly threatened, "If the Gentiles wish to see a few tricks, we have 'Mormons' that can perform them. We have the meanest devils on the earth in our midst, and we intend to keep them, for we have use for them. If the Devil does not look sharp, we will cheat him out of them at the last, for they will reform and go to Heaven with us." It was rumored Brigham actually got pleasure out of spilling Gentile blood, and those who did it for him were proud.

Isaac Haight was Cedar City's Stake President, which made him the most powerful priest in the area. His words and commands were as those of Brigham Young, and he was not to be disobeyed. It did not matter whether Haight's orders were right or wrong. No Mormon was permitted to question him. Their duty was to obey him or die.

Chapter Ten

Cedar City
July 1857

The night sky bristled with stars, but there was no moon. A coyote howled, but no other coyote answered. The desert was still. The bay horse John rode, a borrowed horse, was jittery as he rode through the desert grass and sagebrush with three other men. Brother Zeb was on his big, flashy, dappled gray. Zeb's nephew, Bud, was riding a young, only half-broke mustang, and Brother Henson was on one of his draft horses. They were not only saints but were Avenging Angels with a mandate from God.

There were no trees or hills to hide them, only darkness as they approached the distillery that night. Guided by a lantern in the window, the only light for miles and about a hundred yards away, the four stopped in the dead grass of a small opening in the sagebrush, and dismounted.

"Might be here awhile," Zeb told them. He reached into his saddlebag and removed a golden glass, whiskey flask. He pulled the cork, took a nice long drink and handed it to his nephew. "Never hurts nothin' to have a swig or two 'fore doin' God's work. Does it, Bud?"

In response, Bud took two swigs. Satisfied, he handed the flask back to Zeb.

"Either 'a you care to," Zeb asked John and Brother Hensen, offering them the flask.

Brother Hensen shook his head. "Not 'til it's over." He was shy and not much for talking. He was considered a loyal Angel, yet he let none of them get close to him and never shared what he was thinking.

"Thanks. I'll have some," John said, taking the flask. He wiped the thick lip with the palm of his hand, put it to his mouth, and swallowed. He coughed as he drew it away and handed it back to Zeb.

From inside the distillery was a noise, something falling. Startled, they stared. Zeb stepped toward his horse, reached for his rifle, and cocked it.

"What happened?" Brother Hensen asked, but no one answered.

Examining the darkened perimeter of the distillery and everything they could see through the window, they waited. A man appeared in the window, picked up the lantern, and put it back.

"What's that mean?" Bud asked, his voice strained.

"Nothin'," Zeb told him. "They was just telling us everything's all right."

"How much longer 'fore we go," Hensen asked him. "They oughta' be ready by now."

"Just hold onta' yer britches," Zeb said. "Won't be long now." He looked back at the distillery window and examined the half-opened front door. Parked about twenty feet away was a flatbed, freight wagon. "Get mounted."

Shoving his rifle into the saddle holster, Zeb mounted his big gray. "So what are you waitin' for?" he demanded. John, Hensen and Bud had not yet moved, but responded immediately. "Want us arriving the same time, so get astride me," Zeb ordered as the men mounted, and in a line, they waited.

From inside the distillery, shouts and laugher, the sounds of drunken partying drifted toward them.

An hour later, the noise subsided and the distillery was quiet. "Signal's comin'," Zeb told them. "Watch for it but don't move 'til I tell ya. Understood?" He stared at Bud.

"Yeah, yeah, I understand," Bud told him.

Long moments passed. A man appeared at the window, picked up the lamp and took it away.

"Go slow and stay with me," Zeb ordered. Gently pressing his spurs against the gray's flanks, the gray quietly walked forward, each step a cushiony fall.

Only Bud's mustang resisted, crow hopping and sidestepping, whinnying in protest when Bud tried to hold him back. Aroused by the struggle and spoiling for a fight, excitement gleamed in Bud's eyes. He suddenly spurred the mustang into a run and galloped toward the distillery. Jerking back the reins when he got there, forcing the mustang to slide to a stop, Bud dismounted in front of the freight wagon. He reached toward the front axle. Yanking the kingbolt out of its seat, he wrapped his hand around the fifteen-inch long, two-inch diameter, iron rod and ran to the distillery. The door already opened for him, he rushed inside.

Spurring their horses to catch up, Zeb, John and Hensen immediately galloped after him, dismounting just as Bud ran inside. Within the distillery, sprawled on top of bags of grain was a body, blood gushing from its cracked skull. They looked up. A few feet away, against other bags of grain set out as a backrest, was a second man. In a drunken stupor, barely able to comprehend what was happening, he was looking up at Bud, his eyes dull and questioning. In that instant, Bud glared at him, drew back his hand and swung, the kingbolt striking the man just above the temple. His skull smashed, his blood spraying onto Bud, he lifelessly stared as, like so much blubber, his body tipped and fell over.

Two Mormon men, sent to lure these Gentiles to them with promises of liquor, stood quietly in the corner, removing themselves from the bloodshed. A third man, the other Gentile, able to stand and upright was readying to defend himself. Fists clenched, feet spread apart, he searched the room, looking for a way out or for a weapon. Finding neither, he waited for them. He was a big man, and he was braced to fight. It would take all four assassins to kill him.

John stepped forward, and with Zeb and Hensen surrounded him. Covered with blood, and still holding the kingbolt, Bud hung back.

"What do you want? Why? I don't have any money," the big man told them. "I'll get on my horse and be gone. You'll never see me again." His eyes shifting from one man to another, he watched them. His hands were shaking. There were tears in his eyes. "Leave me be," he begged.

Suddenly from the corner, the two Mormon's who lured him there rushed him and tried to push him to the floor. Stronger than they, he resisted. He was about to get the best of them, when John and Hensen tackled him. All their strength and weight against him, the four dragged him down. Biting and kicking, squirming and cursing, the Gentile fought like a bull for his life. He lost when Zeb stepped forward, calmly put the rifle barrel to the Gentile's ear and shot him.

To kill was a potent elixir for John and the other three men. The Gentile's blood all over them, they were breathless when they stood. The three Gentiles were destitute. The Mormons thought they were spies for the approaching army. Considered dangerous, the Avenging Angels' tribunal had decided they were to be 'put out of the way'.

As far as the Mormons were concerned, Gentiles were the cursed of God. Killing them was virtuous. Told the elimination of these three Gentiles was the will of God, John and the others righteously agreed to kill them. Believing in the Doctrine of Blood Atonement, they thought they were spilling the Gentiles' blood to save them from their sins, to assure them a place in heaven. Yet, as John and the other saints who held this Gentile down stood over his body, they seemed anxious. Breathing hard and fast, John especially seemed affected. As they calmed, the flow of their adrenaline diminishing, they were deadly quiet. Their faces turned pale, and they looked fearful. The Mormon men they killed went almost willingly. This man was the first who struggled for his life, and they were obviously troubled.

"Even those who resist must find their way to God," Zeb reminded them, breaking the silence "These Gentiles would have destroyed us if we'd let them go. This way, even if they didn't want it, we've done them a favor. They would have gone to hell, if we hadn't stopped them. You've gotta' remember that blood on the floor is their atonement. They should thank you for their salvation."

Guilt seeking to overtake him, John refused it. "That's right," he said, as if inspired. "It was God's will that this man die. It was His will that we be His messengers. This Gentile fears hell no more because we have saved him."

When John came home that night, hours after Hattie and the girls had gone to bed, Anna was waiting. His clothes were red wet. Sweat had dried on his face and was sticky. Blood was caked in the creases of his face, on his hands, along his cuticles, and beneath his nails. He reached for her, but she turned away. "Your bath water's outside," she coolly told him of a barrel out back. "Give me your clothes, and I'll wash them."

Stripping to his spiritual undergarment, John handed her the same clothes he'd worn to all his meetings. With a patchwork of stains and fresh blood no amount of scrubbing could remove, she took them silently and sadly. She knew someone had died. Were she courageous or able to do anything about what was happening, or even convinced the Priesthood was wrong, she might have asked John who was killed that night. Yet, she was none of those things. In any event, she would hear about the murder tomorrow in town.

Chapter Eleven

Present Day Portland, Oregon
8:00 p.m.
April 24

Kevin James was at Susan's kitchen table, a solid pine table with matching chairs, all painted white. Alex was napping on the couch in the living room, more comfortable there in the center of activity than in the double bed Susan made up for him in the guest room. Though Susan took the news about Wayne and Kim better than Sharon expected, Sharon stayed close to her mother, sitting with her legs tucked in an overstuffed chair in the corner.

Kevin rolled the medallion between his fingers, put it between his teeth, and softly bit into it, verifying to himself the piece was 24 karat gold. Placing it on the table, Min side up, directly under the bright light of a tiny halogen lamp, he examined it through a magnifying glass.

The relief of Min the Beekeeper was unmistakable. The Mormon's connection to the red crown he carried was also unmistakable. The Egyptians called the red crown 'Deseret'. Deseret's connection to the Mormon Church and to the red crown was also unmistakable. Deseret meant honeybee. The Mormons not only named their territory Deseret, but they use the bee and beehive as their symbols. He recalled the verse in the Book of Mormon that talked about the bee. 'And they did also carry with them Deseret, which by interpretation, is a honeybee, and thus they did carry with them swarms of bees', he recited to himself. 'They' were the Egyptians. The Mormon verse clearly referred to the people who migrated to Egypt from the Middle East, the people who created the Egyptian civilization. The honeybees they carried came to symbolize reincarnation. The Deseret came to symbolize the secret of reincarnation, which only the Pharaoh possessed. He and the entire Egyptian empire was called 'Deseret'. To them, the honeybees provided nourishment when the old world was destroyed and the new world begun. What did it mean to Wayne? What did it mean to the organization he belonged to and which he feared, the organization that descended from the Sons of Dan.

Kevin put the medallion aside and unfolded the inventory, Samson's inventory. *So, who the hell is Samson?* He asked himself.

He went back to the conversation he had with Sharon and Alex in his office. The only connection he could think of then was what the name Samson had to an ancient riddle about the bees. "As the story goes," he'd said, "Samson posed this riddle to his enemies, the Philistines. 'Out of the eater came something to eat, out of the strong came something sweet.' When the Philistines couldn't come up with the answer, they went to Samson's wife. She told them Samson discovered the carcass of a lion infested with bees and ate the honeycomb."

There was a Greek myth Kevin thought explained what Samson's wife told them. The solution was to kill a heifer and bury its carcass in the earth. Out of the putrid heifer will come swarms of bees, one life snuffed out to birth a thousand. Without knowing why, the whole idea gave Kevin the willies, and he involuntarily shivered.

Frustrated and without any clues as to what happened to Wayne and Kim, Kevin got up from his chair and poured himself a cup of coffee. Restless, he walked toward the door, opened the back door, and stepped out into a drizzle.

From her chair in the living room, Sharon watched her mother search through the old boxes that held their Mormon family records. Susan searched the trunk in the garage in which other family mementos were stored while she waited for Sharon and her friends to arrive. She'd found Great Grandmother Anna's diary there. Opening the supple rabbit skin cover of her Grandma Anna's diary, Sharon read the first lines.

August 2, 1857.

I am driven by conscience to record what I see and to confess what we are doing, Anna began, the pain of her words still fresh through the nearly hundred and fifty years since she wrote them. *John was with them again last night, the angels of God who call themselves His Avengers. Yet all they are all murderers, supposedly acting under orders of our Prophet, Brigham Young. Help me God to understand why men must kill others and, for the sake of their souls, tell themselves the killing is for You.*

John usually feels good after a killing. I do not understand it, but he is grateful he was chosen to help a man to salvation. He talks about the shedding of a man's blood like it was an act of kindness. I've tried begging him to stop, but he won't. He won't even consider it. I have been at a loss as to what to do.

Yesterday, Angels came for him again. He rode off with them with not a word of when he'd come back. It seems the only time Zeb and Bud have anything to do with him is when they want him to kill for them. I don't know what they did, but this time, John was like a wind beaten cloth in shreds when he came home. He was crying. He was sick for whatever he had done.

Chapter Twelve

Southern Utah
Summer 1857

It was midday, and the sky was clear over Nephi, a fledgling Mormon town in the center of Utah. Riding down the main street in a wake of their own dust were six strangers. They'd been spotted miles before entering Nephi, and its citizens were waiting. Fifty of them, divided in two groups on either side of the street, silently stared at them. Nervously turning in their saddles, the strangers stared back. They stopped in front of the general store but did not dismount. In seconds, they were surrounded.

"Who are ya?" A tall man, apparent leader of the pack, challenged the strangers. He had a long, brown beard and wore a broad-brimmed hat set back on his head. The rest of the fifty, all men, were dusty and armed.

"Name's Helker," the stranger nearest the tall man said. "We come up from Sacramento to do some huntin'." Helker was hatless, sunburned and peeling. His eyes were light blue. His hair was dark brown, but his short, well groomed beard was streaked with gray.

"Ya' come alone?"

"'Til' about two days ago we was with one a' yer wagon trains. They was given us protection through Indian country."

"Ya' say ya' come from a Mormon wagon train?" the tall man asked.

"Yeah," Helker confirmed.

"Ain't no train of ours gonna shield no Gentiles," the tall man spat. "You ain't no hunters.

Yer spies for that damnable army a Gentiles headin' for us, ain't ya?"

Suddenly coming to attention, his eyes examining every man around him, Helker denied it. "We ain't no spies. We don't know about no army. You got us mixed up with somebody else."

"Yah, sure." The tall man tipped his head only slightly, and his pack attacked, ripping the Gentiles off their saddles. Ropes in lassos dropped over their heads, were pulled tight, then wound around their wrists. In seconds, the Gentiles were hogtied. "You're under arrest."

"Search 'em," the tall man ordered. "Confiscate anything you find, then lock 'em up. Take 'em to Judiah's house. Take their horses and tack to my place. I'll keep 'em there 'til they're auctioned. I'll handle their money, too."

Helker and the other five Gentiles were imprisoned in Judiah's house under armed guard for days, during which time no one came forward with evidence they were spies. One night, at dusk, as if a miracle, the Mormon wagon train with which the Gentiles traveled rolled through town.

"Come with me," the tall man ordered Helker, and we'll see what we will see." As the two walked toward the wagon train's encampment on the other side of town, two guards followed, their guns aimed at Helker. "You know this man," the tall man asked the Mormon wagon master. There were at least ten other men in the wagon train standing around them near the master's campfire.

"Yeah," the wagon master confirmed. He was a big chested man with the look of a rancher about him. "Him and his friends come up from Sacramento with us. Left us 'bout forty miles back. Why? They done somethin'?"

"Caught 'em spyin'." the tall man told him. "They're gettin' information 'bout our strength for that army comin' against us."

"No," the wagon master protested, "not these Gentiles. I've known 'em for years. All of 'em lived not more than twenty miles from me. Trust 'em like I would my brothers. They ain't spy'n for nobody."

"The wagon master's right," a man standing nearby added. "These men ain't here ta do ya harm. We come back home to Utah cause we're runnin' from Gentiles. If we didn't trust these Gentiles, why would we bring 'em with us? Let 'em go. They ain't the men yer lookin' for."

"Ya gonna let 'em go?" the wagon master pointedly asked.

The tall man sighed. "Guess we'll have'ta if there's no evidence against 'em. I'll take 'em back to town, hold 'em under guard so none of our folks take to killin' 'em, and send 'em out to my ranch tomorrow to get their horses. Thanks fer yer help." He nodded toward town. "Better get back, 'fore somebody comes lookin' for us."

Helker reached out, clasped the wagon master's hand, and shook it heartily. "Thanks."

The wagon master smiled, patted Helker on the back and responded, "Good luck with that huntin.'

Turning, Helker strode back to town, the tall man beside him. The two guards lowered their guns, and followed. Back at Judiah's house, the five men with Helker waited. Appreciative of the tall man's efforts to confirm their innocence and relieved it was over, they thanked him. That night, they ate a good meal cooked by local Mormon women and, under the protection of the guards the tall man left, slept peacefully.

Before dawn the next morning, a long-bedded, buckboard drew up to the house, and the six Gentiles climbed in back. One of the armed men guarding them that night climbed onto the seat next to the driver. Two other armed Mormons, new to them and not introduced, joined them on horseback.

"Where is it?" Helker asked the driver about the tall man's ranch.

"Down the road quite a bit," the driver told him. He headed southwest, out of town and into a long valley framed by rugged foothills. "It'll take us all day ta get there. Might as well relax." He took a canteen from beneath his seat and gave it to Buck, the strapping Gentile sitting behind him in the bed of the wagon. "Here's water if ya need it. Probably won't eat 'til after sun down, so don't be lookin' for it."

Dust kicked up by the horses and wagon choked the rough and potholed trail south, the constant breeze across the desert unable to clear it. Sitting in the back at wheel level, the Gentiles were caked with it. Their bodies were wracked by the constant jarring of the buckboard. To get away from his discomfort for a moment, Helker stood. Holding onto the seat behind the guard, he looked across the valley, blanketed with sagebrush and desert grass. Near the edge of the foothills, a small herd of cattle was grazing. On the road in front of them, several miles ahead, was another cloud of dust. "Busy out here, isn't it," he said, sarcastically.

Neither the driver nor his armed companion responded.

"Either of you got an extra kerchief?" Helker asked. "Must of lost mine," he said, rather bitterly. The Mormon's who took them into custody confiscated his handkerchief, along with all their other possessions, the total value of the money, stock and personal property they took nearly twenty-five thousand dollars. "We gettin' our money back, too?" he pressed.

Again, neither man responded.

"Be sunset in an hour or so," Helker continued. "We stoppin' soon?"

"We'll tell ya when we decide ta stop," the driver snapped. "Now sit down."

Holding onto the sideboard Helker sat down. There was a troubled look in his eyes.

"Wha'd they say?" Buck asked him.

"Nothin'."

At dusk a calm, narrow river flowing south appeared on their left. Several miles downstream, near the river's confluence with a much larger river flowing west, the buckboard turned and circled onto a worn, wagon-tracked opening in the sagebrush. The wagon stopped about ten feet from the riverbank.

"Chow time," the driver announced, as he reached under the seat for a couple of saddlebags. "Set up a perimeter," he barked at the three armed guards. "You build the fire," he ordered Buck and one of the other Gentiles. "Nobody leaves the perimeter without one of us goin' with you," he demanded. "I'll get some water." He walked toward the steep riverbank, stepped over the edge, and disappeared into the three-to-four-foot tall shadescale and greasewood bushes that lined it. When he got to the rocky river's edge, he turned upriver, following the bank north as it curved around a bend.

There, waiting in the darkness, were John, Zeb, Bud and Henson. "Where are yer horses?" the driver asked. "Can't have them fussin'.

"Back of us 'bout half-a-mile," Zeb told him. "Got 'em tied to the bushes and gave 'em feed bags. They ain't gonna make no fuss."

"What you gonna do?" the driver asked.

"We're goin' back to our horses," Zeb told him. "Signal us when the Gentiles are asleep."

The driver nodded in agreement, turned downriver and walked away.

Two hours later, as a half-moon began to rise, the riders from Cedar City were still waiting. "Gotta' be any time now." Zeb told them. His companions were getting restless.

Kneeling by the river, John cupped his hands, dipped them in the water and drank from them. He took a deep, slow breath. The bishop's council made their decision days ago. The six Gentiles in Nephi were to be 'sent over the rim'. John, Zeb, Bud and Hensen were chosen to send them. John glanced toward heaven. With a tinge of regret for what he was about to do, he sighed. Believing that if he did his duty that night his actions would help him reach the greatest of heavens, he then reminded himself these six men were Gentiles, and as Gentiles, they were destined for hell. He should feel sorry for them. How lucky they were, they were to be saved. How blessed he was to help them. These Gentiles were spies helping an army come to murder his people. The rewards he received in the hereafter for what he did that night would be great. Feeling much better, he stood, wiped his wet hands on his pants and walked back to his horse.

Hours more passed, and the waiting men began pacing, walking up and down the river's edge to calm themselves. "There," Zeb suddenly, whispered. He was perched just below the rim of the riverbank watching the Gentiles' fire. A burning branch had been raised. It was being waved at him. "Let's go."

Leading, Zeb walked along the river's edge. Avoiding the water on one side and the brush on the other, he made barely a sound. John was immediately behind him. Directly below the Gentiles' camp, a break had been worn through the brush and there was a trail up the bank leading directly to it. Zeb stopped at the bottom of it. "I'll get up here," he announced. "You and Bud get ahead a' me, spread out, and climb when I give ya the signal," he told John. "Hensen, you get to my right. Whistle when yer in position."

John let Bud get in front of him, and they positioned themselves five yards apart along the riverbank. Hensen turned back and took position several yards to the right. With quiet, twittery whistles, the three signaled Zeb they were in place.

Zeb whistled back, and they were off, scrambling upward through the dirt and brush to the rim. Springing to their feet when they reached the top, they drew their knives, picked their victims, and slashed the throats of the nearest three men, all sleeping when they were attacked. Helker was next, and John took him. Before he could strike, Helker rolled, sprung to his feet and took off, screaming to warn Buck and the last Gentile. Like deer they fled, all three of them running in different directions.

Shots rang out and one of them fell. Leaving the fallen, Buck got away. Helker kept running. Undeterred, John chased Helker down, pushed him to the ground and rolled him over. Straddling him, John held Helker's arms down with his knees, his head down with his left hand, and poised his knife to cut with his right.

"Don't," Helker cried, his light blue eyes pleading.

Suddenly stricken with compassion, John paused. Filled with doubt for an instant, he could not move. He wavered, and Helker rose up beneath him, butted him with his head, and ran off.

"That's Helker," the driver shouted. He and his three men were standing off to the side. "Get him?"

Dazed, John got to his feet and ran after him. Tackling Helker at the riverbank, wrestling with him as Helker struggled to get over the rim, John frantically half-raised his knife and jabbed it into Helker's throat. Gagging, blood streaming from his wound Helker slumped, and John let him go. Shoving him over the rim with his foot, John watched as Helker tumbled down the steep bank, through the brush, and into the river.

"He dead?" Zeb asked, suddenly there and looking over John's shoulder.

"Yeah. Got him in the throat," John said, as he turned away.

"See the others are dead and get 'em away from the road, Zeb ordered the men from Nephi. The four men from Nephi had done nothing to help kill the Gentiles and were standing in a cluster at least ten yards away. They looked at one another, hesitated, then slowly walked toward the bodies near the river. Each grabbing an arm, looking away from the stark gaze of the two dead men staring at them, their throats slit open, the Nephi men dragged them to the river bank and stretched out their bodies. Leaving them there, the Nephi men divided into two pairs. One pair fetched the body of the other man whose throat was slit. The other pair went out into the sagebrush and fetched the third body, the man that was shot in the back trying to escape. Like the two before them, both bodies were dragged to the riverbank and stretched out next to the rim. With one man lifting a body by the ankles and a second lifting it by the wrists, the Nephi men then threw the dead Gentiles over the bank and into the river.

Searching the area for bloodstains, the men from Cedar City kicked dirt on them, and all trace of the murders from the road was erased. The Nephi men left immediately and headed back to Nephi. Zeb, John, Bud and Hensen rode south a piece and made camp two or three miles below the confluence of the two rivers. They quietly ate a supper of hardtack and dried beef, and slept until sunrise. At dawn, Hensen made a pot of coffee. When their tin cups were empty, they mounted and rode south toward Cedar City.

A few miles behind them, in frigid water, a hand reached for the shore. It grasped the branch of a greasewood tree and pulled.

Chapter Thirteen

Present Day Utah
April 21

The heavy rain subsided and there was but a light drizzle. Tire iron in hand, Elder Roundtree again waded across the frigid, swollen creek and through the dense willows in Little Cottonwood Canyon. Molly Jeffrey's red Mustang was cradled, upside down thirty feet ahead of him, and she was still inside. He must reach her quickly and get her out before the police came to check on him. It had been a good twenty minutes since the aid car left him and there was little time left.

When Roundtree reached Molly's car, Ralph was waiting for him. Shivering, stomping his feet to warm them, Ralph demanded, "What the hell took you so long?"

"I had visitors," Roundtree told him. "A couple of medics out looking for good deeds. They didn't see Molly's car but said they'd have the police come out and check on us. I figure we've got less than thirty minutes." Roundtree looked at Molly through the window. "Has she moved?"

"No," Ralph responded, "but that car's sunk about a foot."

"Here, your stronger," Roundtree said, "you get it open."

The Mustang's convertible top was smashed and pierced by branches. Molly was hanging upside down from her seatbelt. "Molly," Roundtree called, "we're going to try to get you out."

Jamming the tire iron into a gap between the door and canvass top Ralph strained to pry open the door. The window cracked, and he stepped back. "Why don't we just break it and pull her out," he suggested.

"We might hurt her," Roundtree warned.

"We've already hurt her," Ralph reminded him. "Might as well do it while she's out. At least she won't feel it that way."

Roundtree stared at the door and then at Molly. "Okay," he said. "But be careful. If she's alive I want to keep her that way."

"Stand back," Ralph told him, "and cover your eyes with your arm."

"Don't move, Molly," Roundtree instructed. He backed several feet down the trail they had broken through the willows and watched without covering his eyes.

Clutching the end of the iron with his right hand, Ralph brought the crook of the iron behind his shoulder, covered his eyes with his left arm and swung, smashing the glass, exploding it into hundreds of tiny pieces. Scraping the tire iron over the fragments remaining in the frame, he cleared the hole and stepped aside. "Better check her before we move her," he told Roundtree. "If she's dead, we don't need to bother."

Roundtree approached the Mustang and looked inside. In a pool of blood, Molly's head was crammed against the crushed convertible top. Blood trickled out of her ears. Elbows awkwardly bent, her arms were hanging limp beside her head, her hands and forearms resting on the canvass. His hand trembling, Roundtree reached for Molly's neck. He held his breath until he found her jugular. He sighed when he felt a pulse. "We've got to get her help and quick," he told Ralph. "I'm going to release the seatbelt. Put your arms under her and catch her."

Unable to fit through the window frame, Ralph reached for Molly's left shoulder and arm. Roundtree reached up and around her, felt for the release and pushed. As the seatbelt gave way, so did Molly. Like gelatin, her muscles not functioning, she slumped to the ceiling.

"Pull," Roundtree yelled. "I thought I told you to hold her."

Ralph reached around her waist, dragged her from the car, and laid her on the broken trail. The skin and hair on the top of her head was gone, the flesh that was left was raw and red, and blood was bubbling from it. "We've got to get out of here," Ralph warned. "If the cops catch us with this, we're goners."

"No, we're not." Roundtree disagreed. "Give me your undershirt."

"Why?" Ralph asked.

"Give it to me. I know it's not clean, but it's probably the driest piece of clothing we have. I promise I won't use it to bandage her. I just can't look at it."

Removing his light, water resistant windbreaker and his semidry, flannel shirt, Ralph took off his sleeveless, dingy white t-shirt and handed it to him. Lifting Molly's head, Roundtree slipped the t-shirt over her head, covering first the wound and then her face. "There," he said. "Now we don't have to look at her at all." He moved to Molly's feet. "You get that end," he ordered, "I'll take this one. We've got to get her to the car."

"Why don't we just leave her and get out of here?' Ralph asked.

"Because they want her, that's why."

Ralph moved to Molly's head and gripped her under the armpits. "Oooh," he shuddered, as he glanced at the top of her head, "she's bleeding through." Blood was soaking the t-shirt, and in an area six to eight inches in diameter, the t-shirt was turning a soggy, bright red.

"Then don't look at it," Roundtree snapped. At his count of three they picked her up, and with her bottom sagging, struggled down the willow-broken trail toward the highway. At the fast moving, waist high creek, unable to lift her above it, they put her down.

"You think she'd survive if we tossed her across?" Ralph asked.

"What if we don't throw her hard enough, and she drowns?" Roundtree posed. "What if we do, and she dies from the shock of the landing?"

"If she doesn't make it, we can always say she got thrown out and died in the crash," Ralph offered. "They can't blame us for that."

"Yes, they can," Roundtree told him. "They can blame us for anything they want to blame us for. They want this girl alive, and if at all possible, we're going to get her there. Do you have a blanket in the car?

"Yeah, I've got a couple of them. We're quite the football fans, you know."

"Good, we'll float her across." Without waiting for Ralph to protest, Roundtree stepped into the frigid, rushing water. "Keep her head up." Tightly gripping Molly's ankles, with Ralph holding tight to her upper arms and cradling her head against his chest, Roundtree pulled her into the creek.

Without tension, Molly's left elbow fell to her side, and her lower arm stretched out in the current. Her right hand fitfully bounced about in the water.

The current was battering her, the water breaking over her, and the blood on the t-shirt got washed away. Struggling to keep the swollen creek from stripping her away from them when Roundtree got out, as they reached the other side, he and Ralph turned her parallel to the bank and lifted her onto the broken trail together. Another twenty-five feet or so through the brush, they were at the black SUV.

Ready to throw Molly back into the brush if anything was coming toward them, Roundtree looked up and down the highway for any sign of headlights. The coast clear, he unlocked the cargo hold. Safe for the moment, they hoisted Molly inside. Roundtree got in beside her, and Ralph got into the driver's seat. As Roundtree reached for a small first aid kit the engine started.

Chapter Fourteen

Utah 1857

Painfully and tediously pulling himself up the steep riverbank through tough, desert brush, Helker climbed onto the clearing where, the night before, his comrades were ambushed and murdered. Blood trickled from the knife wound in his neck, and he tore a strip from his shirt to bandage it. Whoever tried to cut his jugular vein missed, and the wound was not critical.

The wagon he'd come in with the other five Gentiles and four Mormon guards was gone. There was no trace of them in the clearing, no trace even of their campfire. "Where did they all go?" he asked himself. He looked for signs of anybody, but there were none. There was only the rough, dirt road on which they'd traveled. "They must have thought I was dead," he sighed, "and left me."

He glanced around for signs of their attackers but saw none. There seemed to be nothing alive in the desert but him. "I gotta' get out a here." He walked to the road, looked north in the direction from which he had come, and then looked south. "Must have been outlaws," he figured of his attackers. "Must have followed us from Nephi. How else would they have known we'd be here? Wonder who else they hurt." He looked to the north again. "They're probably somewhere along this road." He gaged the time by the position of the sun and started walking south. "Them Mormons in Cedar City'll help me."

More than a week later, hungry and exhausted, Helker stumbled into Cedar City and was immediately taken to Bishop Taylor's house where he was fed, nursed and given shelter. Within hours, the story of the bandits' attacking and nearly killing him was all over town. Two days later, a second victim staggered into Cedar City. It was Henry, the Gentile who had been dropped by a bullet while trying to escape and who was then thrown into the river with the three Gentiles whose throats were cut. Of those four, Henry was the only survivor.

"I can't believe I missed you," Helker told him, as he sat on Henry's bed. "I didn't see you. I didn't know any of you were there."

Henry had a bullet wound in his back, not more than an inch from his spine. One of Bishop Taylor's wives and one of his daughters had bandaged it, but no one in town would dig into it to take the bullet out.

Bishop Taylor was standing in the doorway. "Quite an adventure you two had," he told them. "It's lucky yer alive." Bishop Taylor and been generous and kind, and he had earned their trust. He was a soft spoken man with thinning gray hair and a long white beard. "How soon do ya think you'll be able ta travel? We'll have ta see about gettin' ya home."

"I could leave tomorrow," Helker told him. "Don't know 'bout Henry, though. He's still kind 'a weak."

"How about we wait a day or two and take you both back to Nephi?" Taylor suggested. "There's a doctor up there that's real good with bullet holes. He'll get Henry back in shape in no time, and the two of you can go home."

"What about the bandits we ran into?" Helker asked.

"No need to worry 'bout them. I'll send men with you to protect ya that won't be surprised like the brothers from Nephi were. No bandits'll bother ya this time."

Early on the morning Helker and Henry were to leave, Taylor's wives cooked them a big breakfast and packed a dozen fresh biscuits for them. The wagon that would take them back to Nephi came to the house just before sunrise. Brother Hensen was driving, his broad brimmed hat pulled low over his eyes. Following on horseback were Brothers John and Bud. Bishop Taylor introduced them just as Helker was about to climb onto the seat. Helker nodded at Bud and Hensen, but the instant he saw John, he paused. A strange look came over his face, and he looked back at Taylor.

"Have a nice trip," Taylor said, his smile almost mocking.

Helker paled, took a long, deep breath and climbed onto the seat. He was staring straight ahead, looking neither left nor right, as Hensen clucked at the horses and drove north toward Nephi. Fearing Helker had recognized him, John lowered his head, delayed, and followed yards behind.

"Conversation was stiff and thin as the small party continued up the same dirt road Helker and Henry had stumbled down to find help in Cedar City. The clearing in which they were almost killed was still tens of miles north. Next to a stream, five miles up the road, was an old, abandoned cabin. Reining the horses left, Hensen pulled to a stop, just feet from a spring. "Gotta' give the horses water," Hensen told them, getting down from the seat.

Helker watched as Hensen walked to the front of the wagon and gripped the horses' reins. He sighed as he saw John and Bud dismount. Turning toward Henry, who was sitting behind him on the wagon bed, Helker resignedly told him, "Prepare yourself, Henry. We're about to die."

Just as Henry turned his head to see what was behind him, Bud pointed his rifle at Henry's head and pulled the trigger. Watching, Helker shuddered and looked up. John was beside him, staring at him, pointing a rifle between his eyes.

"I'm sorry," John whispered, as he blew Helker's head away.

Blood was everywhere, on them and around them, as John and Bud picked up Helker and Henry's bodies and carried them to the nearby spring. "Hensen," Bud called, "Bring us the canvas and ropes."

From a locked wooden box near the seat, Hensen pulled out two five-foot-square canvass sheets and two hefty, ten-foot ropes. He spread one of the canvas sheets next to each body, then helped John and Bud collect a number of big rocks. When there were sufficient rocks on each canvas, Hensen wrapped the canvas around them and tied the rock bundles to Helker and Henry's ankles. The spring was bottomless, and when John and Bud shoved the bodies into it, Helker and Henry disappeared forever.

Chapter Fifteen

Southern Utah
Summer 1857

It was early evening on the night of Helker and Henry's murders, hours before dark when John and Bud stopped two miles out of Cedar City and John dismounted. Henson's cabin was north and west of them, so he'd already left them. "Thanks for the horse," John told Bud, as he handed Bud the reins.

"Yeah," Bud grunted, reining his horse west. It had been a long, silent ride home, and neither of them said anything more as Bud rode off, pulling John's borrowed horse behind him.

Blankly staring, John watched, deeply sighed and turned east toward home. Avoiding the road on which his family and neighbors traveled, he walked two miles out through the brush then paralleled the road home. A thousand feet from the cabin he stopped and sat down in a grove of scrub oak. Downwind from Anna's dog and out of sight of his family, he waited until dark.

"Anybody seen Angel?" Anna asked about her dog. "Haven't seen her for a while." It was about an hour after dark, and the coyotes were yipping. Maybella was in bed asleep. Hattie was in the rocking chair mending Maybella's dress, and Lizzy was at the table reading. "I'll go out and take a look for her." Anna picked up a lantern, opened the door, and reached for the ax. "Angel," she called as she stepped outside. "Come on, Angel." She looked toward their half built barn. "Are you hunting rats?" The roof was on and the tack room built, but the stalls and loft were not finished. Anna slid the door open and went inside.

The floor of the barn was covered with straw. Three of the oxen were lying down. Only Bull was standing. Curious, they watched her. "Angel," Anna called, shining the lantern light into a far corner, "time to come inside."

Suddenly, there was a commotion in the tack room. Ready for trouble, she raised the ax. "That you, Angel?" she cautiously asked. She heard panting and peeked over the shoulder high door. Angel was on the other side looking up at her.

"Guess she got away from me," John said from the shadows. He stepped into the light. Copious amounts of blood had dried on his shirt and pants. Dirt and straw were caked on it. After he helped dispose of Helker and Henry's bodies, he'd rinsed his hands and face in the stream, and dirt now coated them.

Anna knew immediately what he'd done. "You can't go in the house that way," she told him, unsympathetically. "Hattie and Lizzy are still up."

"I know. That's why I'm in here."

"Hiding from them," Anna derisively observed. She lifted the light and shone it in his eyes. Death itself was in them, and he had been crying. There was an ugly, swollen bruise on his forehead. She stepped toward him, gently took his hand and, for the first time, asked him directly, "What happened out there, John? What have you done?"

He searched her eyes, then looked away from her. "I blew an innocent man's head off." His lips quivered, his hands began to shake, and he sobbed. Chest heaving, shoulders hunched, he slumped to his knees.

Eyes wide, her own breath shallow as she realized what he was telling her, Anna knelt beside him and put her arm around him. "Tell me."

"It started a couple of weeks ago, when I was gone for a few days. Zeb took us to Nephi," he began, "to kill six Gentiles. We were told they were spies, and the bishops ordered us to kill them. We ambushed them about twenty miles south of Nephi while they were sleeping. Zeb, Bud and Hensen killed the first three by cutting their throats. Two ran, and Bud shot at them. One got away, but the other one dropped dead. My man got away from me and ran toward the river. When I caught up with him, he fought me. He looked into my eyes and pleaded with me not to kill him. I didn't know what to do. Then while I was thinking about it, he butted his head against mine and got away again. When I caught him, I stabbed him. I drove my knife right to the center of his throat then pushed him over the riverbank. I thought he was dead. We thought all five of them were dead, and we threw the other bodies into the river.

"Turned out, two of them weren't dead. My man and the man Jed shot, names Helker and Henry. They showed up in Cedar City about a week ago. Bishop Taylor took care of them but knew they had to go. By then, we'd found out from Nephi they weren't even spies. That they'd come up from Sacramento with Mormons who swore they were innocent. It didn't matter though. The bishops still wanted them dead. We all talked about it last night at the meeting. Zeb didn't have to go, but Bud, Hensen and I did. According to Zeb, we were the ones that fouled up, and it was up to us to fix it.

"We picked Helker and Henry up from Bishop Taylor's this morning. Told them we were taking them back to Nephi to get Henry's bullet out, but then stopped at old Ragtail's cabin." John paused and swallowed hard before he continued. "I didn't want to do it, but I had to. I'm just sure Helker recognized me from when I stabbed him. If I'd have let him go, he'd have had the Federals on us. We'd been hung for murder. And if the Federals didn't get us, the bishops would have for disobeying them. I'd a been dead for sure.

"You should have seen Helker when he looked at me with those ghostlike blue eyes." Strangling on his tears as he remembered, John paused, then slowly shook his head. "I never shot a man like that before. I never saw a head blow apart like his did." He shuddered. "Pieces of it flew at my face and into my mouth. It made me so sick I almost threw up. It was all I could do to pretend it didn't bother me."

John straightened his back, dried his eyes and gazed into Anna's. "I was hiding because I was ashamed."

"Oh, John," Anna sighed. Repulsed by what he had done, she took her arm from around him and stood. "What happens to us, your family, if the Gentiles find out? What if a Gentile finds their bodies? They'll hang you. They'll hang all four of you."

"Nobody will find them," John assured her, sobering. "Nothing will happen to us unless the Gentile army defeats us. And if that happens, all of us Mormons will be dead." He seemed to be distancing himself from her, saying, "Take Angel and go ahead inside. I'll take off my clothes and come in after the cabin's dark."

One day later, Buck, the third man to survive the assassinations, the man who had escaped Bud's gunfire on the run, stumbled into Parowan, a small town just twenty miles north of Cedar City. Believing, as Helker and Henry had, that their attackers were bandits, Buck went into Parowan believing the Mormons there would help him. He relaxed with them, and as he was fed and given drink, he related the story of the ambush. When he was drunk, Mormons loaded him in a wagon and drove him out of town. Somewhere along the road, Buck must have guessed what they were up to, because when they came after him with slingshots and billies he was ready. He ran like God Himself was after him, swam to the other side of the river, and lost them.

The next afternoon, Anna was in front of Zeb's store when a wild and angry man came roaring into Cedar City. "You damned, cursed, cowardly Mormons," Buck shouted, pumping his fist into the air. "Ya ambushed us and killed us. Ya fooled us inta thinking you were good, then turned on us. Where's the law in this town?" he demanded. "I want'ya hung."

Mormons and Gentiles alike stopped in the street and came out of the stores to see him and listen. "What the he..?" Zeb cursed, as he hurried out of his store and joined them.

Buck angrily stomped down the street, accosting everyone he came close to, demanding to see the marshal. All of them pointed toward Zeb. "I want them damn Mormon's arrested," Buck demanded, inches from Zeb's face. "We wasn't doin' nothin' but huntin' and the damn Mormons murdered us. Get the army down here. Get the hangmen and hang every one of 'em."

Zeb looked away from him and at the people staring at them. Their faces told it all. The Gentiles were angry. Mormons who knew nothing of the murders were astonished and troubled. Those who knew were alarmed. Anna was terrified. "I'll help you, but come inside," Zeb promised, reaching for Buck's arm. "You're upsetting everybody."

"I hope to shit I'm upsetting everybody," Buck shouted, pulling his arm away.

"I can't do nothin' til you sit down and tell me about it," Zeb reasoned. "Now come inside."

Buck paused, took a deep breath and conceded. "Okay."

Once Buck was inside the store, Zeb closed the door. Outside the window, Anna was staring, her face sheet white. As she hurried home, men and women on the street were gathering in small, agitated groups and talking.

The murders of the six Gentiles no longer a secret, without mentioning John's involvement, Anna told Hattie what happened when she got home. "That's what's been bothering John, isn't it?" Hattie asked. "There's nothing wrong with him that I can tell, but he's been hit by something hard. Didn't even eat his breakfast. Been poking the straw in the barn all day and won't talk to me when I ask him. It's what he got himself into with that pack of murderers he's been traveling with, isn't it? They did this, didn't they?"

Anna was shocked and ashamed. She had no idea Hattie knew what John was doing or that she had been lying to her. Unable to face her, Anna looked away.

"What are they going to do?" Hattie asked. "There's no law here but the men who murdered them. There's no place else that man can go except to the Federals. Zeb's already lured him into that store. He going to kill him?"

"I don't think so," Anna told her. "Every Gentile in town heard him. Anything happens to him, and there won't be any question who did it. The Gentiles would tell, and the Federals'd come after us anyway. Don't know what they're going to do, but they've got to do something. I'd better go talk to John. If it ever gets out John was with them, we'll lose him."

"I'll come with you," Hattie told her, heading for the door.

"No," Anna said, taking Hattie's arm. "John's really upset by what happened. He'd be even more upset if you knew he was a murderer. Let me talk to him alone this time, okay?"

Flashing with anger, Hattie's eyes fixed on Anna's, looked deeply into them for a moment, and then looked down. Taking a deep breath, Hattie sighed and then stepped back.

Inside the barn, John was grooming Bull. "Did Zeb say anything about wanting to see me?" John asked, when Anna told him what had happened in town. She shook her head and, as if she had said nothing, John went back to brushing Bull.

"Aren't you going to say anything?" Anna demanded. "What are you going to do? What if they come after you?"

John turned back to her. Looking as if he was about to cry, he started to say something then turned away. "Go back to the house and forget it," he told her.

That day passed. Late in the afternoon the next day, Anna and Hattie walked to town together. Careful not to ask a soul what was going on but gravitating to people talking in the street, they just listened. Oddly, no one was talking about what happened in the street the day before. In Zeb's store, they explored everything new on the shelves but bought nothing, waiting and listening for what might come and learning nothing. Hattie finally told Zeb, "Heard there was a crazy man in town yesterday. He all right?"

"Yeah," Zeb casually told her. "He's out back gettin' some rest. Want ta take him some hardtack? He's been mighty hungry."

"Sure," Hattie said, taking from him two hard, dry crackers. "Where is he?"

"Out in the shed."

Hattie peered through the open back door, saw a stranger dressed in his underwear through the shed's window and declined. The door to the shed was open, and the man was unrestrained. "Maybe you'd better give them to him. He's not dressed." She smiled and returned the biscuits to Zeb's outstretched hand. "We'd better get home and start supper," she said to Anna.

Anna and Hattie were nearly out of town when, from the north, a rider galloped into town, slid to a stop in front of Zeb's store, and ran inside. They waited, and in a few minutes, the rider ran out of the store, mounted his horse, and galloped back in the direction from which he'd come. Anna and Hattie looked at one another, expectantly. "But we can't go back," Anna said. "Zeb already knows we're snooping. It can only get us in trouble."

Hattie looked longingly at Zeb's store. "Whatever's going to happen is happening now," she observed. "Come on." She took Anna's hand and led her into the alley that ran behind Zeb's store. "We can watch to see if Zeb goes into the shed. See if he does something," she suggested.

"We can't do that. We'll be seen," Anna reasoned.

"But we have to know," Hattie told her, "for John's sake."

"John's out of this," Anna argued. "He's not going to go with them again. This is Zeb's business, and for all of us, we'd best stay out of it."

Chapter Sixteen

Utah
Summer 1857

Inside the General Store, Zeb was angry and pacing. In his hand is a letter. Within hours of Buck's tirade down Main Street word of it reached Brigham Young, and he was angry. The letter to Zeb was from him. Bracing himself, Zeb read it again.

"You boys have made a bad job of trying to put these Gentiles out of the way," Brigham wrote. "One of them is in Cedar City making a big stink. You men are at fault. Fix it so there's no more stink. Get him out of the way and use him up, now."

***

That night, hours after dark and the household was asleep, Zeb's nephew, Bud, knocked on Anna and John's door. He said nothing as he motioned John outside. Watching out the window, Anna could see Bud had an extra horse with him but couldn't hear what he was saying to John. A moment later, John came back into the cabin, reached for his rifle, and left, saying only he wouldn't be back until morning. Leaving as he always did, stone faced and determined, couldn't tell how he felt. Yet she knew his mission was murder. She glanced at Hattie, and troubled, the two sat down to wait.

***

In present day, Oregon, as Sharon sat in her mother's arm chair reading Great Grandma Anna's diary, she sipped her coffee, disturbed by what she was reading. Great Grandpa John was a murderer, an assassin, and Anna was frightened.

When John got back that morning, Anna wrote, *he confessed what he had done and held me in his arms. He told his mother, but she would have nothing to do with him. She took the girls outside and didn't come back for an hour.*

I saw how John grieved that night in the barn. I know how blowing off that man's head hurt him. Because I know, because I thought he would never murder another man, I stayed with him. I fixed him breakfast and listened.

After Bud came for him last night, they rode back to town and to Zeb's store. So the horses wouldn't be seen, they left them in Zeb's stable. The shed Buck was in was dark, so they figured he'd gone to bed. The door was unlocked, so Bud knocked, and he and John ran inside. Bud shouted, "Get up," and Buck woke up all confused. Bud told him that gang that tried to kill him was comin' for him and that they'd be there any minute, meanin' to kill him.

Bud lied, telling Buck he and John were Gentiles there to rescue him. He needed to come with them right away. Still confused, Buck grabbed his hat, put on his pants, and followed them to the stable. Zeb had saddled a horse and it was waiting for him. John told me Buck was asking all kinds of questions, but he and Bud didn't answer them. They just left him in the barn and started riding hard toward the edge of town. Just like they'd planned, Buck followed them, and the three of them road north and then west a piece to a deserted shack. John didn't tell me what happened next, except that he and Bud held Buck down and killed him. John didn't even tell me what they did with Buck's body.

After that, John changed. Trying not to blame himself for what they did, he started preaching to me about his duties to God and the Priesthood. He told me about the threat God and the bishops said these six Gentiles posed to the Church and that he was just carrying out their orders. He repeated every excuse he could think of for murdering them, but it didn't help either one of us.

John knew he had murdered those men in cold blood, and he was suffering for it. God help us, if the priests tell him to kill again.

Chapter Seventeen

Present Day Utah
April 21

It was an hour before midnight. The big, black SUV Ralph was driving headed west, turned north, then reversed its course to head east on highway 190, the only highway that ran completely through Little Cottonwood Canyon. Less than a thousand feet down the road a patrol car passed them, headed west. Through the side mirrors, Ralph saw it turn onto the road they had just left. "Do you think they're the cops those medics sent to check on us?" he asked Roundtree, who had been watching the patrol car through the cargo door window.

"I don't know, but we have to assume it is."

"Odd they didn't stop when they saw us," Ralph observed. "There can't be that many SUV's like this on the road this time of night. There are hardly any cars at all."

"Guess they didn't want to bother. Besides, if they're checking up on us, they're looking for an SUV with car trouble, parked on the side of highway 210."

"Think they'll find the mustang?" Ralph asked.

"Not before morning," Roundtree told him. "It's too far from the road. And by now, it's probably sunk in the bushes. Besides, if they're looking for us, they'll be looking down the road. There's no reason for them to turn their lights into the brush."

"Okay," Ralph accepted. "But, what happens tomorrow when the cops find the car and Molly's not in it. They're bound to search for us."

"Don't worry," Roundtree promised. "I made sure those medics didn't get a look at our license plate. But if there is trouble, I'll take care of it. It'll take time for them to figure out what happened and find us. By then, I'll already have the processes in motion."

"She still alive?" Ralph asked, changing the subject.

"I suppose," Roundtree told him. "She's breathing, but that's about it."

Ralph's sleeveless t-shirt already ruined, Roundtree had folded it, pressed it onto Molly's head wound and taped it down with the white adhesive tape he had found in Ralph's small first aid kit. Having wound the tape over the t-shirt on one side, he brought it down under her chin and up the other side to secure the t-shirt to her head. With blood still oozing from the wound, his makeshift bandage was soon saturated with it.

He examined her arms, lifting each one by its hand. Unresponsive, Molly showed no reaction. He turned them over, first the left arm and then the right. On the underside of her right forearm, halfway to her elbow, through torn and mushy flesh was the tip of a broken bone. Roundtree gagged. "Oh, God,' he murmured.

"What's wrong?" Ralph demanded. "What happened?"

"She's got a compound fracture," Roundtree told him. "What do I do?"

"She bleeding to death?" Ralph asked.

"No, there's blood but not a lot of it."

"Then leave it be. There's nothing we can do for it. Funny we didn't notice it when we got her out of her car. We'd have seen it if it was there, wouldn't we?"

"Maybe it just hadn't poked through yet," Roundtree guessed. "Maybe it didn't come out until we lifted her into the car. But what does it matter, anyway? That would just be one more thing we'd have to explain." He glanced at her legs, pressed his ear to her chest to hear her breathing, and started to climb between the seats. "Nothing more I can do," he announced, as he crawled into the passenger seat.

Fifteen minutes later highway 190 became a gravel road. Six miles down the road it was again paved. Two and a half hours later, still hours before sunrise, the black SUV pulled into a semicircular drive at the side of a single level, unadorned, beige building. A door opened, and a gurney came through it pushed by a man who was nearly fifty and who had dyed his clearly graying hair brown. His name was Jake.

"He's inside," Jake told them, without them asking.

With Ralph on one side and Jake on the other, they pulled Molly out of the SUV, put her on the gurney and wheeled her inside. Roundtree followed. The entrance smelled of sweet, flowery deodorizers and of Purex. The door to the room in front of them was open. Inside, at the foot of an examination table, a man in his mid-forties and in light blue scrubs was waiting for them. "Put her there," he ordered, gesturing to the table.

Dr. Philip Reed's freckles and youthful face made him look much younger. A large decal of a liver coated German Shorthaired Pointer with a pheasant in its mouth dominated his scrubs. He glanced at Molly, then at Roundtree and Ralph. "How long has she been unconscious?" he asked.

"Several hours," Roundtree told him.

"Has she lost much blood?"

"Seems like quite a bit," Roundtree said. "But I don't think it's enough to kill her."

"What happened to her head?"

"She landed upside down and was scalped when the convertible top was crushed. Her right arm's broken, too."

"Get me blankets," Reed ordered Jake, the man who helped Ralph bring Molly in. "Why is she so wet?" he demanded of Roundtree.

"We were in the wilderness, Phil. She got wet when we were bringing her back out to the highway."

"Did you cover her at all?"

Shaking his head, Roundtree confessed. "We didn't think of it."

"All right, I'll take it from here. You staying?"

"No," Roundtree told him. "If I don't show up by ten, they'll start asking questions. It's bad enough I have to make up excuses to my wife."

"You want me to call you when I know something?"

Roundtree looked at Molly, her body flaccid on the examination table. "No, I don't want to know. Come on, Ralph. We've got to get back." Hurrying out the side door, they climbed into the black SUV and pulled away.

When Jake returned with three blankets, he wrapped Molly in them. While Dr. Reed examined the wound on top of her head, Jake kept it clean. The wound was an oval four inches long and three inches wide. Her scalp and a bit of bone had been sliced off as if by a butcher knife, the layers of skin clearly visible at the edges. "Suprafascial avulsion," Dr. Reed pronounced. "She's going to need a skin graft."

"Do you know how to do that?" Jake asked.

"No," Reed acknowledged, without looking up and without pausing. "Get me a magnifying glass."

Not equipped for delicate examinations or surgery, the only magnifying glass in the office was in the Nurse Ray's desk. Behind a half wall next to the waiting room, a nine by nine foot room with small prints of red and yellow flowers in the rug and on the wall paper, Jake searched her drawers for a hand held magnifying glass. He quickly returned with it. "What are you thinking?" he asked, but Reed did not answer.

Holding the magnifying glass close to Molly's head wound, Reed bent down and examined the fine details of the wound. "I was afraid of that," he said. He stood, laid the magnifying glass on a nearby table, and announced, "Her skull is fractured."

"Is it bad?"

"Yeah," Reed said, "the crack fragmented, and it's depressed. There's probably brain damage."

"Brain damage?" Jake gasped. "What are we gonna do? She going to die on us?"

"No, at least not now," Reed told him, "but that's why she's unconscious."

"She going to be any good to us?" Jake asked.

"I don't know that, either."

Jake stared at her. "If it turns out she's no good to us, what are we going to do with her? We don't have any way to treat her."

Not responding, Reed lifted the sheet and examined her right arm. "Compound fracture," he determined at first glance. "She's going to need surgery." His voice revealing his frustration, he added. "We'll need a whole battery of x-rays."

"We can't do all that, we just don't have the facilities," Jake reminded him. "If we take her anyplace else, there's going to be trouble."

"What would you propose we do?" Reed asked, sarcastically.

Very somberly and in all seriousness, Jake said, "Get rid of her. She means nothing but trouble. If we do it now, nobody will know. Roundtree and Ralph aren't interested, and if anybody else asks, we can tell them she died of her injuries. She's just too much for us."

As if considering what Jake proposed, Reed paused, took her left hand in his, and lifted it to his cheek. "Looks like this arm's broken, too." Completely ignoring Jake's morbid proposal, he told him, "We'll get her bandaged, then move her. Set out what we'll need while I make the arrangements."

Alone with Molly, her body perfectly still, Jake tried to wake her. "Molly." He slapped her face, and her head rolled. He shook her at the shoulders, and it bounced up and down. Her wound resumed bleeding, and he stopped. She was like a rag doll. "Sorry, Molly." Quickly checking the open door, Jake took from a nearby cupboard a pillow, placed it over her face and pressed.

Chapter Eighteen

Salt Lake City, Utah
Late Summer 1857

The dry, dusty main street of Salt Lake City was as wide as parts of the Missouri River when Carrie Drake and her family strolled between the two-story buildings that lined both sides. Clapboarded and shingled, filled with an array of goods, the shops in the city were almost as sophisticated as the stores she had seen back East, in towns along the Mississippi and Missouri.

Carrie was not quite twenty-eight. Her rich, brown eyes reflected the joys in her life, her almond face the sunshine. She was dressed in her Sunday best, a dark blue dress with tiny, white, polka dots and a broad brimmed, straw hat with matching ribbon band and bow. She was in the prime of her life, slender and strong. Though her calloused and sun-spoiled hands showed years of hard work, her spirit was as alive as it was when she was sixteen, on the day she first met Lyle.

Lyle walked beside her, a man of thirty. He was tall and sinewy. His shoulders were wider than his hips, and he was strong enough to do the work of two men. He was wearing the red plaid shirt Carrie made him for his birthday and tight fitting, blue trousers, which emphasized his taut, muscular thighs and buttocks. He'd worn his knee high boots all the way from Arkansas, but buffed and polished, they looked almost new. Always proud to walk beside him, she took his arm.

Out in front of them was their nine-year old daughter, Alice Elmira, named after her two grandmothers. For their day in the city, Carrie had specially curled Alice's flaxen hair in long ringlets and dressed her in a fresh, yellow dress with white collar.

Alice was busily minding her little brother. Afraid the toddler would stray too far in any direction, she kept herding him. Hovering over him like an ancient goose over her last gosling, she blocked his every advance. When he tried to escape, she grabbed him by the scruff of the neck and made him angry.

He screamed. Squealing so loud the entire block heard, he turned on her and kicked her in the shin.

"Mom," Alice shouted, limping about in a circle.

"Will you stop that?" Carrie put her hand on Alice's shoulder, brought her to a halt, and reached around her toward the toddler. "I'll take him. You walk with your father. This is the first outing we've had in months, and you two aren't spoilin' it."

Alice's eyes welled with tears, and Lyle knelt beside her. Taking her hand, wiping away a tear drifting down her cheek, he soothed, "Mama didn't mean ta scold ya. She knows yer just tryin' ta help." He brought her close and hugged her. He grinned. "I have an idea. Why don't we all go get a piece a' pie." His children never refused an offer of treats and for them pie was a panacea.

Her dimples deep and enchanting, Alice grinned back at him. Seeming to forget her hurt feelings, she enthusiastically accepted. "Okay."

The toddler, little Theodore Chatfield whom they lovingly called 'Teddy', agreed. 'Me too. Me too'. Despite long, hard months on the trail, Alice and Teddy were as healthy as they were when they left their home in Fort Smith, Arkansas.

Carrie and Lyle were each the youngest children of German immigrants who settled in northwest

Arkansas about the same time Fort Smith was established there, around 1817. The country was rough and lawless, and life there was hard. In constant fear of reprobates seemingly immune from the law and of the lustful, leering soldiers at Fort Smith she had to deal with when she was growing up, Carrie did not want to raise her children there, especially Alice. She and Lyle tried to keep the extended families together, but when Carrie's mother died, her only surviving parent, and when Lyle's two brothers preceded them to California, Carrie and Lyle decided to move. California held the promise of a good life and fortune, so they packed up everything they owned and followed. Lyle's cousins, Robert and Alexander Fancher, were headed west with several other families from Arkansas, and Lyle arranged to join them. They had been months traveling, and while the teams rested and while other travelers got supplies, Lyle and Carrie decided to see the city the Mormons called 'New Jerusalem'.

There was a coffee shop on the corner, its storefront flush with windows. Inside the shop, two big, kerosene lanterns hung from the ceiling over a dozen square tables with chairs. Several small lanterns extended from the walls. Its wood floor was covered with sawdust. A short, bald man with a fringe of bright red hair was behind the counter using his long, white apron to wipe silverware. No one else was around. When Carrie and Lyle came in with the children, he looked up and stared but didn't greet them.

"Four pieces of apple pie, two coffees and two cups of milk," Lyle cheerfully ordered.

"Teddy can't eat a whole piece of pie," Carrie said.

Lyle winked at her and grinned. "I'm countin' on it."

She rolled her eyes and smiled. "Let's take a table by the window. I want to see the people walk by."

Once seated, they waited patiently for the man behind the counter to bring them pie, staring out the window at poor people, working people, and people of means who walked or rode by. When the pie didn't come, Lyle spoke up. "Mighty hungry over here," he said to the man behind the counter, who in the last fifteen minutes hadn't moved.

The storekeeper looked up and slowly wiped and laid a fork on the counter. "Berry, wasn't it?" he asked.

"No, apple," Lyle said. "All around."

The storekeeper reached to a shelf shock full of pies, took one of them down, and cut out four pieces. After pouring the coffee and milk, he put everything on a large, round tray and served. "Berry pie all around," he said, as he plopped the dishes down.

"Apple. We wanted apple," Lyle told him.

"You Mormon?" the storekeeper asked, looking at them suspiciously. "I keep the apple in reserve for saints. Don't have any for anybody else."

Angry with the man's blatant favoritism and disappointed about the pie, Lyle told him with distaste in his mouth, "No, we're not Mormon. We're outa' Arkansas, headed for California."

"Takin' the north trail?"

"No, too late in the year. We're taken the trail south."

"Got cattle with ya?"

"Yeah, a big herd of 'em. One a' the reasons we have ta go south. Them cows don't move too fast."

Lyle chuckled. "If we try to take 'em north into those mountains, we're likely ta get trapped in the snow. End up like them Donners I heard about."

Without continuing the conversation, the storekeeper nodded and walked back to the counter.

Lyle stared at the pie. "Got any ice cream?" he yelled after him.

"Nope. Reserved."

"Just eat your pie," Carrie whispered. "It's good."

Lyle picked at the pie before he tasted it. "You're right, it is good." He eyed Teddy's piece. Teddy had been working hard on his pie, and the piece was almost gone. "Watch you don't get sick from all that," Lyle warned.

Teddy's spoon was overflowing, and his face was covered with dark, blue juice. He grinned. His green eyes sparkled as he shoveled another sloppy, dribbling bite into his mouth.

Outside the coffee shop, drums rolled. Everyone on the street stopped and watched as an armed militia of a hundred men marched by. "Just like at Fort Bridger," Carrie whispered. A few miles this side of Fort Bridger they had past three militia companies, each a hundred men strong. At Fort Supply there were four hundred armed Indians waiting for Brigham Young's orders.

"What they for? More men to fight that army the President's sendin' against ya?" Lyle verbally jabbed the storekeeper.

The man glared at him and came to the window. "You bet. And, that's not all of 'em. There's thousands of us."

Carrie's heart stopped.

"You people ain't fixin' to go after anyone else, are ya?" Lyle asked, with a growing concern for his family. "There aren't no civilians in yer sights, are there?"

"We're only defendin' ourselves as is our right," the storekeeper argued. There was hate in his eyes. "Them that don't bother us, we don't bother."

The wagon train from Arkansas had done nothing to bother them. As she realized it, Carrie breathed a little easier, but still, she would be glad when they moved on.

"How much do I owe ya?" Lyle asked.

"Quarter each for the pie," the storekeeper began.

Angry, Lyle shouted, "A quarter?" Barely containing himself, he pointed at the menu board behind the counter and shook his finger at it. "That there says a dime."

"That was yesterday's price. This here pie will cost you a dollar," The storekeeper pressed.

Lyle dug into his pocket for the precious money. "Here, take it," he said, slamming the silver dollar down on the table. "Hope it curdles your precious ice cream. "Come on. We're gettin' outa' here." Cradling Teddy in his arms, he carried him outside with Carrie and Alice following.

Rounding a corner two blocks down the street, its drums still beating cadence, the militia disappeared, leaving in its wake shock waves of hate. Obviously being from the Gentile wagon train encamped out of town, as Carrie and Lyle stepped from the shop, passersby glared at them with threats in their eyes. The hate all around them palpable, dangers they had not sensed before immediate, Carrie and Lyle retreated. Cutting their outing short, they hurried the children back to the wagon train.

***

More than two weeks later, traveling through dry, uneven country flush with low lying shrubs and short, brown grasses, the wagon train stopped for provisions at Buttermilk Fort, a Mormon settlement. "I'll need sugar if I'm gonna make you that pudding I promised," Carrie told Lyle, as the train circled outside the fort. "Thought I could wait 'til mornin,' but I checked the tin this afternoon, and I'm out. "I'll take Teddy with me while you and Alice set up camp. I won't be long."

When the wagon stopped, with Teddy in tow, Carrie joined Pearl Jones and her oldest daughter, Beth, and the four of them ventured into the Fort together. They were only a few yards inside, when Beth blurted, "Ma, why they all starin' at us?"

Everyone in the fort seemed to have stopped what they were doing to glare at them as they were joined by other women and men from the wagon train needing food for supper or grain for their stock. Uncomfortable about the unwarranted and disconcerting scowls, Carrie and her companions didn't tarry. Joining others from the wagon train, they quickly and quietly headed for their destination. Every Gentile among them hurried, everyone except a man named Spears.

Spears was a big, bully of a man from the State of Missouri, one of several men who had joined the wagon train from Arkansas in St. Louis. Always looking for a fight, Spears stopped, and with fists clenched, glared back at the gawkers. When no one came forward to meet his challenge, he advanced on the feed store. Outside on the loading dock, a man much smaller than Spears, packing a fifty-pound sack of grain on his shoulder, was staring. "Heh, you," Spears spat, as he approached, "yer eyes don't seem to be movin' right. You got trouble with 'em?" Only inches from the man's face, Spears stiffened and sneered. Shoving his middle finger between the man's eyes, he threatened, "Want me to ram this up your ass?"

Spears was a giant man, well over six-foot-four. Each of his feet was almost as long as the small man's grain sack, the breadth of his belly was as big any two men's, and he was too big for his clothes. Tufts of scraggly, black hair stuck out from his gut and splayed through the buttons holes of his stretched, plaid shirt. His belly hung over his belt. Unshaven and never clean, he and his dozen or so friends were a rough lot. Calling themselves 'Missouri Wildcats', they had been nothing but trouble since they joined the train. Just like the rough men of Arkansas, they were the kind of men from whom Lyle and Carrie were escaping.

The man carrying the sack, the crown of his hat barely reaching the height of Spears' chin, backed away. He then joined several other men who were standing in front of the store behind him. "You want somethin', mister?" one of them asked, taking in his hand a menacing, five-pronged pitchfork.

Without his belligerent companions, Spears backed down. "Too bad my partners ain't with me. We'd show you some a' that hospitality we showed yer kin back in Missoura."

Several of the Mormons in front of the store had relatives murdered in Missouri by thugs like Spears, and as Spears strategically retreated from them through the gate, he mocked them. Constantly watching his backside, he taunted them with real or fabricated details of the murders, and their anger boiled.

Seeing the encounter unfold, Carrie picked up Teddy and hurriedly carried him away from the feed store, in the opposite direction to the general store. "Don't know why we didn't leave that man and his friends in Salt Lake City and let them go on to California on their own," she told Pearl. She hurried inside the store and set Teddy down. "As long as they're along, nobody's gonna welcome us."

Two Mormon women, also there for sugar, were at the counter. "How much you want, Sister Grace?" the proprietor asked one of them.

The shelves in the store were loaded with stock, and in the corner, was a barrel of giant, dill pickles. While she waited her turn, Carrie eyed them. She had not had a pickle since St. Louis.

"A couple of pounds," Sister Grace said, handing the proprietor an empty tin, ignoring the women from the wagon train pouring through the doorway. As Carrie and Pearl got in line behind her, the store was crowded with them.

"Here ya are, Sister," the proprietor said, as he scooped two pounds of sugar out of a full, fifty-pound sack. "'Spect that'll do ya for a few days." He closed the tin and gave it back to her.

"Put it on my husband's credit. He'll be in on Saturday to pay you."

"Sure thing, Sister Grace." The proprietor smiled then recorded the transaction in a tablet he kept next to the money box. "Don't forget the picnic on Sunday," he reminded her. "We're all expectin' ya."

"We won't. I'm bringin' a big potata' salad. Ask Emily if there's anything else she wants me to bring." Sister Grace glanced behind her at the bevy of Gentile women patiently waiting their turns. "You want me to get my son? He's at the feed store."

The proprietor looked behind her and scowled. "Never you mind, Sister. I can handle this."

Carrie did not catch the exchange and, as Grace left with her companion, stepped to the counter to order. "A pound of sugar." She looked longingly at the barrel in the corner. "And one dill pickle."

Pearl laughed. "Don't blame you a bit. Kinda' partial to them things myself."

Carrie looked expectantly at the proprietor who, with cold eyes and curt manner, said, "I'm closed."

"What?" echoed through the store.

"You ladies get outa' here. There's nothing in here I'm gonna sell ya."

Shocked, trying to understand what was happening, the women from the wagon train did not move.

"You Gentiles aren't wanted in these parts. Damned if I'm gonna help ya by feedin' ya. Now get outa' here." He moved through the stunned crowd, opened the door, and motioned them to leave.

"Never heard the likes before," Pearl said. "What kinda' place is this?"

"I'm gettin' my husband," another woman threatened, but all of them left as the proprietor closed and barred the door behind them.

Outside, Spears had returned to the feed store from the wagon train and was no longer alone. He brought eight of his Missourian companions with him. Arkansan Gentiles were at the feed store too, trying to buy grain. The men from Arkansas didn't come to make trouble but only to get feed, yet the store proprietor denied them entrance and refused to sell it to them. While the Gentile women were being thrown out of the general store, at the feed store, angry Gentile and Mormon men were squaring off for a fight. The men from Arkansas were on the right, the men from Missouri on the left. A dozen Mormons blocking the loading deck were glaring at them.

"You clap passin' bastards," Spears yelled over all the other curses shouted from both sides. "We're gonna rip you morons off that deck and hang ya. Right here, in front of yer kin," he threatened. Just as angry but not threatening, the Arkansas men stood ten feet from him, talking among themselves as they figured out what to do.

Glaring at the proprietor, shaking his fist at him, Spears warned, "You damn hide son of a whore. You get us what we want, or we'll burn the whole place down. We got two dozen horses needin' to be fed," Spears shouted on behalf of the Missourians. "Ain't a one of 'em that's done a damn thing to you."

"No one asked you to come here," the proprietor yelled, his bulbous cheeks and wide forehead flushed, his eyes as round as silver dollars. "No one wants you here. We ain't responsible if you got problems."

His fists balled, Spears told him through clenched teeth, "No god damn wonder we run ya outa' Missoura, you and yer whores. You people'd fuck yer own mothers if ya could get 'em ta lay down fer ya."

The proprietor's face turned violet. His eyes steamed with anger, and he stepped into the store. Reaching for something near the window, he came back out with a long handled, twenty-pound sledgehammer.

"Don't," one of the Mormon's grabbled his arm and warned him. "They'll kill ya."

"Not before I kill him," the proprietor spat, glaring at Spears.

"No," another Mormon pleaded as he took the proprietor's other arm. "Get outa' here," he yelled at the Gentiles. "You boys ain't no match for all of us."

"You ain't so tough," Spears shouted. "You ain't no better'n that whore born Joseph Smith, and we didn't have no trouble killin' him. Died like a squealin' baby, that 'un. Cryin' so hard I put four shots in him myself just to put him outa' his misery."

Spears' confession he murdered the Mormon prophet, whether true or not, was like a spark flicked onto a pool of kerosene. The Mormons ignited. Scrambling off the loading deck, they leaped on the Missourians. Their fists and feet flailing, they incited every Mormon in the immediate area to join them. Attacked from every side, the men from Arkansas fought back, and the brawl began.

Fearing Teddy would get hurt, Carrie scooped him up and, with the other Gentile women and their children, quickly and cautiously skirted the violence, and headed for the gate. Once there, they ran for the wagon train. "Lyle," Carrie yelled, as she and Teddy got within hearing distance of their wagon. "Get the team harnessed. There's trouble." Teddy's arms and legs were tightly wrapped around her as she carried him through the brush, repeatedly stumbling but not falling. Lyle came out to meet her and by the time she reached him, she was panting. "We've got to get out of here."

"Why? What happened?" Lyle quizzed her. She was struggling to stand, so he took Teddy from her and put him down.

Anxiously searching in all directions, Carrie shouted. "Where's Alice?"

"Gettin' cow chips. Why?"

Her voice shaking, Carrie rattled, "The Mormons wouldn't sell us any food, so the Missourians egged 'em into a fight. They're in there with our men, killin' each other."

Lyle looked up and to the Fort. "You all right?"

"Yeah, but let's get outa' here."

"Ta where?" Lyle asked. "We've gotta' stay with the train.

"I'll get some of the other men and see if we can't put a stop to the fightin'. You stay here. Alice should be back in a minute."

"Don't go in there. You'll only get drawn into it and hurt."

"I can't stay here." Lyle gave her a glancing hug and hurried away, unarmed.

She stared after him, as more than a dozen other men from the train headed for the fort. Pacing, afraid she would never see him again, she nervously waited.

Less than half an hour later, bloodied and limping, the brawlers came out of the fort and made their way to the wagons. Their reinforcements followed, Lyle among them. They, at least, came back unharmed. "What happened?" Carrie asked him.

"By the time we got there, the Missourians and our men were in full retreat. All we did was shield 'em while they got away."

"What do we do now?"

"Gettin' too late in the day to go on. We'll have to stay here for the night."

They heard banging behind them as the gate to the fort closed and was locked. "Me and some of the other men are gonna stand guard tonight in case there's trouble. If they don't come after us, we'll be headed out 'fore sun up."

Word of the altercation with the Gentiles at Buttermilk Fort and that the wagon train carried one of Joseph Smith's murderers spread through Utah like wildfire as the Arkansas emigrants headed south. When the news reached Salt Lake City, the Church sent Elder Jacob Tuttle to investigate. Jacob was to follow the train and report its activities.

He rode hard to Buttermilk Fort where the citizens confirmed the reports sent to Salt Lake City. The Mormons' only regret was that they had not killed the Gentiles. As Jacob rode south from Buttermilk Fort, he discovered the Gentile wagon train had caused trouble all along the way. He heard that the Gentiles called their oxen 'Brigham Young' and 'Heber Kimball'. As they passed settlements refusing to sell them supplies, they cursed Church leaders and turned their cattle into Mormon fields. The Missourian, Spears, not only bragged he was carrying the very gun that killed 'Old Joe Smith', but bragged, along with his companions, that they would send troops to wage war in Utah once they reached California.

At Corn Creek, about a hundred miles north of Cedar City, something poisonous got into the grass or water, and as the train passed, resident cattle died. Because they skinned and ate the cattle and drank the water, Indians got sick, and a Mormon boy died. The Indians and Mormons blamed the Gentiles, and as the wagon train passed south, rumor spread the Gentiles poisoned the water. As the wagon train moved closer to Cedar City, an Indian shot at them at Beaver, and the Mormon bishop barred the train from town. Twenty miles out of Cedar City, the walled town of Parowan was closed to them, and they were forced to break new trail to go around. Spiteful words were exchanged. In return, the Missourians threatened to go back to Salt Lake City and hang 'Old Brigham' and the other Church leaders.

The Mormon's hatred of the Gentiles boiled and bubbled in the desert sun. As the wagon train continued south to Cedar City, that hatred fed on itself until it was totally out of proportion to any harm the emigrants had done. A murderous crisis was on the horizon, and Carrie and Lyle were driving into it.

Chapter Nineteen

Cedar City, Utah
August 30, 1857

It was Sunday night. Beneath the waning crescent of the moon, the desert was cooling as Anna sat at the table alone, writing in her diary. Angel was protectively lying in front of the door, and everyone else was in bed. All were soundly sleeping.

The sun was very bright this morning, she wrote. *It was as if it was trying to spark a fire in the red and orange desert clay. The air was dry, and like yesterday, the heat got almost intolerable. Yet it was a wonderful day. Lizzy called me 'Mama' for the first time, and I loved it. She called me 'Mama' again tonight after supper.*

I know I'm the only mother Lizzy has ever known, but until now, I never thought she felt that way. I hope it means something. I hope Lizzy isn't just saying it because she wants to be included. I hope she really feels that way. Maybe Maybella's calling me 'Mama' made it easier for her. But then, what does it matter? All I know is that my heart melts every time I hear it.

Before church this morning, Lizzy and Maybella asked me if they could wear their Sunday dresses outside. Lizzy wanted to take Maybella down to the creek to play with the water skippers. I was afraid they were going to get them dirty, but Lizzy promised me they wouldn't. It was probably asking for trouble, but I let them go anyway. If they got dirty, they got dirty. I'd rather have them happy than clean. Besides, playing kept them occupied until John was ready to go.

As time passes, we worry more and more about the armies approaching us. Colonel Dame told us there is not only the original column of twenty-five hundred troops marching from Washington but hundreds more. At least six hundred dragoons are following them, and there's a third army coming against us from California. For a month, we've done nothing but prepare to defend ourselves.

While I was watching John clean his rifle this morning, he loaded it. He's been ordered to carry it with him everywhere he goes, and he usually does. I know I shouldn't be, but I'm terrified of it. I hate it. That gun is a constant reminder of what John has done and what lays ahead of us. I couldn't stand it any longer, so I asked him to leave the gun home just for today. He reminded me he'd get into trouble, but I begged him. I told him to tell them it was broken. That the hammer's jammed. To tell them anything, just please let's not go armed to God this morning.

He gave in to me and did what I asked, chose me over the Church and put the gun against the fireplace. At least this morning, he went to church not as a soldier but as a man, the man I used to know.

Every Mormon man in this area had to join the Iron Battalion, and John was no different. The high priests in Salt Lake City have commanded the Battalion to be ready to march at a moment's notice have even ordered them to be equipped for a winter campaign. Colonel Dame keeps telling us an attack is imminent.

There is drought and locusts are coming. The wheat and corn won't be ready for two weeks. If the locusts attack before the harvest and before the food

*is hidden, we may not survive the winter. I fear we
are all going to die.*

*The wind was restless this morning, constantly
blowing dust in our eyes and into our clothes as we
walked to town for Sunday meeting. The desert
flowers are long since dead, and all that's left is
brush and powdery dirt. Even with the windows
open, the meeting room was too hot. Saints sat
fanning themselves with their hands and with the
latest copies of the Deseret News. The paper is
running stories about Joseph Smith. All our Sunday
meetings talk of hate, memories of Illinois and
Missouri and of Joseph Smith's murder.*

*I do not like this talk of revenge and war, and I
no longer like going to the meetings. Not having
lived through the persecution, I sympathize with my
brothers and sisters, yet I do not feel the hate that
flows from their experiences. I do not understand
why the only answer is more violence, either. I
especially do not like that John has been forced to
kill for them.*

*No one talks about making peace. To the
brothers and sisters who came from Illinois and
Missouri the feud with the Gentiles is personal, and
they don't want peace. They forget there are
children here.*

Anna paused and sat back, silently reliving the
troubling meeting of that morning.

Isaac Haight, Stake President, presided. Mormon
General George A. Smith was visiting.

After recanting for the thousandth time over the
last few months the Gentiles' murder of Joseph
Smith and his brother, Hyrum, Zeb accused the
Mormon men present of having done 'absolutely
nothin'' about it. "You lily-livered, egg suckin'
weaklings," he called them. "You ain't no more use

to us than spent up old hens," he shouted. "Them Gentiles are shittin' on ya, and yer not doin' nothin'. Ya outa be getting' up off yer asses, raisin' up on yer toes and whippin' 'em. Ya gotta' kill 'em. Every one of 'em."

"Hang 'em for murder," someone in the congregation shouted, encouraging those all around him to rise.

Hate engulfed the room. Revenge became the prayer, vengeance the sermon. "Seed our borders with guns and kill 'em all."

As anger raged uncontrolled, Anna became frightened and drew Maybella closer. She took John's hand.

"Kill 'em. Kill 'em," Zeb led the chant. He then suddenly lifted his hand and stopped it. "Apostle and General George A. Smith has come to us from Brigham Young with news and with orders," he introduced, as an old man with a full and square face stepped forward. His short beard was a flat ridge below his lip line. His taut, curly hair was parted and fully fluffed on his left side, smoothed flat against the crown of his head and delicately puffed over his right ear.

Apostle General George A. Smith was one of the most powerful men in Utah. He began, in low, slow, quavering tones. "Some of our young boys in Parowan were publicly whipped for stealing fruit. Stealing was wrong, but whipping these boys was not right. I told the people of Parowan the boys' stealing was their fault and the boys' parents' fault for not planting more fruit. It was the scarcity of fruit that made the boys do it. When they asked me where the fertilizer would come from to grow the fruit, I told them to fertilize the soil with the bones of the approaching Gentile armies."

Just as Smith planned, the room exploded with cheers. He smiled triumphantly. Waiting until the noise died down, he continued, "You must be strong, for the greatest of God's tests is before you. The armies of the United States are coming to attempt our destruction. But, be comforted. God will fight with us and will destroy them here.

"In preparation for the attack, you are to burn your property, take all that you have, and hide in the mountains. Leave nothing to them they can use."

"I'd rather throw my farm into hell than let them Gentiles have it," a man shouted.

"Give me a torch, and I'll burn mine now," another yelled. "Glory to the fires that will starve them."

"You are good, courageous people," Apostle Smith praised them, his orders as sacred as God's commandments.

Taking a deep breath and letting it exhaust in a controlled, silent trickle, he waited for utter silence. "The Gentile armies have sent a wagon train to prepare their way," he confided. "It is traveling toward you now. It is bringing viper and sword to kill you, and you must resist. The Gentiles in the wagon train look much like you do, hardworking God fearing people, but they are not. Do not be fooled by them. They carry with them one of the men who murdered Joseph Smith, and all through Zion, he has bragged about it. They spy on us, and when the information is gathered they will report it to the Gentile Armies coming to destroy us." Apostle Smith glared at his audience, spell binding them as he continued. "You must stop them. You must bury them under their own villainy. Strike them down and clear Zion of them. And don't worry, whatever you do, be comforted you will not be alone.

"Days ago, I delivered instructions to the Indians at Santa Clara directly from Brigham Young. He has advised and reminded them that if they do not help us, the United States will kill us both, Indians and Mormons alike. He has promised them we will keep them from want and sickness, give them guns and ammunition to hunt, and help them slay their own enemies if they help us. In return, they have promised to fight for us. Twelve of their chiefs have been taken to Salt Lake City where Brother Brigham will bind them to that promise. The Indians are our friends, and as surely as we planned, they will become for us the battle-ax of the Lord. They are waiting for you. Use them."

Anna tightened her grip on John's hand. She trembled when the congregation broke into a battle song:

In thy mountain retreat,
God will strengthen thy feet
On necks of thy foes thou shalt tread
And their silver and gold,
as the Prophets foretold

Shall be brought to adorn thy fair hair.

Anna cringed as she realized they were not only to kill these Gentiles, but they were to rob them, strip them of everything they had and make it their own. The forces for the defense of Zion were gathering for war, and there was nothing she could do about it. It was as if the saints had forgotten their promise of an open gate to Heaven for everyone, as if they had forgotten heaven at all. For, they were knocking on the doors to hell.

It was Saturday afternoon, September 5, nearly a week after Apostle Smith's speech. As Anna and Hattie walked down the road into town, the light breeze barely shifted the dust beneath their feet. Headed to Sister Greta's ninetieth birthday party, Hattie carried a small, colorful embroidery marking the occasion, Anna a large bowl of potato salad covered with a linen towel and tied with a colorful string. From the dry grass and sage, flying grasshoppers crackled.

As Anna and Hattie approached the outskirts of town, a group of young men working on an irrigation ditch stopped what they were doing to watch the lead wagons of a large wagon train draw near. Anna stopped in her tracks, took Hattie's arm and pulled her back. "That's the Gentile train, isn't it?" she asked. "There are no other trains due through here."

Hattie stared at the wagons, studying them, but said nothing. Riding toward the young men were two older, rough-looking men from the train, clearly on an errand. The first was a thin, scruffy looking man, whose dense, black whiskers were interrupted by a scar running from his earlobe to his lips. The second was a big man on a big, gray mare. "Name's Spears," the big Missourian told the young men. "You boys got any whiskey with ya?"

Brother Zeb's nephew, Bud, was carrying his shovel in front of him, balanced in his hands like a weapon. He stepped forward, glared at Spears and said, "No."

"Sorry to hear that," Spears said. "We're mighty parched. Ain't had nothin' but water in days.

Couldn't get you boys to buy some for us, could we? We'll give ya a couple 'a silver dollars if ya do."

"Not if ya gave us a pure gold ass," Bud said, his feet spread, his hat cocked back on his head.

Spear's oily voice oozed with threat, "You meanin' to fight with me, boy?"

Bud's sun-browned neck turned crimson. "I ain't meanin' to do nothin' with ya. 'Specially give ya whiskey."

"Gettin' damn tired a' you Mormons on yer high horses. Think I'll get down and knock you off yorn." Spears made a move to dismount, and the young saints came forward with shovels eager to meet him. Reconsidering, he stayed in the saddle. Patting the rifle he carried in a leather sheath, he sneered, "You know this here gun's the one that killed Joseph Smith, don't chuh? Better be feelin' lucky I'm not usin' it on you." He turned his horse away and then turned back. "You boys outnumber us now, but we're coming back, and when we do, we're gonna bring a passel 'o soldiers to wipe out every god damn Mormon we can find. You think on that." Tarrying no longer, Spears and his friend rode back to the wagon train and out of sight.

Bud and the other young men gathered in a group and watched them. They huddled, then Bud and one other left, hurrying on foot toward Zeb's store.

"There's going to be trouble," Annie said, as still, Hattie said nothing. Cautiously giving the wagons that passed them plenty of room, they hurried toward Sister Greta's. At a narrow spot in the road where thick brush crowded the shoulder, a wagon came very close to them. They looked up, and a man and woman glumly stared down at them.

"Get up," Lyle Drake told his horses as they hesitated.

Chapter Twenty

Present Day Portland, Oregon
10:00 p.m.
April 24

Sharon looked up from her Great Grandmother Anna's diary, thoughtfully stretched her arms and legs and put her feet on the floor. The overstuffed chair in which she sat was getting uncomfortable. "Grandma was with some pretty extraordinary folk," she told her mother. "She says Grandpa John was a murderer. He was an Avenging Angel and took part in the Church's blood atonement murders. The Mormon's had to have been pretty desperate men to have taken the lives of so many of their own. What started it, anyway? Was it Joseph Smith's murder?"

Susan was still going through the old boxes containing their Mormon family's history. She stopped what she was doing and told Sharon, "It was a number of things. In those days and with those people there was a lot of blood shed even before he was murdered. I think mostly because of his corruption. Non-Mormons hated him. And I think they were afraid of him, too. He ran for President of the United States, you know, and I think that terrified non Mormons."

"When was that, Mom?"

"Just before he was murdered," Susan told her.

"What happened?"

Seemingly to reflect on what she had learned about it through the years, Susan paused. "I suppose it began right after Joseph founded the Church. In the fourteen years before the founding and his murder, he pushed the Gentiles beyond anything they would tolerate. There was his philandering and polygamy. There was the failure of his bank where Mormons and Gentiles alike lost their money. Even voting was a problem. When Mormons settled in an area, they took control of it by block voting. When he declared his War of Extermination against Mormons who didn't surrender their properties to him and started killing not only them but the Gentiles, he turned the entire State of Illinois against him, and they drove him and his followers out. He was a tenacious sort, though. Not to be discouraged by the violence and hatred all around him, he ran for President. I think it was 1844."

"How'd he do?" Sharon asked.

"Not too well, I'm afraid. It culminated in his murder."

"Why that?"

"His platform was pretty scary. He wanted to take control of all of the United States and its territories with power to send an army into any State he wished without the governor's permission. He wanted to make Missouri give back to the Mormons the land it took when the Mormon's were driven out. Most frighteningly of all, Joseph Smith wanted the power to destroy every government except his so he could establish God's true government on their ruins."

"Good Lord," Sharon gasped.

"That's one of the main reasons why I didn't want anything to do with the Church, even after Kim married Wayne," Susan confessed. "Six months after Joseph announced he was running for President, he was locked in the Carthage jail with his brother, Hyrum, and nothing short of an army could have stopped the mob that came after them from killing them."

"Wow," Alex said from the couch. He had been listening. "That's quite a story. You got anything in those boxes that might be proof of any of that?"

"No, but it's no secret," Susan told him. "It's part of Mormon history. Our family didn't get involved with the Church until Joseph Smith was dead and the Mormons were settling Utah. My grandparents were just emigrants from Europe caught up in what was happening out there. They probably didn't even know about the real Joseph Smith."

"If it is the Sons of Dan or Avenging Angels, or whatever they're calling themselves these days, who kidnapped Wayne and Kim, we've really got our hands full trying to find them," Alex observed. "And, we're going to have to be careful."

Alex's smartphone buzzed and vibrated. Drawing it out of his pants pocket he glanced at its face. "It's a text from Herb Brown." Alex opened 'text message', viewed the message from his editor and slowly, his hand shaking, he handed Sharon the phone. *Hank Blanchard murdered. Call me,* the message read.

Sharon read it, gave the phone back to Alex and told Susan, "Wayne and Alex's friend, Hank, has been murdered.

Tears welled in Susan's eyes. "Oh my God. Kim? Wayne? Are they dead, too?"

Sharon left her chair, knelt beside her mother and put her arm around her. Gazing up at Alex, she asked, "Are you going to call Herb back?"

"If I don't call him, we won't find out what happened. Who did it? We won't find out anything."

"You can get online. There has to be something about it in your newspaper," Sharon suggested. "I don't think you should talk to Herb. Remember what happened to us the last time you called him. He might have gotten us killed."

"I can't believe Herb's responsible for those bozos who were chasing us. I've been working for him for years, and it's just not his style."

"Try the paper first. If not there, Hank's murder should be somewhere on the web," Sharon told him. "You don't need to talk to Herb. Don't take the chance. Where's Kevin? He might have discovered something. Let's talk to him first."

Chapter Twenty-one

Southern Utah
September 1857

Cedar City was the last settlement of any size the Gentile train would pass through before reaching the deserts of California and was the last possible source of supply. Stopping there was imperative.

Dust rose and was suspended in the heat, as Lyle and six other men from Arkansas went, hat in hand, into Brother Zeb's general store. "Beggin' your pardon," Lyle said, as Zeb turned his back to them. "We're headed into the desert and need supplies."

Ignoring them, pretending not to hear, Zeb counted aloud the tins of beans he was stocking. "One. Two. Three...."

"Please, mister, we gotta' have 'em. We'll lose our stock. Our women and children will starve without 'em." Lyle never begged for anything, and he hated it. Forced to swallow his pride for the survival of his family, he was now groveling to a lousy excuse for a man who would not even look at him.

Feeding on the Gentiles' plight, proud the Mormons had kowtowed their kind, Zeb surreptitiously smiled. Still hiding his satisfaction, he turned and, in a quiet, rancorous tone, told them "I'd go ta hell and be grateful 'fore I'd sell you scum'mer's a thing."

Even if Zeb had been inclined to help, he would not have helped. Any saint daring to help Gentiles was being excommunicated, beaten or worse. "I'd give my wheat to locusts 'fore I'd let you or that filth you spawned eat a grain of it. Now, get out, 'fore I set the militia on ya."

"You Bastard," a man shouted, as he broke ranks and went after him, setting in motion a row.

Scattering, colliding, men jockeyed for position as they looted flour and sugar, hardtack and pork, saddles, harnesses, plows, and guns. "Better get in here if ya want some," someone shouted to the Gentiles waiting outside. By then, Zeb was beat up and unconscious. The militia was out of town on maneuvers, and there was no one to stop them.

"You stole that food?" Carrie challenged, as Lyle lobbed two slabs of bacon into the wagon.

"Didn't want our money," he said, adding sacks of flour, beans, and sugar to the larder.

"What does that matter? You stole. What kind of example are you setting for our children?"

"That Mormon'd see our children starve 'fore he'd sell me food for 'em," Lyle seethed. "Is that what you want?"

She quieted, mumbling beneath her breath, "I don't know what I want. I don't know what is right or wrong in this place."

The sun was a flame, the meetinghouse an oven, at services the next morning, as Mormons vented their anger over what happened at Zeb's store. Sitting between John and Hattie, holding Maybella on her lap, Anna sensed a fury in those around her greater than was justified over the incident. Their wrath could mean the beginning of war, and with the militia back in town, they were ready.

In front of them, solemn and intent, Isaac Haight, the word of God and Brigham Young in Cedar City, led them, his voice reverberating revenge. "We have been visited by those who persecuted us, killed our Prophet, and drove us from our homes in

Missouri. Traveling with them are men from Arkansas where our apostle Parley Pratt was stabbed to death this year. With the devil in their hearts, these men have now robbed us, tread on us, then departed to bring an army against us from California."

Tall and muscular, his frame stretching as he spoke, Haight had their full attention. "Years ago in Missouri, they drove us out to starve. When we pled for mercy, the massacre at Haun's Mill was our answer. When we asked for bread, they gave us stone. We left the confines of civilization and came far into the wilderness where we could worship God according to the dictates of our own conscience and without the interference of Gentiles. We are etching His kingdom in this wilderness, yet even here, they hound us.

"The Gentiles came among us asking us to trade with them and, in the name of humanity, to feed them. All of these we have done. Now they are sending an army to exterminate us. So far as I am concerned, I have been driven from my home for the last time. I am prepared to feed the Gentiles the same bread they fed us. God being my helper, I will give my last ounce of strength and, if need be, my last drop of blood to defend Zion.

"Let us pray from Doctrines and Covenants, Section 98, verses 23-32: '...Thine enemy is in thine hands; and if thou rewardest him according to his works, thou art justified; if he has sought thy life, and thy life is endangered by him, thine enemy is in thine hands and thou art justified.' Amen.

"We are called upon by God to correct the wrong that is in our land. So whatever we do to our enemy is justified." He paused. "Immediately after service there will be a meeting of the Stake High Council, and we will decide."

Sweat born of fright as much as the heat beaded on Anna's brow. She dabbed it with a handkerchief, then reached for John. His arm was as cold as death. His muscles were flexed in knots. She turned, her eyes embracing him.

Reflecting deep, morbid thoughts, his face was pasty white. His lips were stone gray. Fear as great as hers was in his eyes, yet his eyes did not move from the lectern.

"John," she whispered, but he did not hear. He was distant until the service ended. When others filed out of the room, John did not move.

"What are you going to do?" Anna whispered. Hattie and the girls stood with them.

"I'm staying for the meeting," he announced.

"They won't let you, will they? You're not a member of the council."

"Doesn't matter."

As the room emptied, leaving only those men who would attend the meeting inside, a familiar, unsavory figure approached them. "Brother Jacob," John said, "what brings you to these parts?"

Jacob Tuttle was quite a bit shorter than John and had an oversized head. His graying black beard was longer than the last time John and Anna saw him and was unusually unkempt. His thick, dark brows were bushy. As usual, his square jaw was clenched, and his smile was insincere. When he answered John, his pallid brown eyes were sensually gazing at Anna. "I've been following the Gentile wagon train that pulled through here yesterday since they left Buttermilk Fort. Brother Isaac wants me to tell the council what they've been up to. You staying?"

"Yes."

Jacob tore his eyes away from Anna, and stared at John, studying him for an instant. "Stay as my guest."

As if he had held his breath a very long time, John exhaled in a deep, bottomless sigh. "Thank you." He turned to Anna. "Best take the girls home. I'll come when the meeting's over."

Anna and Hattie rushed the girls outside, but Anna had no intention of leaving. "Take Lizzy and Maybella home," she told Hattie at the door. "I'll wait for John."

Apparently, Hattie had no intention of leaving, either. Turning to Lizzy, she told her, "You heard your mother, take Maybella home."

Lizzy must have sensed the importance of the meeting going on inside and did not argue. "I'll get dinner." She took Maybella's hand and, with Maybella skipping along beside her, started home.

Outside the meeting place, men gathered beneath windows to listen. Women gathered behind them. Anna and Hattie wasted no time in joining them. Inside the meeting house, members of the council were scattered here and there among the benches. No one made a sound as Jacob stood before them and addressed them.

"They are carbuncles on our flesh," he began, "and their puss boileth over. They taunt us and bleed us. They steal all we have and wish to destroy us. I know. I have seen them. I have followed them all the way through Utah, and they are the most evil of evils. They take whatever they want, threatening our people, gang beating those of us who resist, and stealing what they refuse to buy. They poisoned a creek along the way, leaving behind them murdered Indians, cattle, and an innocent Mormon boy. Worst of all, they carry with them and protect one of Joseph Smith's murderers."

Straightening his shoulders, raising his chest as if rearing, Jacob glared at every man in the room and then at the men staring through the windows. "Imagine, one of Joseph Smith's murderers in our grasp. Imagine the day he died. He and his brother, Hyrum, were being held in the Carthage jail for crimes trumped up by the devil himself. Lying Gentile sheriffs were promising to protect them. But the Prophet and his brother were defenseless. They were praying and studying the Book of Mormon when a heathen, Gentile mob came after them. The sheriffs did nothing but watch as those damned, cursed Gentiles dragged Joseph and Hyrum from their cells and murdered them, leaving them in the street like vermin. When the saints claimed them and brought their bodies back to Nauvoo, they were stretched out and prayed over. God was demanding revenge, and we promised it."

Jacob paused, then quickly but earnestly predicted, "These Gentiles in the wagon train are part of the evil that forced us into the wilderness. If they return with an army as they promise, they will drive us out again. Our children will starve. Many of us will be murdered. We must stop them before they leave Utah."

"We already got a militia," someone shouted. "Let's use it."

"What about the armies coming against us from the East? Shouldn't we defend ourselves against them first?" someone else asked.

"If we don't take care of this situation first, we'll have to worry about facing two armies coming from different directions" Jacob argued. "I move we deal with the Gentile wagon train now, so they cannot send an army against us from California. That threat gone, we can then meet the armies from the East at full strength."

"Seconded."

"In favor?"

The motion carried.

"What are we going to do with the Gentiles in the wagon train once we defeat them? If we arrest and punish them, we'll have to guard and feed them," Brother Isaac reasoned. "They'll consume our stores and we'll be worse off."

"Then do away with them," Jacob said, coldly. "We must forever urge the Lord to avenge the blood of the Prophet. These men not only boast that they killed him but taunt us with the murder. Are we to forget our oaths of vengeance and let them go?"

"No," Brother Zeb responded. His right eye was bruised and swollen shut from the beating the Gentiles gave him. His lip was split. "Look at me if you question their intent. Go into my store and see that they have stripped it clean. They've poisoned our water. They've murdered our Prophet. They promise they will not rest 'til every one of us is dead. For our very lives, we must eliminate them."

"If you kill those Gentiles, you're no better than the worst of them," John said, standing. "There are many innocent among them. There are women and children. You cannot in God's name kill them."

"Brother John's right." A tall man with spectacles stood. "What can you be thinking? There's no law in all of God's Kingdom that allows the murder of innocent women and children. No matter what the reason."

Though nervous and frightened by the council's reaction, Anna beamed with pride at John's bravery, amazed he had the courage to publicly take issue with the Priesthood. A few of the eavesdroppers outside the open windows agreed with John, but others did not. There was murder in their eyes, and their sights were now on John.

"I move we send an urgent message to Brigham Young to let him know what's happening down here and to get his directions. No action to be taken until the messenger returns," the tall man suggested.

"Seconded," John shouted.

Although the militant among them were hesitant to delay, this was a compromise with which they all agreed.

"We'll send a messenger this morning," Jacob said, "but we should also send another messenger, one to Major John D. Lee requesting that he come and manage the Indians. We might need them."

"Seconded," Isaac Haight called, and the motion was carried. "Every man here, every man in the militia, is to make himself available and ready to move out at a moment's notice. Brother Zeb and Brother Jacob will remain to help me draft the messages. This meeting is adjourned."

Feeling he'd done everything he could to stop them, John walked to the aisle where the tall man met him. Without stopping as they passed, they nodded. The council's agreeing they needed authority from Brigham Young before acting legitimized their objections. Having risked their very lives in making them, they mistakenly breathed easier.

"You've never felt the sting of starvation, have you, Brother John?" Jacob was behind him and angry. "You've never had your brother murdered, have you? Because if you had, you wouldn't turn your back to his murderers. You wouldn't let the same mobsters that killed him run you off your land again. Better think about that, John. Might be your family they murder next time."

Jacob gestured toward the windows and the onlookers outside. "People here don't take kindly to anybody standing up for those thugs. Don't take kindly to their trying to keep us from defending ourselves. Some might even call their trying treason." Restraining the full force of his anger, Jacob's left eye twitched. His threat was not veiled as he crowded John with clenched fists, stilled his eye and glared at him, seething, "Better watch you and yours on the way home."

"Maybe you better get to writing those messages," John said, disdainfully. Goading Jacob, he stepped closer, his large frame making Jacob look diminutive. Showing no fear of the threats Jacob had made toward his family, John added, "If you're the messenger, you got a long ride ahead of you." He turned to leave, purposefully brushing Jacob's chest with his muscular arm. "See ya."

Anna and Hattie were waiting outside. "We're proud of you, son," Hattie told him, as Anna took his hand.

John kissed Hattie on the cheek. As they walked down the trail toward home, he put his arm around Anna.

"Brother Brigham wouldn't let them murder those Gentile families, would he?" Anna asked.

"Not likely," John assured her. "We aren't the kind that kill women and children. It'll take a couple of days to get Brother Brigham's answer. By that time, those hotheads will have cooled down, and there won't be any killing."

As they walked the road home, dust coated Anna, Hattie and John's clothes and faces as a brief wind picked up from the south. As the wind died away, they stopped to brush the dust off. That was when they heard the sound of hoof beats behind them. They were being followed.

"Who is it?" Anna asked, as they all looked down the trail.

At a distance too far away to identify them, three horsemen had stopped and seemed to be waiting. "Who are they, John?" Hattie asked.

"Can't tell."

"We'd better get home," Anna said. She took John's arm, "Come on."

Not taking his eyes off the riders, he went with her. The horsemen slowly followed.

"What do you think they want?" Hattie asked.

Whenever John stopped, the horsemen stopped. "They mean to scare us," he decided, though he seemed not to want to believe it.

"They've sure done that," Anna said. "But, why?"

"They probably didn't like me standing up for the Gentiles. Didn't like me going after Jacob much, either." John shaded, then squinted his eyes trying to identify the riders.

"Those men wouldn't hurt us, would they?" Anna asked. They were alone with nothing to defend themselves, and she was scared.

"Don't know. But, I think we'd better get home." John took their hands and started walking. "Can't outrun them, so don't try. If they come at us, stay close to me. Don't want them catching you by yourselves."

Their pace quickened, and with each step, John looked back. The cabin was more than a mile away.

"You don't suppose they'd go after the girls?" Hattie asked. She was ready to bolt. "I'll kill them if they touch my girls."

John tightened his grip on her. Best way to make 'em try to get to the cabin before we do is to run. Just keep walking. We'll be there in a minute. Wish I'd brought my gun," he mumbled.

The road seemed to stretch ever longer, as with their every step, the men stalking them kept pace. It seemed they would never reach the cabin, but soon, they were within fifty yards of it. "Run," John shouted. Anna and Hattie took off, and he followed them.

"Lizzy. Maybella," Anna called, as she pushed the door open.

Maybella was playing on the dirt floor with Angel. Lizzy was at the cooking fire. Frightened by Anna's entrance, they looked up.

"Bolt the windows," Hattie yelled, shuttering the first one.

Immediately behind her, John grabbed his rifle. "Come on girl," he called Angel, as he stepped outside.

Heat waves floated over the trail blurring the horsemen's retreating images. They were gone, yet their point had been made. John and his family were at their mercy. He better not challenge the Priesthood again.

***

Back in town, Isaac Haight finished and signed the final draft of the message to Brigham Young. "Ride quickly," he urged, as he handed the letter to Jacob. "We all may die if you delay."

Jacob put the envelope in the inside pocket of his jacket, hurried to the meeting house door, and left.

"We gonna wait forever?" Brother Zeb asked Isaac. "If we just sit here on our thumbs, those damnable Gentiles are gonna get away."

"No," Isaac responded, "we're not waiting. Brother Brigham has already told us what to do through Apostle Smith. Remember what he said? He admired our spirit and told us we would not be condemned for taking matters into our own hands. He told us to destroy the Gentile wagon train if we are threatened, and told us that whatever we do, we will not be alone. I sent that message to Brigham Young only to appease the council and to confirm his order. There's no need to wait for his answer. Come first thing, we act."

Taking a second sheet of paper from his private stock, Isaac wrote, *Dear Brother Knight.* Samuel Knight was one of their missionaries to the Indians. *You are hereby ordered to ride south right away. Instruct the Indians to arm themselves and immediately attack the emigrant wagon train that went through Cedar City yesterday.*

Chapter Twenty-two

Present Day Portland, Oregon
11:00 p.m.
Present Day

Gusting winds came out of the dark dashing sheets of rain against the windows of Susan Marshall's home as Kevin sat at the kitchen table examining Wayne's medallion. He was certain there was more to the markings on the piece than that which was obvious. He had been studying them for hours. Sharon, Alex and Susan were in the living room. Wayne and Kim's children were sleeping upstairs.

Kevin's dark green eyes were tired and strained. The images on the medallion of the eagle and Min the Beekeeper carrying the red crown were blurring even under the magnifying glass and the bright halogen light. He began to see in the engravings things that were not there, faces and flowers, letters and trees, ghosts of his imagination. His long, tendril like bangs hung limp over his forehead, and he rubbed his eyes. He put the medallion down and walked to the cupboard. Sharon's mother, Susan, kept an automatic grinder there and coffee beans in an air tight canister. He'd helped himself to them all day.

When the coffee was made, he poured himself a cup and walked to the window. He watched as, with the wind, drops of rain as big as dimes flew out of the darkness and struck it. Standing quietly and unthinking, his freckled face drawn, he rested while he sipped, feeling at home. The cup emptied, he poured another and went back to the medallion, turning it to the image of Min.

"Min the Beekeeper," he said aloud. "The Egyptian symbol of the bee, the red crown, 'Deseret'. What could this mean to a man like Wayne? What meaning could it hold for the descendants of the Sons of Dan? They're all Mormons, but Mormons use the symbol of the beehive, not the red crown. Why don't these new Sons of Dan use the beehive?"

He opened his laptop and searched, bringing up a detailed image of a beehive symbol used by the Mormons. Enlarging it as much as possible, he studied every line engraved on it but found nothing out of the ordinary. The lines on the exterior were simply round circles with short, diagonal lines through them probably representing honey combs. The multiple etches inside the darkened entryway, a maze too hard to distinguish, had gotten him nowhere. Yet, in his fatigue, the lines seemed all of a sudden to translate themselves.

Order came. A picture broke through. "Couldn't be," he whispered to himself. He rubbed his eyes, gulped the rest of his coffee, and examined the etches more closely.

"Alex. Sharon," he shouted. "I've found something."

"What?" Alex asked, as Sharon and Susan came with him to the table.

"Look through here. See if you don't see it, too."

Alex replaced Kevin in the chair and peered at magnified image of the entrance to the beehive.

"See," Kevin directed, impatiently waiting. "The image is in the etches?"

Alex stared. "What image?"

Fearing what he saw might have been his imagination, Kevin looked to Sharon. "See if you can't find something in the entrance."

Reluctantly relinquishing his place, Alex stood and let Sharon try. Taking her time, manipulating the image to different perspectives, she too saw an image in the threshold. "An inverted five pointed star. A pentagram."

"I knew I wasn't still imagining things," Kevin said.

"You've been hallucinating?" Alex asked, sarcastically. "Better let me take a look."

"Start from the top of the entrance and go straight down," Sharon instructed. "See the long point?"

Sure enough. There was a pentagram in the threshold, the longest, thickest point aimed into the center of the beehive. "How obvious is that?" Alex quipped. "A star makin' it with a beehive."

"Is he right, Kevin?" Sharon asked.

"Could be. Pentagrams are often associated with black magic, devil worship, and satanic cults, but if you go back to Ancient Egypt, which makes some sense here, pentagrams are symbols of the sun, the phallus, and fecundity. When mixed with female fecundity, the phallus or pentagram is believed to have the power to produce a new race after the old one has died." He paused.

"What's 'fecundity?'" Susan asked.

"It means capable of producing an abundance of offspring," Kevin told her. "The symbol of female fecundity is the bee."

"You don't think the Sons of Dan intend to replace the rest of us with a new race, do you?" Sharon asked.

"Well," Kevin said, not giving her a direct response, yet thinking aloud, "the name of their project is 'Samson'.

"The Greek legend on which Samson's riddle was based told about new life rising from the dead, swarms of bees coming from the rotting carcass of a heifer. One life snuffed out so thousands could be born. Yes, I think you could say these Sons of Dan may intend to replace us."

"We've got to get back to Utah and talk to the authorities," Alex said. "They'll want to hear this."

"I'll get my things," Sharon said, already halfway to the living room. "Anybody going to see us leave?" She peered through a space at the edge of her mother's heavy, satin drapes and into the night. "They're here," she sighed.

"Who's here?" Susan asked.

"The men who were following us," she told her mother. "We've got to go." Her face flushed as she hurried back into the kitchen. "The white Impala's outside."

"How did they find us here?" Alex asked, rushing to the window and checking for himself.

"They must be tracking us," Sharon presumed. "They could have planted a device on my car before they broke in on us at the motel. They probably knew where we were all along."

"How are we going to get to the car? They'll see us even in the dark." Kevin asked.

"How fast can you run?" Alex asked him.

"I can't outrun a bullet, if that's what you mean."

"We can't leave Mother and the kids even if we could get to the car," Sharon reminded them.

"Susan, is there some place safe you and the kids can go?" Alex asked.

"Aunt Jenny's. She lives just three miles east of here. The garage opens onto the back alley. I can get the children and sneak out back without them seeing us."

"Good," Alex said. "Go to their room and wake them but don't turn on any more lights. Tell them you're playing a game or something. Get them dressed but hurry."

Sharon took hold of her mother's arm. "Are you sure the men in the Impala won't see you?"

"Yes, dear. Just make certain they don't come near the house before I leave. If they go into the alley, I'll be trapped."

Sharon nodded. "All right, Mother."

As Susan hurried up the stairs, Sharon watched apprehensively, blaming herself for putting her mother and the children in danger. Deciding she had better help, Sharon followed her upstairs.

"Sh-h-h," Susan said, as she and Sharon awakened the children. She reached into the crib and scooped baby Emily into her arms.

"It's still dark outside, Grandma," five-year old Martha whined. "We're not supposed to get up yet. Daddy doesn't like us to get up at night. He spanks us."

Sharon swallowed hard. She knew Wayne was a disciplinarian, but she never dreamed he abused them. "Daddy isn't here," she told Martha, "and Grandma and I want you up. You and Grandma are going to see Great Aunt Jennie. Remember her? She's going to take you and Grandma to a carnival. You like carnivals, don't you?"

"Yes," Martha said, scrambling out of bed. "Come on, Keith," she said, shaking her brother. "We're going to the circus."

"I'll explain the difference between a carnival and a circus in the car," Susan whispered to Sharon.

"I'd have to drive for miles to get to an amusement park." She grinned, "Besides, Jennie abhors them."

"Mom?" Sharon quietly nudged. "The only important thing is that you get away from here and quickly.

"Of course it is," Susan told her. "I'm just trying not to alarm the children. Philip," she called to the still sleeping two year old, as she began to change Emily's diaper. "Martha, would you get him up?"

"If you'll carry Philip, I'll take Emily," Susan told Sharon. "Come on kids. Martha, you lead."

"We gotta' lose that tracking device," Kevin said, still at the window in the living room staring at Sharon's convertible.

"What do you suggest?" Alex asked.

"It's got to be under one of the bumpers or maybe below the doors. They didn't have time for anything tricky."

"You know what a tracking device looks like?"

"No. Do you?" Kevin queried.

"Can't say I do. But, even if we don't, we ought to be able to find some palm sized object that doesn't belong there."

"So, which one of us is going to go out there?" Kevin asked. He reluctantly eyed the pools of water on the lawn between them and Sharon's car. The only way to remain unseen was to crawl.

"I get ya," Alex said, realizing he would have to do it himself. "But let's wait until Susan and the kids are clear."

As if on cue, Sharon, Susan and the children came bumping down the stairs. Emily was in her portable car seat, rhythmically bouncing between the wall and Susan's leg. Martha stopped at the bottom of the stairs, stared at Alex and Kevin, and frowned. "Are they going to the circus with us?"

"No, dear. They're Aunt Sharon's friends. They're going to stay here with her. Now keep moving. Great Aunt Jennie will be waiting for us. What do you say we go have pancakes at Albys after we pick her up?"

"Oo-ooh, I like paneggs."

Sharon helped usher the children through the kitchen and into the garage. When they were seated and buckled in, she opened the garage door and peered into the alley.

"Good luck, Mother," she told her, touching the car as Susan backed out.

"Take care of yourself," Susan said, as the car rolled past. "I don't want anything to happen to you."

"I will, Mother. I'll call you the minute I know something."

Several yards down the alley, in a direct line between Susan's house and her next door neighbor's, was her cross alley neighbor's security mirror, a large fish eye trained to catch and reflect everything going on in that alley. As Susan backed her decade old, gray Honda Civic out of the garage, the rain and fog in the dimly lit alley seemed to absorb it. As she drove away, the shadows of her small, vulnerable passengers quickly faded.

Believing they had escaped and were safe, Sharon pulled the garage door down and hurried back into the house. Across the street, the chisel faced redhead on the passenger side of the Impala immediately opened the car door and got out. Holding his jacket over his head for protection from the rain, exposing the revolver he held in his other hand, he ran twenty feet up the curb, through the soggy grass, and stopped. He searched through the darkness, his eyes roving about the house and between the houses into the alley. Suddenly, with the intensiveness of a dog locked on its prey, he looked up, his line of sight to the fish eye mirror unobstructed.

"We've got to stop him. He's going to get them," Alex cried, as he just as suddenly realized what was happening.

"Susan," Kevin shouted, hurrying through the kitchen. "Stop them."

Chapter Twenty-three

Utah
Present day

It was nearly 5:00 in the morning. Dr. Reed was on the phone making arrangements for Molly's diagnosis and treatment. Jake was in an examination room with Molly, pressing a pillow against her face. "You're just trouble," he whispered, his voice strained because of the exertion. It took a lot to kill someone, even someone who was unconscious.

"Get the ambulance, Jake," Dr. Reed shouted, his voice coming from his office, two doors down. His voice was enough to startle Jake, make him stand up straight and take his hands off the pillow. "I'm leaving a message for Ray," Reed continued. "She'll be worried if I'm not here when she gets here. She'll have to cancel all my appointments. Call Toastmasters and let them know I won't be speaking today."

Glancing at Molly, her face still covered with the pillow, Jake studied her chest. "Damn," he seethed. "She's still breathing." He checked the door to see if Reed was coming, heard his footsteps and panicked. "Son of a bitch." Quickly ripping the pillow from her face, he slid it beneath her head and pretended to fluff it as Dr. Reed walked in.

"I told you to get the ambulance," Reed scolded. "We've got to get her out of here before any early risers see us. I don't want any questions. Understand?"

"Yes, Doctor." Jake was still seething.

Molly was still unmoving but alive. From beneath and about the pressure bandage covering the raw flesh exposed when her scalp was severed, her hair was matted with blood, her curly, red hair sheathed in thick, coagulated clumps. On her right arm, wide, white tape wrapped around a splint protected the compound fracture from further damage. Not yet black and blue, her right cheek was inflamed and swelling where Jake slapped her.

"I didn't notice that before," Reed said, as he lightly touched the cheek. "Did you?"

"Yeah," Jake told him. "She had it when they brought her in. I didn't say anything because I thought the other wounds were more dangerous."

"Okay, but make a note of it. I want to take an x-ray of that cheek. Looks like it might be broken. Now go get the ambulance."

It was late morning and miles away as Jake and Dr. Reed drove onto a dusty circular drive in front of a single-storied, adobe-walled facility, painted beige. Molly had not moved. As the ambulance approached the entrance, an older woman met them and ushered them through the doorway. Three hours later, Molly's blood tests and x-rays were complete. No diagnostic equipment for soft injuries was available.

"Ambiguous Head trauma resulting in an extended loss of consciousness." Reed entered into his private computer, listing his diagnostic findings. "Cracked and fragmented skull at location of a serious suprafascial avulsion where her scalp was severed by the convertible top crushed during the automobile accident. Compound fracture of the radius of her right arm, and split ulna at the hinge joint of her left elbow. An orthopedic surgeon is required to repair these bone fractures. I do not have the necessary skills. A neurosurgeon is required to evaluate her for and repair possible brain injuries.

She is breathing on her own but is unresponsive. Blood tests normal in every respect. Please advise." Selecting the diagnosis, Reed copied it and pasted it into an email. Tenting his fingers over his nose and mouth, his elbows on the desktop, he took a deep breath and paused. Sitting back in his chair, he clicked 'send' and waited.

"What did he say?" Jake quizzed, when Dr. Reed returned to the examination room where Molly lay on the table. "He said, do it."

Jake stared at him. "You're kidding."

"No."

"What about the surgeries she needs? Is someone coming?"

"No," Reed stoically told him. "It's up to us to do whatever we need to do to keep her alive."

"Are you going to operate then?" Jake asked.

Reed almost snarled at him, as he responded. "No. We'll just have to keep her wounds clean and immobilize her."

Jake stared hatefully at Molly, wordlessly fussed for a moment, then protested, "Those arms are in really bad shape. If she doesn't get surgery, she's likely never to be able to use them again. We'll have to feed her and wipe her ass. We'll have to cater to her like servants. With all we have to do around here, they can't be serious. They can't make us do that, can they? It's not our job."

"Our job is to do whatever they tell us to do," Reed smoldered. "Now, go get the instruments. We have work to do."

Chapter Twenty-four

Mountain Meadows
Southern Utah
September 1857

Isaac's message informing Brigham Young of their intention to destroy the Gentile wagon train was burning in Jacob's pocket as he galloped north to Salt Lake City. At the same time, on Isaac's orders, Samuel Knight was riding south to enlist John D. Lee and the natives for the attack.

***

The Gentile wagons, with Carrie and Lyle's among them, were in the meantime climbing out of the Great Basin into hills six thousand feet high and into a long, green valley. Eight miles further was an area known as Mountain Meadows, a respite from the dry, dusty, sage clogged landscape of the mountain desert through which they passed. Across the meadow was a bubbling spring that flowed southward. Refreshed by a skim of surface water, the grass was deep and rich. On nearby rolling hills, brush and sage gave way to junipers, and scrub oak grew in washes.

The Gentiles were some thirty-five miles south of Cedar City and the trouble there. A place of solace, Mountain Meadows was the perfect place to rest and feed the livestock before driving them into the Mojave Desert twenty miles south. There, food and water would be scarce. Believing they had left the Mormons behind them, the Gentiles chose not to circle the wagons.

"How long do you think we'll stay here?" Carrie asked. It was late afternoon. Alice and Teddy had run off to play with friends, and Lyle was unloading the wagon.

"Don't know how long we'll be here, but it'll be a while." He nodded toward Spears and the other Missourians. They were riding out, stopping only long enough to feed and water their horses. "Guess 'a while' is too long for them."

"You people can stay here all winter if ya want," Spears shouted, as they remounted their horses and rowdily rode through the middle of camp. "We're goin' ta California." He suddenly spurred his horse to a gallop and let out a yelp. Inciting the Missourians behind him to do the same, they yelped and wahooed like drunks, spurring their horses through small, individual camps already set up and destroying them. Waving his hat over his head, Spears shouted something, but whatever it was, it was drowned out by the pounding of horses' hooves and the shrill whoops of his companions.

Carrie and Lyle watched as the Missourians reached the last of the wagons, waived a final goodbye and rode south. "Hope they keep headin' south when they get to California," Carrie said. She and Lyle would head north. "I'd rather have rattlers for neighbors than them."

"Wouldn't worry about them," Lyle said. "Doubt those buzzards'll settle anywhere long enough to have neighbors." He smiled wryly. "They'll keep movin' 'til they get ta hell."

That evening, as the night turned cold and everyone retired to their own wagons, Carrie put more wood on the fire, while Lyle took his juice harp from a special box he kept it in beneath the wagon seat. "Play 'Camptown Races.'" Carrie eagerly suggested.

Teddy was in her lap, and as Lyle played, she took Teddy's hands in hers and clapped in rhythm to Lyle's song. Clearly and joyously she sang, "Camptown ladies sing this song, Doo da, doo da. Camptown racetrack's five miles long. Oh, de doo da day." She picked up Teddy and danced with him. "Come on," she invited nine year old Alice. "Come dance with us."

Hearing Lyle's tune, Cousin Alexander brought his fiddle, his wife, and his four children and joined them. Soon, Cousin Robert and the Dunlaps came with their five children. Mrs. Tacket brought a pie, Mrs. Camron a ten pound cake, Solaman Wood a near full jug, and the event became a party.

Alice and Teddy were asleep by the time the last dance was over and everyone left. Carrie was breathless. "We'll have such fun when we get to California," she told Lyle. "There's not one of these folks I don't care for. How much longer before we get there?"

"Well," Lyle calculated out loud, "we got a few days here. Not likely we'll tarry through the desert. It'll take a good week after that to get to my brothers.' But we oughta' see 'em before the month's out." He grinned. "Almost over, Honey. A few weeks more, and we're there. No more travelin,' forever." He took Carrie in his arms, kissed the nape of her neck, and asked her, "What's the first thing you want when we bring in our first harvest?"

She put her head on his shoulder. Taking a deep breath, she sighed and whispered, "A hundred years more with you."

Carrie and Lyle Drake slept peacefully that night. In no hurry to rise the next morning, they let the sunlit peak above the hills to the east without them. They even nodded back to sleep until..."When's breakfast?" Alice asked. "I'm hungry."

"Me too," Teddy cried.

Carrie and Lyle were used to rising well before sunup, so they could be ready to move at first light. Breakfast was more than an hour late. "In a minute," Carrie told them. "Let us rest a little while longer." The dawn held a chill, and she and Lyle were snug and warm beneath their comforters.

Alice peeked outside, "But, everybody else is gettin' up."

"All right," Carrie said, surrendering. "If you're that hungry, get the fire started. Take Teddy with you to get wood and see he potties. You can use that towel to clean him up." Carrie pointed to an old, blue, hand towel, worn and faded, hanging on a nail just inside the wagon.

Alice lowered the tailgate, grabbed the towel, and climbed out. "Come on, Teddy," she called, once she was out of the wagon. Teddy crawled to her and, when he reached her, held out his arms to her. The surrounding hills were quiet as they headed toward a nearby stand of scrub oak. The ground was crowded with tick bearing sage and riddled with varmint dug mounds and holes. Alice did her best to guide little Teddy around them, but he was still unsteady on his feet. He stumbled along and, trying to keep his balance, grabbed onto the nearest sage.

"Dad's gonna get a fire stick after you if you don't stop that," Alice threatened. She referred to a small stick Lyle would heat in the campfire and touch to any tick imbedded in Teddy's flesh to drive it out.

Once in the privacy of the stand of scrub oak, they chose a likely spot and Alice took off his pants. "Mama's gonna be so proud of you when you don't spoil them," she told him. "If I hold them, it doesn't matter if you miss." Teddy wet and as he settled down to poop, Alice took care of her own comfort. Patiently waiting for Teddy to finish, she gazed out over the sagebrush.

"What's that?" she whispered. "Did you hear it?" There was something in the brush, something disturbing the sage as it passed. When Teddy opened his mouth to answer, she hushed him, putting her finger over his lips. She listened, trying to hear the sound again.

The only sound was that of the nearby spring. She peered over the brush and across the meadow and observed, "Why aren't there any birds?" She stared at the hillside. In the soft, emerging light, something moved. She started. There was more movement. She could see men taking up positions. "Mama!" she screamed. "Indians!"

Everyone awake in camp looked first at Alice and Teddy running back to their wagon, then up the hill. Scores of natives armed with rifles were stealthily moving through the brush setting up positions. "We're being attacked," someone shouted.

"Get your guns and form a line," Robert Fancher yelled. "They're coming."

Lyle leaped from the wagon in his long johns, Carrie behind him screaming for Alice and Teddy. They ran to her, and she wrapped her body around them. "Get under the wagon," she told Alice. "Don't let Teddy out of your sight. Papa and I'll be right here."

She reached for Lyle's shotgun and followed him to the firing line. With barely time to aim, she fired, dropped the barrel, and reloaded. Raising the butt to her shoulder, she aimed and fired again, propelling a barrage of pellets into the native running straight for her. His chest burst with blood, and he fell. Revolted by what she had done and convulsing with sobs, she paused.

"Keep shooting," Lyle yelled, when she hesitated.

Another native was coming at them, his dark body covered in bright colored paint. Carrie raised the shotgun, pulled the trigger, and fired.

Chapter Twenty-five

Mountain Meadows
Southern Utah
September 1857

Terror and pain in his eyes, his voice a hollow cry, the native Carrie shot pointblank blew apart. Chunks of flesh and splinters of bone splattered everywhere, spraying her face and getting in her mouth. "AAAHHHH," she cried, scrambling to get away as he fell on her. "Get him off me. Get him off me!" she screamed.

Lyle was there, pulling at the native's arm, throwing him to the ground next to her. "Take hold of yourself," he told Carrie. "They're still coming. You've got to shoot." He handed her the shotgun she had discarded and went back to his post.

Whimpering, repulsed by any and all measure, she took a deep breath, got to her knees, took up position, and retched. Still gagging, she reloaded as the natives retreated, taking with them all the wounded they could reach.

"Circle the wagons," Robert Fancher ordered. "Now. We've got to move while they're retreating."

Not bothering with the horses, Lyle and Carrie grabbed the tongue and physically pulled their nearly empty wagon fifty feet into the forming circle. Alice carried Teddy in front of them. Hobbled for grazing, the horses were already inside the circle.

"What about our things?" Carrie asked, as she saw them exposed and undefended at their campsite.

"I'll get 'em after dark," Lyle promised. "We can't worry about 'em now."

In disarray, gathering in groups on the hill just out of range, the natives stood watch. "Get whatever you own out of the wagons and build yourselves a barricade," Robert shouted. "They'll be comin' back."

Yet the natives did not come back. Instead, they stayed on the hill watching as the settlers built embankments, reinforcing them with mattresses and boxes, barrels and well-worn saddles. When the barricades were up and ready for another attack, the natives melted into the brush and disappeared.

Carrie and Lyle had made a veritable fortress, scavenging from their wagon its floorboards and the mattresses they slept on. When their barricade was complete they got into position, their eyes and guns riveted on the hillside. Alice and Teddy were between them.

At dusk, when after the long day they had not eaten and had no more bread to give Teddy, Carrie dug a hole just behind the wagon and built a tiny, cooking fire. "Better make us something that will last several days," Lyle told her. "No telling when we'll be able to get out of here." She gazed at him, between them passing a hundred doubts and fears, each one of them mortal. "We gonna be okay, Mama?" Alice asked.

Carrie's eyes softened, making them strong and sure as she took Alice in her arms and promised, "Yes, dear. As long as we stay inside our circle, we'll be fine." With an assurance she tried to believe herself, Carrie added, "When the Indians realize they can't get to us, they'll leave. We just need to be patient and keep our heads down. Want to help me make some flatbread?" She glanced at Lyle.

His eyes welled with tears, and he nodded his approval. He waited until a few hours after dark and until the children were asleep, then told Carrie, "It's time I get out there and get our things."

"I changed my mind," she told him. "They're not worth the risk. Leave them where they are."

He was rubbing dirt on his face. "But, almost everything we own is out there. If the Indians sneak down the hill and steal them, we'll have nothing."

"We'll have each other." To hold his gaze she stared at him but he did not look at her. He turned to leave and glanced over his shoulder. "I've got to do this, Carrie. Cover me."

He stepped on the wagon wheel and leaped outside the barrier. As he did, Carrie felt a rattling in her chest and fear so great her hands shook. She dropped to her knees. Her hands still trembling, she stuck the shotgun through a narrow gap between the floor boards in the barricade and looked for him. He was already at their campsite picking up all he could carry.

The moon was a slim, bright sickle, and except for an occasional cough on the line, the night was silent. His hands full, Lyle turned his back on the hillside and started running back. Before Carrie even heard the shot, he was down, kettles and food scattered everywhere.

"Lyle," she screamed, scrambling over the wheel. She was at his side in an instant, pulling at him, tugging at him to make him stand.

Hands reached out to help her. She on one side, Robert Fancher on the other, they dragged Lyle back inside the circle.

"Lyle," Carrie whispered, as he woke at dawn. He had a nasty shoulder wound and could not move his left arm, but he was alive. She wanted to kiss him until his lips hurt, but she was too angry with him for taking the risk. "You ever do that again," she threatened, "and I'll shoot you myself."

He faintly smiled, reached out with his good arm and patted her hand. "Sorry."

By late afternoon, he could stand. He returned to the barrier with his arm in a sling and in pain. As he propped his rifle between the boards and took his place on guard, he quipped to her, "Good thing I'm right handed."

Carrie was not amused. "Good thing you're not dead," she said flatly, leaving her post to spend some time with Teddy.

Throughout the day, hidden in the brush, the natives took shots at anyone fool enough to expose himself, but they did not launch an attack either that day or the next. In siege and surrounded, their courage waning, the emigrants were restless. At a meeting held next to Robert Fancher's wagon on Wednesday evening, they decided to send for help.

"Take this with you," Robert said, as he handed young William Aiden a letter signed by every lodge member in the train. The letter was specifically addressed to Masons, Odd Fellows, Baptists and Methodists, and to all good people everywhere, imploring them to send help. Aiden joined the Gentile wagon train in Provo and had previous experience dealing with the Mormons, so he with two other men had been chosen to carry the letter. Specifically, they were to first try to deliver the letter to Cedar City. "The people in Cedar City may not like us," Robert told him, "but I know they ain't gonna turn their backs on fella' Christians."

"What if we can't reach Cedar City? What if it's too dangerous?" Aiden asked.

"If ya don't think ya can reach Cedar City, head for California, and hurry."

The sky was a little clearer, the waxing moon a little brighter, as young Aiden and the two other men rode out of the wagon circle, skirting the natives. Once the danger was behind them, the three rode north. Despite the risk of being seen, hoping to reach Cedar City by dawn, they used the main trail. Believing the natives were their only threat, they were caught unaware when they were ambushed by Mormons.

Aiden was murdered. His companions were wounded but escaped, riding west toward California. "Find and kill them," were the Mormon's orders.

***

In Cedar City, Isaac Haight called a meeting of the council. "The Indian attack isn't going well," he told them. "They've been in siege for four days, and they're doing nothing but waiting. The wagon train's barricaded, and the Indians are refusing to attack. Apparently, they didn't expect much of a fight, and they weren't ready for it. They've got killed and wounded. They're scared, and they're angry. Their blaming us for sending them, and if we don't do something to help, them Indians are gonna turn on us. We've got to decide what to do."

Zeb had a suggestion. "Just tell them cowards to go home. We'll kill the Gentiles ourselves."

"There aren't enough of us," Isaac told him, "not with the defenses they built. The braves that came with the news told me the Gentiles have built a fortress around their wagons. They also let me know the Indians aren't about to leave without avenging their dead. We don't give them the chance.

They won't take it too kindly. We could find ourselves in a heap a' trouble with them.

"There's something else we have to consider. I just got word saints killed one of the Gentiles the train sent to us for help and the two men with him got away. If those two reach California, or if we let the train go now, all the Gentiles will bear witness to that murder and come after us. California will have even greater cause to send an army against us."

"Then we gotta' get that train. We have ta' kill everyone in it." Zeb urged. "We don't need ta worry 'bout them two on the run. They don't have a chance against us."

"Before we do something like that, shouldn't we wait to hear from Brigham Young?" one of the other men asked.

"There isn't time," William Dame, commander of the militia, told them. "We need to move now. I'll send a detachment to Mountain Meadows this morning to reinforce the Indians and let them know we're coming in force. A larger detachment will follow tonight with Major Higbee in command."

Chapter Twenty-six

Present Day Portland, Oregon
2:00 a.m.
April 25

T he wind passing through had blown itself out, yet the downpour continued as Alex surreptitiously peered between Susan Marshall's drapes at the white, nondescript, four door Impala parked across the street and at the armed, formidable, redheaded man who got out of it. "Sharon," he heard Kevin call her as Kevin ran to the garage, "stop them," he yelled, referring to Susan and the children. "They've been spotted."

The redhead was staring at the alley and at the neighbor's fish eye mirror, which reflected everything that went on in the alley. Susan and the children were out there, exposed to him. They were trying to get away, and he was carrying his gun. Standing at the curb, squinting his eyes, he raised his revolver and aimed it right into Sharon's path.

"He's going to shoot them," Alex gasped.

At the end of the alley, Susan's exit was blocked. A neighbor's pickup was parked in the way, and she could not get around it. In repeated K-turns, she turned around, her Honda looming larger and larger in the fish eye as she approached the back of her house.

Pausing, jaw clenched, his look determined, the tall, stocky redhead sighted his revolver at the image on the mirror. Slowly and quietly rotating his shoulders away from the mirror, he aimed the gun waist height at every inch along the side and front of Susan's house.

The barrel of the revolver rotating toward him, Alex quickly closed the drapes. He waited, but there was no gunfire, no sound. After a moment passed, he slowly and cautiously peered outside.

The redhead was still at the curb. He was stooping. From a paper cup, he was pouring a dark yellow liquid down a storm drain. "Jesus," Alex said in disgust. "He's dumpin' his pee."

"Too bad we didn't know what he was doing in the car," Kevin said, when he returned and Alex told him what happened. "We might have used the opportunity to escape. Susan and the children got away fine." Keeping a close eye on what was happening outside, they watched as the redhead slid back into the passenger seat of the Impala.

"Doesn't look like they're going anywhere. If we're going to get out of here, we'll have to do it right under their noses," Kevin observed. "You all ready to crawl out to Sharon's car?" Kevin asked, reminding Alex they had a tracking device to find.

"Think thin," Kevin said, as Alex unsuccessfully tried to force his shoulders through the dog door in the lower left, wood panel of the front door. "You can't be that much bigger than a retriever."

"Wanna bet?" Alex snapped. "I can't even see how the retriever got through. The opening can't be more than a foot wide." The route to the convertible from every other door in the house was easy to see from the Impala, so was the front door if opened. With the convertible blocking the line of sight from the Impala to the dog door, the twelve by fifteen inch hole was the only way Alex could get out without being seen.

"Mattie wasn't very big," Sharon told them of the golden retriever who was Susan's dear and loving friend for over fifteen years. "We'll have to take out the frame. I'll get Mom's screwdriver and a hammer."

"Hurry," Alex told her, again peeking out the window through the rain and at the Impala. The balding man with the unnaturally thick neck was behind the wheel and looked to be asleep. His head was resting against the side window, opened a crack so all the windows would not fog. His redheaded partner was sitting sideways, staring at the house. Alex would have to be careful.

"This should help," Sharon said, once the frame was out and half-an-inch gained on all sides. She rubbed the inside of the opening with liquid soap. Still holding the soap dispenser in her hand, almost daring Alex to get through, her look was steady and reassuring. "If you can't squeeze through, I'll go."

Alex wore only a short-sleeved tee shirt over tight fitting jeans. His head at the dog door, he lay on his side. Hunching his back, extending his arms through the hole and bringing his shoulders as close together in front as possible, he folded himself lengthwise and pushed. With Sharon and Kevin shoving, he forced himself through the hole diagonally, bruising himself against the rigid door. His legs useless until he got them through the hole, he wriggled over the front step and onto the lawn and was immediately immersed in deep, wet grass. Soaked to the skin, he crawled toward the convertible, the rain sheathing over him. The lawn was a cold, aquatic growth of mud rich puddles.

While Alex skimmed across the grass, Sharon and Kevin were on hands and knees watching through the dog door. Alex's shoulders had been seriously abraded when they shoved him through the unforgiving frame, and blood was seeping in patches through his T-shirt.

"Who are those guys, anyway?" Kevin asked her of the two men in the Impala.

"They didn't say who they were," she quipped. "But they've been chasing us ever since Alex got here. No matter what we do, we can't seem to lose them. They turn up everywhere we go."

"You told me you've been running from them, but shouldn't we try to at least talk to them and find out what they want?"

"Don't forget they've got guns and that the redhead aimed his at this house knowing we were in it. If all they wanted was to talk, they could have done that at the motel, but they kicked our doors down. Given what happened with Wayne and Kim, we probably don't want to find out what they want with us. And I sure as hell don't want to visit with them."

Always keeping the convertible between him and the Impala, Alex slithered across Susan's yard. Sopping up the moisture out of the grass, sponging out the water in puddles, his clothes were soaked. He shivered.

The middle class, older middle-aged neighborhood was deathly quiet until a small dog two houses away became aware of him. It was frantically pawing at the window between the drapes, and its shrill, incessant bark could have awakened the deaf. Lying very still, Alex peered beneath the convertible, watching the Impala for any sign the two men were getting out. Seconds later, a voice as shrill as the dog's shouted at it. "Shut up." There was a loud bump as something hit the window, and the dog was silenced.

Alex continued to watch the Impala, but neither of the men seemed to have moved. Wasting no time, Alex moved quickly but stealthily to the convertible.

Arriving at the curb on the driver's side, a surging stream of runoff below him, he stuck his head between car frame and gutter, searching with his hand all along its edge and to the front bumper. Carefully following the lines of the bumper from wheel to wheel, he found nothing. Retreating, reexamining the driver's side to the rear, he then examined the back bumper. There, beneath the street side corner, was a small, battery powered, 63x57x35mm metal cube, magnetically attached and less than eight feet from the Impala.

Now, what? Alex thought, realizing he would expose himself to the redhead, if he attempted to get the device. He looked about the yard. Maybe there's a stick.

The wind and rain had blown down fledgling leaves and twigs but nothing long enough or strong enough to help. He looked at the house and at the two faces peering at him through the dog door. He shrugged.

"What's he doing?" Sharon asked Kevin, as Alex repeatedly pointed toward the back bumper, turned his closed fist upside down, and jabbed.

"What?" Kevin mouthed in response.

Alex jabbed again, and spread his hands apart.

"He needs something long," Sharon said, flashing Alex an 'okay' sign. "I'll get the broom."

She was back in a flash, shoving the kitchen broom through the dog door and onto the step. Easily sliding through the dog door, she got on her belly and followed. Crawling on hands and knees with broom in hand, only her hands and her legs below the knee getting wet, she covered the stretch between the door and convertible easily.

"Thanks," Alex said, extending the handle beneath the car and forcefully dislodging the box.

"So how do we get Kevin and our things out of the house?" Sharon asked him. "We don't dare go back."

"Guess we should have talked about that before I came out here." Alex thought for a moment. "One thing for sure, Kevin's never going to fit through that dog door." Pointing to Kevin, Alex started gesturing to him with his hands, drawing the outline of the computer in the air and going through the motions of tucking the computer and papers under his arm, and running with his fingers.

Nodding as if he understood, Kevin disappeared.

As Alex and Sharon waited, the rain constantly sheeting, they heard a car door open and then slam shut. "The Impala," Sharon whispered, not daring to move. Praying Kevin would not chose that moment to come out of the front door running, she anxiously listened for whomever got out of the Impala, hoping he would get back in and close the door.

Across the road, the balding man from the Impala was outside, leaning against the car door. The expression on his pale face was obscured in the rain and in the darkness, yet they could see his head was pointed toward the house. It was obvious he was watching, looking for signs of them in the house, maybe ready to enter it. He stepped away from the car door, walked down the road to the edge of Susan's property and then walked back, always watching the house. Seeming to be studying every avenue of escape, he silently motioned his partner to join him.

Only feet away from Alex and Sharon, the passenger door opened and slammed shut.

"Is he back in the car?" Sharon whispered.

"No," Alex mouthed, putting his finger to his lips. Pointing beneath the car he directed her gaze to four big shoes.

"Kevin?" she quietly blurted.

Quickly glancing toward the house she saw the front door slowly opening. "Don't," she prayed.

"What was that?" the balding man asked. He must have heard their voices. "Something's happening. I can feel it. Better check in back."

Alex and Sharon could hear the slap of the redhead's shoes against wet pavement as he walked toward her car's bumper. Pressing their bodies tight against each other and to the convertible, they hurriedly tucked their legs beneath them. Immediately on the other side of small, narrow car, they were trapped, with no place to hide.

As the redhead rounded the bumper splashing through a puddle, he stopped only a foot away from reaching their side. If he looked down, he would see them. The rain both curtain and friend to them, he shielded his eyes as he searched the house and its perimeters, looking everywhere but next to him.

"Whew," Alex whispered, as the redhead suddenly ran to the left and around the house.

"Kevin." Sharon's whisper was a gasp, as the front door opened, and he appeared.

"Hurry," Alex shouted, jumping to his feet as the bald man ran past them, headed for Kevin. "Start the car," he told Sharon, as the balding man reached for his gun and turned toward Alex.

"Thump" was the sound of Kevin's lap top case hitting the back of that big bald spot.

"Run," Alex yelled, as the balding man stumbled and fell.

Scrambling over the slick and soggy grass, Kevin reached the convertible and scrambled inside as Sharon revved the engine. With Alex already in back, Sharon gunned it, and with tires squealing and neighbors lights turning on, she sped away from the curb.

The balding man was still down on the lawn, his hand on the back of his broad, ugly neck. The redhead was racing toward the Impala.

Chapter Twenty-seven

Mountain Meadows, Utah
September 1857

S uspended on the horizon over a dusty green sea of brush, the sun delayed dawn as Higbee's Militia detachment rode south from Cedar City toward Mountain Meadows and the Gentile wagon train's encampment. The dust churned up by the horses was a curtain which never parted, and riding far to the rear without a kerchief to protect him, John squinted and coughed incessantly.

The horse Brother Zeb supplied him was a bay over sixteen hands high and slow. Steadily falling behind, John prodded it, kicked it with his spurless boots and slapped his reins at it. Brother Higbee and Jacob were in the lead and nearly a mile in front of him. If he did not hurry he might lose them.

As soon as Jacob delivered the council's message to Brigham Young in Salt Lake City advising him of the pending attack, Jacob turned around and rushed back to Cedar City not waiting for an answer. If there was to be an answer another rider would bring it. He'd traveled over five-hundred miles round trip, but as he rode into town, seeing the Militia organizing, he joined it and rode out of town with it.

John and most of the other men had been told nothing of what was happening at Mountain Meadows, nothing of what they were expected to do. Orders came in the middle of the night through Zeb's nephew, Bud, and two others, possibly the same men who stalked John's family home on Sunday. They brought with them Zeb's horse and had refused to leave without him. There was no time to take anything but his rifle and the small bag Anna quickly stuffed with salt pork and bread, enough food for only a day.

After Anna, Hattie, and the two girls waved good-bye to him and as they went into the cabin, Hattie asked Anna, "What if they keep John out there for days? He's got hardly nothin' to eat with him, and he'll go hungry."

"I know," Anna agreed. "We'll pack enough for a week, more if we have it. We can put it in one of the empty grain sacks. I'll take it to him. It shouldn't be that hard to follow them, they just left."

"What do you suppose they're up to?" Hattie asked. "Those three that came for John looked like they'd packed quite a bit. Looked well-armed too. Bud not only had a rifle in his saddle holster, but he was wearing a revolver on each hip."

"Those guns weren't all. That blanket tied to the back of his saddle had a musket wrapped in it," Anna added. "The man to Bud's right, had three guns on him."

Hattie flooded Anna with questions. "They told us just last week that that army from Washington isn't anywhere near us yet, so what do you think they're doing?" she asked. "Where are they riding off to? Do you think there's an advance party out there? And, why did John and the others ride south and not north? Is there an advance force down there? What if the war is beginning, not from the north but from the south?"

"I don't know, Hattie, but I'm going to find out. John's in trouble, and whatever that trouble is, I have to know. I have to be there." She picked up the half-filled grain sack. "Can we spare any more venison?" From the bed she and John slept in, she took a pillowslip and tore it into strips. "If John's wounded," she told Hattie, "he'll need bandages. I'll be there, and I can bring him home in the wagon."

While Anna hitched the four oxen to the uncovered wagon, Hattie fried in bacon fat the corn bread she'd mixed the night before, cut a big slab of bacon, picked from their stock a pound of venison jerky, and packed them with some of the hardtack they had stocked for the coming war.

"I might not be back for a while," Anna told her, as she climbed onto the wagon. "If there's fighting, I want to be with him."

"Then wait," Hattie said, rushing back into the cabin.

She returned with a full jug and an old, gray dress. "Use this for bandages too," she said, as she handed the dress to Anna. The mash was John's favorite. "You'll need it to clean wounds, and to make him feel better." Her eyes deep with worry, she took Anna's hand. "Be careful and take good care of him. I'll see to everything here."

Already significantly behind John, Anna pulled out just before dawn. Fretting about all the things that could happen to him, her heart fluttered. Her mind raced to follow him, but her wagon did not. Hardworking, lumbering animals that would give her their all, the oxen could move no faster than a walk. After three hours, looking anxiously down the road south without seeing any dust, she frustratingly resigned herself to the oxen's pace. She was on the main road, and she told herself, aloud, "I can't miss them."

The militia climbed onto the foothills surrounding Mountain Meadows, left the trail and headed east behind the hills. Below one of the crests, out of sight of the Gentile wagon train, was an encampment of over three hundred natives. The detachment of Mormon militia which had arrived earlier that morning under the command of Brother John D. Lee, was camped nearby. With Higbee and his militia's arrival, the Mormons numbered fifty-four, and the command changed hands to him.

As John dismounted near Jacob, he heard isolated gunshots from the other side of the hill. He looked at the native encampment and saw that several of the natives were wounded. The men around him were unsaddling their horses and tying them to a hitching rope strung between two scrub oaks. "What's happening here?" he asked Jacob.

"That Gentile wagon train we were talking about on Sunday is on the other side of this hill. The Indians have attacked them, and we're here to help."

John looked toward the militia's camp. Just outside it, Major Higbee was standing in the sagebrush shaking Brother John D. Lee's hand. It was clear there was some kind of tension between them. "What do you mean 'help them'?" John asked, suspiciously. He was recalling the gist of Sunday's meeting. It was the Mormon leadership who wanted to attack the Gentiles, not the natives. John waited for Jacob's response.

Jacob ignored him. Without responding, Jacob dropped his saddle and blanket in the dust and hobbled his horse. Looking not at John but at John's big mount, Jacob told him, "Brother Zeb holds a pretty high value on that gelding. Better tie him. Sure would hate to see you have to pay for him."

Irritated but determined, John was not to be put off. "What are we doing here, Jacob?"

"Major Higbee's been issued orders. He'll tell us what they are." Jacob pushed his round brimmed hat up and off his forehead, picked up his things, and walked off, letting his hobbled horse graze.

As John uncinched the gelding's saddle, a hundred unanswered questions battered his mind. Higbee had orders, but from whom? Had they already heard from Brigham Young? What were the orders? What did Brigham say? Most of all, John was suspicious. Just who are we going to help? The Gentile settlers? Or the Indians? His instincts were demanding he run, so John was slow to unsaddle and brush his horse. When the meeting was called, he was tying his gelding to the picket line. Though John joined the rest of the militia gathering around four campfires, he hung back in the growing darkness. Staying outside the firelight, he came just close enough to hear what John D. Lee was saying.

"The Indians attacked the wagon train on Monday," Brother Lee began. Slightly derisively, he then told the militia, "They've been sittin' here ever since, nursin' their wounded and buryin' their dead. Gettin' more frustrated all the time. At first, they wanted to kill the Gentiles down there 'cause they poisoned the water back at Corn Creek. Now they want to kill 'em 'cause some of their own were killed when they attacked. We've had real trouble containin' 'em. Can't seem to finish the job themselves and can't get us to help 'em. Make matters worse, one of our men killed one of the Gentiles when he was goin' for help."

The fires were crackling. The nightly cry of desert coyotes was noticeably absent. Mosquitoes were circling in flocks, and the air smelled of sage.

John D. Lee glared at the man standing a few feet in front of him and announced to the militia,

"I've been relieved of command by Major Higbee." Lee sneered, squinted his eyes and demanded of Higbee, "Jist so's everybody knows what we're about, I'm askin' him right here and now what orders he brought." His look piercing, Lee's face was ablaze in the firelight.

In baggy, cotton britches, a leather vest and brown, homespun shirt, Higbee, not quite thirty, squared his shoulders and faced not Lee, but the militiamen who were watching them. "After discussing the situation with Colonel Dame," Higbee pointedly and unemotionally told them, "Stake President Isaac Haight has ordered all the Gentiles in the wagon train, save those too young to bear witness, be put out of the way."

Seeming to be reflecting on what they had just heard, nearly every militiaman there held his breath. Everyone that is, but John. "No," he said, under his breath. "I won't do it," he shouted.

Higbee glared at him, commanding everyone's attention. "Yes, you will." Higbee then swept his hand over everyone there. "You all will. You are soldiers in God's militia. You will follow the orders we give you," he seethed, "or you will be shot."

"Go ahead and kill me then," a militiaman on the other side of the fires shouted. "I ain't murderin' no women and children." It was a remarkable moment. For the first time since Brigham Young's reign of terror began, men were daring to say, "No," to the priesthood.

Higbee inhaled but did not immediately let the breath go. While he hesitated, others shouted protests.

"We ain't women killers."

"No way in hell I'm gonna kill a child."

"No one wants you to kill the innocent," Higbee soothed. "We will not ask you to kill women and children, for none of us wants to do it. The Indians will take care of what needs to be done to them. You're only responsible for the men. Through God and by our act, the Gentile men will atone not only for their own sins, but for those of everyone in the wagon train."

John quickly surveyed his surroundings, counted the men standing near him, and glanced back at his horse. The wagon train was on the other side of the hill. To get to the wagon train, he would have to go back for his horse, turn it back toward the fires, and run it through the militia without being stopped. Even if he did escape to warn the Gentiles, the militia would be right behind him, and they'd have no time to defend themselves.

Finally, John understood. Blood atonement was not blessed by God. It was nothing but murder. Standing there, realizing he could do nothing to help the emigrants below them without getting killed, he recognized the evil that lurked in the Church, and he froze.

The camp was deathly quiet, the only sound the crackling of the fires, chirping crickets in the sage, and the light buzz of mosquitoes. "Let us pray," someone said. Gathering in a circle, the sage and starlight their church, the men of the Mormon militia knelt with Brother Lee in prayer.

"Dear God," Lee began. "Thy path is difficult, Thy will contrary to our spirit. How will we achieve it? How are we to step before Thee with your native children and kill? Guide us. Give us a sign so we know You will be with us. Grant us the strength to do that which is Thy will."

John clenched his teeth. As far as John was concerned, God had nothing to do with this. Believing Lee, Higbee and all the others were guided by Satan, John did not pray. While the militia stood with their heads down, he slowly moved away from the crowd, quietly sidling toward the horses.

Maybe if I gallop down the hill, he reconsidered as he neared the line where his horse was tied, *I could reach the wagon train.* He glanced at his mount and instantly reconsidered. Zeb's bay was too tired and too slow to reach them. He paused and hung his head. Trying not to picture the coming slaughter, he prayed for every Gentile in the wagon train. They were about to be murdered, and there was nothing he could do about it.

John heard John D. Lee say the "Amen", and the militia echo it. Their prayer was over. He had to get out of there. He planned his course as he slowly backed into the darkness toward his saddle. He could ride west, away from Cedar City, and escape in the dark. If he did not go home, the militia would not find him. He could circle to the southeast then to the north and hide in Cedar Breaks, wait a few weeks, and then go back home. He could have his entire family in California by December. He was only a few steps from his tack, when he hit an obstacle. Jacob was waiting for him.

"You're not leaving, are you?" Even in the dark, Jacob's eyes were menacingly cold. He reached for his revolver and drew it. "Your business is here. Better get back to the fire before there's trouble." Poking his gun into John's ribs, his breath on the back of John's neck, Jacob pushed him toward the campfires.

"Brother Lee has asked God to give us guidance," Higbee said, as the prayer died away and everyone resumed their places. "So He will, and so He has." Reverently, as if it were the Bible itself, Higbee held up a piece of paper for all to see. "I have in my hand orders from Brother Haight, who with God's knowledge and counsel, has devised a plan." Brother Haight, was the most powerful priest in the area. Handing Haight's orders to John D. Lee, Higbee then ordered Lee to "Read them aloud."

With clarity and resolve, John D. Lee read the details of what was to happen and the description of each officer's duties. Yet, when he got to the orders describing his own role, his face turned white. His hands went limp, and the orders fell to the ground. "I can't do this."

Higbee bristled, stepped toward Lee and picked up the orders. Clearly unsympathetic to Lee's opinion, he shook the orders in Lee's face. "You dare challenge the will of God? You dare spout your refusal in front of us. What you suggest is a sin. A sin you will die for, if you do not recant it." Higbee turned to the militia, raised the orders to heaven and demanded, "You, all of you, will follow these orders. You are soldiers of God and the Church, and God and the Church have issued them. God has spoken through Brother Haight and Brother Haight has signed them. You will do what you are told, and you'll do it tomorrow. Let us pray."

His head bowed, his heart heavy, John reached for God. *Forgive me for what I am to do,* he silently prayed, *for I will have no choice.*

John looked all night for an opportunity to escape or warn the emigrants what was to happen to them, but there was no chance. Having rolled his blanket out beside him, Jacob was alternately sleeping and watching him, never letting his gun out of his hand. The camp was being closely guarded by those whose loyalty and determination were unwavering. By morning, John was too late to do anything to stop it.

As the natives spread out on either side of the main trail, the militia marched in formation to the crest of the hill in sight of the wagon train. John D. Lee was to be the militia's negotiator. He was to be accompanied by William Bateman. With Bateman carrying a flag of truce, they walked down the hill together. They were met by two men from the wagon train.

"What do you think they're saying?" Carrie asked Lyle, as they watched the meeting taking place about two-hundred feet in front of them. Believing Aiden, their messenger, had gotten to Cedar City and the Mormons on the hill had come to rescue them, Carrie and Lyle hurried, along with dozens of others, to meet the four men as they started walking into the wagon train's circle.

"This here's Mr. Lee and Mr. Bateman," Robert Fancher, the train master, told them. "They've got an agreement with the Indians to leave us alone if we follow their instructions."

"What do we need to do?" Lyle asked, his wounded arm still in a sling and aching.

Lee responded. "To be allowed to leave unharmed, and for the lives of your loved ones, you must surrender to the Indians your horses, your cattle, and all of your belongings."

Chapter Twenty-eight

Mountain Meadows, Utah
September 1857

Sixty of the Gentiles' cattle had been shot during their battle with the natives. Their rotting carcasses were strewn about the meadow. Their stench was overwhelming. Yet most of the herd was still alive. The emigrants' horses had been hobbled inside the wagon circle and were unharmed.

"What are we gonna live on?" someone from the wagon train asked of the natives' terms of surrender. "If we give up everything we own, how are we gonna get to California?"

"As for your eatin', we'll see to that," John D. Lee, the militia's negotiator, assured them. "We'll see you get to your destination, too," he promised. "Sure don't want you settlin' in these parts." He grinned as if he had made a joke, eliciting from the emigrant's only a smattering of nervous laughter.

"Don't got much choice, I guess," Robert Francher, wagon master, said. "If we coulda' gotten outa' here without ya, we'd a' done it by now. No tellin' how long we'll be here if we don't take the help yer offerin'." He looked directly at Lee. "Young Aiden send ya?"

"Yeah," Lee lied. He could only have been guessing the young man from the wagon train the Mormon's killed was Aiden. "Got himself banged up a little and stayed in town."

"He gonna be all right?"

"Yeah, just a few bruises." Lee had to put them at ease about everything. He had to make them trust him. "One thing though, to make this deal work, you gotta' give up your weapons."

"Give up our weapons?" Lyle challenged. "Why don't we just let them shoot us and get it over with?"

"They ain't gonna shoot ya," John D. Lee promised. "I got their word."

"What good's them Indian's word to us?" Robert asked. "They'd just soon see us dead."

"I know how you must feel," Lee told him, his voice fatherly and sympathetic. "Guess if somebody'd been shootin' at me for days, I'd have a hard time trustin' 'em too.

"How 'bout if we Mormon men stray with ya all the way back to Cedar City. Escort ya, like. They won't bother you as long as we're armed. You have my word on that." Lee's eyes were warm and sincere as he offered Robert Fancher his hand.

Hesitating to take the hand John D. Lee offered, Robert asked the opinion of the emigrants who gathered around them. "Is that what you people want to do?"

A rider came galloping down the hill, left his mount outside the barricade, and ran to Lee. "Brother Higbee says it's gettin' late. The Indians are restless. Best get movin' if we're gettin' outa' here." The young man's eyes were cold and angry as he looked at the Gentiles surrounding him.

Lyle recognized him as being one of the young men who had been working on the ditch just the other side of Cedar City. He did not know he was the nephew of the storekeeper they'd beat up and robbed.

"You've got to decide now," Lee urged. "There ain't nothin' we can do for you here."

A few folk grumbled about leaving their belongings, but everyone agreed. "Okay, Mr. Lee," Robert said, finally taking the hand Lee had offered. "What do we do?"

Lee turned to Bud. "Tell Brother Higbee to get the men down here. It's time we move out." As Bud galloped up the hill with the news, Lee told the emigrants, "Empty out two wagons and get them hitched. Put the children six and under in one, and the lame and wounded in the other."

Not wanting to be separated from her toddler, Carrie protested, "If there's trouble, I want Teddy with me."

Lee snapped at her. "If there's trouble, you want him to get away, don't you? Get your best team to pull that wagon, and I'll get you my best driver."

Fear flared in Carrie's eyes, and she exchanged that fear with Lyle. Always before, she and Lyle were Teddy's best protectors. "We can't let strangers take him when he needs us," she told Lyle. "He's just a baby. He needs us. Being without us in this place will just scare him."

"But what if something does happen?" Lyle softly asked her. "If Teddy's in the fastest wagon we'll have, he might just get away and wouldn't that be worth it?"

John D. Lee and all the emigrants gathered around them were listening. "You should keep in mind too if you don't let him ride in the wagon, you'll have to carry him," he added, when she hesitated. "He's too little to walk all the way to Cedar City. If something happened, you'd both be captured for the weight of him."

"We have to walk all that way?" Carried asked.

"You've surrendered your wagons and horses to the Indians," Lee reminded her. "There's no other way out."

Lyle nodded. "Let Teddy go with them, Carrie. He's got a better chance in the wagon."

Resignedly, Carrie lowered her eyes. "I'll get his blanket."

Leaving their horses, the militia walked down the hill. A third wagon was hitched, and the Gentiles loaded their weapons in it. When every one of the emigrants was disarmed, one of the saints turned the wagon north, toward Cedar City and drove off with it.

"I want the men in a group over here. The women and older children over there," Lee ordered, pointing to areas about thirty feet apart.

Carrie balked. Now she was to be separated from Lyle. "I want to be with my husband," she said. "What is this?"

Mormon women did not question a man's authority, and Lee responded in anger, shouting not only at Carrie but at everybody else. "The Indians have to see the men will not harm them. You women will only be in the way. Come on now. We gotta' move. Your belongings won't keep the Indians busy long, and when they tire of 'em, you'd better be out of sight."

As the Mormon militia flooded into camp, instantly and with brief goodbyes, husbands parted with their wives and their daughters and sons over six. The two groups then rushed to the areas Lee assigned them.

One of the newer wagons, pulled by stout, young horses, was loaded with Teddy and the other children under six. When all seventeen were inside and settled, the drawstring around the canvass opening was closed so few could see out, and the wagon was driven off. The second wagon Lee ordered was loaded with three emigrant adults, a woman who could not walk and two wounded men. That wagon followed the first with John D. Lee, well-armed, walking between the wagons.

In a ragtag formation, many holding hands, the women and children over six followed a short distance back. Determined not to lose Alice, Carrie held tight to her, their hands perspiring.

John joined the militia formation. He had intended to escape as the men left the campsite to go down the hill to the wagon train. He changed his mind when an older militiaman, not far from him, opened fire and shot his own son when his son refused to join them and began to walk away.

"This is not a democracy," Higbee coldly reminded the militia. "This is an army. If you desert or refuse to obey orders, you will be shot."

The militia horses left behind on the hill were being guarded by two of the youngest men in the militia, to be collected after the Gentiles were disposed of. His rifle was an evil weight as John approached the wagon train with the other militiamen, and his conscience was burning. Outside the circle of wagons, the Gentile men waited in a cluster, gratitude and welcome in their eyes.

His soul in torment, John wanted to tell them to run, take their families and flee. Yet he knew his warning was too late. The emigrant men were already separated from their families. They were no longer armed, and the natives were in position.

Someone pointed to a tall, lanky man with his arm in a sling, and John went over to him. "Lyle

Drake," the man said, as he shook John's hand. "Thank you for helping us."

The tension inside John was explosive. He was so distressed he was near tears. He could barely look at the man and did not respond except to nod. Showing Lyle to their place in line, they joined the Mormon/Gentile pairs of men in front of them.

"How long you think it's gonna take to get outa' here?" Lyle asked. "I wanta' get back to my family."

The word stuck in John's desert dry throat, "Soon," he said.

The women had walked nearly a quarter of a mile before the men, in single file, an armed Mormon militiaman beside each one, started walking behind them. The noon sun was hot and unforgiving. Flies circled the column like vultures as the emigrants and their Mormon guards walked through knee-high brush and across the grass of Mountain Meadows. Peaceful and compliant, the Gentile emigrants were entrusting their lives to men who intended to murder them.

As the militiamen had been instructed, John carried his rifle in front of him, the butt in one hand, the barrel in the other pointed at Lyle, his finger resting on the trigger. "There'll be but an instant to shoot. Try not to miss," they'd been told. "Whatever you do, don't let them take your weapon away from you."

John's grip got tighter and tighter. He clenched his rifle so hard, he shut off the blood to his fingers. The priests' order to kill was trumpeting in his head. The man beside him was young and vital, fully trusting in him. This was wrong. So, very, very wrong. Without John's even realizing it, his finger recoiled and moved off the trigger.

Nearly half of a mile in front of him, the wagon carrying the children under six went over a hillock and out of sight. The second wagon, with the lame woman and wounded men, followed, and it too disappeared. As the two wagons went over a second hillock, the women and older children walked over the first. When the women and older children were in the depression between the hillocks, in a stretch where dense clusters of scrub oak lined both sides of the road, each of the three groups was out of sight of the others.

The timing perfect, from the midst of the men's group, Brother Higbee suddenly ordered, "Halt. Do your duty."

Instantly, the scrub oak on both sides of the women came alive. Natives, yelling and whooping, emerged from it, attacking the women and children over six with axes and knives. In the long line behind them, the Mormon militiamen turned to the men they guarded and shot them point blank. Running to the rear of the second wagon, before they could respond, John Lee shot to death the woman and wounded men inside.

Scores of men, women and children fell.

John met Lyle's eyes, and all the faces of all the men he killed stared back at him, accusing him of murder. In that moment, he decided. He would not kill again, even for God. "Run," he yelled. He shot into the air and then sat down.

Lyle looked at the road ahead and, hearing the women's screams, ran toward them. Faster and faster his legs took him. They suddenly collapsed when he fell, refusing to get him up when he struggled against the weight that held him. A native was standing over him, his foot on Lyle's chest holding him down. The native's rifle pressed against his forehead, it fired.

Yards up the road, the women and older children still alive were scattering. Terrified, Carrie ran through the scrub, dragging Alice behind her. Fighting brush, running from the slaughter all around them, blood flying everywhere, they both screamed as only feet from the road, four natives surrounded them.

Still dragging Alice, Carrie darted left, then right. Jolted to a stop, she saw Alice fall, her skull split open, a native with an ax standing over her. Unable to let go of her, Carrie fell to her knees and sobbed. There was a crack, a split second of blindness, and with her last gasp, Carrie cried "Ly...l...e".

Slumped on the ground, the breeze stirring dust about him, John watched and listened in horror to the massacre around him. Helpless to stop the killing, he dropped his head, closed his eyes, and covered his ears. Yet he could not hide from the death screams. Near the point of breaking, he sobbed.

***

Half a mile behind the slaughter, on the other side of a hill, Anna heard the first gunshots. "My god," she gasped. "The army from California has come, and John's in a battle." She immediately drove off the road and into a cluster of scrub oaks, hiding the wagon there. Grabbing John's binoculars, she scrambled off the seat and ran to the crest of the hill where she could see the entire scene. Between two hillocks, women and children were cleaved and hacked to death or screaming in terror and running for their lives. Behind the second hillock, were the bodies of scores of men with parts of their heads blown off, strewn in long lines down the road while men she knew stood over them with rifles. "The wagon train," she sighed. As she viewed the bloodbath, the wind suddenly crowded with screams. Her heart started racing. Gorge came up in her throat, and she vomited.

As she composed herself, she saw through scrub oak lining the road a wagon approaching, heading toward her. Engulfing it were the cries and screams of small children.

Further down the road a second wagon stopped. The driver and the man next to him on the seat, a man covered with blood, were talking, pointing to a clump of scrub oak about forty feet below her and twenty feet off the road. "Yeah," she heard the driver say. He dropped the reins, and he and the man beside him climbed down onto the road. Each placed a block under the front wheels and walked to the back of the wagon.

"I don't know why we couldn't just throw them out with the others," the bloodied man complained.

"Because John D. ordered it, that's why," the driver told him. "Let's just get it done and get back." He lowered the tailgate, reached into the wagon, and took hold of the lame woman's ankles. The bodice of her dress was covered with blood from Lee's shooting her through the heart, but her legs were unspoiled. "I'll take this end," he told his companion. "You take the other." He dragged her toward him, and when her shoulders reached the gate, his companion lifted her out by the shoulders.

"She stinks already," the companion announced. He looked inside the wagon at the two men John D. Lee had shot in the head. "I ain't gonna carry them this way," he said.

"Well, I'm not gonna do it," the driver declared, as they carried the woman off the road and toward the scrub oak.

"Then, neither of us will do it."

"What do you mean?" the driver questioned, as they unceremoniously and disrespectfully threw the woman into the clump of scrub oak.

"This won't be any trouble at all," the driver's companion told him when they got back to the wagon. He reached inside grabbed the first body's ankles, dragged him to the gate and onto the ground. "Here," he said, handing the driver a foot. "You take one. I'll take the other and we'll drag him into the brush." The man grinned. "See, I told you there wouldn't be trouble."

When they had deposited both corpses in the scrub oak, they mounted the wagon, turned it around and headed back to the scene of the massacre. Anna watched in horror. Again sickened, she covered her mouth. "My God." Revolted, she watched transfixed, unable to believe what she was witnessing. When the last woman fell, her head split in two by an axe, Anna looked up and without looking for him, saw John, a slumped heap in the road, not moving.

"Oh, no," she was nearly hysterical. "They killed him, too." Sobbing uncontrollably, not knowing what to do, she paced back and forth in the brush, oblivious to the danger of being discovered. The natives might think her a straggler and kill her before the Mormon men knew. Mormon men, panicked because she saw them, might quickly do away with her to keep her from bearing witness against them. Yet Anna did nothing but pace, mumbling to herself, screaming at John for the fault of it. John was dead in the road, and the butchering was all around him. Blood raced from her head to her wildly pounding heart, and she fainted.

Chapter Twenty-nine

Utah
Present Day

A single, bright spotlight from a bowl shaped fixture shown down from the ceiling onto Molly Jeffreys. She was lying on her back on a procedure's table, comatose and bare. At her left, an intravenous line from an IV tree with two bags hanging from it was inserted into her wrist. Her arm was tied at her side, immobilized by two three-inch-wide nylon belts tied to the table. At her right, the arm with the compound fracture was stretched out as much as possible, underside up, on the cold, unpadded surgical arm that extended from the table. There were no blankets in sight. The redheaded and freckled Dr. Reed was at the sink washing his hands. Jake, a menopausal man with dyed brown hair, was arranging Dr. Reed's instruments on a nearby tray.

The dull, tan room they were in was large and mostly bare. The lighting in it other than the spotlight was fluorescent. There were two small cabinets along the far wall, three wheeled instrument trays, vitals monitors and a long, wheeled table. There were no windows and only one door, and the door was closed.

Reed turned away from the sink, glanced at Molly and snapped, "I thought I told you to cover her up. You idiot. You'll send her into shock again." He hung back, arms crossed, waiting, while Jake rummaged through drawers that were empty, left the room and came back, carrying a single blanket with him. Still waiting while Jake covered

Molly up, Reed stepped to her head. "Forceps," he ordered. "And get me some gloves."

With gloves on and forceps in hand, Reed gingerly removed the pressure bandage he'd put over her scalp wound. The flesh beneath it was raw, the blood inside it and in the matted hair around it had crusted and formed solid clumps. "Shave off her hair and get that wound clean," he ordered Jake.

"You want it all shaved off?" Jake asked.

"Yeah, and we'll keep it that way. No reason to be fussing with her hair while we're taking care of her. She's not going to see it."

Jake took the razor from the instrument table and plugged it into an outlet in the floor. Starting at the area immediately surrounding the area scalped in the accident, he began shaving off all of her curly, red hair. Without first sweeping the floor, he quickly and roughly wiped the wound clean with sponges. "Done," he told Reed, who was watching him. He grabbed a broom, swept Molly's hair toward the door, and returned to the instrument table.

Reed adjusted the overhead spotlight to shine directly onto the open, oval wound. At the deepest most grievous area, where her skull was exposed, were cracked and fragmented pieces of bone. "Has she had any seizures?" Reed asked.

"Not that I know of," Jake told him, "but she was alone in here for almost an hour while we were getting something to eat.

"She needs to be evaluated by a specialist. She could be this way for life, if we don't do something. She could die on us. Wish they'd have sent someone. I can't even give her a graft. We got any anticonvulsants?"

"Don't think so," Jake told him. "Never needed any."

"Well, order some and have them delivered to the office. Charge them to Hospice. You can bring them with you tomorrow when you come out to check on her. In the meantime, start her on an antibiotic drip." Reed reached for a tube of hydrogel, coated the wound, applied fresh dressings and bandaged it. For the protection of both wound and bandage, he wrapped Molly's head with pink, four-inch-wide vet wrap.

The compound fracture of Molly's right arm was also problematic. "How are we going to keep that bone from shifting every time she moves?" Reed asked, thinking out loud. He was studying the inch of sharp, splintered radius bone sticking through the lower arm halfway to her elbow. Looks like it missed the artery. X-rays show the upper bone stable. Let's just strap the whole thing down," Reed offered. "We'll take some of that vet wrap you've got and immobilize it, put a cast over that, and tie her down.

He hesitated. "We've got no choice." Selecting a roll of two-inch-wide vet wrap from the instrument table, Reed wrapped Molly's arm several times running the wrap beneath and over the exposed bone. He then splinted it through the elbow, immobilizing it. "We can put a cast on if and when the swelling goes down," he explained to Jake. "We'll splint the left arm too. Tie both of them to her bed when you get her to her room.

Reed ran his fingers across the bruise on her cheek. "X-rays were negative, and it looks like the swelling's going down. Keep an eye on it, and let me know if there are any problems."

"Who's going to take care of her?" Jake asked. "She's gonna need a catheter and routine care. We're just not staffed for that."

Reed rubbed his brow with the back of his forefinger. "Keep her care to the essentials and figure it out. Not my problem."

"What about the other thing? What do we do about that?" Jake pressed.

"Let her rest a few days. If her heart and blood pressure is fine, start the injections."

Chapter Thirty

What seemed an eternity after they began, the screams and gunshots at Mountain Meadows subsided into isolated occurrences. Thereafter, in a few brief, torturous moments no sound was to be heard. Wrapped in a ball, his forehead against his knees, his hands held tightly over his ears, John opened his eyes. Pausing, taking several slow, deep breaths and wiping away his tears, he raised his head and peered at what was on the road in front him. As if a starting bell had rung, militiamen and natives, like wolves tearing and ripping apart their kills, started stripping the clothes off the Gentiles' bodies, taking anything of value, and discarding everything that was not. Sick, he crawled off to a nearby bush and retched.

Over the hill natives were stripping and robbing the women and children. In barely fifteen minutes, the Mormon militiamen and their native accomplices had executed a hundred and twenty-four men, women and children. Before the dust settled and as the Gentiles' bodies were being desecrated and stripped, other natives began looting the encircled wagons.

"They can't do that," Zeb shouted at Higbee. Zeb was carrying into the circle of wagons a chin-height load of bloody clothes. He dropped the clothes on a tall stack of them, and repeated his protest. "They told us they'd divide the spoils with us," he said of the natives. "Look," he pointed to a native with four blankets and a slab of bacon, wrapping them in a fifth blanket and putting the bundle on his horse, "they're taking it all for themselves."

Higbee immediately responded. Drawing his pistol, he pointed it in the air and shot four times. Not surprisingly, everyone in the circle stopped what they were doing and stared at him. "Those things you're taking," he told the natives, "are to be divided between us. Take them off your horses and put them here," Higbee ordered, pointing to a clear spot on the ground. "This looting is going to stop."

The natives looked to one of their leaders. When he nodded his agreement, they reluctantly unloaded their mounts and brought what they had taken to Higbee. The plunder they piled next to him was significant. As he surveyed it, the native leader who accepted his order, approached him. Without saying a word, he stood beside Higbee as an equal, folded his arms, and waited.

"Take a couple of men on the other side of that hill to make sure the Indians don't take anything there," Higbee told Zeb. "We're gonna wanta divide that stuff too."

Zeb quickly chose two militiamen from the five or six nearby and rushed out of the circle toward the dip between the hillocks where the women and children were massacred. They had not gone two feet beyond the wagons, when the native standing beside Higbee, nodded to two other natives, who then followed.

Shouting to a militiaman nearby, Higbee ordered, "Take five men and a couple Indians and round up those cattle. There're at least four-hundred head scattered across this valley, and I don't want to lose any of them."

Sitting in the road with dirt and blood all over him, John did not move except to stare at the plundering of the dead around him. Nearly all were stripped clean by the time he got to his knees and stood. Wandering through the slaughter, stumbling back up and over the crest of the hill to the militia's horses, he found the gelding Zeb loaned him and embraced him. Dazed and in shock, John hummed to him and, with hands bare and shaking, repeatedly and obsessively stroked the warm, living flesh of the gelding's neck.

From his position over the hill John could not see what was happening at the site of the massacre, but the shouting, the arguing over the spoils, and the hoof beats and lowing of moving cattle were clear. John stayed near his horse, cuddling into him, for almost an hour, then walked to an outcrop of rock on the other side of the hill overlooking the massacre. Sitting, with his knees at his breast and his arms around them, he watched and waited. "How on earth," he whispered to himself, "will I ever be able to make amends for what I have done today."

Distraught and equally in shock, other Mormon militiamen straggled up the hill. Repentant and quiet, the scene below reflected in their eyes, they said not a word as they sat beside him.

A couple of miles up the road, the wagon which carried the children under six the Mormon's had spared from the massacre pulled to the side of the road. Brother Knight and the other militiaman with them tried to calm them. Yet the children would not calm and kept crying. Among the children was a toddler his family called 'Teddy'. Brother Knight was driving Teddy and the other surviving children north to Brother Knight's ranch outside Cedar City.

Off the road, hidden in the scrub just a mile from Teddy's wagon, was another wagon. Though it was not party to the massacre, it had borne witness to it. The wagon was Anna's.

Traumatized by what she had seen and believing John was dead she had fainted. Moments later she woke and immediately started crying, the dust coating her face flowing in muddy rivulets down her cheeks. She knew what was down the hill and could not bear to look again at the slaughter. A witness to the butchering and mutilation of nearly every woman and older child in the wagon train, witness to parts of the men's heads being blown away, she finally came to realize the danger she was in if somebody saw her. "I have to get out of here."

Trying to dry with her sleeve tears that would not dry, she stood. John was dead, murdered like every man lying in the road about him. "The Gentiles didn't kill him. They weren't carrying any guns," she reasoned aloud. "One of us must have killed him." She paused, covered her face with her hands, and trembled at the thought. "But why?" She looked to heaven and thought of hell. "The only reason they would have killed him is because he refused an order." She released a slow, deep breath of relief and smiled. "That's it. He refused to shoot the Gentiles."

She did not want to abandon John, but she was a threat to the murderers, and she'd seen what the natives did to women who were no threat to them at all. Terrified they would do the same thing to her, she hurried back to her wagon. Turning her head toward the bottom of the hill but not looking at the massacre, she promised John, "If Zeb and the others don't bring your body home, when the dangers past I'll come back for you." Dazed, she climbed onto the wagon, turned it around, and pressed the oxen homeward.

More than an hour later, Jacob and Bud came up the hill for some of the militia's horses. They abruptly stopped when they saw John and four others who had retreated from the massacre quietly sitting on the outcrop.

"What are you doing?" Jacob demanded.

Not waiting for an answer, Bud pointed his rifle at them and cocked it. "You ain't gonna get outa' nothin' sittin' here?"

As if to encourage Bud, Jacob gave him a nod and aimed his own gun, specifically at John.

"Now git," Bud ordered. "You got work to do down there."

John and the other four men had clearly had enough. Yet they were still captive. Having nowhere else to go, doing as they were told, they walked down the hill to the site of the massacre. By the time they reached the site, the natives were gone. Brother Higbee had sent them away. Allowed to take with them the loot they'd already plundered and some of the cattle, they were satisfied with Higbee's promise he would divide the rest of the booty with them later. Triumphant in their victory and not interested in the paperwork, they returned to their villages.

Scattered down the road and in the brush, were the naked and still clothed bodies of the Gentile men, most of them shot at close range through the head. Over the knoll and just to the side of the road were clustered bodies of butchered women and children, many of them having held each other as they died. In the shrubs were the isolated bodies of the rest of the women and children, those who tried to run away. All had been cleaved to death with knives and axes.

As he walked down the hill, John could see the entire scene, and looked away. With the other four, he was directed to the encircled wagons being, coldly and efficiently, emptied and inventoried. Put to work helping, John built a fire in the center of the circle. As men brought him handfuls of the Gentiles' documents, he sorted them. He then threw them into the fire, burning any that might help identify the people they'd murdered. The stripping of the dead continued, and from the bodies, the militiamen brought back to the wagons money and knives, watches, bracelets, and bloody clothing, all to be inventoried and packed.

It took all afternoon to claim, inventory, and organize their loot. By evening, after having touched and looted the dead all around them, the pungent odor of death stagnant in the air, all the wagons and the plunder they carried inside were taken away. The remaining cattle were driven behind them.

As the militiamen sat around the fires that evening, few talked about what they'd done. Most of them were unable to eat. In an attempt to raise their spirits, Higbee spoke to them. "The time will come when you will be glad you took part in the killing of these enemies of our people, the very enemies who come to take our lands and our kingdom away from us. Enemies who come to murder us. Brigham Young tells us God led us here, and upon His commandment, we will create Zion, our heaven, the final gathering place of all His believers. When we are through, Zion will stretch from the crest of the Rocky Mountains over the crest of the Sierra Nevada and to the Pacific. All peoples but us will be excluded. Gentiles do not belong in the same land as we, the faithful. Nor will they be invited to join us. Their intrusion onto these lands is against God's will. Scripture requires that we drive them out and, if need be, kill them.

"Let us pray. Lord God, your people are gathered and upon this earth shall build a kingdom to serve you, pure and subservient, rich and full, to spread from across the mountains to the Pacific. Give us strength to fulfill your wish. Give us the power and will to drive all evil from this land and bless us for this day. As was Your will, people who sent their armies against us and poisoned our stock and our children are dead. Amen.

"God demands that all who deny the faith and doctrines of the Church of Christ of Latter Day Saints be slain. The sword of vengeance shall shed their blood, and their wealth shall be given as spoils to our people. We have done God's bidding. Praise be He lets the time for us to enjoy the riches of earth be near.

"While we wait to reap our treasures, however, we must keep this act of vengeance a secret from the Gentiles. Keep the details even from our own," Higbee advised. "We must devise a story that will exonerate us."

There were nods of approval among the ranks, murmurs of agreement. Suggestions were offered and rejected, and after much discussion, Higbee announced, "Then it is decided. We will tell the world that the Indians massacred the settlers. That our militia came after the killing was done and that all there was left for us to do was bury the dead."

"If what we did today was what God wanted, we should rejoice in it," John shouted. "We should not hide from the truth like the murderers we are." He was sweating and at the same time cold. His hands were shaking, and his voice began to quiver. "I am disgusted by the lie, sickened by the brutal killings I took part in. Yesterday, I thought myself a good man, a saint on earth, having only killed men for the sake of God and their salvation. Today, I am a coward, a murderer, and I spit on your story as will God."

***

After dark and miles down the road, certain the danger of being discovered was past, Anna let the oxen slow to a crawl. Fear driving her, she had for the time been distracted by it, able to force herself to think of things other than what she saw that day. Yet as the wagon slowed and her fear waned, the massacre and its savagery came back to her, rushing into her mind and heart like a flood. Grief, guilt and nausea, all hit her at once. She screamed. Hysteria overtook her, and she sobbed.

John was dead, her love lost, her heart broken. She panicked. What if the militia doesn't bring his body back to me? What if they leave him? If I abandon him, I might not be able to find him among the other dead when I come back to get him. He'll be lost, unclaimed for eternity. She gasped. "Oh my God, he might be eaten." She shuddered as she thought of the wolves. As she shook, she began to whimper.

"How could I ever tell Hattie and the girls why I left him? How can I even begin to tell them how he died? I've got to bring him home with me." She found a wide place in the road and turned the oxen around, but as they started south, she reined them in and stopped. "What am I doing? I can't go back down there, even for John." She trembled as she relived what she saw. Empathizing with the women who were butchered, she became one of them in her imagination, suddenly running through the shrubs in terror with Lizzy and Maybella. Watching them cut to pieces, hearing their death screams.

She saw men falling, their brains blown away, and she became hysterical. Through her torrent of tears, the road blurred. Without changing direction, she dropped the reins, letting the oxen go on their own. Halfway back to the massacre, still traumatized and uncertain about what she was going to do, Anna pulled some distance off the road to rest for the night and to decide what to do.

***

On the hilltop overlooking the massacre, among other restless and sleepless militiamen, John sat on his blanket, his legs crossed, his head buried in his hands. He sat there all night, his gaze locked in horror, only occasionally lifting his head to become mesmerized by the campfire. His face pale, the bags under his eyes like sagging bruises, he watched without moving as dawn broke and his accomplices woke. Breakfast was coffee. While others drank, John brushed and silently saddled Zeb's gelding. Already mounted when the order was shouted, he waited stoically for the militia to mount. He followed as it rode back to the massacre.

Time and the hot sun of the day before had turned the site ghastly. Bloated and rigid, a cloud of stench and flies hovering over them, the more than a hundred bodies were waiting for them, a vivid reminder of what they'd done. His head light, his senses overpowered, John swayed on his horse, almost fainting as he neared them.

The Mormon militia initially intended to leave the Gentiles where they fell, their bodies exposed to a desert that would ultimately devour them. Yet burying the Gentiles had become part of the lie to cover the murders, so they had to make a showing of doing the decent thing. It was the only thing they could do if they were going to convince people the Indians had already killed the Gentiles by the time the militia arrived. The plunder from the massacre organized, sorted and packed in the emigrant wagons the day before, the wagon in which the shovels were packed was easily identified. Brother Zeb rode directly to it.

While he was passing the shovels out, he told the militiamen, "Dig 'em shallow. We ain't makin' this place no Gentile cemetery," Zeb told them. "Don't dig down more than a couple a' feet, just enough to cover 'em. We gotta' get outa' here."

Once John got his shovel, he rode toward the body of the emigrant he'd tried to save the day before. Lyle was barely recognizable. His head was half blown away. He was rigor-distorted and naked. His body was bloated to nearly half again his natural size, and he was fly and maggot ridden. Yet John found him.

Immediately saying a prayer over Lyle's body, John then covered what was left of Lyle's face with a handkerchief. Unable to straighten Lyle's legs or fold his arms over his chest because he was so stiff, John stopped trying and started digging. Without tarrying, quickly and against Zeb's orders, John dug a grave three feet deep.

"Would you help me lift him?" John asked Bud, who was dragging bodies to a nearby gully.

"I got my own to do," Bud told him. "Use yer feet and shove him in. He ain't gonna care."

Avoiding Lyle's brain splattered head, not touching again his rubbery, blue gray flesh, John measured the thickness of Lyle's body with his hands. "Too shallow," he mumbled, stepping into the grave and digging it a little deeper.

"Get the move on, Brother John," Jacob said, as he came over on foot and inspected the grave. "We said, 'shallow'."

John did not say a word. He simply climbed out of the hole, took a deep breath, and swung, landing his fist, square and hard against Jacob's chin.

Staggering, Jacob fell. "Dissentee," he cried. He reached for his revolver, pointed it at John, and fired.

Chapter Thirty-one

Near Mountain Meadows, Utah
August 1857

Confused and revolted by what she'd witnessed and in deep mourning for John, Anna was as a leaf in a hurricane, destroyed. She could not stop crying. Except for Hattie and the children, everything she valued in life was gone. She no longer trusted the Church to which she had committed her soul, nor could she trust John, the man to which she surrendered all else. Yet in the end, the only thing that mattered was John. By dawn, she was determined to find him.

She had been awake all night, and since this was the only road back to Cedar City, she knew the militia had not yet passed her. Only heavily loaded, slowly moving wagons had past.

She had no idea how many miles she had put between herself and Mountain Meadows, but she decided to retrace them, to return as quickly as possible for his body. Yet she must move slowly. Afraid she would not be able to get off the road in time to avoid the militia she knew was coming, she walked, leading the oxen and wagon along the rocky riverbank. Six miles downstream, where the bank divided and a high ridge formed, she parked. Leaving the oxen and wagon out of sight, she found cover on the ridge and waited. She did not have to wait long.

After two hours under the broiling hot sun, a large group of riders veiled by dust, with Brother Higbee in the lead, galloped down the road like the devil was after them. Anna could not tell who the other riders were but she knew, because they were with Higbee, they were the militia, and she could see from the silhouettes that none of the horses carried dead bodies. They must have left John's behind. "I wonder what they were going to tell me when next I saw them?" she bitterly muttered. She ducked her head and hid until they were past.

Along the riverbank, wary of stragglers and natives, she traveled two more hours to reach the site and the hill from which she witnessed the massacre. Driving off the road to the very scrub where she had stood, the air choked with a skin coating stench, she raised the binoculars and explored the entire scene.

The natives and Mormons were gone, and fresh graves marked the bodies of those slaughtered. Relieved she would not see the dead or have to deal with them except for John, she exhaled. When she was confident she was alone and that there were no survivors needing help, she allowed her mind to relive the moment she saw John's body. Certain they had not bothered to move him, she mentally identified the grave most likely to be his.

She drove to the site and pulled the wagon to a stop within feet of what she thought was John's grave. Kneeling beside the grave, saying a prayer not to her new god but to her Protestant one, she pawed at the loose and powdery dirt covering it. As she neared the corpse, the odor was unbearable. Taking Hattie's dress from the wagon, she tore a long strip from it, poured a little mash whiskey on it, and used it to cover her nose. I'll use what's left of the dress as John's shroud, she decided.

She had hoped diluting the odor would help, but when she returned to his grave, she hesitated. Forcing herself to resume, she delayed by scooping out handfuls of dirt gently along the edges before she could dig any deeper. Afraid she would expose John's face before she was ready for it, she dug a foot-and-a half down from what she thought was the top of the grave. Moments later, fingers hit flesh that was stiff and bloated. Revolted, she shuddered.

Only her love for John was forcing her on. She uncovered a shoulder then a chest before she realized the body seemed different from John's. It was much thinner. She stopped digging. Maybe it isn't John's.

She swallowed. There was only one way to find out. Wanting to know, yet not wanting to uncover what was left of his head, she slowly took out in small handfuls the dirt covering his face. When his features were exposed, she gagged. The man's head was half gone, and he was not John.

"Oh-h-h-h-h-h," she whimpered, scrambling away from the hole and into the brush. Hysterical, she crouched. Her knees pressed tightly against her chin, she sobbed. "What am I going to do?" she asked, when she got enough control of herself to think.

She dragged herself to the wagon, grabbed the jug of mash and gulped as much as she could swallow. When she was able to face Lyle's body again, she went back and methodically, respectfully, refilled the grave, first and slowly covering his face with dirt. When his body could no longer be seen, she pushed the rest of the dirt back in with her feet.

When she had reburied Lyle, she looked around at the other mounds of dirt, shallow graves with rotting, mutilated, men in them. She realized then that she could not force herself to dig up another one, not even for John. She'd failed him. She'd failed herself. As she drove the wagon north toward

Cedar City, exhausted and bereaved, a forever kind of emptiness crept inside her.

The heat never having broken, the air stagnant, it was near dawn. The sky was turning a light shade of gray as Anna drove the last mile toward home. The cabin in the distance, she lifted her eyes.

Devastated by grief, by everything she saw and did at Mountain Meadows, she was numb. Exhausted, she did not push the oxen faster. She was eager to get home but not to tell Hattie and the girls that John was dead. She let the oxen go at their own pace, hoping to postpone her arrival.

A quarter of a mile before the wagon reached the door Angel started barking. As the door opened and the firelight shown through, Angel squeezed between the door and frame and raced toward her. "Angel," Anna sighed. Expecting to see Hattie, she looked up and saw someone else running toward her.

"John?" she whispered in disbelief.

"Anna," he shouted, his smile broad and gleaming.

"John." Quickly climbing down from the wagon, she ran to him, embraced him and forgot, for an instant, all but him.

Their emotions were overflowing. When there was finally a breath between them, he kissed her. They made room in their embrace for Hattie and Lizzy as the two joined them, and all of them cried.

"Where's Maybella?" Anna asked, not seeing her.

"Asleep in the cabin," Hattie told her. "She waited for you all night."

"I didn't think I'd ever see you again," John said, still holding her. "Where were you?"

Anna blinked as he jarred her to recall, and the massacre flashed through her mind like lighting.

The images repugnant, her day and night grieving him torture, she suddenly pushed him away. Her gaze cold, she accusingly told him, "I was at Mountain Meadows."

As if she had cleaved him, he stared at her, his eyes dark with guilt. "You saw?"

Her face as gray as the sky, she nodded.

"Must have been awful," Hattie said, believing the natives had massacred the wagon train, just as John told her. "Those poor people."

John's gaze never left Anna's. Studying her, he ventured, "We think it was Indians up from Mexico. You must have gotten there right after it was over." He seemed to be trying to gauge her reaction and appeared more hopeful than convinced.

Jacob missed John with his first shot. Before he could take a second, John D. Lee stepped between them. "There's been enough killing," Lee had told them. Neither John nor Jacob had been injured.

Still staring at John, nearly choking on her tears, Anna glared at him as she told him, "I saw the whole thing."

His face flushed and then turned ashen. Sweat beaded over his lips and brow, and all John could say was, "Oh."

"What's the matter, John?" Hattie asked, suspiciously. "What didn't you tell me? What happened out there?"

"Why don't you go inside and start breakfast?" he asked Lizzy. "I want to talk to Anna and Mum for a minute." John smiled reassuringly, but she was disappointed.

"Why can't I hear, too?" she asked. "I'm grown up."

John put his arm around her, patted her shoulder, and kissed her on the cheek. "I know you are. Just go make breakfast." He watched as she returned to the cabin and closed the door, and then he turned to Anna. "What did you see?"

"Our militia, angels and saints every one, killing the poor, unarmed men in that wagon train. Indians butchering innocent women and children, and you," she accused, "right in the middle of it, the dead all around you."

Stunned, Hattie gasped but just listened.

Anna was trying to sort it out. If John was not a victim of the massacre, she reasoned to herself, he had to have been one of the murderers. She cringed, and all the revulsion of the massacre came back to her. Anger erupted inside her. I thought he was dead because he disobeyed them, but he wasn't dead at all. He was murdering those people just as they were. I mourned for him. I cried for him. I even dug up a dead man looking for him. Why should I have grieved for him at all? "You're a murderer," she accused him.

"Did you see me shoot anyone?" he asked, his only defense inaction.

For a moment Anna's anger was allayed as she remembered where he was when she saw him. He was a heap in the road, unmoving, appearing to be dead as others murdered the Gentiles. She had to acknowledge, even to herself, she had not seen him kill anyone. "No, I didn't," she responded.

"You didn't see it, because I didn't shoot anybody. I couldn't. Those people never did anything to me. One of the Indians killed the man I was supposed to kill. All I could do was sit there, watching."

Fully realizing what happened, Hattie scowled at him, demanding, "What were you doing there at all?"

"I didn't have a choice, Mum. They didn't tell us why we were going until we got there. Then, they wouldn't let any of us go. I would have left if I could," he implored. "I was tired of killing. I didn't want to kill anybody else."

Needing to have her faith in him restored, Anna wanted to believe him, yet the scene was still fresh, the murders too grievous to put aside. She was not ready to forgive him. There was so much for them to think about, so much to consider.

"We're all too tired to talk now," Hattie said, unwilling yet to hear the details. "Let's go inside and have breakfast. We can talk about what happened later."

There was no joy that morning, no peace. Though each of them suffered alone while tension surged among them, for Lizzy and Maybella, they pretended nothing was wrong. John was distraught and pale. Refusing to eat, he went down to the stream and sat, fully clothed, in the water. An hour later, still unwilling to talk, he came back inside and, without taking his wet clothes off, sat for hours in the rocker, blankly staring into the cold, empty hearth. As if everything was normal, Hattie darned. Oblivious to what was going on, Maybella sat at her feet clumsily weaving long strands of dry grass. Mountain Meadows was a grim, despicable shadow over their home and nothing more was said of it all day.

"Look, Daddy," Maybella said. She had slipped a woven grass necklace over Angel's head.

John looked at her and forced a smile. Normally, he would have summoned her to his lap, had her explain how she made such a wonderful thing, and showered her with praise. Today, all he could do was nod and say, "That's pretty."

After hours of relative silence, Anna picked up her diary. In ink, she expelled her emotions on its pages.

Chapter Thirty-Two

Outside Cedar City
August 1857

Anna and John did not sleep that night. Anna was afraid to face the nightmares that plagued her all day, and John was restless, apparently tormented by night with whatever tormented him all day. His accomplices made it clear to the entire militia they were expected to take their families to Sunday services the next morning. So sometime after dawn, John, Anna, Hattie and the girls solemnly walked to town.

Outside the meetinghouse, they were greeting their neighbors when suddenly the pounding of hooves and the bumping of wagons broke into the morning. John D. Lee and a number of natives were rolling into town on horseback, gleefully, almost festively, escorting through town the wagons plundered from the Gentiles. Heavily loaded, the wagons were full of bedding and tin ware, chests of valuables, and bloody clothes.

"My God," Hattie whispered. "We robbed them after we murdered them? Are we animals?" Shocked, she and Anna expectantly and accusingly looked at John.

Avoiding them, he turned away and went inside. Every non-participant in town coming to services had heard the story of the Gentiles massacre. Every one of them had been told the natives did it. With a mix of disgust and morbid curiosity, all of them watched as the spoils were paraded before them. Except for Hattie and Anna, few of them would have known their own militia was responsible for the mass murder.

The plunder was to be stored at the Mormons' tithing office until auctioned. The horses and wagons were had already been spoken for, and in a few days, the Gentiles' herd of cattle would be wearing Brother Lee's 'JDL' brand. The wagons were being driven that day to Fort Harmony where Brother Lee would show the booty to his neighbors. As the wagons went on ahead, he shouted, "Thanks to the Lord God of Israel. He has delivered our enemies into our hands." While virtually everyone in town watched, he rode to the meeting house and dismounted.

Among the onlookers suspicions were immediately raised and questions asked. If the natives massacred the Gentiles in the wagon train, what was a Mormon doing with their belongings? Why was Lee talking about enemies and deliverance? Why was he riding with the very natives who killed them?

Anna caught Hattie's angry gaze when, inside the meeting house, Brother Lee confirmed to the Ward it was the natives who were responsible for the massacre, that the 'Indians' did all the killing. The militia arrived too late, in time only to bury the victims.

The men who participated in the massacre kept with the story they'd fabricated, and despite the onlookers' suspicions, no one questioned Lee. The massacre was regrettable. However, the Gentiles' wagons, livestock, clothing and food were needed for the Mormons. War was coming.

When Lee finished telling the story, Brother Higbee added for the surviving Gentile children, "Those Indian-orphaned babies are gonna need homes. Who can take one?"

"We can," John shouted, even before he stood. At least a dozen others stood with him, all men of the militia.

Anna stood beside him. Taking a child was the least they could do.

The surviving children were at Brother Knight's ranch. Along with some of the other adoptive parents, John and Anna came straight from the services and were shown to its expansive living room.

In a corner, sitting on the wood floor amidst a group of the orphaned toddlers was Brother Knight's first wife. Her hair was askew, and she had a mad grin on her pale, senseless face. When she looked up and saw her visitors, she put a rag doll in her mouth and sucked on it. As they filed inside, her eyes grew wide and vacant, and she gazed blankly into the distance.

Sister Knight had been this way since Friday. She had been taken suddenly ill when her husband brought the crying, orphaned children home, one of them wounded.

The militia had not been instructed to lie about the massacre until after Brother Knight left the scene with the children. Not knowing he was supposed to blame the natives, he told his wife the truth. In shock, she collapsed. She had not spoken since, oblivious to anyone but the toddlers.

In a way, Anna envied her. She walked to her side, bent over her and stroked her hair. "It'll be all right," she whispered.

With guilt and grief in his eyes, John looked on as if secretly adding Sister Knight to the burden on his conscience. He merely glanced at the children. "You pick," he told Anna, abruptly going outside.

The room was full of the orphaned children and families willing to adopt them. Anna approached a toe-headed toddler with big, green eyes, refusing to let go of his blanket. It was the last thing his mother, Carrie, had given him.

"Is he spoken for?" Anna asked one of Brother Knight's daughters.

***

A tale of atrocity and murder known by so many could not be kept secret long. As the weeks passed, everyone in Cedar City and all of Utah knew what really happened at Mountain Meadows. Worse yet, the Gentiles knew.

Another Gentile train, the Mathhews-Tanner wagon train, was in Cedar City the day Brother Lee and the natives boldly paraded their plunder through town. To keep the Gentiles from seeing the site of the massacre, Mormon militiamen volunteered to escort them south. The wagon train was led past the site at night so the travelers would not see the remains. Yet, there was no hiding from them the stench.

While in Utah the Gentiles did nothing about what they learned, but when the train reached California, they reported all they knew and more. News spread, and the story was supplemented by succeeding emigrants. Within two months, word of the massacre flowed to the East. Fearing retaliation from all sides, Brigham Young declared Marshall Law in Utah.

***

The cabin was dark, the late night still. The rise and fall of Anna's breasts as she breathed was tantalizing as John lay quietly beside her. Her body, subtle and sensuous, called to him. His groin tightened and his member responded. His flesh was driving him toward her. Beads of perspiration crowded his brow, and as his heart tore in two, he turned away.

Rigid, Anna lay very still waiting for him. When John turned away, she was relieved. The memory of Mountain Meadows was like an ice block between them, their love trapped inside it. Every time she thought about what happened, which seemed almost constantly, John came out responsible. Even if what he told her was the truth, he was partly to blame for the massacre. Reliving the horrors she witnessed, reliving too, her agony when she thought he was dead, she was always brought back to the Gentile man's grave and her touching him. Revolted by the memory, her skin crawled whenever John made love to her. She tried not to relate John's body with the dead man's but could not help but feel that way. The more John pulled away from her the more distant he became, the easier he was to blame.

It was late on a dark afternoon in mid-September. The clouds were black with rain. Strings of lightning threaded their way to the ground, and the sky burst into thunder. As Anna and Lizzy ran into the cabin, Hattie was watching the storm from the window. A toddler, one of the survivors from the massacre, was in her arms. They would never know that his name was 'Teddy', or that he was Carrie and Lyle's little boy, but they were beginning to love him, and they called him 'Jimmy'.

Maybella was on the floor playing with her rag doll. Angel was lying at her side. John was sitting at the hearth repairing the oxen's yoke. Tightly wrapping the crack in it with a wet, leather strap, he looked up when he heard Anna and Lizzy outside the door. He looked away as they came inside.

Still and somber, John said little the last few days, completely detaching himself from everyone around him, pushing them away when they tried to get near. Seeming to have little use for, or patience with any of them, he treated Lizzy like a stranger and had not once held Jimmy. Only Maybella, and occasionally Angel, could get a loving response from him.

Lizzy's eyes were red when she and Anna opened the cabin door and came inside. The instant she saw John, she started sobbing.

"What's wrong, Lizzy?" he asked, looking up at her.

Having nothing to do with him, she ran to Hattie and tightly embraced her, sandwiching little Jimmy between them. Her small brow furrowed, Maybella stopped playing with her doll and watched.

"What happened?" Hattie asked Anna.

"She knows," Anna said, her voice falling, and that's all she said. She would not relate the story of how Lizzy found out, at least not in front of Maybella and Jimmy, especially not in front of Jimmy. It was too horrible.

Three men passing through town that day described what they saw at Mountain Meadows. They told all of Cedar City that wolves had disinterred and eaten the emigrants' bodies, especially those of the women and children, and that the wolves had left only tufts of hair on their skulls. In town that day, Sister Knight was one of the people who overheard the three men and was shocked back into her senses. Suddenly remembering her husband's confession to her, she became hysterical and blurted out the entire story to everyone in town.

"Yer just like the rest of 'em!" Lizzy accused her father, her tears nearly strangling the words. "Yer nothin' but a murderer," she angrily shouted.

John flushed, then turned ash white. "Didn't you tell her?" he asked Anna.

Anna's perception of John and his role at Mountain Meadows had become a mix of expectation and blame. She was no longer certain what John had and had not done. "I thought you should tell her."

Lizzy looked at him expectantly, tears spilling from her eyes.

As if God willed it, the room got dark and silent. "I can't," he told her. He returned to work, busying himself with the leather. That failing to calm him, he slammed the yoke to the floor. Unable to settle, he paced. Unable to face her, he picked up a long, iron poker and ran out into the storm.

Lightening was all around him. Standing in the downpour, his shoulders squared, he raised the poker, thrust it as far as he could toward heaven, and beckoned God to strike him down. "I am doomed to your justice and I want it now," John cried. "Take me. Have mercy on me and take me."

Bolts of lightning forked. Thunder shattered the sky, shaking the ground he stood on. Yet God ignored him. Long moments later, John was still alive. Soaked to the skin, he dropped the poker, and without looking back at the family who watched him from the cabin door, he walked off toward the hills.

Angry and disappointed, hurt and disillusioned, even after several hours, Lizzy refused to speak to anyone. She'd discovered the man she trusted and loved was a monster.

The thunderstorm cleared. As the sun was setting, Hattie and Anna went outside to look for John, but there was no sign of him.

Gray and disheveled, as if he had stumbled through the brush all night, John came back to the cabin the next morning. His eyes were red and puffy, and there were dark, bloated bags beneath them. He was some distance from the cabin, when Angel ran to meet him, barking her greeting. He was still yards away when Maybella rushed to him and hugged him. He was but feet away, when, much less enthusiastically, Hattie walked out to meet him. Gently patting his back, she put her arm around him and walked him inside. Unmoving, Lizzy and Anna watched from the fireplace. As Hattie brought him toward them, Lizzy turned her back to him, hesitated, then walked outside.

Though Hattie inquired, he would not tell her where he had been. "Then are you hungry?" she asked.

John put his arm around her and nodded. Tears filled his eyes. "I'm sorry, Mum."

Her eyes full of sorrow, Hattie put her hand to her lips as if to keep from crying and looked toward the fire. "Sit down and have your breakfast." She took his arm from around her waist and turned toward him. Her eyes were cold, her lips quivering as she told him in no uncertain terms, "I want this settled, John. I want you to tell us everything."

Appearing to delay the inevitable, John picked at his food, a thick slice of bacon, an egg, and four biscuits with gravy. Hattie and Anna quietly and patiently sat at the table with him. Lizzy ignored him. It being too wet for her to stay outside very long, she had come back and was sitting on the bed in the corner, nervously fussing over Jimmy and Maybella. After only a few moments, she drove Maybella, out of frustration, to break away from her and to sit on the floor with Angel. Though John repeatedly glanced in her direction, Lizzy did not look back at him.

When he had eaten all he wanted, Hattie poured him another cup of coffee. Walking to the hearth, staring into the expiring fire, he cradled the cup in his hands and took a slow, thoughtful sip. "They didn't tell us what they were going to do when we left here," he began. "When we found out, they wouldn't let us go."

Anna and Hattie were unimpressed. He had told them that before.

"There were over fifty of us and nearly four hundred Indians. The Indians attacked the wagon train days before we got there, but the Gentiles were holding them off. They mighta' survived if we hadn't come."

He paced between the table and hearth, and Lizzy turned to listen. "They were just families. People like us. They trusted us, and we murdered them."

"I'm taking Jimmy and Maybella outside," Anna interrupted, not wanting them to hear. She picked Jimmy up, and Maybella followed them outside.

Pacing ever faster, his emotions in full boil, John told Hattie and Lizzie every detail while they stared at him. When he was finished, with sweat pouring from his brow, he knelt before Lizzy. "Please believe me, Sweetheart. I didn't want to be there. They forced me. But, I didn't kill anybody." As he wrung his sweaty, trembling hands, his eyes clouded with tears. "I couldn't tell you the truth before," he sighed.

"I believe you, Daddy," Lizzy sighed, as she put her arms around his neck and sobbed. "I trust you."

At the hearth only inches away, Hattie sniffled, cupped her mouth with her hand, and turned away. With one deep breath and a sigh, she opened the door, walked outside and brought Anna back with her. "We're going to thrash this out," she announced. "It's gotta' stop. We've gotta' quit blaming ourselves and each other for what happened down there. We're going to forgive whatever we've done and be a family again."

They looked at her expectantly but said nothing.

"The men who did this are animals," Hattie judged. "So is the Church that ordered it. We should blame them, not John." Her eyes softened as she told him, "Quit tearin' yourself apart. There was nothin' you coulda' done to stop what happened."

Anna had been so distraught about John, she had pushed all thought of the Church aside, and was neither forgiving nor condemning it. Yet what Hattie said was making sense, everything was falling together. "She's right," Anna blurted. "It was the Church to blame. The militia and the Avenging Angels were only lackeys. John, those emigrants, all of us, were its victims."

Feeling that slate was washed clean, her love for him exposed, she rushed to him and embraced him. "I'm sorry, John. Please forgive me. I should have understood."

Warm and strong, he embraced her. They kissed, and on their cheeks, his tears mixed with hers. He felt good to her again.

Tears still welling in his eyes, he put an arm around Lizzy, looked at Hattie, and smiled. "Thanks, Mum."

The emotions Hattie dammed up inside were released in a flood of laughter and tears as she turned toward the door, dabbing her eyes with her apron. "We may be bruised and troubled," she mumbled to herself, "but we're whole again."

"So, what do we do now?" John asked.

Hattie did not hesitate. "We've got to make this right."

"How?" he asked, exasperated. "Those people are dead."

"Not all of them," Hattie said, discreetly gesturing toward Jimmy.

"Jimmy?" John whispered.

Never wanting to touch him, never wanting to sully the toddler with hands that helped murder his parents, John's conscience never allowed John to hold him. Yet he needed to hold Jimmy now. Picking him up, cuddling him, John kissed him on the forehead. "I'll try to make it up to you, Jimmy. I promise." He pressed Jimmy's cheek to his own and sobbed.

"Maybe we should go to the Federal Marshal," Anna suggested.

Immediately attentive, John lifted his head. "No, I'd have to give myself up. I'd have to confess. The Marshal hates Mormons. He'd hang me for just being there."

"What if you went to California? They'd listen to you there."

"Maybe. They might not hang me if I turned in the men who ordered it. But, how can I get to California? The Angels'd hunt me down and kill me before I got halfway. They're criminals now, and if they're caught, they'll hang. They'd have to protect themselves. They'd kill me before I even yoked the ox."

"Then what do we do?" Hattie asked. "Wait 'til the U.S. Army gets here? 'Til armies from California come across our border to get us? Let them hang you for what others have done?"

"Even if I didn't murder anyone in the wagon train, I was there with a gun in my hands, sorting through their belongings," John reminded her. "I did everything the others did after the Gentiles were dead. If I told the army what happened, I'd just give them an excuse to do what they came here for, kill Mormons, maybe even you and Anna."

"Then, we'll hafta get out of here," Anna concluded.

"We know too much," John said. "If we leave, the Avenging Angels will hunt us down. They'll kill me for sure, and they'd probably kill all of you too. They're not gonna let any of us tell what happened."

"Well, I won't stay here," Anna vowed. "I don't want to raise our children among murderers, and I won't lie to protect them."

"You're right, John," Hattie said. "Whether we stay or not, we might lose our lives. But, if we stay, we're sure to hell lose our souls."

He thought for moment, then, he agreed. "All right, but first let me see what I can do. We've got to be careful. In the meantime, don't say anything. Don't trust anybody. Whatever we do, we can't let on that we're leaving."

Chapter Thirty-Three

Present Day Portland, Oregon
3:00 a.m.
April 25

T he sports car's tires were plaining dangerously over deep puddles of rainwater flooding the freeway. Visibility, already less than a quarter mile, was quickly decreasing as thick, milky fog began swallowing everything around them. After leaving her mother's house, Sharon turned the convertible and backtracked, then traveled in an ever-widening circle until she lost the white Impala pursuing them. Driving east on NE Killingsworth, south on Interstate 205, east again onto Interstate 84, she, Alex and Kevin were away, heading west toward the Cascade Mountains and the Pacific Crest, across the Oregon desert and into the Blue Mountains.

As they entered the last vestiges of winter snow, several thousand feet up a mountain pass, Sharon pulled into a rest stop. "Why don't one of you drive for awhile?" she suggested. "That'll give me some time to read more of Grandma Anna's diary."

Alex drove. While Kevin dozed in the passenger seat, Sharon wrapped the wool blanket she kept in the car around her shoulders. Stretching out on the backseat, her back propped against the door, she picked up Anna's diary.

Not yet realizing Anna's diary held not only a clue but the very key to what happened to Wayne and Kim and to what was happening to Sharon now, she let her fatigue capture her. Exhausted and without reading any of the diary at all, she fell asleep.

***

Cedar City, Utah,
February 1858

At the table while her family slept that night, Anna was writing in her diary.

There is a strangeness between John and I, an unsteadiness that brings me great sorrow. I've tried to forgive John for all he has done, for I know he thought he was killing those men for God. I've even tried to forgive him for not preventing the massacre, and I have, for the most part. Yet, there is something inside me that holds me back. Something between and about us that isn't right.

Blood atonement, murder, it was all wrong. If John was a good man, he would have known that from the very beginning. His conscience would have told him the murders the priests ordered him and the others to commit were evil. He certainly would not have helped them. If it had to come to that, he should have died trying to stop the massacre, especially the murders of those women and children.

I know. I know. I say that now, but then I remember how I felt when I thought John was dead. How I cried for him and grieved for him, and even searched for him in a dead man's grave. I'm glad he's not dead. I could never wish him harm. Yet, how can I ever trust him again? How can I ever be proud of him? He's a murderer and a coward. He's for all who will see through him Satan's lackey.

He has so much guilt inside him, I do not know how he sleeps, yet he is sleeping now. He has been looking for a way for us to escape the evil that surrounds us, but so far, has found nothing.

Brigham Young has declared what he calls 'martial law' and has ordered if the United States Army enters Utah, we are to desolate the territory. We are to conceal our families, livestock, and personal property in the mountains. We are to burn everything, our homes, every structure on our land, our crops and harvests, and everything else we can't take with us. He wants us to become what he calls 'guerillas'. Men following his orders are already burning towns and supply points north. In our land, in Southern Utah, the men are looking for the protective oasis in the desert Brother Brigham envisioned for us. John goes with them. No one has yet found the oasis of Brother Brigham's dreams, and John has not yet found a way we can get out of here.

In October, we heard the U.S. army's supply route was burned. An early winter was setting. We successfully delayed the invasion of Salt Lake City. The army marching against us from the East was stalled.

Tensions eased in the north but not in California where there is an ear shattering cry for revenge for the Mountain Meadows Massacre. A newspaper in San Francisco has called for a crusade against us, and we have been tagged the beast of heresy. It has demanded the beast be crushed and that all of us be exterminated. Brigham Young was so frightened for our settlers in San Bernardino, he ordered them back to Utah. He has called on those of us south to help them evacuate.

The first refugees from San Bernardino arrived in Southern Utah late in November. Hundreds followed. Anxious to see what routes of escape lay south, John volunteered his ox and wagon to help them.

In mid-December, additional wagon trains arrived, and he joined twelve other teams to meet them at Fort Santa Clara, the native mission. The trail was so crowded with wagons coming north and the wagons sent south to help them, John told me any escape that way, at least for a while, was impossible.

The natives, too, are angry with us. They still are very upset that some of their people were killed at Mountain Meadows. Our missionaries are trying to control them, but they are dangerous to any white people traveling alone. Only Mormons traveling in large groups are safe. Even if there was an escape for us, the natives would kill us.

John and I know time is growing short before the Gentile armies arrive, and we are desperate to escape. Yet we are carrying on as usual, trying not to give the slightest hint of our plans. We worry about Lizzy. Though she would never intentionally tell anyone of our plans, she is so young she may not be clever enough to avoid someone bent on tricking her. So I keep her by my side. Except on Sundays that is, when I have no choice but to let her join the other youngsters for religious instruction.

I can hardly force myself to go to Sunday meetings, yet I dress the children just like always, pray aloud with the other brothers and sisters of the congregation, and smile. At first, I wondered how the other women felt. How they could stand next to husbands they knew were ruthless murderers. How they could sing out in front of the men who ordered their husbands to kill while the toddlers of those they murdered sit beside them. Then I remembered the Church's instructions. Men must obey the will of God and women their husbands.

Maybe the women stayed with their men because that was what was required. Maybe they believed that, like John, their husbands didn't participate in the killing. They thought their men were helping the Gentiles find salvation through atonement. Yet, how could that be? Many of the men are denying they were at Mountain Meadows at all.

Sitting through the meetings is like chewing bitter herbs. Although I keep my expression pleasant and accepting, I try to remove myself. I try to separate my love of God from my Church and the men who control it. I feel God is no longer among us, and I do not pray sincerely until I get home.

Refugees from San Bernardino continue to line the road south. With several other men, John always volunteers to go get them, waiting for the road to clear. He told me last night, when he came back from the last trip, the stream of refugees has slowed to a trickle. There are only stragglers on the road, and the time for our escape may be nearing.

I hope so. When spring comes, the armies from Washington and California will come, and we will be trapped. We will be captured, tortured, the truth will come out, and John will be amongst the murderers they will execute.

Please, God, forgive us for our part in this and let us go.

Chapter Thirty-Four

Present Day Boise, Idaho
11:00 a.m.
April 25

Dill's Truck Stop was a hundred-acre site two miles west of Boise on Interstate 84. Its facilities were arranged like a giant wheel with spokes. The diesel pumps for tractors and trailers were some distance from the gas pumps for passenger cars. A small, single story motel with fifteen units, each with a full bath, was a barrier between them. The hub of the wheel was a giant diner where big, greasy breakfasts were a specialty and were prepared twenty-four hours a day. It was all too much for Sharon, Alex, and Kevin who came in for lunch.

Inside the Diner, the seventies western decor was faded orange and brown. It wasn't filthy, but it wasn't clean either. The customers wore cowboy boots and plaid shirts.

"Let's take that one," Alex said, pointing to a booth next to a semicircular one in the corner.

Kevin grinned. "I haven't eaten in a place like this for years." When the waitress came over to take their order, he told her, "I'll have coffee, a hot turkey sandwich, and a piece of apple pie a la mode."

"Hungry?" Alex quipped.

"Absolutely. I'm not going to let an opportunity like this slip by."

"Maybe we should start a taste test between diners," Alex quipped, thinking of that grimy diner south of Salt Lake City. "I'll have a cheeseburger basket, heavy on the onions." He glanced at Sharon. "Hope that car of yours has plenty of ventilation."

"Are you kidding? I'm putting the top down."

"Anything to drink?" The waitress must have been forty something, but her leather like face and deep jowl wrinkles made her look sixty.

"Yeah," Alex said. "A vanilla shake."

Picturing the outlandish portion sizes of their orders, Sharon asked, "You have anything lighter?"

Apparently having little patience with thin women with delicate appetites, the waitress snapped, "You got the menu. Look for yourself."

"I'll have a cottage cheese and fruit salad, and an ice tea."

As if they had a direct line to the kitchen, their meals arrived in less than five minutes. "Want some French fries?" Alex offered, reading the hunger in her eyes.

"Thanks," Sharon said, gratefully plucking a few greasy strings from his plate.

"Guess this isn't the place to come for an abundance of health food," Kevin teased, plowing a fork into the huge mound of mashed potatoes. He was eagerly eating them when the waitress brought him a huge piece of pie with three scoops of ice cream.

"Think we got away from those two guys?" Kevin asked, when he finally took a breather.

"If we hadn't, we would have seen them by now," Alex said, glancing toward the parking lot.

"They probably went south," Sharon added, "retracing the route we took to Portland. I doubt if they even considered we'd go directly east."

"I've been doing some thinking," Alex began, as he finished his burger. "That Greek legend you told us about. Didn't you say swarms of bees came out of the carcass of a heifer?"

"That's right," Kevin confirmed.

"What exactly is a heifer?"

"A female cow. One who hasn't yet borne a calf."

"There was a news story out of Utah not too many years ago about a woman who gave birth to sextuplets after taking fertility drugs," Alex told them. "I remember thinking how irresponsible the doctor was for letting that happen. The Church's involvement in the Olympic scandal was still fresh, so I was viewing everything that happened in Utah a little suspiciously. It crossed my mind then that someone might be experimenting with that woman and her multiple births. Isn't it true, the more children a Mormon man has, the greater his glory?"

"Wayne was researching preemies," Sharon reminded them. "You don't suppose that group of his, those descendants of the Sons of Dan, had anything to do the woman's condition? That they might have been experimenting with multiple births? Do you think that's how they intend to replace the rest of us?"

"Makes sense," Kevin added. "It wouldn't be the first time Mormon women have been treated like breeding stock." He thought for a moment longer. "Given Wayne's medallion...But let's find out for sure." Getting the waitress' attention, Kevin waved her over. "Got 'wifi' here?"

She stared at Kevin with an enigmatic expression, her dull, brown eyes totally blank.

"She doesn't know what he's talking about," Alex murmured to himself.

Her brown eyes snapping to life she glared at him, "You mean 'wireless fidelity' don't you?" she said, flatly. "What do ya want with it? Don't usually let anybody but truckers sign on."

"How about us?" Kevin asked. He made his eyes big and wide and his lips pouty like a spoiled little boy's. "We have to look up something important." He smiled. "Please."

Reading him perfectly, she raised her lip in disgust. "Let me see if I can get the password." Casually wiping down every empty table along the way, as if making certain no one suspected her purpose, she made her way to a windowless door about thirty-feet away, opened it, and walked into a hallway. She was out of sight for less than a minute and returned directly. "How much tip was that?" she asked, waiving a torn piece of paper.

Kevin dug in his pocket for a five.

"Make it ten and you got it," she said.

Moments later, they were online, Kevin at the keys of his laptop. "Search 'multiple births Utah'," Alex told him.

The search brought up a document entitled "Final Data for 2009 Centers for Disease Control and Prevention." As he read, Kevin summarized the article. "Over the last three decades there has been an extraordinary rise in multiple births, especially births of more than three babies. That increase is being associated with advances in and greater access to fertility therapies. Women who undergo in vitro fertilization, especially women over thirty, are especially inclined to have multiple births even without fertility treatments. Many of them are born prematurely and do not survive the first year. Enhancements of fertility treatments lower the risks of multiple fetal pregnancies and may encourage more multiple births."

"That must have been where Wayne came in," Sharon said, as she and Alex started reading over Kevin's shoulder. "He must have found some way to reduce the risks to preemies."

"Look here," Kevin directed, "It goes on to say the Birth rate in Utah was higher than any other state in the Union, twenty-one births to every one thousand people, more than twice the birthrate in Vermont and Maine."

"If Wayne's Sons of Dan were successfully experimenting with multiple births, wouldn't those birth statistics be even higher?" Alex asked.

"No," Kevin said. On screen was the National Center for Chronic Disease Prevention and Health Promotion's report for 'Utah's Center for Reproductive Medicine'. "Look, for the year 2000, where in vitro fertilization was used, 29.5 percent of the live births in Utah were with more than three infants."

"So?" asked Sharon.

"Look at the footnote," Kevin said, pointing his finger to footnote 'd'.

"In Utah, a multiple infant birth is only counted as 'one live birth.'

"Don't you see? Those twenty-one births out of a thousand could actually be a hundred or more births for every thousand, and most of them would be preemies.

"If Wayne found some way to keep the preemies healthy, babies could be flooding Utah, and there'd be no record of it.

"Pretty clever, huh?"

"Don't you think we may be reading more into this than is there?" Sharon asked.

"No," Alex said. "In vitro fertilization. Bees. Multiple births. Maybe Wayne came up with a serum or something that eliminates the risk of premature births. I've heard of women carrying and conceiving as many as seven without help. Think about that Greek legend, a heifer is the carcass from which bees will swarm."

"The 'Vessels' in the inventory," Sharon gasped. The 'vessels' are the hosts, surrogate mothers of multiple fetuses carrying them to term. Heifers. Kim must be one of their hosts. She's still alive."

Alex fumbled in his pocket for the single sheet inventory. "Location," he read of the 'loc' in column two. "UTVR," he read. "AZPG."

"Of course, Utah. Arizona," he concluded. But, where? What's VR? What's PG?"

None of them were familiar with Utah. Not one had a clue. "We need a map," Kevin said. "A good one. Maybe we'll find it there."

"Wait. Before we do that, enter 'VR Utah'," Alex suggested.

The results were disappointing. All they found was Virtual Reality Panoramas, a seemingly endless list of people whose last names begin with Vr, the Vocational Rehabilitation Program, and the Voter Registration System. Not much help there.

"My screen's too small to make a comprehensive map of Utah useful," Kevin said. "But, there's a food mart connected to the diner that might have one."

"Let's just keep going," Alex suggested. "VR could mean anything. A residence. A hospital. A clinic. Who knows?"

"It's time to get the authorities involved," Sharon said. "We should contact Utah's Attorney General."

"I don't know if I want to involve him or not," Alex told her. "I've read all about him. He seems to be pretty supportive of Mormon Fundamentalists. He made it public some time ago that he had no intention of enforcing the laws against polygamy. He said there were just too many polygamists, something like tens of thousands in the West. He said he'd rather work against the crimes committed inside the Polygamist communities than try to break them up."

"Remember?" Kevin asked. "Polygamy was the means by which Joseph Smith and Brigham Young intended to populate their Kingdom of God. The more children, the more glory, the more land they would occupy and control.

"Maybe you're right, Alex," Sharon said. "Better not deal with the State. Our time might be better spent with the Feds. The U.S. Attorney in Salt Lake City will have the resources to find out what 'VR' is and to help us find Kim. We'll go see him."

Chapter Thirty-five

Cedar City, Utah
February 7, 1858

It was hours after dark. Everyone in the small cabin not far from town was in bed and asleep when a thunderous knock shook its only door. Rifle in hand, John answered with Angel beside him. "Who is it?" Anna was standing behind him with Jimmy in her arms. Hattie was with the girls in the bed at the far wall. They were frightened, and she was embracing them. A visitor this late could only mean trouble.

"It's Jacob." He was in the doorway, light from the coals in the fireplace flickering against his face. "Get dressed and meet us outside," He told John.

"Be right there," John said, closing the door on him.

"What does he want?" Anna asked, in a whisper.

"For me to go with him somewhere, I guess." As John rested the gun against the wall, he slipped on his pants. "He must be going to a bloodletting." John's face was solemn, his eyes subdued by despair. "Don't wait up for me this time." He looked toward the door and then looked back. Love poured from his eyes as he surveyed them. "Be back before breakfast."

Outside, about ten yards from the cabin, Jacob waited on foot with young Bud, who was mounted and holding the reins of all three horses. "Get mounted. We have God's work to do," Jacob told him. "Word has reached us that Brother Hensen is about to desert, to go to the governor of California and to confess all. We have to stop him right away.

His wagon's in his shed already loaded, and he's leaving with his family at dawn."

Demanding John's attention, Jacob reached toward John, took hold of his arm and squeezed. "You know all those trips he took with us looking for Brigham's oasis? He's been using them to plan his escape. All the refugees from San Bernardino he saved? He just wanted information from them. He's deceived and betrayed us, so we must save him."

John sighed but said nothing. He was being ordered to murder again. As he mounted the gelding they brought for him, he turned and through the cabin window saw Anna and Hattie watching. He knew if he refused to go. Jacob had grounds to kill him. He might even kill him here, right in front of them. It was better to delay, to hope God would intervene somehow, to hope maybe he could stop them before they murdered Hensen.

"Let's go," Jacob ordered.

Miles away, half-buried in the side of a large, isolated, sagebrush covered hillock, Brother Hensen's cabin was pitch-black when Jacob, Bud and John rode up to it sometime after midnight. The shed in which Hensen's belongings were packed must have been somewhere in back. Everything looked peaceful, but even before they dismounted it became obvious they were expected. Hensen and William, his seventeen-year old son, were fully dressed and armed, and they were waiting for them behind a trough.

"Evenin'," Hensen said from the darkness, his voice low and even. "You boys come for anything special?"

"We wanna see yer shed," Bud blurted. "Now."

William stepped to one side, leveled his gun at John, and paused.

"Help yerselves," Hensen invited. "I'll show it to ya myself." He inexplicably winked at William. "See you boys don't get lost 'tween here and there."

Jacob, Bud and John dismounted. They tied their horses to a hitching rail out front and followed Hensen around the cabin to the shed out back.

Half buried in the same hillock, the wood structure contained every food stuff, farm implement and oxen Hensen owned. The walls were stacked sapling poles tied together with rope. The crevasses between the poles were mud filled. The roof was sod. On the way inside, Hensen lit a lantern. As they entered, the shed revealed the most obvious of its contents, a large wagon, uncovered and empty. Two oxen were in their stalls for the night and chewing cud. Clearly, no one was going anywhere.

John sighed. Maybe there would be no atonement. Maybe they'd let Hensen be.

"What are you trying to pull?" Jacob demanded of Hensen.

William came in behind them, closing the door.

"Just what you told me," Hensen answered. His sad gaze fixed on John, and at that instant, Bud and William leaped, tackled John, and knocked him to the floor. Turning him, they forced him onto his stomach. William sat on his ankles. Hensen tied his hands behind him, and Bud sat on the back of his shoulders, pinning his head to the floor.

A quarter again as big as either Bud or William, outweighing Hensen by over twenty pounds, John thrashed and kicked. He threw them off of him and got to his knees, but Jacob was behind him. As he tried to get his feet, with a full and powerful swing, Jacob hit him in the back of the head with a shovel.

When John came to, he was tied to the shed's center post and naked. With pressure deep and painful, his temples throbbed. Jacob and the three other men were blurs. "What are you doing?" John asked.

Jacob's eyes were shining, creased at the corners with delight, as he told him, "You have breached the covenants you made with God. You are the one deserting and betraying us. You are the one looking to escape. And you openly disobeyed orders at Mountain Meadows, refusing to kill our enemies. All of them unforgivable transgressions."

John's head was pounding so hard he could barely open his eyes. "How did you know we were leaving?"

"One Sunday at instruction, Lizzy was talking to one of the refugee boys out of San Bernardino. She asked him if all the wonderful things she heard about California were true and told him she might see them someday. The boy told his father, and his father told me. After that, I had you and Anna followed. For the last two months, we had Zeb keep track of your purchases at his store. We figured you'd bought at least three weeks more food than you needed. Wasn't much to guess why."

Jacob leaned close, his breath a smothering pillow, his eyes sharp blades of scorn. "Prepare yourself, Brother John. God is upon you."

Chapter Thirty-six

Present Day Salt Lake City, Utah
7:45 p.m.
April 25

The Federal Office Building in Salt Lake City, Utah was a 41,439 square foot building at the corner of South State Street and East Second. Being Sunday, and considerably after hours, all the double glass entry doors were locked.

It was almost dark as Alex, Sharon and Kevin stood outside looking into the atrium while, from inside, two well-armed security guards, standing abreast, stared back at them. "Come over here," Alex said to them, with a wave. "Come on," he shouted, when they did not move. "We need help."

The guards conferred then one of them walked deeper into the atrium, unlocked a windowless door, and entered. He returned a moment later carrying an ugly looking M16A2 5.56mm rifle. Spreading his legs for balance he lifted the rifle to his shoulder and aimed it at them.

"Ooh," Alex said as he stepped back. "Get back." he warned Sharon and Kevin. "That's no toy he's got there. That thing's built for combat. It can fire ninety rounds in a minute, and each round can cut a hole in a man a quarter-inch wide." As if to surrender, he put his hands up. "We just want to talk," he shouted to the unarmed guard. "We're looking for the U.S. Attorney."

"Maybe we'd better find him somewhere else," Kevin suggested, stepping back.

"No. Look. He's coming out," Sharon told them of the non-belligerent guard who had walked to the main entrance and was unlocking one of the doors.

"Show me your identifications," he demanded, walking outside and approaching them with one hand outstretched and the other hand resting on his holstered handgun. The guard with the M16 moved closer to the door, and he too stepped outside, remaining at the entrance.

"All we want to do is talk to the U.S. Attorney," Sharon explained. "Do you know where we can find him?"

"You got ten seconds to hand over your I.D.'s," the guard said, his cold, brown eyes glaring at them. "Or, we're taking you into custody."

"I'm an attorney," Sharon said, reaching into her wallet and stepping forward. "Here are my driver's license and my California State Bar membership card. I'm involved in an investigation and these men are assisting me. It is imperative we see him today."

The guard examined her identification. Breasting the licenses, he asked her, "What's your bar number and date of birth?"

"238762. 12/15/77."

"Wait here," the guard ordered, turning on his heels.

While the other guard watched them, rifle still at the ready, the guard with her licenses went back inside, locking the main door after him. Walking into the security office, he picked up a phone and entered a number. Nodding once or twice as he talked to whomever answered, he looked back at them. He was engaged with whomever he called only moments, then he brought the phone outside. "Either of you two Alex Caldwell?" he asked of Alex and Kevin.

"Yeah?" Alex told him, seemingly puzzled by the inquiry.

"He wants to talk to you."

"The U.S. Attorney?" Alex confirmed with the guard. Covering the receiver with his palm he whispered. "What's his name?"

"Mr. Mark Ellis."

"Mr. Ellis," Alex greeted the man on the other end of the line.

***

Some distance away in a suburb, the relatively young U.S. Attorney, no more than forty, his dark brown hair graying early, responded, "Alex Caldwell?"

"Yes."

"I received a call late yesterday afternoon from your editor, Herb Brown. He says he's worried about you." Dressed to the hilt, only the onions and garlic on his breath, boldly challenging the blend of odors from his cologne, distracted from his perfect look.

Caldwell's voice was warm and friendly, yet immediately after Caldwell mentioned Herb Brown, Alex's body went rigid. The last time Alex had anything to do with Herb those thugs chasing them in the Impala showed up outside Kevin's office at Berkeley. "Oh?" was all he said in response.

"We had quite a talk about you," Ellis went on about his conversation with Herb. "Asked me to keep an eye on you. Are you still with that Marshall woman?"

"How do you know Herb?" Alex asked, very cautiously.

"Herb and I go way back."

"Back where?"

"Not important. What's important is that you've come looking for me. In need of help, I assume. So, what can I do for you?"

Alex's face got very taut, his eyes very narrow. "The guard must have misunderstood us. We just wanted to check in, leave you a message to let you know that Wayne and Kim Hoffel are missing and we still can't find them."

"Have you discovered anything?"

"Nothing, really. Been going in circles mostly."

"Well, keep in contact with me and let me know if you learn anything that might help find them. There's nothing I can do officially until and unless there's some proof they were kidnapped or there's evidence suggesting any criminal activity crossing state lines. A federal law has to be broken before I can get involved. Where are you going next?"

"Back to San Francisco. We think they might have headed there."

"Why there?" Ellis would not let go.

"We think Wayne and Kim caught a connecting flight at the airport. We believe its destination was San Francisco."

"Call me when you get there."

"Yes, sir." After disconnecting and handing the phone to the guard, Alex told him, "Mr. Ellis says I should contact the FBI, talk to the Special Agent in Charge of the local office. Where can I find him?"

"That would be Special Agent Carter, Neil T. Carter," the guard responded, unquestioningly. "Agent Carter called just this morning. Said he'd be shutting his cell phone down tonight between six and ten but that he could be contacted at Herbie's

Athletic Club in the 2400 block of 56th Street West."

"Great. Thanks," Alex said, ushering Sharon and Kevin away.

"Why didn't you tell Ellis what we found out? That we think Kim and Wayne were kidnapped? That's a federal crime and would have given him reason to get involved." Sharon asked, desperate to find Kim.

"Because I didn't trust him," Alex said. "I'm not telling that guy anything. I think Ellis and who knows how many others in the U.S. Attorney's office here are involved in their kidnapping. It looks like Ellis is working with Herb Brown, too. If we want help we'll have to go to the FBI. If we raise a fuss, the FBI will have to investigate."

Chapter Thirty-seven

Present Day Salt Lake City, Utah
April 25

Herbie's Athletic Club was a modern, well-equipped gym catering to the local upper middle class. It was a private club, and Sharon, Alex and Kevin were abruptly stopped at the reception desk.

"We'd like to see Neil Carter," Alex told the receptionist. "We were told he was here."

"Is he expecting you?" a very young and shapely blond asked.

"Should be," Alex told her. "We were sent by U.S. Attorney, Mark Ellis." That lie worked with the guard at the federal building, why not with her?

"Wait here," she said, turning on the intercom. "Mr. Neil Carter, please pick up a courtesy phone and call the front desk. Mr. Neil Carter, please..." she repeated. "There are two gentlemen and a lady here wishing to see you," she said, as she answered his call. "They said Mr. Mark Ellis, U.S. Attorney sent them."

"Mr. Carter will meet you in the juice bar," she told them, when she hung up. "Two doors down the hall and to your right."

Behind the first door, a surround of windows overlooking a well-kept, fully lit private garden, half-framed a bistro full of singles and couples having a casual dinner. The juice bar next door was small and windowless, nature having been brought inside by a canopy of tropical plants and trees. A 'U' shaped bar with tall, bamboo stools was at its the center.

"Let's take that table over there," Sharon suggested, pointing to one in an island of tables to the left. It was surrounded by a manmade waterfall.

"I'll have tomato juice," Kevin told the waitress.

"Put their juice on my tab," a man coming up behind her said.

His thick, black hair was wet and combed straight back. He was wearing a white, terry cloth, knee-length robe and blue flip-flops. A thick, white towel was draped around his neck. "Hope you'll excuse my dress. I was in the pool doing laps." The pupils of his dark, rich walnut eyes were huge in the subtle light. "I'll have a strawberry rhubarb slush," he told the waitress. "Special Agent Neil T. Carter," he told them, borrowing a chair from the next table and sitting down. I understand Mark Ellis sent you."

"Let's just say he gave us the idea," Alex responded.

"I certainly hope he did more than that. This is my day off," Carter said, leaning forward. His smile had become a frown.

"We came to you because we think Ellis may be involved in a kidnapping, or worse."

Carter threw his head back, broke into a grin and laughed. "Mark?"

Not to be discouraged, Alex continued. "He's been in contact with my editor, and I think my editor's involved too."

"Ah-uh," Carter said, condescendingly. "If you'll notice, I haven't asked who you are."

"You already know, don't you?" Sharon challenged.

"This can be a very small community," Carter said, no longer laughing. "When people like you start alleging a renowned scientist like Dr. Wayne

Hoffel and his wife have been kidnapped, we tend to take a look at the situation. So far, we've found nothing. The report came to me just yesterday morning. On Wednesday, April 21, a man and a woman traveling under the names Wayne Hoffel and Kim Hoffel, together with his laboratory assistant, a Mr. Arthur Johnson, boarded Delta Flight 1821 from Salt Lake City to Cancun, Mexico at 10:00 a.m. That flight arrived in Cancun about 3:30 in the afternoon. The three of them spent the night in a local motel and at 1:30 p.m. the next day boarded Inter Grupo Taca's flight 977 to Flores, Guatemala. They arrived in Flores a little after 3:00 p.m. They were picked up by a car sent by the Minister of Science and were transported to an undisclosed location further inland. There, they are to begin research on the prenatal diet of the indigenous Q'eqchi. I think your kidnapping theory is a bit farfetched, don't you?"

"No, sir. I don't," Alex told him, refusing to be made a fool. "For one thing, we've been trailed for two days by a couple of bozos in an Impala who seem to stop at nothing to follow us."

"Um..m. These two?" Agent Carter gestured toward two men in the hall just outside the juice bar, a balding man with overgrown pectorals and biceps and a tall, stocky redhead. They stood side by side with their hands behind their backs. Their sport coats were buttoned, but it was obvious they concealed revolvers in shoulder holsters.

Carter smiled. "Mark Ellis asked me to keep you out of trouble. Apparently, he's had his eye on you for a couple of days. He picked these two agents himself to watch you. The bruiser on the left is Agent Brundy. The red head's Agent Haskell. They tell me you were more trouble to them than they anticipated." He laughed. "They told me you lost them."

"If they were just trying to keep us out of trouble, why didn't they identify themselves?" Sharon angrily asked. "Why did they knock our doors down at the motel?"

"They didn't tell you who they were because Ellis asked them to be discreet," Carter responded. "Though, I think you've established they don't know what that means," he added sarcastically. "They knocked your doors down at the motel because the motel manager said he'd seen someone follow you upstairs. They thought you were already in trouble, and they were trying to save you."

Alex was not convinced. "But how did you and Ellis know we were coming? Why did you think we'd cause trouble? Wayne and Kim didn't tell anyone, not even Sharon, whom they saw the night before they disappeared, they were moving to Guatemala? How did you know they were kidnapped? Or even that we thought they were?"

"Those movers Ms. Marshall followed to the tithing storage facility reported her to the police, and when the storage unit in which Wayne and Kim's possessions were stored was broken into, she became a suspect. Alex, you met the description of the man who was with her. The FBI got involved because Wayne and Kim were traveling abroad.

"But what about this?" Alex quizzed, slamming Wayne's medallion on the table. "What about these symbols?" he argued. There was motive for Wayne and Kim's kidnapping, maybe even for their murder. Alex showed Carter the images engraved on the medallion. He told him about the Cult of the Bee, the promise of fecundity, and the Sons of Dan.

Terror and conviction gripped Alex's voice. "The Sons of Dan were murderers, and their descendants are murderers now. They're planning to take over the country with multiple births and baby farms, using women like Kim to breed them."

"Whoa," Carter said, withholding a chuckle. "Do you hear yourself?

"Only a lunatic would buy all that, especially when all you've got to prove your theory is a medallion that may or may not refer to myths and old, imagined histories."

"So, you're not going to help us?" Sharon asked, beginning to doubt their sanity herself.

"You haven't given me anything with which I can justify an investigation. I'd lose my job if I went chasing theories based on myths," Carter told them. "Tell you what I can do, though. Let me take the medallion to our cryptographers. See if the images mean anything to them."

"Not yet," Alex said, putting the medallion back in his pants' pocket. "We need to talk among ourselves first."

"Suit yourselves, but I'm sure there's nothing for you to worry about. I'll be in my office tomorrow. If you want our cryptographers to examine the medallion, you can bring it to me then."

"Just one question," Kevin asked Sharon and Alex as they drove out of the parking lot, "If the FBI doesn't believe there's been a kidnapping and doesn't believe there is a criminal conspiracy, why are they involved at all? They don't handle minor break-ins even if the owners of the property are traveling abroad. So why are they trailing us?"

***

Sharon glanced in the rearview mirror. Keeping pace, two blocks behind them, was the white Impala.

Chapter Thirty-eight

Present Day Somewhere in Utah
2:00 p.m.
April 25

A single engine, turbo prop, a cargo pod mounted on its belly, flaps down. With engines nearly idle, it glided out of a mountain framed sky and onto a landing strip, a long, narrow channel cut through knee high grass and covered with dirt. Once safely on the ground, its engines revived, the plane turned, backtracked, and taxied toward an unmarked white ambulance.

"In one piece and in good condition," the pilot said, as he met a tall man walking toward the plane. Handing him a clipboard with the shipping order on it, the pilot told him, "Just sign here." The cargo was identified "Quantity: 1 Description artifact."

"Let's take a look," the tall man said, withholding his signature until inspection. A strand of his dark, wavy hair blew in the breeze, tickling his brow.

The pilot gestured toward the open cargo door, starboard side. "It's in there."

"Rough flight?" the tall man asked, making conversation.

"No more than usual. Took a while, though, had to skirt a couple of thunderstorms over the Midwest."

The cargo hold looked empty until the copilot, sitting in the cockpit, exposed a concealed lever beneath his seat, lifted it, and opened the hatch to a secret compartment beneath the hold. Inside the secret compartment, securely strapped to the bulkhead, was a large, canvas bag, tied with a drawstring. It was the only cargo the plane carried in its four hundred and fifty cubic feet of cargo space.

Cautiously loosening the drawstring, the tall man opened the canvas bag and peered inside. Reaching down and about, he felt the arms and hands of the figure inside, the breast and pelvis, then the face. After slowly drawing the sack closed, he reached for the board on which the shipping order was clipped and signed.

Chapter Thirty-nine

Present Day Salt Lake City, Utah
2:00 a.m.
April 26

Between clean, crisp sheets on a queen-sized bed in a motel room near the Mormon Temple, Sharon raced through the pages of her Great Grandmother Anna's diary. With grotesque interest, she read about the blood atonement murders and the Mountain Meadows Massacre, beginning as she continued, to read Anna's entry for February 8, 1858.

I was at the window in the first hours of dawn looking for John, Anna wrote, *and in the distance, I saw a rider. 'He's here,' I told Hattie, thinking it was John. We were so relieved he had come back, yet we worried too. What had John done while he was gone? Who had he murdered? With mixed feelings I looked at Hattie, yet she did not look back. Turning away from the door through which he would come, she went to the hearth and started fixing his breakfast. So Hattie and I could talk to John alone, I told Lizzie to take Angel and the children outside. John was usually covered with blood when he came home from a killing, and I did not want the children to see it.*

As he rode closer, to calm my nerves I fed the fire, hung a pot of water to boil, and half-filled the wash basin with what warm water was left from earlier on. Lye soap and a good scrub would have the blood off his clothes and ready to hang in minutes and the children could come back inside.

I was very frightened by what Jacob might have forced John to do that night, and I didn't want to know what it was so I delayed going back to the window. I didn't look at John again until he opened the door.

I turned, and though the sunrise behind him nearly blinded me, I knew instantly, the shadow in my doorway was not John. It was Jacob. He was haggard and dirty. Malevolent dark red stains of the kind I had seen before on John were all over him. 'Where's John?' I demanded. I looked out the window to see if he was there, and when I didn't see him, I demanded again of Jacob, 'Where is John?'

Jacob ordered me to 'Sit down,' quickly closing the door and shutting out the sun. 'I have something of importance to discuss, he told me.'

'Why? Where's John?' I again demanded.

As usual, dear Hattie said nothing to him. She just stood there, her back to the hearth, keeping her eyes on him.

"Ignoring her, Jacob stepped toward me and took my hand. He guided me to the table and stood beside me until I sat down. 'When is John coming home?' I asked. I did not like Jacob here alone in my house and sorely wished John would come back right then.

As I watched him, Jacob circled the cabin as if taking stock of it, making himself at home as if he owned it. He then took it upon himself to sit as bold as you please in John and Erich's rocker. I wished John was there to throw him out, but I said nothing.

Making Hattie and I wait to hear why he had come, he lit his cigar, took a puff or two, then struck out at me. 'You seem to be in the habit, Sister Anna, of choosing husbands who are, and always will be, less than gods, men who lack faith, who are too weak to earn godhoods. It is where you are most flawed. It is for this reason, and for others, you are to be bettered. *Despite your past mistakes, we have determined to help you. And through our efforts, you will reach the Kingdom of God. I was given permission to save you, and I have saved you. From now on, you are mine.'*

I was so shocked by what he told me, I stopped breathing. I was so frightened I started sweating right in front of him. Hattie must have been frightened too, because she stepped to my side to protect me. Her face turned a brilliant bright red. Her hand was trembling as it touched my shoulder. Squaring herself to face him, she threw out her chest, crossed her arms, and demanded he tell her, 'What do you mean?'

But Jacob didn't pay any attention to her. He was only looking at me, treating her like she was not even there.

'Where's John?' I shouted at him.

'Brother John broke his covenants to God of loyalty and obedience,' Jacob explained. 'He lost his way to salvation and would have perished for eternity if we had not intervened. Now through us and because we helped him over the rim, he will find that salvation.'

My heart beat so fast I thought it was going to strangle me. It pressed against my ears, and I heard nothing. I couldn't even feel Hattie's hand again touching my shoulder. Trying to keep from fainting, I shook my head. My heart beat just as fast, but I could suddenly hear and feel again.

Jacob was talking, and I heard him saying, 'John also failed in his duty to populate God's Kingdom. He took you away from me and wasted you by not giving you children. We have seen that he has atoned for that too.

'You have three days to collect and give away what belongings you will not need. You, Jimmy and Maybella will live in my house. You will finally become my wife. Jimmy and Maybella will become my children. You will break your celestial covenant with John, and you will be forever sealed to me! Brother Jeremy wants Lizzy for his wife, and Brigham Young has approved it. The five of us are to return to Salt Lake City on Tuesday. Brother Zeb has agreed to take Hattie as his wife, so she will stay here.'

I was angry and afraid. I wept so hard, tears would not come. I was entering hell and dragging my family in with me.

Jacob stood and walked toward me. Leaning over me, the smell of blood all over him, he gripped my arms and made me stand. His arms enfolding me until I could not move, he forced my face to his. His fat, wet lips closed over my mouth, his drool flowed into it and clung there.

Utterly revolted, I pushed him away and tried to hold him back. 'No!' I cried.

"Yet, he only laughed. 'You'll learn to like it.' His lips curled to a smile, and then he threatened me, 'It doesn't matter what you think or what you do. You have taken an oath to obey, and if you do not obey, you will be destroyed.'

He took a leather pouch from his pocket. Inside that pouch, was another pouch, bloodstained and filthy. Holding it out to me, he opened it, saying, 'I brought these to you to help you remember your vow. They're part of the price John paid for his disobedience.'

Jacob pulled something out of the bloody pouch and dangled it in front of my eyes, gloating with a smile, 'They're John's bollocks.'

I tried to run away, but Jacob grabbed me and wrenched my arm behind my back. I was sick, so very sick, matter filled my mouth and I vomited. I couldn't look at them. But, I couldn't look away, either.

Jacob released me, and out of the corner of my eye, I saw him take a whittling knife from his other pocket. I heard flesh give as he pierced one of the bullocks he held. He turned his back to me, and I heard a thud as he pinned John's parts to the door.

'Don't touch them,' Jacob ordered us. 'I'm putting them here so you do not forget what he did or where you are going.' As I finally looked up, he glared at me. 'So you do not forget you are mine.'

He had torn out my heart, and when he came back to me, I couldn't help myself. I reached for the hearth, grabbed the fire iron and hit him in the head, knocking him to the floor. God help me, I wanted to kill him.

I brought the rod over my shoulder to hit him again, but he was too fast for me. He grabbed the iron, threw it aside, and hit me with his fist. I went down, and as I turned to get up, he got on top of me, pinning my hands to the floor. Spread out on top of me, he pressed his chest against my breasts, brought his fat lips to mine and kissed me again. His pizzle stiffened, and I thought he was going to rape me. Kicking and twisting, I screamed for help.

I remember Angel barking and growling at the door, and Lizzy crying as she opened it. Desperately worried about them, terrified for Maybella and Jimmy, I hardly realized the full weight of Jacob's body pressing me to the floor.

Chapter Forty

Cedar City, Utah
February 8, 1858

*W*hen I realized Jacob wasn't breathing, I dared look at his face. His eyes were fixed. His mouth drooped open, and he smelled like uncured deer skin. Still sprawled on top of me, he suddenly got excruciatingly heavy and strangely gelatin. I felt fluid dripping onto my breast, and I suddenly panicked. Shoving, forcing him away with my hips, shoulders and knees, with all my strength, I threw him off me.

I sat up, looked toward the door and saw Lizzy in the doorway. She looked like she was in shock. Sweat dripped from her brow, her lips were turning blue, and she was deathly pale. I looked beyond her. The little ones were still playing outside. I became aware that Angel was by my side and that Hattie was standing over me.

Hate like I had never seen before was in Hattie's eyes. In her hand, she held the blood soaked knife she had used to cut Jacob's throat. As I watched, she bent over his body, her voice cold and even as she said to him, 'Rejoice Brother Jacob. For we have saved you.'

All the grief I felt for John instantly turned to fear. I knew we had to get out of there.

Chapter Forty-one

Present Day Somewhere in Utah
7:00 a.m. Monday
April 26

S he was delivered yesterday," Dr. Philip Reed told Jake, his assistant, who was standing next to him dressed in nurse's scrubs. "She came in from Atlanta," he continued, referring to a prone, heavily sedated woman just wheeled into the procedure room. Outside his practice, Reed was known to spend his nearly every waking hour hunting and for spending thousands of dollars buying and training his dogs. He was ruthless if they did not hunt to his expectations. He hunted and competed with the dogs who did, then bred them until they were spent and no good to him. "What's her number, Jake?"

Opening a locked drawer of the pink, stainless steel cabinet by the door, Jake pulled out a blue, nine by twelve inch, three ring binder and opened it to the first and most recent page. Taking his reading glasses from his pocket, he put them on and leaned forward, his gray roots showing as the bangs of his dyed brown hair fell over his eyes.

"How many times do I have to tell you to cover your hair?" Reed disciplined.

"I don't have anything in here. I left my cap in the coffee room," Jake confessed. "Want me to go get it?"

"Just get a paper clip or something out of those drawers and pin it back"

Jake fumbled inside the thinner, top drawer, pulled out two large paperclips, divided his bangs and pinned them back on each side of his forehead.

Quickly going back to the notebook, he read Reed the woman's number, "60156. Wow," he exclaimed, "we've had quite a few come in this month. That's at least ten."

They were in a small examination room containing only the basic instrumentation and equipment they would need including a large, bright, overhead light. A long cord hung from the ceiling connecting to what looked like a small drill.

When Jake returned to the examination table, he took the sedated woman's pulse and lifted her eyelids to check her pupils. He then listened to the beat of her heart through his stethoscope.

Emily Brighten was in a semiconscious state. At his prodding, she opened her eyes and seemed confused. As if she was unable to connect her thoughts to the blurry images she must have had of the freckled faced man leaning over her, she mumbled, "Where...who...where...What?" she finally blurted, when Jeff told her, "This won't hurt a bit."

She turned her head toward the second man and appeared to read the embroidery on his pocket, now just inches from her face as he leaned toward her. "Dr. Philip Reed, M.D."

Gently lifting her hand, Jake stretched her arm onto a stiff armrest and flattened her palm against it until her wrist was flat. With easy-to-release nylon straps, first over the breadth of her hand above the knuckles then at a point four inches up her forearm, he secured her wrist to the armrest. "Here's the needle," he quipped when her wrist was completely immobile, handing Reed an electric powered, vertical vibrating instrument that was plugged into the ceiling.

"What'd you say that number was?" Reed asked.

"60156, Doctor."

"60156," Reed repeated, as he drew black pigment into the instrument's wide, fountain pen-shaped needle. Placing the point of the needle near her skin, just above the cluster of bones connecting her hand to her forearm, he injected the ink into the second layer of skin at a rate of 2,000 times per minute, tattooing a '6' on the back of her wrist. "Ready for the sample?" Reed asked, when he finished tattooing all five digits.

"Here's the ultrasound we took this morning," Jake told him, switching on the lighted screen. A gray, shadowy mass that looked like some kind of hive appeared. Inside, were two circles that looked like part of a honeycomb. "This is the right ovary," Jake explained, pointing to the delineation on the bottom edge of the screen. "Looks like it's already released two follicles."

"I see that," Reed told him, quite impressed. "Was she taking fertility drugs?"

"Not that we could determine."

Reed laughed. "Looks like she won't need any from us, either. She'll be a good one. Any follicles developing on the left?"

"Not yet."

"Well, we'll improve that," Reed promised. "Any infectious diseases or genetically transmitted conditions?"

"Nope."

"That's what we like to see."

With no further direction, Jake put Emily's heels in the stirrups at the end of the table, gripped her at the waist and pulled her toward them. Fully opening her hospital gown in front, he bared everything.

"Mm...m," Reed said, tantalized by what he saw, "not bad."

Yet Jake was the first who got to touch her. First rolling up his sleeve, he caressed her as he lathered her groin and shaved her, brushing his elbow against her breast whenever possible. "You sure she's taken?" he asked.

"Yes," Reed told him. "Someone better than you and me is going to breed her. So don't get too excited."

When Emily's groin and belly were clean, Jake spread a clear, light gel over them. He then positioned the ultrasound mouse to the left and immediately over her right ovary.

Standing in front of her spread and bent knees, Reed inserted a stainless steel speculum into her vagina and expanded it, making himself a workspace. His gaze glued to the ultrasound screen, he then inserted into it a long, wide bore, aspirating needle. With care, he guided the needle through the top right hand side of her vagina and into her ovary.

Locating the first developing follicle, Reed inserted the needle and drew all the fluid from it. He then moved to the second follicle and withdrew the fluid from that one. The unfertilized eggs inside her follicles, too small to see with the ultrasound, were sucked up along with the fluid.

"Take them to the lab and give them to Henry," Reed told Jack of the aspirated eggs. "If there're no problems, go ahead and donate them. Once they've been implanted in the recipient, nobody but you and me will know the difference."

Two hours later, her head pounding, her wrist and groin aflame, Emily Brighten woke and looked around. She was in a blue bedroom of some kind. The wall in front of her was papered with giant, yellow, baby duck designs, so intrusive as to be almost frightening, while an array of colorful cartoon characters stared up at her from her bedspread.

"Nightmarish, isn't it?" asked a slim woman with blond hair and rapturously beautiful blue eyes sitting on the bed next to hers, the only other bed in the room.

"Quite," Emily said, turning to stare at her.

"I think we're cellmates," the woman said, somewhat flatly. Her Barbie doll nightshirt design was more appropriate for a child than a full grown woman, and Emily was staring at it. "You think mine's bad. Take a look at yours."

Emily looked down. Her pink, flannel nightgown was covered with Poohs and Piglets. "What's this all about?" she asked. "What do you mean cell mates?" The last thing Emily remembered was being in her kitchen in Atlanta and answering a knock at the door.

"The door is locked and there aren't any windows," her roommate told her. "Our meals are brought to us. We get outdoors only once a day for exercise and fresh air. There are guards at the gate and along the compound wall, and we're not allowed to leave. I don't know where we are, but I suspect, wherever it is, we're going to be here a long time. Look at your wrist."

Sore and swollen red, the black numbers on Emily's wrist seemed to rise and hit her in the face. "My God, look what they've done to me."

"Me, too," the woman said. She slowly raised her wrist, displaying her own tattoo, number "60154".

"But, why? Where are we?"

"In a concentration camp. Cellmates. I don't know. Whenever I ask for an answer, they tell me not to worry, that I'll soon find out. But nobody's told me anything yet. I don't even know what happened to my husband.

"By the way, my name's Kim Hoffel. What's yours?"

Chapter Forty-two

In the grip of Great Grandmother Anna's story, Sharon threw off her sheets and turned to the next page. Hattie murdered Jacob, and she and Anna were preparing to run. It was well after midnight. The motel was quiet, the well-lit street was still, and Alex and Kevin were asleep in the room next door. Beads of sweat formed on Sharon's brow, and she held her breath as she read from Anna's diary, *I retched as I struggled to my feet, Jacob's body beside me, my vomit splattering onto his face.*

Blood was everywhere, on the floor, on my dress, and on my face. Hattie was covered with it. The spattered walls seem to close in on me and the room to reeked with filth and shame. If we were caught for this, we'd die. Sooner or later, our brethren would execute us.

Lizzy was still in the doorway, her eyes wide and struck with terror. Angel was sniffing at Jacob's wound. Before I could even speak, Hattie told Lizzy to take Angel outside and to stay with the children. She was not to tell them what happened.

Lizzy's face was flushed. Her hands were shaking. She looked like she was going to faint. She called Angel and when Angel did not come, walked to Jacob's body. She pulled at Angel's collar and, without saying a work, took Angel outside.

I wasn't nearly so calm as Lizzy. My entire body was shaking. My knees were giving way, and I could taste Jacob's blood and even his drool. I was going to vomit again, but then I stopped myself. I had to think. What were we going to do? We had to run. We had Jacob's horse, our wagon and our oxen, but where would we go? Would there be time to find a hiding place before he was missed? And after we were away, how would we survive? If the Avenging Angels didn't kill us, the Indians would.

Hattie handed me the canceled promissory note I signed to Jacob four years ago, the one where I promised to pay him for Angel's food on our trip West. 'Use this to buy us time.' she told me. 'I'll take care of Jacob.' She dragged him to the door, leaned outside and told Lizzy to take the children out back to the creek. Angel usually stayed with the children, but she must have sensed we needed her more and went with Hattie. Tugging at Jacob's clothes, she even helped Hattie drag him into the brush.

The promissory note was in Jacob's handwriting. I needed only to mimic his scrawl to write something else. I ripped a blank page from my diary and with tedious attention to his hand wrote, 'Brother Haight, I am taking on poor Brother John's family as my own and must return to Salt Lake City to make preparations. I will be back in two weeks to get them. Do not worry about them. They have plenty of food and provisions until I come back. Please tell Brother Zeb to let Sister Hattie spend this time with them. I will bring her to him immediately upon my return. I prefer these women not be allowed to attend Sunday meeting without my direct supervision for I am afraid of what they will say. Best leave them be until I return. Thank you. Yours truly, Jacob Tuttle.'

Since Hattie was the calmest of us all, Anna wrote, *she delivered the note to Brother Haight. I removed the blood-soaked, earthen floor from the cabin, threw the dirt into the brush, and replaced it with fresh dirt. By the time Hattie came back, the wagon was nearly packed. Lizzy and I had packed everything we could fit, mattresses and bedding, clothes, tools, a plow, all our food, plenty of water, and John and Erich's rocker. We had to leave everything else.*

Once the oxen were harnessed, we pulled out. Lizzy, astride Jacob's horse. Hattie, Angel and I walking beside the wagon, and Maybella and Jimmy on the seat. By midafternoon, we were moving south, knowing we would be followed.

Chapter Forty-three

Present Day Salt Lake City, Utah
7:30 a.m.
April 26

Alex was just opening his eyes, his hands behind his head, trying to decide what he was going to have for breakfast when the door to his motel room suddenly rattled. Someone was knocking.

"What the hell," Kevin growled, waking up in the other bed. As Alex was peering through the peephole to see who was there, he sat up and yawned.

"Alex. Kevin." Sharon shouted, as she continued to rap. "Open up. I've got something to show you."

Wearing just boxers, only a smattering of dark, curly hair on his long, narrow chest, Alex turned the knob and let her in. "What's up?"

"I've been reading more of Grandma Anna's diary," she began, "and it's there. What the new Sons of Dan are doing and their motives." She grabbed Alex's arm, squeezed, and yanked him toward her. "There's nothing they wouldn't do to further their ambition.

"What do you mean," Kevin asked, walking over to them.

"They want what Brigham Young and Joseph Smith couldn't get," Sharon told them. They want to control part, if not all, of the United States."

"How are they going to do that?" Alex challenged, his voice rife with sarcasm.

"They're going to do it by controlling the vote and by force."

"What vote?" Alex demanded.

"The country's vote." Sharon wouldn't back down. "Think about it, the original Sons of Dan and their successors did horrible, unscrupulous things to get for Joseph Smith and Brigham Young whatever they wanted. What they wanted most was to substantially increase their member population so they could strengthen their army and extend control of their territories. Once their vote is in place and they infiltrate the army, the entire country can be theirs.

"Wayne and Kim's disappearances have something to do with it. I don't know why they've taken Kim, and I don't care what proof Agent Carter thinks he has that she and Wayne went to Guatemala. I know they've got her, and they've probably killed Wayne. Whatever we do, we can't stop looking for her. We find her, and we find out what they're up to. She walked to the table in the corner and spread out a detailed road map of Utah. First brushing out the creases, she pointed to an area in the northeastern desert, inside the triangle between the Wyoming and Colorado borders. "She's got to be here somewhere." Sharon was referring specifically to the area south of Ashley National Forest and west of the Dinosaur National Monument. The tip of her finger was pointing to a town called 'Vernal'.

"Give me the inventory," she directed Kevin. When he handed it to her she pointed to one of the designations they believed identified the location. "UTVR," she said, repeating the abbreviation under 'loc,' on the inventory. "'UT' is Utah. 'VR' is Vernal. As far as I can tell, there's no other 'V' on the map. It's a small, isolated town and would be the perfect place to hide a baby farm."

Alex and Kevin looked over her shoulder, studying the map for themselves. They came to the same conclusion. "How long do you think it'll take us to get there?" Alex asked.

"Three and a half to four hours. We'll know better when we see the condition of the roads. There're only two lane roads and dinosaur fossils out there."

"We'd better not take that hot car of yours then," Alex told her as he put on his pants. "It rides pretty low and might not make it. There's a rent-a-car across the street. You can park yours at an overnight garage." He slipped on his jacket, "I'll get us an SUV."

***

In the middle of the green and rugged Wasatch Range, at the western edge of the greater Rocky Mountains, Sharon turned the rented, dark blue SUV right, off of interstate 80 and onto U.S. Highway 40. From there they traveled south along the east edge if the Wasatch Range and south of the high wilderness known as Uinta. They then turned east where a series of strata deposited one hundred and forty-five million years ago became a massive graveyard for dinosaurs. Squeezed by rock when the Rocky Mountains formed, the dinosaurs' sandstone tombs became ridges. Worn down by rain and wind, they became giant rock formations laced with color.

"How much further," Kevin asked from the back seat.

"About half an hour," Sharon told him. "You need to stop?"

Kevin's only options out there in the wilderness were alfresco. "No, thanks. I can wait. I suppose there're rattlers around here, too."

"You could say we're in rattler heaven," Alex remarked, spotting at least ten holes in nearby rocks where snakes were probably lurking.

For as far as they could see, they were the only vehicles on the road. "So, where's all the traffic?" Kevin asked, "Doesn't anybody live around here?"

"We're just about in the valley," Sharon said. "There should be farms there and at least a few cars on the road. Might even be a tractor or two," she teased.

"See, there's a car behind us already." She observed in her rear view mirror. The desert haze, though not severe in April, made the closing vehicle look small and blurry. "Boy, they're really coming fast," she observed through the rear view mirror. "Guess there's no reason to enforce speed limits out here."

Alex turned and as the approaching vehicle got within a hundred feet of them at speeds reaching ninety recognized the big, white Impala and its occupants. "Christ...." he blurted. "They're back."

"How do you suppose they found us?" Kevin asked. "They couldn't have put another tracking device on us. We just got the car."

The Impala was only a few yards off their bumper, when Agent Brundy, the balding man, started waving them over from the passenger seat.

Sharon looked for a shoulder on which to pull over, but there was none. "Here?" she questioned. The road was on a steep, rock shelf. There was a hundred foot rise on their left and a twenty foot drop on their right. "I'll have to wait until I get to some kind of turn off."

Brundy and Haskell were not waiting. Crossing the double, yellow line, putting all their lives at risk on that narrow, curving road with limited visibility, Haskell turned into the oncoming lane, caught up with them and kept abreast. Brundy was still waving them off. "Pull over?" he shouted. "Now."

"Must be some kind of emergency," Kevin said. "Maybe we'd better do as he says."

"But it's not safe," Sharon insisted. "I can't stop in the middle of the road." Attempting to let Brundy and Haskell know she was cooperating, Sharon pointed ahead and yelled out the window, "I need more shoulder."

Without responding, Brundy rolled up his window, turned away, and said something to Haskell. Abruptly, the Impala slowed. Putting some distance between them, it got back into the right lane and followed. As the SUV approached a blind curve, the Impala pulled back farther.

"Wonder what they want," Alex said. "Carter must have sent them."

"How did they know we were here?" Sharon asked. She was driving about twenty-five miles an hour into a sharp curve to the left. Immediately to the right was a forty-foot drop. Through her open window, the sound of squealing tires drew her attention.

The white Impala, aimed to hit them broadside, raced to within twenty-feet of them, then braked, skidding directly into Kevin's door. "No," he shouted, as the impact crushed his leg.

The crash sent the SUV flying, hurtling over a three-foot metal rail and off the brink of the forty-foot-high edge. Everything whirled in slow motion as they tumbled, rolling over and over down the sharp and brutal slope until, half-pancaked, the

SUV finally came to a stop, upside down at the bottom. Dust was everywhere, and as the SUV came to rest, a curtain of powdery dirt immediately closed around it.

Sharon opened her eyes, but dust billowing into them immediately blinded her. "Alex," she called, groping for him. Finding his arm, she felt upward along his shoulder. Her hand traveled up his cheek, and she found his eyes. They were closed and unmoving. "Alex?" Her body was waking from the impact, and she was beginning to experience pain, a deep, steady ache in her joints and chest, an unmerciful throbbing in her left arm. She let her hand fall from his face. "Please, Alex, wake up."

He groaned. "You all right?" he asked, his eyes open and searching her.

"I think so. But we'd better check on Kevin."

Kevin was limp, hanging by the threads of a seat belt cut nearly in two by collapsing metal.

"We've got to get him out of here," Sharon said. She tried to push the door open, but the pain in her arm was suddenly excruciating. Immediately pulling back, she tenuously touched the area from which the pain was coming. A rough, half-inch piece of bone was sticking through her torn and bloody blouse. "My arm's broken." She took a deep, almost tearful breath. "I think my door's jammed, too. I'll have to come out your way."

"Cautiously releasing his seat belt, Alex braced himself as he fell onto the SUV's pre-formed felt ceiling, landing on his sore, soft tissue. Taking a few seconds to quickly examine himself to find only bruises, Alex pushed at his door and opened it.

Leaning back toward Sharon, he supported her while he got her free of her seat belt and from underneath the wheel that nearly trapped her at the knees. She groaned but said nothing, the pain in her arm clearly agonizing for her. Moving her as gently as he could across the ceiling, he pulled her out the passenger door and onto the fringe of the rock slope. Helping her to stand and walk off the rocks, he got her to the adjoining field, sat her down against one of the boulders and looked past the SUV, up the slope, and to the road. Standing behind the bent rail, in the very spot where the SUV hurtled it, stood Brundy and Haskell. They were staring down at them, watching.

"Let's go," Brundy said, as they walked away from rail and got into the Impala. "We gotta' get down there."

Chapter Forty-four

Present Day Northeastern Utah
1:20 p.m.
April 26

Barely able to focus, feeling like a spike had been driven into and was twisting inside her arm, Sharon tried to calm her trembling body, to breathe naturally, and not to cry. She was seated and leaning against a four-foot slab of rock. Alex had left her several feet below the SUV and to the left, against big rocks at the edge of a huge alfalfa field. He then went back to the pancaked SUV and was trying to extract Kevin from his seat. Her blood pressure dropping, the misery in the rest of her body a backdrop for the pain in her arm, Sharon waited, unaware the three of them were no longer alone.

Inside the overturned SUV, Kevin's left knee was crushed, his left leg torn in several places, his skin hanging in chunks. The scalp over his left temple had been half ripped off by the doorframe.

"Is there any way you can help me?" Alex asked. He was fumbling with the seat belt release, supporting Kevin's entire weight with his shoulder.

"I'll try," Kevin told him, as he attempted to make himself lighter, feebly pushing himself against the upturned ceiling.

"There's no cell coverage here," Alex explained, "so I can't call for help. Once I get you out of here, Sharon will have to take care of you while I walk to Vernal."

"How far is it?"

"Ten. Twelve miles, maybe," Alex told him, as the belt released and Kevin fell on top of him.

"Agh...h...h," Kevin cried.

"I'll take him from here," a deep voice from behind them, calm and reassuring said. "We're really sorry about this. Our brakes failed coming around the curve. We tried to steer clear, but there wasn't time." Haskell's chiseled face was uncharacteristically soft, his brown eyes seeming genuinely regretful. "Brundy's bringing the car down, so we can take you to the hospital."

"You all right with that?" Alex asked Kevin, suspicious of Haskell's offer to help.

Kevin had fallen on his shoulders, his crushed leg dangling excruciatingly in his face without means to move. "Sure. Yes. I don't care who it is, just get me out of here." Sweat flowed from his pores, cold gripped him, and he was trembling uncontrollably.

"All right, but be careful with him," Alex demanded. "You're a lot bigger and stronger than I am, 'specially after I've been bounced around that car, thanks to you. But just in case you have trouble, I'll be right outside the door." Quickly scooting across the ceiling, he crawled outside, changing places with Haskell.

As Haskell cradled Kevin like a baby, gently pulling him away from the wall, blood from Kevin's leg ran down his torso and flowed onto his face. As he eased Kevin's legs down onto the ceiling, Kevin whimpered and shuddered with pain. Remnants of the seat belt were wrapped around his calf, holding him.

"I'll have to cut you down," Haskell told him.

Alex was pressed against the window, watching. "Be careful," he reminded.

Supporting Kevin with his left arm, Haskell pulled a three-inch switchblade from his right pants pocket. Putting the handle between his teeth, he sprung open the blade. With the knife in his right hand, lethal edge down and out of Alex's view, Haskell then slid the blade down Kevin's leg. Tracing the contour of Kevin's thigh, Haskell dragged the blade down the length of it, over Kevin's knee, and to the remnant of the seat belt which held him. Then, like a boning knife through flesh, it quickly severed the two inches of nylon that remained.

Kevin's leg suddenly free, it bounced off the ceiling like rubber. "Aaggghh," he screamed.

For an instant, Alex had diverted his attention to Kevin's face. "Hold on," he called. "You're almost out."

His courage and nerves worn raw, Kevin closed his eyes.

Finding footing on the rock outside, Haskell put his knife away, took hold of Kevin's shoulders and guided him toward the open door. In obviously sharp, tortuous pain seeming to get worse with every inch he moved, Kevin crawled slowly but steadily across the crunched, uneven ceiling to where Alex and Haskell were waiting, his head dropping, his pale, bloody face always down, his eyes toward the ceiling. When he reached the door they both took a shoulder and pulled him out. As they were setting him on the ground, he went limp.

"Kevin," Alex called, "wake up."

Kevin's face was deathly pale and bloody. He opened his eyes, acknowledged Alex with a brief, feeble smile, then slipped into unconsciousness. Quickly, Alex and Haskell carried him off the rocks and to Brundy and Sharon, who were waiting at the edge of the rubble.

"The Impala's over there," Brundy told them, pointing further east and about ten feet into the field. "If you two can carry him, I'll help her."

Fear and doubt clouded her gaze, as Sharon looked to Alex for assurance. "Go ahead," she told him, when he hesitated, "I'll be fine."

Brundy made her a sling with his black, polyester tie, put his arm around her waist, and helped her over the two to three-foot thick, jagged rocks into the bowels of the Impala, which nearly killed them.

"How many more miles?" Sharon asked, after what seemed an hour. Between sharp bursts of pain, her arm was throbbing. Kevin was lying in the back seat beside her, his head on her lap. "Kevin's really limp. When need to get him to a doctor."

"It's about five miles more," Haskell told her from behind the wheel.

Alex was in front, on the Impala's bench seat, sandwiched between Haskell and Brundy. The front windows were open, and Sharon was freezing. "Got a blanket up there?"

Haskell glanced at her in the rear view mirror. Her trembling was getting worse, and she was a lot paler than when they started. "Sorry," he said, rolling up the windows.

"We'll be there in about ten," he said, taking a corner at twice the recommended speed, then accelerating, pushing the Impala to a hundred miles per hour on the straightaways.

Outside the town they were entering, large and cartoonish replicas of dinosaurs advertised local businesses. The main street was wide, yet only a few blocks long, and was lined with one story, brick buildings most likely built in the 1950's. Small, rain-deprived trees were evenly dispersed along the sidewalks. Halfway down Main Street Haskell turned right onto a residential street lined with small houses.

"Where's the hospital?" Sharon demanded.

"Isn't one," Brundy told her. "There's only the town doctor."

"What," Sharon burst, "Kevin needs a hospital."

"We'll let Doc Reed decide that," Brundy said.

Haskell turned into a semicircular drive at the side of a single level, unadorned, beige building, where there was a sign that read, "Dr. Philip Reed, Family Practice."

"What are we doing here?" Alex asked. "They both need a hospital."

"Like I said, there's no hospital," Brundy impatiently told them, "there's only Dr. Reed. Gotta' stop here first."

Alex looked back at Sharon, and their gazes locked. Something was not right.

"Tell Doc we're here," Brundy ordered Haskell. "Alex and I'll bring Kevin in."

Sharon waited patiently, as Brundy pulled Kevin's flaccid, unresponsive body off her lap and out of the car. Managing to take care of herself, she opened her door and followed them inside. A nurse was waiting.

"My name's Ray," the nurse said, just briefly glancing at Kevin. She was middle-aged and maternal, in white polyester pants and a flower print blouse. Her red hair was proudly graying, and her figure was the product of years of fried, country cooking. "Doctor's waiting in Number One," she told Brundy. "You go ahead. I'll see to the lady." Long coils of her hair, swept up and away from her face, were held in place by two sky-blue, plastic combs corralling them in a bun at the top of her head. The combs were fastened there by a cluster of hairpins and a traditional nurses' cap.

"Come with me," she told Sharon, leading her down a short hallway. Passing the door to the examination room into which Kevin was taken and in which all five men were gathering, she took Sharon one more door down and into a smaller room across from Dr. Reed's personal office. "Sit here," she instructed. Nurse Ray's strong hands and forearms eased Sharon onto the paper lined and padded examination table. "I'll help you get ready." She laid a clean, folded hospital gown across Sharon's lap, then eased Sharon's arm out of the sling. Proceeding to cut from the left cuff to the shoulder and through the neck, she gently removed Sharon's blouse.

***

Next door, Dr. Philip Reed lifted Kevin's eyelids, and with a tiny, white light, peered into his pupils. "Why don't you wait outside," Reed told Alex, without moving. "I'll be with you in a minute."

"Can I see Sharon?" Alex asked, as Haskell ushered him out of the room and directed him away from Sharon and to the small reception room just inside the front door.

"Just wait out here," Haskell told him. "Doc will let us know if there's anything we can do for her."

On Haskell's word, Alex abandoned Sharon and Kevin to people he had no reason to trust, and as he waited, he restlessly paced. The small, floral prints of the rug and wallpaper in the nine-by-nine-foot room were crushingly claustrophobic, the sweet, flowery deodorizer coming from a dispenser plugged into an outlet nearby suffocating. His hands and brow were sweating, and his face was turning bright red.

***

Inside the examination room, Dr. Reed removed the blood-soaked tourniquet Haskell tied above Kevin's injured knee just before they left the scene of the accident. He then cut the hem of his pants leg and ripped it open to the thigh, exposing his smashed knee and several ugly gashes. Reed then ran his fingers over a gaping wound a few inches above the rest. The wound was above the tourniquet and had not been protected by it. It had been bleeding profusely since Haskell helped Kevin out of the SUV. "Didn't do much good, did it," Reed laughed.

While cutting Kevin free from his seatbelt, Haskell surreptitiously made a small slit in Kevin's femoral artery. He then intentionally tied the tourniquet too low to stop its bleeding.

"Examining the cut, Dr. Reed poked his finger through Kevin's ample flesh. "Not exactly a mountain climber, was he?" Reed criticized. "Sorry about your car, Brundy. Must be a mess in there."

"That's all right, I needed a new one anyway. Think I can get one on the house?"

"I'll see what I can do."

"What are you going to tell Caldwell?" Brundy asked.

"The truth," Reed told him. "The rest is up to you."

***

In the waiting room, finding the flower print in the carpet more irritating with each step, Alex stopped pacing.

"Why'd you come here, anyway?" Haskell asked, still watching him.

"We were headed to Colorado," Alex told him. "Sharon has a great aunt in Craig she wanted to see. Kevin and I just came along to keep her company." As if preparing for a fight, Alex squared himself, displaying his full breadth to Haskell. "How come you and Brundy tried to stop us? How did you even know we were here?"

"We've got a trace on your credit cards," Haskell told him. "When you used yours to rent that SUV, we knew you were going to get yourselves into some kind of trouble, so we followed you to prevent it."

"What kind of trouble?" Alex asked.

"This kind," Haskell said. "The kind that can kill ya."

Dr. Reed interrupted, as he joined them "I'm afraid your friend with the crushed leg is dead. Bled to death."

Brundy was standing outside Sharon's door.

"How can anybody bleed to death with a tourniquet?" Alex challenged.

"He'd lost too much blood by the time the tourniquet was applied. There was nothing you could have done to save him."

"I want to see him."

"See that he's given as much time with his friend as he likes," Dr. Reed told Haskell.

"The woman you brought with you has been stabilized. As soon as we give her something for pain, we'll transport her to the hospital. From what

Brundy told me, she'll need surgery on that arm. You're welcome to follow with Haskell if you like. Otherwise, feel free to stay here. The ambulance is out back."

Alex looked sadly down the hallway to the room in which Kevin lay and told Reed. "I'll follow."

"Then, don't take too long with your friend. Nothing more you can do for him anyway."

"What are you going to do with Kevin's body?" Alex asked.

"My nurse will call the local mortuary. His remains will be taken there, where you can claim them later. Ready Haskell?"

"Right with you, Doc." Haskell started toward the examination room where Kevin lay, not so subtly signaling Alex to hurry. Quickly opening the door, he hurried Alex inside.

"I'm Dr. Reed," Reed told Sharon, as he walked into the room where she was waiting. "Compound fracture," he observed to Nurse Ray, after removing the temporary bandage with which Nurse Ray had covered the wound.

"Yes, Doctor."

Gently holding Sharon's forearm, he more closely examined the piece of splintered ulna sticking through her skin at a forty-degree angle. "You'll need surgery," he told her. "Any other injuries?" he asked Nurse Ray.

"Just bruises and soft tissue injuries."

"We'll give you something for pain, then transport you to a hospital for care. Have you ever had morphine?"

"No."

"Are you allergic to anything?"

"Not that I know of." His professional manner and easy, gentle voice comforting, she relaxed.

"Lay back."

Nurse Ray handed him a syringe half full of clear liquid.

"I'll take her from here," he told Ray, strapping a rubber tube around Sharon's arm and injecting her. "You call the mortuary."

As Sharon's body absorbed the dose of sodium pentothal, she tasted onions. "Mortuary?" she sighed as her eyes blurred and her mind receded into darkness.

Chapter Forty-five

Present Day Vernal Utah
6:00 p.m.
April 26

O h, that man in there," Dr. Reed told Nurse Ray. He was referring to the nearest examination room and Kevin's body. "Just before he died," Reed continued, "he told Mr. Haskell he wanted to be cremated and his ashes dispersed by his family in the Great Salt Lake."

Several feet away, Brundy was pushing the gurney Sharon was on out of her examination room, out the side door, and into an outdated, white ambulance, void of markings. Alex was with Kevin, while Haskell stood watch outside the door.

"Advise Mr. Crawford at the mortuary," Reed continued, "that I'll personally guarantee these were the dead man's desires and ask him not to wait for the paperwork. Mr. Haskell will pick up his ashes for transport to the family in the morning. He'll bring the necessary documents then."

"Is there family I need to call?" Nurse Ray asked.

"No. I'll call them myself after the surgery."

Once Reed's instructions were carried out, there would be no body, no autopsy, no murder. Perfect.

"What is the deceased man's name?" she asked.

"Ralph Goodloe, that's with an 'oe', of Grand Rapids, Michigan. He told me he'd come to Utah on a personal pilgrimage to the Temple and came here to see the dinosaurs."

"What about his bill?" Nurse Ray asked.

"No bill. There was nothing I could do for him."

She smiled. "You're such and good, decent man. I wonder if these people realize how lucky they are to have found you this day."

"Thank you, Ray, but your mind should be on Mr. Goodloe, not on me. He has suffered and he has died, and it is our responsibility to help him find peace. Go ahead now. Do what I've asked, and I'll see you tomorrow. Call and reschedule my appointments. If there are complications with the surgery, I'll let you know."

"Yes, Doctor."

As Reed passed Kevin's room, he took Haskell's arm and drew him away from the doorway. "Everything's taken care of," Reed whispered. "His body will be disposed of without a trace, and there'll be no record of his death." He glanced toward the examination room where Alex was leaning over Kevin. "There won't be any witnesses, either."

Kevin was as pale as the white sanitized walls around him, as still as the table on which he lay. His eyes were closed, and as if with his last breath he had tried to speak, his mouth was open. The khakis he had worn for days were split from ankle to groin. The hair on his leg was matted with blood.

"Must have bled internally," Alex queried aloud but very quietly, as he viewed him. "It's odd, though. "I don't remember a wound that big, or him losing enough blood to kill him. I don't even remember a bruise other than at his wounds. There wasn't even that much blood in the SUV." He looked closer.

The left side of Kevin's knee was crushed. A broken chunk of the knee cap was protruding through the skin. "So where was all that bleeding?

Anatomy. Let me think. The femoral artery. The big one goes down the inner side of the leg." Alex began touching the area around and underneath Kevin's knee, concentrating on the inner side of it. The bones in the joint were in pieces, but there was not much blood. "Where is that artery?" He demanded of himself. He put his hands around Kevin's calf, gently sliding them toward the ankle. No wound and only minor bruises. He reached higher, cupping his hands just above the knee, slowly sliding them upward.

Suddenly, a strong, meaty hand dropped onto his shoulder and squeezed. "The ambulance is leaving," Haskell said. "Time to go."

Alex looked helplessly at Kevin's lifeless face, reluctantly letting go of Kevin's leg. "How's she doing," he asked Haskell of Sharon, never taking his eyes from Kevin.

"She's hurting. That's how she feels. And we're not waiting on you. If you want to go, you're gonna have to go now.

The ambulance Sharon was in, Dr. Reed in the passenger seat, drove passed the window. "Sorry, Kevin," Alex told him, as he hurried out of the room. "I have to go."

By the time Alex slipped into the passenger seat of the Impala, the old, unmarked ambulance carrying Sharon was halfway down the block. The stores in downtown had closed, and, at 5:00 p.m., the town was deserted. In the neighborhood, everyone was home having dinner, and so, it too was very quiet. The siren just as silent, the ambulance turned onto West 100 and headed east. "Hurry," Alex urged, as Haskell slowly backed down the drive.

Looking behind them, Alex's gaze fell on a dark red stain on the backseat. "Kevin bled to death in here, didn't he?" Alex sighed. "While his head was on Sharon's lap."

Ignoring Alex's discovery and the grief in his voice, Haskell said nothing.

"I thought the tourniquet would hold him if there was trouble," Alex murmured, his guilt overflowing. "I was less than two feet away from him all the way in to town, yet my back was to him. I didn't even turn around. He was dying, and I did nothing to help him."

Haskell seemed to be paying no attention to him at all as he backed onto the street and followed the ambulance east and then north through town.

"I can't believe it," Alex continued, not watching where they were or noting which streets they were taking. Only by chance did he look up to see a one-story brick building with a circular drive at the edge of town. The entrance was identified in bold red letters as "Emergency".

He stared at the ambulance transporting Sharon. It was driving past it.

"Heh, isn't that a hospital?"

"Ashley Valley? Yeah, but Doc's not taking her there."

"Where is he taking her?"

"He has his own facility in the country. She'll get better care there."

"Reed told us the town didn't have a hospital," Alex challenged in anger. "That one even has an emergency room. What the hell is he doing?"

"He didn't tell you because that hospital doesn't have an emergency doctor on staff. And he calls the doctor on-call this week 'birdbrain'. His hospital can give her good care. This one can't."

"Even if that's the case, wouldn't Dr. Reed be her surgeon?" Alex asked. "What does it matter who's on-call in emergency?"

"Don't know one way or the other. Just know Doc's takin' her to his." The instant the Impala crossed the town limits, Haskell stepped down hard on the accelerator, almost catching the ambulance carrying Sharon.

"How much further?" Alex asked, reluctantly sitting back into the seat.

"Not far," Haskell said. "Relax. Doc's taking care of her."

East was Dinosaur National Monument and the Cleveland-Lloyd Quarry where anyone with a permit could dig for fossils. The ambulance turned north onto highway 191, and Haskell followed.

The setting sun was bright in the sky behind and to the left of them as they drove through the rolling and desolate, sagebrush terrain of the Great Basin Desert toward Flaming Gorge. Fifteen miles further, the ambulance left the road and turned west onto an unkempt, rugged dirt road breaching the very heart of the desert. In a matter of seconds, it disappeared in the thick cloud of dust that trailed it.

"Reed have a monastery out here or something?" Alex asked, anxiously looking across the wilderness they were entering. When Haskell did not answer, he studied him. Haskell had not said a meaningful word since they left Dr. Reed's. Feeling nervous, Alex quietly searched for Haskell's gun, his eyes darting toward the holster Haskell wore on his belt. It was empty. Sweat poured from his brow as he casually, yet frantically searched the seat between them and the floor. He then peered into the trash-filled compartment in the driver's door. Nothing.

Haskell's left knee was bent. His foot was hugging the base of the seat. His left thigh was higher than his right. Beneath and behind the crook of his left knee, at mid-thigh, a bit of the gun handle was exposed, a dark, dull piece of metal easy to reach if needed. It was Haskell's 9mm, and its barrel was pointed toward the door.

Alex quickly turned away. "You sure you guys are FBI?" he quizzed.

The look in Haskell's eyes was hostile as he turned toward Alex. "What do you mean by that crack?"

"Nothing," Alex back peddled. "Just wondering."

"My wallet's in my breast pocket. Take it out and look for yourself."

Alex hesitated.

"Go on. I won't hold it against you."

Alex slowly reached into Haskell's pocket, drew out his wallet, and put it on the seat.

"Go on. Open it up," Haskell badgered, almost daring him.

Alex paused, picked up the wallet and slid it back into Haskell's pocket. "S'okay, I'm satisfied. Sorry I doubted you."

As they went deeper into the desert, dust swarmed through the Impala's vents, cracks, and any crevice through which the powder could penetrate. Breathing was difficult. The haze caused inside further limited the already dismal visibility of the road up ahead, and the ambulance became a blur.

"Not very air tight, is it?" Alex snapped. Each mile into the wilderness would make his options fewer, any imprisonment more secure.

"You'd leak too, if you rammed an SUV," Haskell blurted, his choice of words incriminating.

"Rammed?" Alex pressed. "You said your brakes failed. That you couldn't stop. By the way," Alex realized, "there hasn't been any trouble with the brakes since then, has there? Or, do they just fail when convenient?"

Haskell glared at him, pressure within his temple squeezing the lid of his right eye closed. "Better watch what you're saying," he warned. "'Cause you're makin' me mad." His fingers drummed the steering wheel, nervously and unpredictably, until his right hand released it and slid down the rim, coming to rest on his right thigh immediately across from his gun.

Alex eyes were riveted on Haskell's hand. "You shouldn't take what I say so personally," he soothed. "I didn't mean anything. With Kevin dying and Sharon hurt, I'm just upset. Had to blame somebody, didn't I? I know you didn't mean to hit us. Forgive me?" he appeased, his gaze now fixed on the gun

With a deep, full-breathed sigh, Haskell left the gun where it lay and put his hand back on crest of the steering wheel, clearing the tension. Without referring to the incident again, he paused, took a second deep breath, and rolled down all the windows. Resting his left elbow out the window, he leaned toward it, stretched his head back, and breathed deeply once more. "Might as well let her fly," he laughed, as fine, billowing dust and the cold evening air engulfed them.

Air slowly streamed from between Alex's lips as he pursed them in a whisper and sighed, "Whew."

The dust outside was a light brown cloud limited to the range of their headlights. Darkness fell, and the sheer rock bluffs on either side became mere shadows. His face and clothes coated, his lungs full of fine powdery dirt, Alex coughed. "How much further did you say?"

Haskell checked his odometer. Yet seemingly tired of the question Alex had already asked a dozen times before, he didn't answer.

All around them was darkness and dust, with no visible landmarks or clues to give away their location. Broken through snake infested territory and leading nowhere, the road seemed endless. Then suddenly the dust cleared. The road ahead was empty. Sharon and the ambulance were gone.

Chapter Forty-six

The Great Basin Desert
Present Day Northeast Utah
9:00 p.m.
April 26

There was nothing in the distance against which the headlights of the Impala could reflect except a giant, sheer walled, red bluff. Skirted by huge granite rocks, it was a massive silhouette against the three-quarter moon. "What happened to the ambulance?" Alex asked, near panic.

"The ambulance did what we're going to do," Haskell wearily told him as he turned right onto a second dirt road, more primitive even than the first. Down the high, bottom-busting center, were thick, broken growths of weeds and sagebrush. Bumping and scraping them, the Impala rounded the bluff and headed north. In front of it, at the edge of its high beams, reappeared the now familiar trail of dust.

Alex glanced at the odometer, if nothing else, he would know how many miles were between that turn and the next. He rubbed his eyes and sat back. His body beginning to feel the soreness resulting from the accident earlier that day, he leaned back and relaxed, his eyes not straying from the ambulance ahead of them.

"Got an aspirin?" Haskell asked, apparently sore himself.

"Don't carry any."

"Look in the glove box. Maybe there's some in there."

Alex dug inside the large, cluttered lock box, through and around the papers, flashlight, tissue, screw driver, pliers, flare and more, and finally found a small bottle of aspirin. "How many?" he asked.

"Three."

"Mind if I have a couple?" Alex asked.

"Help yourself."

With nothing to drink, they swallowed their aspirin dry and whole.

"What kind of place is this anyway?" Alex casually asked about their destination, willing to venture one more query.

"A private hospital."

"Any other doctors besides Dr. Reed?"

Haskell reached for his visibly throbbing temple and rubbed it with the palm of his hand. "Have one of those damned migraines," he blurted. "Feels like my heads gonna blow off."

"Sorry about that. Too bad we don't have anything stronger than aspirin," Alex soothed. "You have any hand warmer gels or muscle relaxers you could massage onto the back of your neck?"

"Don't have anything, not even a first aid kit," Haskell moaned.

"Want me to drive so you can relax?"

Like a rattler, Haskell turned his head toward Alex and struck, glaring with a venomous, threatening stare.

"Okay, okay. You drive. I'm just trying to help."

"All we need is to have you get us lost out here or hung up on this god damn center strip."

Alex paused, waited a few minutes and asked again, "So," he repeated, "are there any other doctors at Dr. Reed's hospital?"

Haskell sat back, pressed his hand against his temple and told him, "No, but Jake, the nurse practitioner, is on duty almost all the time."

"So there's no orthopedist to repair Sharon's arm?" Alex asked.

"Don't need one. Dr. Reed can do it. He's repaired plenty of broken bones."

"Coming from a big city, I guess I'm just spoiled. There probably aren't any specialists out here, are there?"

Haskell did not answer.

The dust cloud ahead of them seemed to move closer as the ambulance slowed and turned into a drive that led into an adobe walled compound. As the ambulance reached the gate, Haskell pulled up behind it and stopped.

Through the windows in the back doors, Alex could see Brundy get out from the driver's seat, walk to a box mounted on an adobe column and speak into a microphone. "Dr. Reed and Wes Brundy with a patient," he said, waving to a camera mounted near the top of the wall.

"Let the Impala in behind us."

Brundy got back behind the wheel, and the gate slowly opened. Rolling onto the graveled, circular drive of a beige, single-storied, adobe-walled facility, the ambulance stopped in front of what must have been the patient's entrance.

Alex looked for any identifying signage, but there was none. "What's the name of this place?" he asked, as Haskell parked the Impala a few feet away from the door.

"Hospital," he said, somewhat hostilely, shutting off the car and any further questions. No longer hiding its location, he drew the gun out from under his thigh. "Let's go. Don't know about you, but I could use some soup." Still holding the gun in his hand, not pointing it in any particular direction, he waited. Not pressing him, Alex got out of the car and took a quick look around.

With the bright security lights around the perimeter glinting off the rolls of concertina wire strung along the top of the compound walls, Dr. Reed's hospital looked like a ranch style asylum. The glass entrance was protected by steel-barred gates, locked by remote control from the reception desk inside. Haskell waved at the receptionist on duty, and she opened them.

"Wait over there," Haskell told Alex, pointing to a stale corner lined with industrial gray, metal chairs with thin padded cushions. Not seeming to care whether Alex went over there or not, Haskell turned his attentions back to the receptionist. "Got any soup left," he asked the grandmotherly woman behind the desk.

"Just some canned stuff," she said, lip curled. "Kitchen's closed. Cook's gone to her room." She watched as Haskell headed for the kitchen door, calling after him, "Just don't touch the clam chowder. That's mine."

The walls in the reception area were a high gloss, emerald green enamel. The floor tiles alternated between mustard and white. Alex smiled. "Contractor must have been color blind," he mumbled. There were no magazines in the room and only a few plants, all behind the desk with Grandma. "Not exactly hospitable," Alex murmured, no longer amused. Pacing back and forth, searching for Sharon, he peered down the halls on either side of the reception desk. "Where'd they take her?" Venturing to explore the hallway on the left, he walked down it and past several locked and windowless doors, their occupants, if any silent. He was about thirty feet down that hall, when Jake, the nurse practitioner, came up the other hallway, the one on the receptionist's right.

Summoning Haskell out of the kitchen, Jake told him of Sharon, "We've got her ready for the operating room. "Where's Caldwell?"

As if suddenly remembering Alex, Haskell quickly looked into the reception area. "Where is he?" he demanded of the receptionist.

"Down there," she gestured, never having lost sight of him.

Jake grinned. "Lost him, huh? Better hope Doc doesn't find out."

. "He's no more lost than I am," Haskell argued.

"Doc says we don't need him anymore," Jake told him. "Got her here without a fuss. Got him here without anybody knowing his name, and nobody's the wiser. Got to say, I was beginning to think you guys'd never catch 'em."

"I was just going to have some soup," Haskell whined. "Can't I at least eat first?"

"Doc says, 'now.' You can eat when you're finished."

"Isn't anybody going to help me? Where's Brundy?"

"Doc told him to call Samson to let him know what's happening. I've got to handle the anesthetic. You're on your own."

Haskell sighed in disgust. "The usual place?"

"Yeah, and hurry. The sooner you finish, the sooner we can all have something to eat." He handed Haskell a twelve-inch-long zip tie. "Use this."

Haskell then turned, and following Alex down the hall, called, "Hey, Caldwell, Sharon wants to see you before her surgery."

"Where is she?"

"In prep. I'll take you there."

Dropping his guard, Alex unquestioningly followed Haskell through the reception room and down the second hallway, where the colored floor tile was dark green and the walls were a glossy, ugly mustard. "Nice place," he quipped. "How's she doing?"

"Fine."

They walked about forty feet and turned right, down a hall with light blue tile and glossy, pink-orange walls. Alex counted at least twenty windowless doors as they passed. "Glad my stomach's empty," Alex critiqued, "all these colors are making me nauseous." He followed Haskell to the end of the hall and to a door marked "Procedures."

"In here." Haskell gestured to the door as he stepped back to let Alex go first.

Peering through a small, wire mesh window in the door that revealed basically nothing, Alex pushed the bar handle. He was brought to an abrupt stop. The door was locked. "What the...?" he questioned. He turned around, right into the barrel of Haskell's 9 mm pistol.

Jabbing the end of it into Alex's chest, Haskell aimed it directly at Alex's heart. "Just do as I say," Haskell told him. Across the hall was another windowless door. Haskell gestured in that direction.

"My cell?" Alex asked, sarcastically.

"Go on," Haskell ordered, handing Alex the key. He removed the gun from Alex's chest long enough to let him walk past, then shoved it into Alex's back, never changing his target. Pressed against the left of Alex's shoulder blade, the barrel was still aimed at Alex's heart. One sudden move, and Alex would be dead.

The doorway led, not to a room, but into another hallway. That hallway was an ugly turquoise. Down it was another collection of rooms, again with windowless doors. At the end of the hall there was a gray, fire door with a green light marked "Exit."

"We'll go out here," Haskell told him.

Through the fire door the night was bright with floodlights. Bordering the building outside was an open strip about ten feet wide paved with gravel. It ended abruptly at the tall, adobe, perimeter wall. Through the perimeter wall, about twenty feet to the left of them, was a small, wooden door. There was nobody else around.

Pressing the barrel of the gun even harder against Alex's back, Haskell demanded, "Go on." In front of the small, wooden door in the wall, Haskell stopped him. "We're going out here. The key I gave you is a master." He prodded Alex to open it. A second door was on the other side of it, a steel door that barred the way to the desert outside the perimeter. There was a spotlight flooding the area, illuminating nothing but desert and sage. Cold darkness was the backdrop.

Haskell nodded toward the left and to a shallow rise, barely visible under the perimeter lights. "Head off in that direction. I'll tell you when to stop."

Alex suddenly turned pale and shuddered. His heart started pounding, his stomach and buttocks to flutter. His muscles lost their tone, and he could hardly walk through powdery dirt that was putting up no resistance.

The rigid mouth of Haskell's gun was bruising in its tenacity, terrifying in its proximity to his heart. To jar it at all meant certain death. To turn or trip or do anything to stop him would be suicide. As if struggling through deep sand, Alex's feet moved slowly and with mincing steps. Sweat poured onto his brow, seeped through his shirt, and down his legs.

In what seemed an instant, time was out. "Far enough," Haskell told him, as they reached the rise.

Frantic, Alex searched for a rock, anything he could use as a weapon. "Why do you want to kill me?" he asked, his voice shaking. "I don't even know what you guys are doing."

"Sure you don't," Haskell said, sarcastically. "There's a box behind the brush. Get the shovel out of it and start digging."

"Oh," Alex sighed, "You're not going to make me dig my own grave?"

His eyes fixed and dull, Haskell stared at him.

"Guess you don't care, do you?" Alex observed, "You're going to kill me, and you don't even care. Chills pricked his spine as he retrieved the shovel from the box behind the brush. Holding it as if it was a club, turning it in his hand, he paused a moment, studied Haskell's gun and then sighed. "So, where do you want me to dig?" he asked.

"Here," Haskell told him, pointing to a spot at the base of the rise.

"All I want to see is your back," Haskell said, as Alex turned slightly, looking as though he was going to throw a shovel full of dirt in Haskell's eyes. "Put the shovel down and turn away from me."

Obediently, Alex dropped the shovel and squared his back to him.

"Go on, pick it up and dig. You turn toward me again and you won't have to dig your grave.

As Alex dug, distracted while he fragilely planned an escape, he did not realize the pace of his digging was increasing. The dirt was soft, and the hole was growing too quickly.

"That's good enough," he suddenly heard Haskell say. "Don't need to meet any burying codes out here."

Startled, Alex stopped. He was rib deep in the hole.

"You don't want to do this," he said. "You're FBI. You're supposed to defend, not break the law."

Haskell's eyes were soft, blurry puddles devoid of conscience. "I do whatever I'm told to do. Whatever's necessary to fulfill the will of God and to protect and defend His people. Gentile laws and organizations mean nothing to me. Now, gently put the shovel on the edge in front of you and get out."

His hands shaking, his buttocks now in a twitch, Alex put the shovel on the far edge of the hole and climbed out.

"Come around here and turn away from me," Haskell told him. "We have to do this quietly."

Panicked, Alex turned, rushed Haskell, and lunged. "Aghh...h...h," he groaned, as he suddenly collapsed.

Haskell had been prepared for him. As Alex lunged, he drove the butt of his gun into Alex's head.

In agony, Alex rolled onto his stomach, helpless to stand. He could do nothing as Haskell pushed his head into the dirt and shoved his knee into Alex's temple. He could not resist as Haskell forced his hands behind his back and tied a zip tie around his wrists.

"On your knees," Haskell ordered, finally getting off of him. When Alex did not move, he picked him up by the elbow, threw him toward the grave and forced him to kneel at the edge.

His head throbbing, his senses in a helpless fog, Alex teetered. His knees sank into the dust. As he tipped to fall in, he felt a hand grab his collar and steady him. He was groggy and only vaguely aware that the hand then moved to his head, took hold of his hair, and lifted. His chin bobbing, his eyes half closed and dreamy, he felt another hand move closer, pressing something long and sharp against his throat.

Chapter Forty-seven

Present Day Philadelphia, Pennsylvania
12:30 p.m.
April 26

T he formal dining room in the two-hundred-fifty-year-old Continental Club was tomblike in its stillness. The white columns and wainscot, the raised figures on mauve wallpaper, were a drastic departure from the dark, somber wood paneling of just two decades ago, a result of the old guard having bowed to the desires of younger members in the 1980s to update and remodel.

Tables were set with fine, white linen, expensive china, and silver flatware made of gold and silver. For long conversations in which the fates of corporations, executives, and presidents were decided, they were deliberately spaced apart for privacy.

A waiter dressed in white approached a table even more isolated than the rest situated only a few feet from the garden at the far end of the room. His shirt and jacket were starched and stiff, and his black, spotless tie was in a perfect bow. Before interrupting the two men at the table, he waited patiently for his presence to be acknowledged. "More wine, Senator?" the waiter then asked of a well-dressed man in his forties with graying, dark hair and eyes like polished walnut.

Senator Kenneth J. Albrecht wore a gray, silk suit, pink shirt, and expensive Italian loafers. He had a soft, friendly look about him and was a favorite among conservatives. He was attractive and a leader in his party. His reelection seemed secure.

As he looked up and smiled, his teeth were beautiful. "Not right now," Senator Albrecht told the waiter. He then whispered, "Do me a favor. Don't seat anyone closer to us than twenty feet and give us about half an hour."

"Yes, sir."

Albrecht waited until the waiter was out of hearing distance, checked about for anyone else who might be able to hear, then in all seriousness, his face turning to stone, he asked his companion, "Where are we?"

"We're completely on track," the other man at the table, the man called 'Samson', told him. Though Samson's new silk suit and sage green tie were in perfect harmony with his surroundings, the strong odor of his citrusy and leathery cologne was distracting.

"I asked you to pick something up for me. Have you?" Senator Albrecht asked.

"Yes, the package was delivered to the factory yesterday."

Albrecht grinned, abandoned the conversational code they had been using, lowered his voice and leaned forward. "How did you find her?"

Samson chuckled at his own cleverness, and he too examined their surrounding for anyone who might hear before he whispered. "Through 'WhoWereMyGrandparents.com.' We planted a virus in the software set to trigger whenever certain names came up during genealogical searches."

"What names?"

"Remember in the 1970s, when researchers at the University of Utah began combining Church genealogical records with public health and mortality records? The database those records created today contain information about 1.6 million people, Mormon and non-Mormon alike. The information in that data can be used all over the country to cross reference families with cancer clusters, asthma, and diabetes. It can even be used for breast cancer and left-handedness. There's no doubt in my mind that in utilizing that data Project Samson will soon realize its secondary objective. In no time at all, we'll be able to cleanse all genetic defects from our membership and ultimately, engineer the perfect race."

As he continued, Samson's voice rose in excitement, "Genetic tissues and embryos are being taken from Caucasians everywhere in the world. From Catholics, Protestants, Jews, and even the unfaithful, all with the aim of identifying those traits and genes that will make us flawless. We already have a catalog of three quarters of a million surnames whose descendants are known to be free of genetic defects.

"When a visitor to 'WhoWereMyGrandparents.com', or any of the related sites asks for information about anyone with one of the names we have identified, the virus captures the visitor's e-mail address. It then invades the user's hardware. From that hardware, the virus obtains and secretly emails us all the personal data stored there. The virus works even if the inquiry is made by someone whose surname matches another family member already in the database.

"If the user is a woman, or the search has been conducted on behalf of a woman, we review the data obtained and determine whether that woman is suitable for participation in the project. Basically, whether she's healthy and is of childbearing age. We have agents planted in fertility clinics on both coasts whose job is to identify and take for our use eggs likely to be perfect. We also have nurses in obstetrics clinics in every major city and in small towns in the Midwest to identify potential surrogates. The nurses see to it that any embryo conceived by an unacceptable father is aborted and that every fetus is miscarried. They also make it appear the surrogate dies during the procedure. The clinic then helps the family arrange for the surrogate's cremation, and another body is substituted. With their family believing her dead and cremated, the vessel surrogate is taken to one of our breeding facilities.

"Sixteen and seventeen year old girls whose families have turned them away because of their pregnancies are the easiest to obtain. Gentile women with blue eyes and red or blond hair are a little harder to secure. Yet we have been able to ship scores of them to our facilities."

"What about Joan's daughter?" Albrecht asked.

"Like I say," Samson continued, "our records contain the names of hundreds of thousands of nonmembers. When you asked me to search for Joan Ashley's daughter, I fed the virus Joan's name and found her."

"Where was she?"

"Atlanta. Her married name is Emily Brighten."

Albrecht lowered his eyes. Very many years ago he had fallen in love with Joan Ashley, a tall, joyful creature of nineteen, with blond hair and green eyes. Though he had been warned she was not a member of the Church and not likely to convert, he let his youthful emotions get away from him. She broke his heart when she said, "No."

"Your donation will be thawed, and in less than three weeks, Emily will be bred with them,"

Samson assured him. "Will you want any of the product for yourself?"

Albrecht paused. He wanted a son, a genetic substitute for the son he would have had with Joan. He could adopt him without scandal. It would be easy to cover the trail of his birth and to hide the truth from the press. Why, he could carry him in his arms all the way to the White House. "I'll let you know," he told Samson.

"Now tell me, if I get the nomination, will I win the Presidency?"

"I don't know Senator. We control the Mountain States. Conservative Republicans and their ultra conservative offshoots control many of the rest, as well as Middle America. You've got your home state of Pennsylvania in the bag. Ohio, Missouri and Florida will be the challenge. Get those states and a few more, and you'll win."

"I don't suppose there'll be much help for me from Project Samson?"

"No, not yet. We won't control that much of the electorate for some time. We've only got five facilities operating in Ohio. At 6.82 products per vessel per year, we can produce only 511.5 there this period. Those statistics also ring true in the facilities we have in Connecticut and Alabama. By this time next year, we will have doubled our output in New York and Missouri. The facilities we've opened in Utah and Arizona are to manufacture products that are to be sent to other states on an as-needed basis.

"But we won't see any exponential growth for years. Not until the feminine products come of age and are old enough to reproduce at the same rate. Voting statistics won't begin to be altered for another fifteen years. So, I'm afraid you're on your own."

"I hope I succeed. A Presidency for us in the next eight years will certainly expedite our plans."

"Keep thinking positive, Senator. Our Prophet believed our destiny was to control this country. If he hadn't been murdered, maybe we'd already control it."

"I can hide the fact that I'm a member of the New Sons of Dan," Albrecht said. "Only a few trusted men know that. Do you think my being Mormon will hurt me?"

"Appeal to the religious right. Talk about God and his commandments. Hold God up before them and pray. People are afraid to challenge anyone who touts God. We can't determine your election, Senator," Samson continued. "There just aren't enough of us yet. But, someday there will be.

"There will come a day when all the generations of sons and daughters we breed multiply into millions. Then we will control the vote. The system of laws we will pass will finally bring to fruition the Word of God interpreted by the Book of Mormon, and we will use our system of courts to enforce them.

"Implementing the dictates of the Lord and Joseph Smith, we will build a new country whose people cringe before them and obey. By the year 2090 our God will be the symbol of this country, and the country will be ours. Time is on our side."

Chapter Forty-eight

Present Day Utah
6:30 p.m.
April 26

As he stirred from unconsciousness, his mind swirled with vague images. Heavy and still, his limbs were like fresh cut wood, his torso an unwilling stump. He forced the images to slow down and tried to remember what happened. Yet, he was weary and dizzy, and nothing in his mind made sense to him. He didn't even know who he was. "Am I dead?" he mumbled.

Inside him a presence was growing, a pressure he did not understand. It was surrounding him, crawling over and about his bones, shooting thousands of wires through his flesh and finally surfacing to catch fire. *I'm not dead. I'm in pain*, he realized.

He wanted to cry, but he had no voice. He wanted to run, but he couldn't move. His only avenue of expression was tears, and from within his closed, unseeing eyes, tear drops flowed across his temple and into his ear.

"On my," Nurse Ray cried, when she saw them. She was cleaning Kevin's face, preparing him for cremation. She stared at the streaming tears, dropped her washcloth, then ran to the examination room next door. Retrieving a stethoscope, she returned and pressed it to Kevin's chest. No heartbeat. "Ooohhh," she sighed with relief. "For a minute there I thought we'd made a terrible mistake."

She grinned, put the stethoscope around her neck and picked up the washcloth. The instant she touched it to his face, his lips began to move as if he was trying to talk. "My God," she cried.

Ripping the stethoscope from her neck, she jammed the earpieces into her ears and placed the chest piece onto the side of his neck, directly over the jugular vein. There was a faint, yet distinctive, series of thumps. "Help us all," she prayed.

Hands shaking, she reached for the phone.

Chapter Forty-nine

Present Day
9:30 a.m.
April 27

Heavily medicated for pain, content to sleep, neither the ache in her groin nor the prickle in her arm were enough to wake Sharon. Not yet knowing where she was, or caring, she drifted in and out of dreams and only gradually awakened.

As her senses began to clear, she became aware of a cinnamon odor. It was at first pleasant and comforting, almost relaxing, though in an unfamiliar way. As it lingered, the scent mixed with that of sage. It became peppery and spicy and was suddenly heavy in the room. As if it was enveloping her, the scent seemed to wrap an invisible shroud around her face. It became claustrophobic. Fear began to rise in her heart, and all it once it suffocated her. She started. Frantically trying to brush the odor away with her good arm, she opened her eyes, felt the sting of the broken arm she was flailing, and woke to a man staring at her. His dark, rich walnut eyes penetrated her soul, and for an instant, kept it captive. He leaned closer. The odor smothering her was his cologne.

"Thought I might have come too early," the man said. His thick, black hair, suffused with pomade, its odor conflicting with his cologne, was shiny and combed strait back from his face. "How's your arm?"

She instantly recognized him. "Agent Carter, what are you doing here?"

"I came to see you. To tell you something."

"How's Kevin? Where's Alex?"

"In due time. You and I need to talk first."

"Did you find Kim?" she asked of her sister.

"Yes, we found her."

"Where is she? Is she all right?"

"She's just fine. As a matter of fact, she's here."

"Wonderful. Can I see her?"

Standing straight, Carter pulled away from her, his expression changing to one of self-satisfaction. "I'm afraid that won't be possible."

"Why not?" Sharon demanded. "I thought you said she was fine." Carter's question and answer game was beginning to irritate her.

"She *is* fine," he emphasized. She just doesn't know you're here."

"Why doesn't she?" Sharon pressed.

Ignoring her question, he smiled, looked aimlessly about the room they were in, turned away from her and walked toward the door. He stopped near her feet and turned toward her again. Still looking about him, as if theirs was merely a casual chat, he conveyed to her, "They told me you were brought to this facility heavily sedated. Do you know where you are?"

Sharon looked quickly around. She was obviously on a gurney, in a hospital or clinic of some kind. She looked to her left. Her broken arm was in a cast. "I'm at the hospital in Vernal, aren't I?"

"Not exactly," he teased. "If you were to look outside, you would discover you're in the desert, some distance north and west of Vernal. At a private clinic."

"Okay," Sharon snipped, impatiently. "So I'm at a clinic. What clinic?"

"My 'investors'."

Surprised and more than a little suspicious something was wrong, Sharon quieted. "Why would investors give an FBI agent money to run a medical clinic?"

"Ah...h...h, now you're asking the right questions," he smugly commented. "They are not giving money to an FBI agent. They are giving money to 'Project Samson'."

As if hit by a blunt, brutal instrument, Sharon flinched. Angry and frightened, she stared at him.

"I thought that would get your attention," Carter grinned. "You, Alex, and Kevin were right about everything."

Even in her drug induced haze, it took Sharon only a moment to put it together. "Then your investors are Sons of Dan? And, you're their leader?"

"No, you might say I'm just a middle manager. I'm only responsible for the Utah-Arizona operation. A much higher authority is in charge of the entire operation, and I report directly to him."

"And, Project Samson *is* the operation?" Sharon confirmed. "If you don't mind telling me, what is Project Samson?"

As if he were considering all the risks involved in responding, Carter paused. "I guess there's no harm in your knowing," he decided. "It's not like you're going to go anywhere."

Sharon's chest began to tighten, her heart to beat faster. What reason could there be for him to say that? Why would they bring me here and set my arm if they were going to kill me? They could have killed me in Vernal. Why here? Setting her jaw, refusing to betray her growing fear, Sharon listened.

"Project Samson is an extension of our Prophet's dream. It's a plan to repopulate the earth with our own people. Beginning here in the United States. This clinic is only one of twenty clinics in various stages of activity. Most of them are located in the Midwest and on the eastern seaboard where people aren't as prejudiced against us. Those clinics are older and more established than the ones in Utah and Arizona.

"It was your brother-in-law who gave us the idea. Wayne's work with preemies, especially in multiple births, was brilliant. His research has helped mothers carry as many as seven to full term, while at the same time, keeping the babies from becoming too large for normal delivery.

"By controlling the mother's intake of sugars, he regulated the levels of insulin binding to the fetal insulin receptors that promote rapid cell division. That, in combination with customized preparations of vitamins, minerals and hormones and with his controlling fetal levels of the growth factor IGF-11, makes normal, healthy deliveries possible. Hundreds of fully developed, three to five pound babies are being born in multiples of four or five. After birth, they are given concoctions that stimulate growth, and within six weeks, they are at normal size and birth weight. Wayne's protocol has proved to be genius," Carter added.

"What happens to the women who bear these babies?" Sharon asked, her concern for Kim suddenly crowding out her own fears.

"Our vessel breeders are carefully selected for the program and are given excellent medical care from the very beginning. When they are brought to one of our facilities they are thoroughly examined to make sure they are healthy and fertile and that they don't carry any infectious diseases or have any genetically transmittable conditions. If a vessel qualifies, and most of them do because we have prescreened them, she is immediately started on injections of Lupron, which will help stimulate multiple egg development.

"On the ninth day of treatment, estrogen tablets and injections of FSH, a follicle stimulating hormone, are added and are continued until day eighteen. FSH and Lupron are then dropped, and progesterone is added. Her eggs are harvested on day nineteen. On that same day, we fertilize the harvested eggs with sperm donated by one of our members. Five days later, the vessel breeder is impregnated with the fertilized eggs."

"I'm not talking about the process of In Vitro Fertilization," Sharon corrected, impatiently. "I'm talking about the women 'vessels' you do this to. What happens to them?"

"After there is a birth, the babies are distributed," Carter patiently explained, "and the process of In Vitro Fertilization begins again. For as long as they are productive, the women themselves remain, relatively comfortable, in a facility like this one.

"We are very proud of our program. The vessels we utilize are so well cared for, we seldom lose one through child birth. As a matter of fact, I don't recall having lost more than two or three in the last three years. Not bad for a fledgling operation, even if I do say so myself. That inventory you've been showing around should tell you exactly how many have died in Utah and Arizona from our inception. That's what the letters 'dd' mean in the column describing the vessels' conditions."

Sharon pictured in her nearly photogenic mind every detail of Samson's Inventory. It showed that at least seven of their captive women vessels in

Utah and Arizona had died. Even when he did not have to, Carter lied. She involuntarily shuddered with anger, yet her voice remained calm. "So, what happens to vessels who are no longer productive?" she continued, determined to learn as much as she could about the Project Samson.

"We haven't crossed that point yet, but when a vessel's child bearing years are over, we'll probably retire her somewhere. You understand, though," he said, quickly, "we'll never be able to free her."

"I understand," Sharon said, unable to hide her disdain for him. "What happens to the women who are brought here and don't qualify?"

He sighed and almost sincerely said, "Regretfully, we have no place for them."

"What do you mean you have no place for them?" Sharon demanded, the anger inside her exploding.

"I mean we have no place to house them and no use for them. Just as we would livestock who come to the end of their usefulness, they are ended. They are brought here, humanely euthanized, and given decent burials in a graveyard outside the compound.

Shivers riffled down Sharon's spine. "So where's Kim? What's happening to her? Did she qualify?"

"Ohh, most assuredly. Kim will be an excellent vessel."

"What about Wayne? Just what happened to your genius?" Sharon wasn't sure how to feel about Wayne. Was he their pawn or did he voluntarily help them with this evil?

Carter's eyes were cold, his manner patient but unrepentant. "Wayne was fine until he started having second thoughts about the way were using the women. When we told him we wanted Kim for the project, he balked. Betrayed us. Broke his covenants to God of loyalty and obedience. He was a transgressor and needed help to find salvation."

Sharon recoiled. She knew exactly what he meant. Great Grandma Anna described the Blood Atonement murders in her diary. Tears welled in Sharon's eyes, and she asked, "Does Kim know what happened to him?"

"No, we told her Wayne was one of us and willingly surrendered her to us to further God's work. He told the children she was dead. We told her by giving her to us as our property, Wayne surrendered all rights to her and he would not see her again." Carter smiled. "Even we were surprised at how readily she believed us."

"What about Alex and Kevin? What happened to them? I don't remember anything after we got to Dr. Reed's office."

"They're dead, too, I'm afraid." Carter told her, still smiling. "We don't have much use for Gentile men here."

Sharon tried to sit up, but he pushed her back down. "My God," she accused, "what kind of people are you?"

"None, a woman need understand," he said, his smile disappearing.

Anger delaying her grief, she defiantly and sarcastically asked, "Have I been examined? Are you going to breed me, too?"

Carter's face was expressionless as he coldly informed her, "No, you're not suitable for the Project."

Stunned, realizing he was sentencing her to death, she lay quietly, waiting for him to continue.

"We want babies born who will grow up to obey us. Unlike Kim, you're stubborn and independent and would be too much trouble. Your product would be as stubborn as you. We don't tolerate renegades and aren't going to waste our resources breeding them."

"Then why bring me here? Why fix my arm?" She was clung tight to her original theory. They would have killed her with Kevin and Alex if they didn't plan to keep her alive for something. Otherwise, bringing her here made no sense.

Like a cold, icy wind battering her with its force, he told her, "When he operated, Dr. Reed didn't know we had already rejected you."

Though heartsick and frightened, Sharon summoned her courage. "You told me everything because you'd already decided to kill me, didn't you?"

"I didn't tell you everything," he corrected, grinning as if he was playing with her. "You're right in that you're going to die."

Despite herself and to his amusement, she gasped. "Is there some personal vendetta you have against me or something?" she asked.

His eyes twinkled, then he laughed. "Ever heard of Jacob Tuttle?"

"Grandma Anna's diary," she sighed, thinking of all the terrible things Jacob had done and of Hattie's finally cutting his throat.

"Let me introduce myself. My name is 'Neal Tuttle Carter'. Jacob Tuttle was my great grandfather."

"What does that have to do with you and me?"

"Your Great Grandma Anna used him. She then betrayed him with a man named John Wickens. Even after John's death, she refused to come to Grandpa Jacob. When he went to rescue her, to give her a home and care for her, she murdered him in cold blood then ran away. She took everything, even her children deserting the Church and condemning them forever. By the time the Avenging Angels discovered Grandpa Jacob's body her trail was cold. In all the years the Angels spent searching, she was never found. Nor have any of Jacob's sons, in any generation thereafter, found her daughters."

Carter grinned. "Until me, of course. When I found you and Kim, I told Wayne to give Kim up so I could finally reclaim Anna's descendants, to return them to the discipline of the Church and to Jacob's memory. I have chosen Kim for myself and to have her bred with my sperm. Through Kim, all of Anna's future descendants will be mine." He put his hand on Sharon's shoulder and menacingly grinned. "Mine and Jacob's.

"As far as you're concerned, my dear Sharon, I have chosen you to be the object of Jacob's ultimate revenge for Anna's murdering him. You, above all Anna's female descendants, will pay the price for Jacob's death."

Fear tore through Sharon like shrapnel, prompting her to run. She spit in his face, threw off her covers, and punched him in the gut as she swung her legs off the gurney, and bolted toward the door.

"Wes," Carter called, and suddenly, Brundy was blocking the doorway.

Chapter Fifty

*The Great Basin Desert
Present Day Northeast Utah
The Morning of April 27*

His cheek was buried in dirt, the powder up to his eyebrows and piled in the corner of his mouth, when Alex woke inside his grave. His knees were pressed to his chin. One arm inhumed in the dirt, the other wrenched behind him and trapped. He was crumpled in a ball and Haskell was spread out on top of him.

Sharp pain ricocheted between Alex's shoulders. His hands were still zip-tied behind him. "Get off me!" He pushed upward and butted his head as best he could against Haskell's chest, but there was no room, no space to make it effective. "What happened? What's wrong?" he demanded when the strain on his neck was too much.

Taking a deep, determined breath he pushed as hard as he could with the arm buried beneath him, straining a struggling to throw Haskell off. Yet, Haskell didn't move. "What is this? What are you doing?" Alex impatiently asked. "Is it some kind of sadistic game?" The walls of the grave were closing in on him. The more he struggled the more loose dirt fell in on him. Claustrophobia was overtaking him.

"Wake up. Get off me, you son of a bitch." Aiming at Haskell's chin drooping down in front of him, Alex spit. When that did not work, he wrestled his legs out from under Haskell and straightened them. Using his legs to help push, he lay on his stomach and shoved his back against Haskell's chest. Yet the man on top of him rose only as high as Alex pushed him, and when Alex stopped, settled back down with him. "Haskell?" There was something very odd about this.

Turning his head as far as he could, Alex peered at the face that now rested on the back of his armpit. Haskell was quite pale. He seemed to be staring at Alex, yet his eyes were as lifeless as glass, his pupils the size of pinheads. Alex worked his zip-tied hands to the closest piece of Haskell's flesh he could reach and pinched him. Haskell was cold, very cold, and his flesh was almost stiff. Off to one side, bent backward and twisted, Haskell's lifeless hand clutched a knife, and Alex remembered. Terrified as much as repulsed, he shuddered, thinking of that knife at his throat. He was about to make his move, about to take Haskell out at the knees when something happened. He remembered rolling, a weight heavier than a boulder shoving him down, and then nothing.

Squirming and sliding backward until his feet were firm against the other end of the grave, carrying Haskell's body with him, Alex pushed against the wall. Wriggling his chest across the ground, he pushed his rear end up cupping into Haskell's belly. Squirming free, he slid under Haskell's legs until his head was between them, lifted his shoulders, and shoved them off. Haskell's body fell in front of him.

First rising to his knees, Alex stood and, with his feet, lifted and pushed Haskell onto his side. Yet, even on his side, the tall, stocky Haskell nearly filled the grave. Able to fit one foot between Haskell's thigh and the wall of the grave, Alex stepped closer to Haskell's head. Turning around, reaching toward Haskell's neck with his tied hands, he felt for a pulse. "He's dead all right," Alex concluded. "Wonder what happened to him."

He looked again into Haskell's vacant eyes, felt for a pulse on the other side of Haskell's neck, and was completely satisfied. "What do you suppose killed him?" Alex examined Haskell's head and his clothing, but there were no bloodstains. "There's not even any blood on the knife. Well, that let's me out. I didn't kill him. Doesn't look like he killed himself, either. There are no wounds at all." Exhausted from his struggle with the dead man, Alex leaned against on the edge of the grave. "Maybe he was hurt when the Impala rammed us. Didn't he have a headache? That's right, he needed aspirin, and all he wanted to eat was soup. If he had a brain bleed, that aspirin could have killed him. He could have hemorrhaged and had a stroke. Wow," Alex breathed in relief. "At least he timed it just right. An instant later, and I'd have had my throat slit. We'd be sharing this grave."

The early morning air was warming, and he began to feel the heat of the sun on his face. "I've got to get Sharon." he suddenly realized.

Unable to climb out of the grave with his hands still bound in behind him, his back to the compound, the edge of the grave chest high, he stepped on Haskell, bent at the waist, and flopped over the edge like a seal. Rolling over, he got to his knees. He was about to stand when the cold, steel barrel of a twelve-gauge shotgun was pressed against his head.

Chapter Fifty-one

Present Day
Great Basin Desert
Morning
April 27

Strapped to the gurney with three-inch wide, nylon belts at her ankles and thighs, wrists, upper arms, and chest, Sharon was helpless to do anything but watch as Brundy opened the door for Doctor Reed's assistant, Jake. In dark green scrubs, devoid of designs and with nothing visible underneath, Jake was carrying a tray with large, plastic bags, long tubes with needles at the end of them, two clamps, and two clear vials with liquid in them.

Arms crossed, his face etched in pleasure, Neil Carter leaned against the wall facing her, almost gleefully watching Jake put the tray on the counter closest to her. "We thought maybe we should cut your throat," Carter grinned, casually and cruelly telling her, "but Jake had a different idea, and we thought we'd give it a try. We've never tried it before," he told her, "so it should be quite the experiment.

"It seems Jake moonlights, drives into Idaho and Arizona every once in a while to assist the State in some condemned guy's execution. Says he gets quite a kick out of it. Wants to branch out into California and Colorado someday so he can get more experience."

Like a child being praised for good grades, Jake turned toward Carter and sheepishly smiled. Their eyes met, and Jake went back to work.

"Wants to try it himself," Carter continued. "Wants to try it here, and he asked us if he could practice on you. After all, you *are* being executed for the crimes your Grandma Anna committed. Not only for the murder of my grandfather, Jacob, but for her crimes against the Church. Since Jake and I don't care about her salvation, or yours either for that matter, we're not going to worry about you atoning for her sins with blood. It's all right with us if you don't shed any. Blood atonement is such a messy thing, and we really can't blame Jake for not wanting to have to clean it up. Since you're in no condition to walk outside for the ritual anyway, we're going to do what's necessary in here."

Suddenly terrified, Sharon jerked, wildly and ineffectively flinging herself against the belts that held her. Her eyes on Jake and then on Carter, she pulled at them with all her might. When it was no use, she stopped. "You can't mean this," she said. Her heart was racing. Her breathing was short and fast.

"Of course I mean it," Carter said, feigning indignation. "Don't be ridiculous. The men in my family have spent generations trying to carry out our pledge to take revenge on Grandfather Jacob's murderer. And after all these years, it's me who gets to do it. That pledge is about to be fulfilled. Grandpa Jacob will finally be at peace, and by the time I'm through with you, my glory before God will increase a thousand times over. Of course I mean it," he repeated.

"Combine Jacob's revenge with the hundreds of children I will father in this facility and the facility in Arizona. Combine with those hundreds the thousands of children I give to the Church who were fathered by others, and one day, I will be a god. I will be as Adam is to earth, and the children born of Project Samson, through my blood and because of my efforts, will serve me forever in my celestial kingdom. "

Carter's usually dark walnut eyes were like crystals of ice, a fire flickering behind them. "Let's do it," he told Jake.

Having added gauze, tape, disinfecting wipes and other instruments to the tray with the plastic bags and tubing, Jake placed the tray on an instrument table and wheeled the table to Sharon's gurney. From across the room, he pushed a bag tree to the gurney and positioned it near the edge of Sharon's pillow. Then, he hung, one at a time, three bags full of various solutions, the solutions that would kill her. On a smaller, sterilized tray, was a three way stopcock, a long tube with two medication ports near the base; two plain tubes without ports, two wide bore catheters, each with a tiny feeder tube about two-inches long, a hypodermic, and a brown mustard colored, rubber tube.

Desperate to watch, Sharon turned her head as far she could to get a glimpse of him as he put together the materials needed for her execution. Yet, she could not see him, and when he reached for her right wrist, she recoiled, making a fist and rolling it.

"Hold still, I've got to reposition you a little." Jack loosened her wrist strap.

As he reached for the strap on her upper arm, she wrenched her hand free and struck out at him. Banging her fist against his arms, slugging him in the face when he tried to catch it, she fought, trying to drive him away while she desperately hunted for the release on her chest strap.

In response, Jake stepped back, cast a disapproving look at Brundy, and waited.

Ignoring the hand whipping in his direction, repeatedly slapping him, Brundy stepped forward, put his right thumb and fingers on each side of Sharon's throat and squeezed, strangling her. When her arm collapsed, Brundy released her and went back to the door.

Gasping, almost retching, as air poured suddenly back into her lungs, Sharon trembled. All fight was gone out of her.

No longer challenged, Jake stepped forward with a six-inch-wide board which was fitted with steel hooks. Placing the hooks over the top rail, he securely fastened the board to the gurney at a ninety-degree angle. Restrapping her wrist and upper arm, underside up, to the board, he tightly tied the rubber tube around her arm just above her elbow, and thumped the swelling vein. Satisfied the vein would do, he picked up one of the catheters, aimed for the bulging vein, and slid the needle inside.

Her heart bumping wildly, her body shaking in terror, Sharon begged him, "Please don't."

With cold, unpitying eyes, Jake looked at Carter for confirmation. When Carter nodded, he proceeded to attach the long, portal tube to the first I.V. and to the catheter's feeder tube. He then inserted the three-way stopcock into one of the medication portals, the point seemingly absorbed by the rubber dike protecting the portal's door. Running the other tubes from the remaining two I.V.'s, he attached them to the stopcock as well.

All the Luer locks, valve like delivery mechanisms, were closed.

Automatically, and without hesitation, Jake opened the Luer lock on the main feeder tube, releasing the drip. He watched as the fluid from the first I.V. slowly meandered into her arm.

My God, Sharon screamed inside. *What am I going to do?*

Sweat streamed from her brow and from between her legs. At the same time, terror turned her flesh cold, making the streams slow and sticky. A moment past, then two. As she stared at the steady drip that would soon take her life, she missed seeing, until near delivery, the hypodermic needle in Jake's hand. Pointing the needle upward, he was pushing the plunger, squirting clear liquid into the air, clearing the bore.

Wild eyed, almost hysterical as the ordeal dragged on, Sharon fixed her gaze on the hypodermic. Jake was inserting its needle through the rubber dike in the second portal. He pushed the plunger, and its contents joined with the fluid of the first drip, quickly flowing into her vein. Expecting pain, searing agony as she died, she gasped. Yet she felt nothing but the prick of the needle, and soon, she released her breath in a long, easy sigh.

"One hundred," Jake counted. "Ninety-nine," he continued, reaching for the stopcock and the lock that held back the third solution.

Fear and consciousness traveled together in the air that exited Sharon's lungs and escaped, leaving her in stillness and in a peaceful, forever kind of darkness.

Chapter Fifty-two

Present Day
The Great Basin Desert
The Morning of April 27

Dull charcoal gray and menacing, the single barrel of the twelve gauge shotgun never wavered as its bore peered into Alex's eyes. Staring back at it, his hands bound behind him, his heels pressed against his buttocks, Alex lay on his back unmoving.

"Over here," the voice behind the gun whispered.

There was a rush, and two more men appeared.

"I figured you'd be dead by now," one of them told Alex. The three men had their backs to the blazing morning sun, putting their faces in shadow.

"Looks like he killed somebody," the man with the gun said. "There's a body in the hole."

"Check him out, Metkers," the man apparently in charge ordered.

Handing an assault rifle to the man standing next to him, the man known as Metkers stepped out of the glare and to the edge of the grave. If it weren't for that powerful rifle, his down vest, plaid shirt, and hiking boots would have given him the look of a hunter. "Looks like Haskell," he observed, as he climbed into the hole. He rolled Haskell over and onto his back, and his observation was confirmed.

"Haskell, all right," the man in charge said.

With the back of his hand, Metkers felt Haskell's cheek. He then checked the jaw for flexibility. Peering through small, round glasses into Haskell's unresponsive and cloudy eyes, he announced, "Been dead several hours. He'll be rigored soon."

On one knee, the man seemingly in charge knelt down next to Alex's right shoulder, gently nudged the barrel of the shot gun away from Alex's forehead, and said in a gentle, almost benevolent way, "You people have been a real handful. You're lucky that's not you down there."

"Who are you?" Alex blurted.

The man in charge tucked his left hand under Alex's shoulder and helped him sit up. He nodded to the man holding the shotgun. The man drew a knife from the sheath hanging from his belt, and with one quick sweep, cut the zip ties around Alex's wrists.

"I'm Mark Ellis. U.S. Attorney. I believe we've met by phone," the man in charge told him.

"Am I glad to see you," Alex said with a sigh. As he rubbed his hands, reclaiming his circulation, he looked around. About a thousand yards away in the brush was a long, nondescript van beside which were four men in camouflage and flack jackets. They were arming themselves with automatic weapons and grenade launchers, putting over their shoulders a number of ten-by-ten inch black packets.

"Time to close this place down," Ellis told Alex. As Ellis stood, he motioned to his men, and moved out of the shadow. "Come on, let's get those women out of here." Ellis was middle-aged with graying, dark brown hair. He was clean-shaven and wore a potent aftershave. His hair was cut short, but his hands were manicured. He looked very out of place in plaid.

"How's Sharon Marshall?" Alex asked. "I know she's in there somewhere."

They were bent at the waist, stealthily moving through the brush, heading for the back door. "We don't know her condition," Ellis told him. "But, we're going to find out, and we're going to find out now."

In front of them and in the distance, dirt clouds billowed in long trails above the road. "Their transportation," Ellis said.

Relieved, Alex sighed, while above them, two helicopters circled, then landed.

Chapter Fifty-three

Present Day
April 27

In the procedures room where Sharon was being executed by lethal injection, eagerly watching the poisonous drugs dripping into her arm, Special Agent Neil Carter suddenly looked up. As if able to see through the ceiling to the helicopters circling over the compound, he reached for the door. "Stay here," he told Brundy, as he hurried into the hallway. "Jake, you come with me," he ordered over his shoulder.

Sharon was comatose. Death was only a threshold away.

"Take care of the files and sound the alarm," Carter told Jake, as they parted further down the hall. "Tell Haskell to arm himself and meet me out back," he added. "And, have him bring a couple of grenades, too. We got real trouble here."

Ten feet further on was a glass and metal box secured to the wall. A small sledge was attached to it for emergencies. Jake pulled the sledge out of the clamp that held it and used it to break the glass panel. Inside the box were two red, toggle switches. He pulled the toggle switch on the right, and instantly an ear-shattering siren, pulsating with alarm, sounded. Its release, starting a sequence of events, set his heart racing.

Steel bars automatically closed over patient room doors. Down each hallway, a nurse gathered patient records out of racks hanging outside the rooms while all the other nurses ran to a pre-designated emergency station. The patients' records were taken to the central file room and given to Jake.

The nurse delivering them then hurried to the emergency station. Having practiced the drill every week for months, everything went like clockwork.

The nurses were gathering at the opening to an escape tunnel. Dr. Reed was with them. In the central file room, Jake was placing the patients' records in a plastic box at the end of the row of file cabinets. Once they were stored in the box, Jake turned away from them, walked a few feet, picked up a crowbar hidden underneath a table, and counted, one stone at a time, as he walked across the granite floor to a stone four feet away with almost undetectable black streak across it.

First lifting the tile with the crowbar, he set it aside, exposing a locked, steel compartment. Inside the compartment were a bright red pushbutton and two more toggle switches. He pulled the first toggle. The floor beneath the cabinets responded, pulling away from the rest of the floor and sinking six feet, enveloping the cabinets. He pulled the second toggle, and a thick, steel plate slid from beneath the adjacent wall and covered them. As the wall then began to move forward, over the plate, narrowing the room, his hand shaking slightly, he pushed the red button. He had just activated a timer set to detonate explosives which would destroy the files in twenty-five minutes.

Digital copies of the records were stored in a cloud. The secret access codes to those records were destroyed at this site when he activated the timer. In less than half-an-hour, all paper evidence against them would be dust, and only Neil Carter could stop the explosion.

"Where's Haskell?" Jake growled, as he locked the file room behind him. "He's supposed to be defending Carter. I've got to tell him to bring the grenades." Jake ran to the next hall over, looked down the passage and did not see him. "God damn it." Maybe he's already with him. There's nothing I can do about it, anyway. If he's not where he ought to be, it's his own fault. Carter's on his own, and Haskell will have to find his own way out. I'm sure as hell not waiting for them." With only fifteen minutes left before the explosion, Jake rushed back to the Procedures Room where Brundy was standing guard over Sharon.

"What's happening," Brundy asked.

"Don't know, but until I get the all clear from Carter, we've gotta' keep going." Jake looked down at Sharon. "First thing's to get rid of her." Jake reached for the stopcock and released the Luer locks for I.V. drips three and four, the ultimate poisons. "Let's get out of here." Brundy was right behind him as he hurried into the hallway. "We gotta' meet Reed and get to the tunnel."

"No," Brundy said. "We've got to get Carter first."

"But the explosives? The hummers are waiting for us," Zake stammered.

"Don't care," Brundy told him, grabbing his arm and dragging him toward the back door. "Carter comes first."

The nurses and Dr. Reed were already half a mile away, down an underground passage crudely strung with dim, emergency lights. Hummers were to be waiting for them to take them cross country to an airstrip hidden near Flaming Gorge. It was fifty miles to the northeast, in a remote location with no access roads. From there, they would be flown to Mexico City, where they would stay until false identities were obtained for them. Once they had those identities, they could return to the United

States and be relocated to other Project Samson facilities.

On a gravel strip between the facility and the fortified outside wall defending it, and toward the rear of the compound, Special Agent Neil Carter watched as two helicopters landed several hundred feet away. He then patiently waited as Ellis and his advance team broke down the door through the fortified wall. Carter's face was calm, but his hands were sweating. "I thought I told you *I'd* take care of them," he growled, as Ellis approached.

"Like you took care of him?" Ellis sarcastically asked, gesturing toward Alex.

Alex's hands were now tied in front of him. Agent Metkers and the man with the shotgun were bringing him in as their prisoner. He listened intently as Ellis confirmed his complicity.

"Your blundering is the reason I'm here," Ellis told Carter. "Your private agenda and ineptitude have drawn attention from the editors of the New York Post. You've allowed three influential outsiders to spread suspicion about the Project. You've murdered Sharon Marshall and that mythologist. And if that weren't enough, you've killed our chief scientist. What on God's green earth were you thinking? These people are going to be missed. Their disappearances will draw investigations. It'll be hell trying to keep Washington out of it. Just how incompetent can one person get?"

Alex's chin dropped. His mouth opened, and he looked dumbfounded. Already stunned by Kevin's death, he had just learned of Sharon's. His head drooped onto this chest, and he closed his eyes. "My God," he sighed.

"You've failed in your duty to God and the Church," Ellis continued in his attack on Carter, "and I've got to clean up your mess."

Carter's face was beet red, his jaw rigid, as he defended himself through clenched teeth. "Don't you talk to me like that," he snarled. "So, some things have gone wrong. Just what do you think you're going to do about it?" Carter challenged.

"What do you think I'm going to do?" Ellis mimicked. "What has always been the punishment for failing your duty to God and Church?" His eyes squinting, vindictively peering at him, Ellis confirmed it. "You are to be taken to Salt Lake City and brought before the Tribunal. There, you will be judged. Both this facility and the one in Arizona will be destroyed. As the Project Manager, I will recommend Blood Atonement for your sins and the harm you have caused."

As if Ellis had bludgeoned the fight out of him, Carter cringed. His back stiffened, and he raised his head. Suddenly opening his eyes, blankly staring at nothing in particular, he visibly closed in on himself. Silent and unresponsive, the transformation taking place right in front of them, he clearly left this world for another to forever retire into its safety.

As Jake and Brundy came out the back door of the facility, two of the men dressed in camouflage came from outside into the compound. Their automatic weapons were at the ready, and they no longer carried the black packets they took from the van.

"The explosives set?" Ellis asked them.

"In place, Sir," one of them answered.

"Good."

Alex raised his head, and shouted, "No. There are people in there.

"Is he right? We blowing up the women, too?" Metkers asked.

"Are you kidding?" Carter said, somewhat annoyed. "They're too hard to replace, and we have too much invested in them. The vans that will evacuate them to our airport will be here any minute. From there, the women will be sent to our other facilities. They'll never know what happened here."

"To which facilities?" Metkers asked.

Ellis stared at him in disbelief. "You know I can't tell you that."

"Too bad," Metkers said. "But, you'll get other chances to tell me."

"What do you mean?" Ellis demanded.

In answer Metkers raised his 12-gauge shotgun and pointed at Ellis' gut. "Mark Ellis, also known as 'Samson', you are under arrest for conspiracy to commit murder, kidnapping, and felony assault. And, don't be surprised if those charges don't mount."

Alex was watching as the men at arms with Metkers raised their weapons and pointed them, not at Alex this time, but at Ellis, Carter, Brundy and Jake.

Turning to Alex, his gun at rest and his hand outstretched, Metkers introduced himself. "My name is Rawley Metkers. I'm special agent in charge of internal affairs, FBI, Project Samson." He smiled. "You're free Mr. Caldwell."

"Excuse me if I'm not just a little skeptical," Alex told Metkers. "But I've been *rescued* before. I've got to say, I'm confused." One of the agents with Metkers was cutting the zip tie around his wrists, releasing them.

Metkers put his warm, reassuring hand on Alex's shoulder. "Don't blame you a bit. But, you're okay now. We're legit. You're free."

"Free or not, I've got to see Sharon. Where is she?" he asked Brundy, glaring at him.

"In the Procedures Room," Brundy told him. "She should be waking up right about now."

"What?" Jake demanded, jerking his head around. "What'd you do?" he accused Brundy.

In response, Brundy grinned at him, "Ya missed, fella. While you were hiding the files, I substituted saline I.V.'s for the two that were supposed to finish her off."

"Why would you do that?" Jake angrily demanded. It was obvious he had forgotten himself, for he was confessing aloud his guilt.

"Because I've been working for Metkers," Brundy told him. "Have been all along. He came looking for me, recruited me three years ago to infiltrate the revived Sons of Dan and to find out everything I could about Project Samson. Born and raised Mormon, I was a shoe in." Brundy then stepped away from him, joining the men holding guns on Ellis and Carter, severing any connection he had with them and everything they stood for, forever leaving his role as avenger and murderer for Project Samson.

Turning to Metkers, Brundy explained about Sharon. "They were executing her with lethal injection. I would have found some way to stop them, even if Jake stayed in the room, but as it turned out I didn't have to blow my cover."

"Are you sure you stopped them in time?" Alex interjected.

"I've witnessed a number of intravenous executions in Federal Prisons," Brundy assured him.

"The process requires three I.V.'s and an injection. The first I.V. they gave Sharon was simply a saline solution, completely harmless. The shot they gave her was sodium thiopental. All that did was make her sleep. Jake was trying to save money, so he gave her a light dose. It was the third and fourth I.V.'s that would have killed her. The pancuronium bromide would have paralyzed every muscle in her body and stopped her breathing. The potassium chloride would have stopped her heart. It was those I.V.'s I substituted with saline solution. It'll take her a little while to wake up, but there's nothing wrong with her except for her broken arm."

"If you were able to save Sharon, why didn't you save Kevin?" Alex angrily accused. "You can't just trade her life for Kevin's and call it all right!"

"I didn't know Haskell cut Kevin's artery until Dr. Reed told me after we got here. I thought I'd already protected all of you when I told Haskell exactly how to hit you with the Impala. I controlled the accident, so you wouldn't be killed when your SUV went over the edge. Kevin wasn't supposed to die."

"I don't think he did," Metkers announced. "At least, not yet. A man by the name of Ralph Goodloe showed up at the hospital in Vernal without any identification, matching Kevin James' description and almost dead from blood loss. Since he came from Philip Reed's office, the victim of an automobile accident in which another man and woman were involved, we assumed him to be your friend. When last I heard, though, he hadn't regained consciousness. He was still in critical condition."

From the helicopters outside, men in camouflage, carrying rifles poured through the back doorway.

Leaving Alex to his own conclusions, Metkers suddenly changed gears, issuing them orders. "Start the evacuation. Get statements from everyone inside. I want those poor women out of here by three this afternoon. If the women want to call home after they give their statements, let them. Tell them they're being taken to St. Mark's Hospital in Salt Lake City, and that their families can meet them there. Forensics is on the way, so put your gloves on and be careful what you touch.

"All records secure?" he asked Brundy.

"Yes, Sir."

Jake looked at Brundy, questioningly.

"I disarmed your little fireworks surprise last night," Brundy whispered, again grinning.

"What about the tunnel?" Metkers asked the men in camouflage.

"Secured, Sir. All suspects in custody."

Chapter Fifty-four

Present Day Philadelphia, Pennsylvania
6:00 p.m.
April 27

Outside the ballroom at the prestigious Hallmark Hotel on Avenue of the Arts, Broad Street, eight hundred people in formal attire and at eighteen-hundred dollars a plate, mingled and networked. Waiters in starched, white shirts, with black bow ties, vests and slacks were serving them champagne in crystal flutes and hors d'oeuvres, Gulf shrimp, mini crab cakes and satay, on silver trays. Near huge, draped windows, on long, linen covered tables were Prime Rib with all the accompaniments, fine imported cheeses, specialty breads and crackers. Nearby, was a hosted bar serving fine wine, artisan beer, expensive liquors, juices, soft drinks and water.

In fashionable dresses or long, formal evening pants, the women attending wore thousands of diamonds competing for the light, their brilliance conspicuous. Only a few of the men wore tuxes, the rest wore two or three-thousand-dollar, tailored suits. Most wore gold cufflinks, and a few, Rolodex watches. Both men and women were using their smart phones. In their midst, shaking hands and frequently laughing, giving each donor a shallow bit of himself, was the man they had come to see, Senator Kenneth Albrecht.

"We'll have to have you and your family up for dinner this summer," he invited a wealthy man whom he had just met. "I'm sure we have a lot in common." He kept a pack of hand sanitizer wipes in his specially lined pockets and, at every opportunity, used them to surreptitiously clean his hands and return them to his pocket. Always smiling, he was ready to shake the next hand.

"Senator," his assistant whispered in his ear, "there's an important telephone call."

"It can't wait?" the Senator asked. There was a noticeable edge to his voice, but he was still smiling.

"It's Albert Matthews, Lieutenant Governor of Utah," his young assistant whispered. "Says he needs to speak with you immediately." Albert Matthews was a member of the Sons of Dan, code name 'Lion'.

The man Senator Albrecht was wooing was in his early sixties. He was a well-dressed, influential, corporate attorney the senator had been pursuing for months. Men of influence did not take kindly to being brushed aside, and when he let the man go, Senator Albrecht grimaced for the loss. "Won't you excuse me?"

"This better be important," Albrecht threatened his assistant, seething as he walked to his temporary office. At the door, he told his assistant to wait. "When I need you, I'll let you know." He reached for the doorknob, then paused and turned back. "If this turns out to be nothing, you're going home. Do you understand me?"

Sweat was beading on the young man's forehead. "Yes, sir."

Inside the small office, two members of Albrecht's personal staff were working at the same desk. "Leave me," he told them. He waited for them to close the door behind them, then took from his inside pocket a cell phone and speed dialed. "What happened?" he demanded of Lieutenant Governor Matthews as soon as he answered.

"Page and Vernal have been raided," Matthews told him. His voice was shaking. His breath was racing with fear. "Samson and Carter are in federal custody. It was Albert Metkers' grandson who betrayed us, set the entire FBI against us. He infiltrated Carter's organization and found out about Ellis. He and a whole legion of FBI invaded both the Arizona and Utah facilities and shut them down."

"Do they know about the other facilities?"

"Maybe. I don't know. I don't think so. At least, not yet."

"Has Ellis said anything about me?" Albrecht asked.

"I don't know that either, but I don't think so."

"Good. He's the only one who knows of my involvement. Carter doesn't know, does he?"

"I doubt it." Matthew told him.

"If either of them identify me, we'll all go down," Albrecht said. "You got access to them?"

"I have a man within ten feet of them."

"They let us down, Al," Albrecht continued. "They've not only endangered our organization but our very lives. See that they are released on bail immediately. Then make certain that they are given the opportunity to atone for their failure."

Chapter Fifty-five

Present Day
Salt Lake City, Utah
Midnight
May 3

It was a beautiful spring night. The moon was full, and stars seemed close enough to touch. Late in the afternoon of April 27 in a remote desert area northeast of Vernal Utah, Mark Ellis, U.S. Attorney State of Utah, and FBI Special Agent in Charge Neil Carter were taken into custody by a team of FBI agents under the command of Special Agent in Charge Metkers. They were then taken by helicopter to Salt Lake City and jailed. Forty-five hours later they were transported to the Frank E Moss U.S. Courthouse and brought before a Magistrate Judge of the United States District Court District of Utah. A total of six high-powered lawyers represented them, and after arguments were heard, bail was set for each of them at only two hundred and fifty thousand dollars. Ellis and Carter's bails were posted immediately, and anonymously, and the two were released three hours later, free from incarceration until trial.

At midnight on May 3, the moon was full and bright, and the stars were as clear as crystals as Mark Ellis sat at his kitchen table. Before him was a piece of stationary and the ballpoint pen with which he had just written his three pre-teenage sons and his five-year-old daughter. They were asleep in their rooms upstairs across the hall from their mother. The only light turned on in the house was the simple, three bulb chandelier directly above him. The only sound was the beat of his heart. Tears streamed from his eyes as he read what he had written.

My dearest Sons,
I am to leave you with your mother for a while. Don't grieve me. With my atonement I will enter the Kingdom of God and find a place in heaven.
As you grow into manhood, remember to obey the Church in all things so that someday you might join me in my kingdom or even have a kingdom of your own.
My dearest daughter,
You will marry someday, and when you do, you must obey your husband and bear him many children. We will never see each other again, but if you are righteous and obedient and if you serve the Church well, you will join your husband in his kingdom.
Do not worry about me, for I will be at peace as long as I know all of you are doing what I ask.

Love, Dad

Ellis startled as someone quietly knocked at the sliding door a few feet from across the table. He stood as he looked up to see two men standing on the deck beneath the flood light peering in, both dressed in white. "I'm ready," he responded.

Neatly folded on the kitchen counter were the clean clothes in which he would be buried. Tucking them under his arm, he followed the men to a waiting car.

Chapter Fifty-six

St. Mark's Hospital
Present Day
Salt Lake City, Utah
11:30 a.m. May 3

H is head was elevated. His left leg was in traction, and he was desperate for something solid to eat. Kevin was staring at his lunch tray. Before him were cartons of broth, juices, and milk, a cup of lukewarm tea, and one lone cup of lime Jell-O. He curled his lip. He had been conscious for two days and had been kept on an intravenous diet of sugar water and drugs. Only yesterday, was he allowed fluids he could drink. "I've gotta' have some food," he complained, his voice loud enough to reach the nurses' station. "Why can't I have something I can chew?" He paused, but no one came to his door or answered. "Anybody there?" he asked, sarcastically. "I can't live on this stuff forever. Hell, a baby couldn't live on this stuff." He sighed, then tried again. "How about some eggs and toast? Maybe a little bacon?" When there was still no response, he pushed the tray aside and pouted.

Alex was in the doorway grinning. "How about a cheeseburger?" He asked, his voice quiet enough so the nurses would not hear. Temptingly, Alex held out in front of him a greasy, brown bag. "*It* has bacon."

Kevin beamed. "And, French fries?"

"We just wanted to bring you something to eat. We didn't want to kill you," Sharon quipped, as she followed Alex into the room and closed the door behind them. Her left arm was held together with staples and pins and in a full-length cast. "Hurry and eat that thing, before we get caught."

Both of them grinned as Kevin dug in up to his cheeks in that half-pound burger and joyously devoured it. They'd almost lost him.

"Nice to have you back," Sharon told him.

"How's Kim?" he asked Sharon.

"A little shaken but fine. She and the kids are staying with mother for a while."

"Any news about Carter or Ellis?"

"They've been arraigned on kidnapping and conspiracy to commit murder charges in the U.S. District Court but are both out on bail."

"Why weren't they arraigned on murder charges?"

"There's no proof either one of them had anything to do with Wayne's murder," Sharon told him. "They can't even prove he's dead. They can't prove Wayne's assistant, Arthur Johnson is dead, either, but he seems to have vanished. For that matter, so has Arthur's granddaughter, Molly. There might be evidence of murder as they dig up the bodies buried in back of the facility, but they doubt it. They've found the bodies of five women, and so far their autopsies show they died of natural causes. Child birth mostly. I've asked if Ellis and Carter couldn't be charged with murder because those women died after being kidnapped, but Metkers says they'll probably never be charged. There's just no energy for it in the prosecutor's office. No desire to tie Ellis and Carter to anyone or anything, and nobody's talking."

"How did Metkers fit into all this, anyway?" Kevin asked.

"Just like Haskell and Brundy, Metkers has been FBI for years," Alex told him. "When choices had to be made, Haskell chose the Fundamentalists. Metkers and Brundy chose our country.

"Turns out Metkers' grandfather is in the Church hierarchy, one of the Council of Twelve Apostles no less. That's why Ellis trusted him. After an inordinate number of middle class Church women disappeared, Metkers began to suspect the Sons of Dan had revived and were up to something. He wormed his way inside the organization, found out about Project Samson, and recruited Brundy, a friend of his from high school, to help him. He told us we fouled things up by keeping the pressure on about Kim and Wayne. Once we'd pressed too hard and our lives were about to be taken, Metkers couldn't wait, even though he admitted they almost waited too long. Apparently, we forced the FBI to conduct its raid before Metkers learned who was financing the Project and where the other facilities are."

"Couldn't they tell where the other facilities were from the inventory?" Kevin asked.

"No, remember? Wayne's inventory only covered Utah and Arizona," Sharon said, "Utah and Arizona was Carter's territory. The idea was for Brundy to find out where the other facilities were by getting Carter to introduce him to Ellis, get Ellis to trust him, and then find out from him where they were. We just didn't give Brundy time enough to do it."

"Really?" Kevin challenged, sparking with anger. "It's our fault the other facilities are still open? We were supposed to hang around and wait until Kim and all these other women were used and possibly murdered by their breeding experiment? They're human beings, not livestock."

"To Carter and Ellis and whoever else was running the operation, they were livestock," Alex told him. "These women were only instruments to them, only incubators in which they would grow hundreds of children fathered by men conspiring to control the world. I think Metkers weighed the safety of the country and the women suffering at all those other clinics against the women here where Brundy could sometimes watch over them and decided to delay as long as it took. He may have been wrong, but that's what he did. He interfered to save us because he couldn't tolerate Carter and Ellis *intentionally* murdering us."

"I don't like it, but I hear what you're saying." Kevin paused as if thinking through what Alex had told him, then asked, "Do they think the Mormon Church might have had any part in this?"

"They don't know," Alex told him. "There's no evidence of the Church's involvement one way or the other. The code of secrecy among the Sons of Dan is so strong, even Ellis and Carter may not know who the ringleaders are. Wayne's medallion isn't much help, either."

"You'd think the Church would be appalled by what's happening in their name," Sharon observed, "but guess who's getting the heat instead?"

"Who," Kevin asked, his eyes big and curious.

"Metkers."

"Metkers?"

"Seems the Church didn't take too kindly to all the bad publicity. While they're investigating the story about the clinics, news people are digging up and reporting all that dirt in the Church's history and all the dead bodies it left behind," Alex chided.

"Metkers' grandfather was so angry with him he led the group that excommunicated Metkers."

"Excommunicated?" Kevin was outraged.

"He and Brundy, both," Alex added.

"So what's going to happen to Carter and Ellis?"

"The U.S. Attorney General doesn't want what happened in the Olympic bribery case to happen in this one, so she's sent a special prosecutor to Utah," Sharon told him. "She's also asked for a change of venue to move Carter and Ellis' trials out of Utah and to Denver to remove them from any Court prejudice. She fully expects her motion to be denied, so she's getting ready to appeal the decision to the United States Court of Appeals for the Tenth Circuit."

"Heh," Alex asked Sharon, changing the subject, "did you find out from your mother how Grandma Anna escaped the Sons of Dan, or Avenging Angels, or whatever they called these Fundamentalists back then."

"She let me read a letter written by Grandma Lizzy back in 1926, when Lizzy was about eighty. It told all about John's murder and Hattie's taking Jacob's life. Grandma Anna knew she, Hattie and the children would never get away unless they found a place to hide for a while, someplace no one would go looking for them. The only place like that was Mountain Meadows. The Mormons and Natives were avoiding the scene of that massacre like the plague.

"Grandma Anna found a gully about a quarter mile south of the meadows, and they camped there until midsummer. By then the Avenging Angels stopped searching for them. When the coast was clear, they moved further south, following the river and staying off the roads until they reached Arizona."

"What about you, Kevin?" Alex asked. "You ever find out why you didn't bleed to death? You should have been a goner."

Faced again with his mortality, Kevin put the last bite of his hamburger down. "The doctor who operated on me told me I would have bled to death if fate hadn't intervened. Apparently, Haskell was a little careless when he cut me. Probably wasn't feeling well. Anyway, he just nicked the femoral artery. Enough to kill me, of course, but not enough for the artery to split. The doctor figured that when Haskell tied the tourniquet beneath the cut, a clot forming inside the artery just above the knee injury was released. The clog was then caught in the blood being backed up by the tourniquet. Traveling up the leg, flowing to the cut with the rest of the blood, the clot acted like a cork, got caught in the hole as the blood flowed through it, and plugged it. He told me he removed a big clot when he sutured the artery closed."

Kevin sighed, then smiled. "I guess it was nature's way of protecting me from death that day."

"It seems like on that day, at least, none of us were destined to die," Sharon added.

Author Biography

Shawna Ryan was born and raised in the Northwest, United States. After obtaining her law degree, she was a corporate attorney and a trial attorney. Though she has traveled extensively, her home is still in the Northwest. She recently retired from practice to devote more time to writing. Always having been interested in the philosophies of religion, she enjoys researching and writing about the histories behind them.

She is a descendant of Catholics, Mormons, Methodists, Baptists, and other Protestants and tries to be both critical and objective about them all. The inspirations for the research that led to her new serial, KINGDOM, were Shawna's great grandmothers, who converted to Mormonism in 1854 and who were among the first European converts to immigrate to Utah. Some of the anecdotes in KINGDOM were based on their own stories.

KINGDOM Book Two is Shawna's fifth thriller. She is also the author of *Kingdom Book One, Destiny's Damned, Satan's Scat,* and *Triumvirate of the Damned,* a thriller trilogy. The initial inspiration for the trilogy was the writing of Joseph Campbell, a well know and respected mythologist who was brilliant in his fields of comparative mythology and comparative religions.

Shawna's goal is to write thrillers that are fun to read and inspire their readers to talk about them with friends. Shawna's favorite thriller writers are Douglas Preston and Lincoln Child.

www.ingramcontent.com/pod-product-compliance
Lightning Source LLC
Chambersburg PA
CBHW071519260626
47170CB00002B/431